OLD MAN'S GHOSTS

Also by Tom Lloyd from Gollancz:

The Stormcaller
The Twilight Herald
The Grave Thief
The Ragged Man
The Dusk Watchman
The God Tattoo

Moon's Artifice

OLD MAN'S GHOSTS

TOM LLOYD

GOLLANCZ
LONDON

The right of Tom Lloyd-Williams to be identified as the author of this
work has been asserted by him in accordance with the
Copyright, Designs and Patents Act 1988.

First published in Great Britain in 2015 by Gollancz
An imprint of the Orion Publishing Group
Orion House, 5 Upper St Martin's Lane, London WC2H 9EA
An Hachette UK Company

A CIP catalogue record for this book is available
from the British Library.

ISBN 978 0 575 13121 7

1 3 5 7 9 10 8 6 4 2

Printed in Great Britain by CPI Group (UK) Ltd, Croydon, CR0 4YY

The Orion Publishing Group's policy is to use papers that are natural,
renewable and recyclable products and made from wood grown in sustainable
forests. The logging and manufacturing processes are expected to conform to
the environmental regulations of the country of origin.

www.tomlloyd.co.uk
www.orionbooks.co.uk
www.gollancz.co.uk

For Charlotte Lily Wright

What has gone before: *Moon's Artifice*

Narin is an Investigator of the Imperial City and a man with more secrets than is healthy for anyone. Credited with saving the life of a House Wyvern nobleman, his star is on the rise and he has been assigned as protégé to the most famous son of the Imperial Lawbringers, Rhe, to be readied for promotion to the rank of Lawbringer. Unfortunately, the rescue he's taken credit for was actually down to his best friend, Enchei, who is a renegade Astaren warrior-mage and wants nothing of the fame such an act might bring. To make matters worse, Narin has fallen in love with the wife of the man he rescued, a man who was castrated during that attack, and as *Moon's Artifice* begins, Narin is told by Lady Kine that she is pregnant with his child.

Before they can make plans, they are disturbed by a sound outside. Narin reacts without thinking and knocks out a man in the street, realising belatedly that he is injured and was likely seeking help. To complicate matters, the Ascendant God, Lord Shield, descends from the heavens and shows an interest in the injured man – a member of the goshe brotherhood that runs both martial arts schools and free hospitals within the city. Lord Shield charges Narin with discovering what the goshe was up to, intending to use Narin to flush out a wider conspiracy, and Narin is forced to drag the man home in secret.

At the boarding house where the goshe had been staying, a young woman called Kesh discovers her sister has been poisoned by a drug in the goshe's belongings. She takes her stricken sister, Emari, to one of the free hospitals, only to learn that Emari's mind has been entirely erased and she is as good as dead. She is forced to flee, pursued by another goshe who shows unnatural abilities and only escapes when demon-possessed foxes save her. She goes to the Lawbringers with her story and Narin is summoned. He takes her back to his home where the goshe is recovering, only to discover the man, who Kesh

1

has learned is called Irato, has woken with no memory of himself. His mind has been affected by a smaller dose of the drug that has left Kesh's sister effectively dead and he can provide no answers for them, but it becomes clear the inner circle of the goshe order are engaged in some sinister conspiracy involving forbidden magics and stolen souls. To complicate matters, an Imperial caste power-broker called Prince Sorote has learned of Narin's affair.

That night they are attacked by goshe members who would have killed them all except for Enchei's prodigious combat skills and Irato siding with his rescuers instead of his former comrades. Enchei's past is revealed to Narin, Kesh and Irato, while Lawbringer Rhe guesses the truth himself. Aware they're likely still being watched, they devise a plan to escape without being ambushed, but the goshe elites still manage to follow them and Narin is caught during the pursuit through the slum of Cold Cliffs.

Enchei, with the help of an Apkai, an order of demons as powerful as any god, and Lord Shield, manages to rescue Narin, but that rescue panics the goshe elite into thinking the Astaren know about them. They step up their plans, believing they are running out of time, and engineer a fever epidemic throughout the city, while sending out demon-like creatures to spread chaos and distract the Lawbringers. The fever is caused by a variant of the drug, Moon's Artifice, and does something similar but it leaves the victim incapacitated as though dying of disease. The goshe publicly offer to quarantine the victims, soon numbering in the thousands, on their island sanatorium a few miles offshore, which will enable them to enact their final plan – to clear memories from their minds and so their rulers can live as gods in the heads of their thousands of followers.

Once a critical mass of linked minds is reached they will be able to inhabit every goshe dosed with Moon's Artifice across the Empire – tens of thousands of people of all castes and races, who will both be divine vessels (potentially disrupting the Empire's rigid caste system in the process) and so numerous even the brutal Astaren warrior-mages will be unable to stop or catch those disembodied leaders.

Lawbringer Rhe leads a force of Lawbringers to attack the goshe island, assisted by a group of minor Imperials sent by Prince Sorote to bolster the firepower of the mostly low-caste Lawbringers who are not permitted gunpowder weapons. The attack is a diversion to allow Narin, Kesh, Irato and Enchei to infiltrate the sanatorium and disrupt a crucial ceremony before it can be completed, but as the goshe unveil more magical weapons, the fight is joined by a unit of House Dragon's warrior-mages, the Stone Dragons, who begin to slaughter the goshe defenders.

Narin and Irato manage to steal the demon artefact powering the ceremony, thanks to the fox-spirits from whom the artefact was originally stolen. They escape out to sea as Lawbringer Rhe, a nobleman of House Eagle, faces down the Astaren of his homeland's greatest rival, House Dragon, and forces them to halt their slaughter. Out to sea, Lord Shield and the Apkai prepare to fight over the artefact now that it is linked to so many mortal minds, but before they do Kesh reveals she's tricked them and already dumped it overboard – the depths of the sea being ruled by beings beyond the power of both demons and gods.

Private Summary of the Moon's Artifice affair prepared for the Imperial Court, subsequently entered into the restricted Palace records.

The Moon's Artifice affair was a conspiracy that violated the natural order of the Empire; that stole souls and scarred an entire generation of the Empire's children. And yet the audacity and execution of the conspirators' plan remains a remarkable achievement. The goshe inner circle operated for decades without infiltration or detection by Astaren spies, quite aside from their initial theft of an artefact from the demonic inhabitants of Shadowrain Forest.

One chance slip brought their tower tumbling, but not before it had been raised almost alongside the Gods themselves. Had one of their elite not fallen from a rooftop in a manner that infected him with the infamous poison he carried, a new god might have been raised to the pantheon of Gods. The elite goshe styled themselves after the blood-drinking demons of Kettekast, the Detenii, and poisoned newborns while they slept, readying the next generation of their servants. With his memories stolen, the elite known as Irato was reborn an innocent and, horrified by his involvement in something so monstrous, vowed to put it right as best he could.

Lawbringer Rhe's role in foiling this plot is already the stuff of legend after his confrontation with a troop of Stone Dragons intent on a massacre, but it was one of his Investigators who first uncovered the mystery of Moon's Artifice, alongside the turncoat Irato. Charged by Lord Shield himself to uncover the secrets of the poisoned elite, the low-born Investigator named Narin was the primary source of the goshe's undoing. Given the resolve and disregard for his own safety shown by Investigator Narin, it is undoubted that Lord Shield watched over his instrument as loyally as he once served Lord Lawbringer in life.

4

In their fear at finally being discovered, the goshe unleashed enslaved demons and an engineered plague on the Imperial City – a last, desperate effort to gather enough souls to sacrifice to their new 'god'. The impact of this is still felt today and hundreds of those stricken have since died, while more than a thousand remain helpless invalids on Confessor's Island under the care of Lady Healer's priesthood. While the Lawbringers heroically drew the attention of the goshe soldiers, incurring terrible casualties in the process, Investigator Narin and the turncoat Irato scaled a cliff and interrupted the goshe's foul ceremony. The artefact was stolen away before the ritual could be completed and Lord Shield effected their escape before casting the artefact into the deep, to ensure its power could be abused no longer.

Had the goshe not been stopped, thousands of their followers, high and low caste alike, would have carried a fragment of the divine in their mind. How the Great Houses would have reacted can never be known for certain, let alone how the caste system of this nation would have survived. Certainly the fallout proved enough to make the massing armies of Houses Dragon and Eagle pull back from the brewing war. Given the legions that would have been at the goshe's command and the intractability of the Great Houses, it remains a chilly possibility the Empire might have found itself at war with its own Gods.

CHAPTER 1

'Nothing that colour was ever healthy.'

Enchei Jen stared into the cloudy glass tumbler resting in the palm of his hand. The tavern lamps cast a flickering light across his table but, dimly-lit or not, the contents of the tumbler remained a dismal murky green.

His fingers closed about the glass and he swept it up to his lips. The liquor slipped down his throat, now half-numb after repeated shots. He scowled and lowered the empty glass.

'Nothing that colour ever tasted good,' he added under his breath.

A finger of breeze washed in through the room as the tavern door opened. Enchei's gaze lifted briefly to inspect the newcomer, old habits dying hard. A man, tall and lean with a thick grey cloak fastened by a black metal clasp. He didn't push his hood back as he inspected the interior of the tavern, just shook off the snow before approaching the bar. A glimpse of green around the man's neck announced him as landowner caste – not high-born, but unusual enough in these shabby surroundings. Enchei couldn't see much of the man's face, just that his skin was paler than the local stock and his beard dark and neat.

Enchei looked away and refilled the glass in his hand. He left it balanced on his palm and breathed in the liquor's faintly sour aroma. Memories blossomed in his head, none of them good, and despite his strength the grey-haired man bowed his head under their weight.

He remained still a long while, eyes closed and hand trembling slightly as screams echoed in his ears, weeping voices pleading for help. Enchei opened his eyes and lifted the glass to his face, touching the wet rim to his forehead in bitter salute.

'My greatest hour,' he said wearily and downed the contents again. 'Here's to the dead I left in my wake. Every last bloody thousand of you.'

The flavour hadn't improved, but tonight wasn't one for enjoyment. No, tonight was for maudlin thoughts and drinking enough to send a regular man blind. It was something of a tradition for Enchei since he'd been a resident of the Imperial City, coming here on this night. Trade was slow for the Gull tavern in winter, a grimy little place that relied on harbour business. Few ships came in when the snow fell so Enchei knew he would be left to his own devices.

Just as importantly, he knew the landlord stocked this rotgut called Ivytail because the tavern was frequented by House Raven sailors. Getting drunk wasn't an easy task for Enchei, inconveniently difficult if truth be told, but on this night the voices of the dead always needed quietening, so Ivytail it was.

He sensed a figure move towards him and old instincts kicked in. The layout of the L-shaped room appeared in his mind. His leg tensed as he shifted his weight – ready to twist and kick the table up at the figure. His fingers trembled slightly, poised to hurl the glass and pull his knife. A flood of strength washed through his body, a familiar sparkle of readiness as the alcohol was flushed from his blood and Enchei readied his savage strength … and then he focused on the face peering towards him.

It was the bartender, an anxious look on the man's face. Brodin, his name was, a sturdily-built retired sailor like half of the residents hereabouts. Never normally a man to intrude, Brodin knew Enchei's face to nod at and had not bothered further than that.

'Ah, a moment, sir?'

Enchei allowed himself to breathe slowly out. 'Aye?'

'Don't want ta bother you, but I got another customer wanting Ivytail and that's my only bottle.'

Enchei felt a cold sensation run down his spine. 'He sent you over?'

'Asked if you might share it – on him, he said.'

'Sent you over, eh?'

Enchei closed his eyes briefly. In his mind, his right arm traced a path through the folds of his coat to the grip of his knife, the left into a long pocket where a dark baton rested.

'Polite of him.'

With an effort Enchi breathed out and glanced back over towards the newcomer at the bar. In his forties perhaps, but wearing his middle years well – on the slim side, but Enchei of all people knew that was no real guide – clothes tailored as befitting the highest of the non-noble castes. A strip of wavering gold brocade down the breast of his tunic added a gaudy touch of wealth while a plain-hilted rapier on his hip told its own story.

7

Not a face I recognise, he thought as he scrutinised the man, *but one I know anyways. That's the face of my past sure enough.*

The man stood with his back to the bar, at the end furthest from the door. He met Enchei's gaze a moment, long enough to give him the faintest of nods before turning away. With a slightly exaggerated movement he faced the bar and placed his palms flat down on the top, well wide of his body.

Enchei narrowed his eyes and checked the rest of the room again. No obvious dangers among them, no one paying any attention past their own drinks.

Stars above, is this really a coincidence? Has he just come looking for the same drink as me or is there a snatch squad waiting outside? Is this bastard just playing a little game of his own – inviting me to run, pretending he's giving me a chance?

Enchei touched his fingers to the battered leather coat he still wore. The interior was a quilt-work he'd sewn himself, several dozen pockets filled with a fine powder. The city outside was gripped in a surly and persistent frost so, despite a fire blazing in the room, it was not warm enough for him to look out of place with a coat on.

'Good a day as any to die,' he muttered.

'I'm sorry, sir?' the bartender asked, leaning forward to hear Enchei better.

'Nothing.' Enchei paused. 'This bottle's on me. Send him over with some whisky and we'll call it even.'

As the bartender turned away, momentarily blocking his view of the man at the bar, Enchei slipped his baton from the coat and wedged it under one leg, handle sticking out. The coat was a last resort – a fallback plan if he was taken or killed.

Determined not to betray his anxiety, Enchei refilled his glass and watched the newcomer approach. He walked silently, hands in plain view, and kept a wary distance even once he'd reached the table. A clear glass bottle and three tumblers was all he carried – lethal in the wrong hands, but those hands could cause enough damage without any assistance.

A tiny sound crept into his ears, the whisper of demons on the edge of hearing. Enchei scowled and ignored the faint chatter, making no indication that he'd even heard it.

'It appears we share a taste for unusual spirits,' the man said in a cultured voice. 'You don't object to me joining you?'

Enchei didn't speak at first. His mind went perfectly blank for a moment while his body screamed to move, to strike and kill. Eventually he composed himself and nodded towards the seat.

'Take a seat,' he said in a gruff voice.

The man inclined his head and slid into the space opposite Enchei. 'My thanks.' He set the whisky and tumblers on the table. 'A peace offering, for the imposition.'

'Peace offering?' Enchei echoed. 'We at war?'

At that the half-smile on the man's handsome features wavered. 'I don't believe so,' he said cautiously, 'but then I don't know who you are, so I suppose I can't rule such a thing out. Are you at war with anyone?'

'I try not to be.'

The man frowned and indicated the bottle of Ivytail. Enchei grunted and the newcomer poured himself a glass, knocking it back in one gulp.

'My name is Sorpan.'

'Aye, sounds about right, that.'

'I'm sorry?'

'Straight out of the old country, that name.'

Sorpan inclined his head. 'And you?'

'I've got a name, aye. Had a few over the years, but I don't fancy sharing any of 'em.'

That prompted a moment of quiet. 'Was that bottle full when you started?' Sorpan asked, picking up the Ivytail again and sloshing the contents around before pouring each of them another shot.

'Was thirsty.'

'Indeed. More to the point, you're not even halfway drunk, by my reckoning.'

'The evening's still young.'

'You know what I mean.'

Enchei exhaled slowly and stared into Sorpan's eyes as he considered his answer. 'You got a point to make?'

Sorpan swallowed his drink and set the glass down. 'No point,' he said at last, 'but it's an unusual drink. Few have a taste for it.'

'Probably because it tastes like shit.'

The man's bark of laughter echoed around the tavern, but was cut short as the keyed-up Enchei twitched. The humour faded in Sorpan's face as he recognised what had almost happened.

'Few have a taste for it,' he continued in a quiet voice, 'I'm one of the few, as it happens, but I know others who drink it. Men and women with hardier constitutions than any sailor.'

'It does get a man drunk,' Enchei acknowledged.

'I must confess to being curious as to why a man needs to get drunk on something he dislikes.' Sorpan pushed the tumblers aside and poured a generous measure of whisky into the remaining glasses, pushing one across the table to Enchei.

As the man sipped his new drink, a voice appeared in Enchei's head. *But enough of being coy – we're comrades, are we not?*

Enchei tightened his fingers around his glass, fighting the urge to touch them to a scar on the back of his skull. Once, speaking that way had been as natural to him as breathing, but no longer. He'd cut out his voice just as he'd cut his ties to his past. Most days he didn't even miss it.

'Comrades? Don't have those no more. My soldiering days are long gone.'

Sorpan shrugged. 'As you wish. If I'm intruding, I'll leave.'

'Think it best I go first.'

That brought the man up short. 'It appears I've misinterpreted matters. My apologies.'

'No need for that,' Enchei said, 'but I don't know why you're here and I'd rather not find out.'

I'm here alone. I'm not in the city on a mission of any kind.

'That's nice to hear, but I'm not going to take your word for it.'

You're a renegade?

'Name-calling ain't nice.'

'But no longer one of us. Retired away from the fold or independent?'

Enchei snorted. 'A fan of fairy tales, are you?'

The derision was shrugged away by Sorpan. 'Still – I somehow doubt this is a holiday from the home valleys.' He frowned down at the bottles on the table. 'Or that this is a celebration. I might have a taste for Ivytail myself, but still I'd just planned on taking the edge off the day before moving on to something else.'

'That's what the whisky's for,' Enchei said.

Sorpan shook his head. 'The whisky's because, now I'm here, you want a drink that won't cloud your mind. Before I got here you were just working your way down a bottle of the hard stuff.'

'Sounds like you're making a point again,' Enchi growled.

10

This time the other man nodded. 'I was looking to celebrate the conclusion of some mundane business. A man who's attacking a bottle of Ivytail when he doesn't even like it, that's no celebration.'

'So I'm not celebrating. What of it?'

'Nothing, I suppose, I'm just curious.'

'No one in the game is just curious.'

'But you're out of the game and still drinking to forget. That's enough to make any man curious.'

'Mebbe I am, no crime in that. We all got ghosts in our shadows; an old man's just got more than most.'

'But he's not a drunk or he'd have a stock at home,' Sorpan mused and nodded towards the door where a trail of snow was melting on the muddy tiles. 'Hardly the weather to be outside by choice however, even with a hardy constitution. An anniversary? You must be two decades older than me and you've a hard way about you. That means maudlin and drunk isn't something you'll do lightly and the worst of what you've gone through was probably before my time.'

'You know what they say about curiosity?' Enchei warned.

Sorpan nodded. 'It's a cliff – safe up to a point and then there's no way back.'

'Loose stones under your feet now. My mood ain't the finest tonight and from this side o' the table there's a knife-edge between curious and theatrics.'

'You think I'm building to some dramatic reveal before I smugly watch a snatch team come through every window? Was that our style twenty years ago?'

'For some.'

'I suppose.' Sorpan hesitated, his face suddenly going tense. Enchei almost rammed a knife into it before he realised the man's expression wasn't a prelude but a flash of insight.

'That's the face of a man thinking too hard.'

'Stars of heaven,' Sorpan whispered, almost not hearing Enchei. 'Not twenty years ago, thirty.'

Enchei eased his baton clear under the table.

'You were there, weren't you? Those are the ghosts you're drowning?'

Despite his readiness, Enchei felt a cold sickness in his gut and distant screams echoed through the frosty streets of memory.

'Some ghosts you can't drown,' he whispered. 'I'm here to remember, not forget.'

Sorpan was quiet a long while. He stared down at his drink for a dozen heartbeats before moving at all, finally taking a long swallow of whisky. Even in his surprise he was careful to move slowly, to not startle Enchei's hair-trigger reactions.

'I'm sorry,' he said in a hoarse whisper. He topped both glasses up and raised his in salute. 'To those who didn't make it.'

Enchei drank left-handed. 'To those I left behind,' he said, finishing the glass with a second mouthful.

Sorpan shook his head. 'There's only rumours, you know that? Every file is sealed, the whole account hidden.'

'And we're back to curious.'

'Can you blame me? The greatest horror in past centuries? More dead than the Ten Day War itself? *No one* outside of the Five knows what happened there, except those who survived. Not thirty-year veterans who deal with every nasty secret the Empire has to offer, not the observers who watch the passes into the valley. Avatars of the Gods have patrolled that place for decades and I half-doubt even they know everything.'

'Some things are best forgotten,' Enchei said heavily. 'Nothing for your generation to learn there, nothing in that valley to benefit the Empire or any House in it.'

Sorpan gaped and leaned forward, this time not even noticing the tightness in Enchei's face as he did so. 'But *three hundred thousand* troops died, without counting the villagers who lived there!'

Enchei grimaced. 'I don't need reminding.'

'And you think they should be written out of history too?'

'Just how they died. If I could write that out of my mind so easily, I would've long ago. That whole celestial month – from the snow storm sealing the passes to the day I dragged myself out. As it is, I can't. All I can do is remember the friends I lost, the folk I met and watched die...'

Enchei lowered his head. The memories washed fresh and sharp over him now. He was aware Sorpan's moment had come; if the man was there to take him Enchei was at his weakest, his most vulnerable.

Part of him wanted it to happen. The ache in his heart grew and grew, threatening to burst out of his chest and set the room aflame. His precautions were in place. They'd never get him alive, and for one brief moment the grief and guilt were so strong that a voice inside him begged for Sorpan to spark that final conflagration.

But it never came. Slowly the consuming horror subsided and Enchei opened his eyes again to see the other man looking aghast. With an effort Enchei pushed himself to his feet, the unnaturally-strong man feeling the full span of years on his shoulders.

'Some things are best forgotten by history. The Fields of the Broken is one of them.'

CHAPTER 2

One year later

Clear, cold light traced the frost-rimed cobbles. The street was still and quiet under the white glare of the Gods. It was deep into the night and the ruling Order of Jester was halfway over the horizon. Lady Spy would be in Ascendancy for another few days. She led Jester's wheel of divine constellations across the sky so her light had already fallen below the horizon.

The cloudless sky wore a milky collar of lesser stars upon which the divine constellations shone like diamonds. By contrast the moon was a dim and sullen shape that seemed to skulk close to the horizon. Two men and a woman stood in the deserted street and surveyed the slender constellations of Cripple and Duellist that flanked Lady Jester.

The mortals were an even less likely trio than cold-hearted Jester, ever-suffering Cripple and proud Duellist. One man was tall and pale-skinned, with neat clothes and a dark beard, a sharp contrast to the woman ahead of him; teeth white against her ochre skin, blonde hair pulled untidily back in a knot. A north-continent man of money, a south-continent woman of more practical means. The woman's clothes were a patchwork of cloth and metal; battered scraps of steel stitched and riveted onto a long coat marked by scorch marks and roughly-repaired rents.

'This is the place?' asked the third man, at last turning away from Lady Jester's light. Enveloped in a heavy silver fur he was also pale, but not of the north this time. Deathly-white skin and grey hair coupled with lilac eyes marked him as a Leviathan, from that House's islands far to the south-west. 'This is where we will find the trail?'

The first man stirred into movement and nodded. With a grey cloak edged in pale fox fur, he resembled a statue in the cold winter light. There was the faint glint of frost on his shoulders and a silver badge gleamed at his throat.

'Here.'

'On this night?'

'You keep questioning me, Leviathan,' he said sternly. 'I'm growing tired of it.'

'That is not my concern.'

'Pissing me off should be. You're not your master.'

The Leviathan turned to face him. 'No, Ghost, I am not – but neither are you. You answer to me as you answer to Priest, and I am yet to be impressed.'

The man from House Ghost regarded him, still barely moving. 'You don't believe me?' he asked with a mixture of amusement and contempt.

'You have shown us nothing, Master Sorpan, nothing but supposition,' the pale-eyed man said with an equanimous shrug of the shoulder. To Sorpan it seemed an oddly neat and understated gesture from the broad man, but characterised what he knew of the Leviathan. 'I am here because this may yet be a trap.'

'A trap, Kebrai? You think I was set up by my own? Unlike House Leviathan we're not composed of paranoid madmen – there are no senseless purges or childish scheming between fiefdoms.'

Kebrai grinned nastily. 'No purges you ever noticed, but such things are as inevitable as the turning stars. Where power gathers, paranoia is but a whisper away.'

Sorpan spat on the ground and nodded towards the side-road they stood near.

'The tavern's there and this is the night, but he's a survivor not a fool. The trail begins here, but you'll not have him tonight.'

'Priest understands patience as well as any alive; just remember your life rides on this. There are too many eyes watching the Imperial City to act here without good reason.'

'If the reason wasn't good, we wouldn't be here at all.'

'It is so.'

They both looked at the woman ahead of them whose eyes had moved from the passing stars to those at their zenith. Sorpan didn't need to follow her gaze to know which constellation she had fixed upon – the Order of God-Emperor was high above them now and the south position was occupied by Lord Huntsman. Though she dealt with demons and cultivated a savage appearance, she was hardly the crazed shamaness he'd expected and she was particular in her honouring of Huntsman.

An icy breath of wind shivered over them, bringing with it the muted sound of voices. Even at this late hour the streets of the Imperial City were not deserted and the Leviathan turned to check on his trailing guards. No signal came from the House Smoke mercenaries who'd escorted them here, so Kebrai nodded.

'Sharish, it is time.'

The shamaness, Sharish, bared her pointed teeth and beckoned to Sorpan. He followed her across the cobbles to stand opposite the side-street's entrance. From there he could just see the tavern, the slender threads of light around the shutters and the sheen of ice on its tiled roof. It seemed an unremarkable place to find an Astaren hero, grown shabby under the battering sea breeze.

A small upper storey and a roof peaked like a prow to part the south-westerly wind, an alley covering two sides. According to the grey-eyed mercenary who'd been sent to scout the place there were three men inside who could be the target, but Sorpan knew none would be as they watched each leave. You didn't get to be an old Astaren by getting sloppy and retirement wouldn't diminish the man's instincts. If anything it would sharpen them.

A loose tile on one of the rooftops clacked noisily as the wind picked up, breaking the hush of deepest night. Old instincts made Sorpan wary; abrupt noises in the dark and dangerous strangers made poor companions.

'Come.'

Sharish had a velvety growl to her voice, one that seemed to match the three long claw-marks down her cheek. Sorpan ducked his head and allowed her to put her callused palms around his bearded face.

'Keep still.'

'No.' That prompted her to curl her lip, a snarl ready, but he smiled and forestalled her anger. Light flickered briefly in his eyes. 'I will give you the scent.'

'I don't work that way.'

'I have layer upon layer of defences in my mind. You'll likely burn your senses out before you get anything.'

He brought her head closer, almost close enough to kiss those full lips, and began to mouth secret words to the night. Her confusion deepened initially but then threads of light began to appear in the air, shifting shapes that twisted and spiralled in no breeze they could feel. These wound their way to her face and he held her still as they burst as delicately as tiny bubbles – minute flashes of light illuminating the muddy-green of her eyes.

'I see him,' she breathed, 'I have the scent.'

Sorpan stepped back. 'Good.'

At her urging he retreated further, finding Kebrai had moved away too. With a gesture the man recalled his mercenary guards; four lithe, light-skinned warriors from House Smoke, a major House within the Dragon hegemony and thus a common sight on the streets of its protectorate city. They silently fell in behind, all watching Sharish as she stepped forward.

In the shadow of an overhang, Sharish unfastened the thong on a long object wrapped in grease-stained cloth. With delicate movements she unveiled a staff which she held out as she knelt. Made of some pale wood, it had sigils scratched into its surface and a head split into three twisted tines. Fat coils of copper wire bunched around the base of those while both the shaft and tines were wrapped in haphazard twists of more wire, creating a bulbous flared shape that reminded Sorpan of a henbane flower.

The winter wind seemed to blow colder as Sharish muttered in some strange dialect of her own language. Behind him the mercenaries began to shift uncomfortably. Sorpan knew she could use demons to hunt a particular scent, but their anxiety triggered a memory of his. His career had been unremarkable thus far – minor work in the greater scheme of things – but his training had been thorough.

Either I'm wrong, or Sharish's more insane than she appears.

His answer came soon enough. The wind's cold fingers slapped across his exposed face, dragging at his coat, and with it came a distant sound to chill the heart. The faint call of a hunting hound, barely audible over the strengthening wind but laden with savage intent. Without meaning to, his hand went to the pistol at his waist and for a moment Sorpan was glad he'd come dressed as a warrior caste, red on his collar and a gun at his side. Then he remembered his suspicions and realised a gun would do little.

He forced himself to stay very still and watch Sharish with horrified awe as she continued her mantra of summoning. Fleeting sparks began to dance around the metal flower-head, swiftly building in intensity. Soon there were fitful bursts of light shuddering within it, the hiss and crackle momentarily drowning out her words and prompting the shamaness to continue her refrain in a louder voice. The distant howls grew no louder, but began to come from all directions, as though whatever made them was circling its prey. With little warning the stuttering burst of light grew to blinding proportions – one great flash, then two more in rapid succession.

At each flash the street was bathed in light – all but black shadows cast in stark relief ahead of her. A glimpse was all Sorpan needed to gasp and fall back in horror – each glimpsed shadow different in size and outline but the smallest still the size of a pony. The suggestion of long lupine snouts and enormous fangs was all he could make out, the sharp line of ears and mass of muscled shoulders with no detail visible.

Gods on high! Sorpan fought the urge to curse aloud, all too aware he did not want to attract further attention. *Gentle Empress and the Lady Pity, what have I just unleashed on this city?*

CHAPTER 3

'Oh Jester's Knives, again?'

Lady Kine Vanden Wyvern closed her eyes, lips pursed and pale against the wave of pain around her belly. With an effort she took a breath, short and ragged, then another. Bent like an old woman, Kine gripped the back of the chair she stood over as though it were a lifeline. Despite everything, between huffs of breath she felt a moment of absurd humour. Standing there, panting like a dog, she couldn't help but hear the disapproving voices of her aunts echo across the sea from her homeland.

A noblewoman must walk with grace – haste is for warriors. Never let your breathing be heard – panting is for dogs and rutting peasants. A noblewoman must never raise her voice – cries and pleas are the domain of the religious caste.

'Look at me now, you shrivelled witches,' she moaned through gritted teeth, 'waddling like a sow, grunting and gasping like a commoner. Shame upon shame staining you all!'

Kine bowed her head as a final burst of pain clamped around her, then it swiftly faded to just a memory in her bones. She gulped down air as she gingerly straightened and looked around the room. Ahead of her stood an elegant desk of polished wood as dark as her own skin – the pearl inlay as clean and white as the teeth she'd been taught to hide from men whenever she smiled.

The things we women do to each other, Kine thought as she took a tentative step towards the window. *Little cuts, every day these little cuts to keep others weakened and bleeding.*

Another step and a phantom breath of cold ran down her spine. *But it's not the little cuts I need to fear now. Never again will I care about petty things.*

She edged round the desk as best she could, one hand on it for support, the other pressed protectively to her swollen belly. Month after month she'd grown used to her burgeoning size, working hard to maintain that elegant carriage her aunts had beaten into her. Now it was all gone and she heaved herself flat-footed across the patterned rugs, past the crackling fire and to the window. Kine hauled back the heavy brocade curtains and felt a gust of cold air like a slap in the face.

Lead-lined panes of glass reflected the dancing firelight back at her. In the centre of each window was a single red pane that bore a blue wyvern, a device that adorned every window in the entire palazzo. Kine grimaced as she saw it – sickened now at the sight of her nation's emblem. She was glad that her private rooms were at the rear of the palazzo, overlooking her husband's jungle-like garden rather than the sandy enclosure in the square where a real wyvern lived.

The beast was a sad sight in Kine's eyes; wings clipped and confined to a rocky home a mere two dozen paces in each direction. She had seen wyverns hunt once. The boldest of the desert noblemen reared a few from birth just for that purpose and the savagery of the swooping predators had taken her breath away.

'As you are too, my little one,' she whispered, looking down at her belly.

Her shift had parted slightly, caught on her protruding stomach, and offered Kine a sight of the paled skin where it had stretched. Kine had grown up knowing her dark mahogany skin could almost pass for the near-black of House Dragon itself and would have been a factor in her marriage to a man of higher station. Raised to be proud of her flawless and even colouring, the sight of it blotchy and pale triggered a childish anxiety inside her.

Her fingers fumbled briefly on the window's brass bolts, the metal so cold it seemed to nip at her fingers as she gripped it. With a little persistence she worked them open and pushed the window wide. The night air was shockingly cold, enough to make Kine gasp as she pulled a white scarf from around her neck. Clear starlight gleamed on the frosted roofs of Dragon District; the snarling statues and peaked ridges picked out in the glistening white of the Gods.

Trying to ignore the biting chill, Kine leaned carefully forward and let the air wash away the last mustiness of sleep from her mind. It was late into the night and high above she could just make out the constellation of General, first among the Ascendants of God-Emperor. Past midnight then, but not so late that there was no hope.

Kine glanced back at the cream damask sofa she'd been asleep on these past few hours, a tangle of blankets and cushions half-slipped

20

onto the floor below. As she did so a warning tingle began in her belly and Kine's eyes flashed wide open – so soon? With the awkward haste of panic Kine gritted her teeth and leaned over the windowsill, hands questing for a hook set into the mortar just below it. At last she found it and slipped one corner of the silk scarf through, tugging hard before tying a knot in the scarf to secure it.

By the time she was done, the pain had intensified and now washed in sharp, piercing waves through her body. Kine jammed her knuckle into her mouth to stop herself crying out, biting down on her hand as the pain only worsened. With all the concentration she could muster and a force of will no less than that of her conqueror ancestors, Kine reached for the open windows and dragged them shut again. Her knees shook, ready to collapse; her arms turned to jelly as she fought the window clasps.

The pain in her belly was white-hot, exquisite and all-consuming. A red haze fell over her vision and the shadows darkened, but somehow she refused to submit. At last both windows were closed and the numbing whips of winter wind ended their scourging. Gasping and heaving for breath, Kine took hold of the floor-length curtain and dragged herself forward, putting much of her weight on it as her knees refused to obey. One brass fitting popped open and she lurched forward, barely catching herself as her fingers clawed and long nails dug into the embroidery for purchase.

Distantly, she was aware of herself keening; a high, animal sound unlike any she'd heard herself make before, but she had only the safety of her baby in mind. Another stuttering half-step brought her within reach of a chair. Just as more curtain fittings burst apart, her slender arm slipped over the thick back of the armchair and she sagged forwards, slipping down to her knees and the safety of the rug-strewn floor. Hands gripping the chair, Kine gasped for breath, desperate for air after the battle even a few paces had been.

Sweat streamed down her face, and a trickle of something warm and sticky coated the ankle folded under her body, but she had achieved victory merely by making it safely down. Now there was nothing but the pain and the fear that followed it. Her entire body was a slave to it, everything a distraction to the bands of pain around her belly. From somewhere she found the strength to suck in another lungful of air and at last she screamed properly – a mangled attempt at her maid's name that was loud enough to make the actual word an irrelevance.

She heard the door crash open, the underwater sound of a voice failing to make sense through the pain and then it began to recede again. Shuddering at the effort of breathing, Kine felt hands under her armpit and howled until they stopped trying to lift her. The red veil faded from her vision and she found herself blinking at the back of the chair, beside which crouched the rounded face of her maid – a shy young girl called Esheke.

The maid's hair trailed loose around her shoulders and Kine was struck momentarily by its length, almost to Esheke's waist. Kine had only ever seen it pinned neatly up.

'My Lady,' the maid wailed, 'is it coming?'

Kine almost slapped her, but a lifetime of reserve interfered so she merely nodded and whimpered at the last sharp twinges. She could feel the sweat run freely down her face and her limbs shake with the effort of staying still, but somehow with Esheke's help she rose a fraction and edged past the chair.

'Get me to the sofa,' Kine whispered, 'then fetch the midwife. My baby is coming.'

And I pray she is not the only one to be here soon, said a voice in the back of Kine's mind as an image of her lover, Narin, flashed across her mind.

There was no chance he could be there, however much she desperately wanted his presence at her side – his anxious, guileless face that shone with a blazing, unwavering love. He had been terrified of this moment for months – unable to sleep for days on end or even enjoy the Emperor's own command that raised him to the rank of Lawbringer. And now the day they both feared most had come, and he could not be here without certain death at the guns of her husband's guards.

But let someone come, Kine prayed desperately as she crawled onto the sofa and her maid darted off. *God-Empress, let someone come.*

It would not just be the midwife Esheke fetched, there could be no doubt of that. Kine's cuckolded husband had hired doctors too and they had barely left the palazzo since Order's Turn. A pair of quiet, sharp-eyed men from the homeland, their skill as physicians she had been unable to fault, but she knew why they were truly there. Castrated in the attack Narin had saved him from, Lord Vanden had hidden the injury from his peers, knowing the shame such a thing carried in Houses Dragon and Wyvern. Once the baby was born, Kine would have only moments to live – her last days won only by the chance of a male heir so desperately craved by her husband.

Lady Chance save my child she found herself crying out in her mind, fear for a daughter more profound even than her own life. *I beg you, save a life tonight – just one. If this is a girl, I'll gladly give my own.*

The pain returned and all thoughts of prayer fled.

Bredin looked up from the bar at the empty room ahead. The last patrons had left for the night and he'd bolted the doors already, and yet … He frowned and touched two fingers to the club cradled on hooks underneath the bar. The fat bar of wood was there as always and its presence was enough to reassure him.

He'd run the Lost Feathers for a decade now, long enough to know the settle and groan of its timbers like he knew the face of his wife, Sennete. She had already retired for the evening, leaving Bredin with the takings and that tiny slip of a maid, Feerin, to sweep and wipe. By now she would be asleep, drained by a long day with dawn's chores always too close at hand.

'Feerin?' he said out loud, fingers still on the club.

As though in response there was the bang of a door at the top of the tavern. The hatch to the loft, where Feerin slept.

'Must be just getting old then,' Bredin said with a weary smile.

His fingers never left the club, but that sixth sense of being watched had faded. The tavern room was still and quiet, full of shadows now the lamps were turned low and the fire burned down to embers, but he'd never found anything to fear in those shadows. The tables were scrubbed down, the floor swept. All was in order and with a shake of the head he went back to the pile of coins on the bar.

Almost ten years older than Sennete, Bredin had never been much for education and only bothered to learn to count when his ten-year bond on a merchant ship was almost up. Despite that, he finished quickly, the tally half in his head already as little Feerin couldn't ever be trusted to make change right.

The last of the coins swept into his palm and deposited into a battered strong-box, Bredin locked it and re-hung the key around his neck. Just as he did so he caught a faint sound, one strange enough to make him look up. Few people in the city had dogs; there wasn't the space for them. Aside from the hunting hounds of House Wolf you rarely saw anything other than a ratter keeping the dock's vermin in check. And yet, faint in the distance, it could almost have been a wolf's howl he'd just heard.

'Strange thing to hear,' he muttered to himself. 'But I s'pose, after the demons of summer, maybe not so strange as all that.'

On a whim, he brought the club with him as he carried his strong-box all the way round the bar and back to the kitchen door. By the grace of Lady Chance, they hadn't been affected by the goshe fever-plague the demons had borne in their wake, but Brodin had seen one with his own eyes and lived for days fearing the worst. As he'd watched the Lawbringers pursue it through the streets, converging like hungry ghosts in the evening gloom, he'd only been able to think of the fever cutting a path through his home district as it had across the city.

As he reached each of the lamps, Brodin turned the wick right down so their light was extinguished. The room was already chilly as the first real bite of winter was upon them, but it seemed to get colder still when the light drained from the room. A final inspection revealed a room in good order, tables and chairs silhouetted by the orange ghost-glow of embers still formed in the shape of the logs they had once been.

Just as he turned his back, the embers spat out a spark across the stone hearth. Brodin flinched at the sound then felt his guts turn to ice as it was followed by a low rumble like a growl – as quiet as the distant howl, but now close at hand.

'Anyone there?' he asked, raising the club.

Brodin peered around the room. He could see nothing out of place but would have sworn on Lawbringer's stars that he'd heard some sort of dog. From where he stood he could see the whole room except behind the bar he'd just come from – there was nothing there, only a glow on the stone floor that he went to tread out after a moment's pause. After another check around the room he set the strong-box down on a table and used his club to break up the remaining embers. The orange light flared brighter while he dragged an iron fire-guard across the front, casting its light up towards the ceiling beams while the lower half of the room became incrementally darker.

Brodin turned back to the strong-box and froze. The shadows around the table had changed. He could still see the chairs on either side and the strong-box on the bare tabletop, but some part of his mind wanted to form a different shape out of the darkness there. A rounded shape that swept down behind, the hint of a protrusion ahead. The hairs on his neck prickled up as Brodin blinked.

Just a shadow, he told himself, able to see the line of a chair-back through the darkness.

He reached out with the club, heart hammering with childish dread, and waved the tip through the darkened air. It met nothing, no resistance at all as he moved it back and forth and feeling foolish he lowered it again.

Behind him there came a noise. A growl – quiet, but this time unmistakable.

Brodin felt his chest tighten as a bitter taste filled his mouth. He watched the club waver as fear sapped his strength, but before he could turn or even move, the shadow in front of him shifted.

In the fireplace there was a crackle and hiss as a finger of yellowed flame appeared over the embers. The shadows below the line of the fire-guard deepened, intensified. Brodin saw it now, the curve of a neck, the thick muzzle and ragged snub ears.

Two red glowing eyes turned his way. There came a second growl behind him but he was transfixed and in the next instant the shadows leapt forward. The hot lash of tearing teeth whipped across his face. Brodin fell back, swinging the club wildly but hit nothing as the shadow-hound pounced.

Claws tore at his arms like burning nails while his own blow passed unnoticed until it hit the brick chimney and was jerked from his grip. Brodin hardly noticed as a second set of teeth tore into his cheek – he screamed with all his strength, then jaws of crackling fire closed about his throat and snuffed the sound out.

Light flashed before his eyes as the pain drove deeper into his mind and eclipsed all thought or feeling. Images and faces flooded through his last moments of life – a bottle, a glass, greying hair, a weathered face. Then deeper – the stains of tattoo-ink on fingers, a mark of the Imperial House.

Then it all faded. The light drained away and all was black as the last of Brodin Catter, proprietor of the Lost Feathers, died. The growls in the tavern continued a few moments longer, before melting back into the shadows and once more becoming just a distant howl on the wind.

Kine lay very still, pain, exhaustion and terror draining what little strength she had left. The sounds in the room were garbled and distant, the faces around the sofa looming and monstrous. The midwife, head down and focused as she tended to Kine – unaware of what was playing out around her. The fat young wet-nurse at her side, commanded into silence by the stern doctors who attended the child.

My baby.

Kine wanted to cry out, but she barely had the strength to breathe. She could see little, lying on her back with her head wedged back against a cushion. There was blood, she could feel that and see smears down her thighs, but how much soaked into the padded seat she didn't know.

The head of the taller doctor turned towards her, his mouth a thin, hard line. His words were garbled in her ears, Kine couldn't make out the order he snapped at the midwife but she saw the shock in the woman's face. The doctor's hair was scraped back and tightly bound. Kine could see scars disappearing beyond the hair line; ugly, jagged marks that spoke of violence. His companion was cherubic by comparison, skin so dark he could almost have been House Dragon – darker even than Kine's – and so smooth and clean it seemed to shine in the lamplight.

The doctors wore white aprons, now stained with blood, over expensive clothes. Lace cuffs had been rolled up to be kept clean and secured with gold pins embossed with the constellation of Lady Healer. Kine could see the detailed braiding on the blue collars that declared their caste, symbols of Healer, Pilgrim and Chance worked into an elegant design.

How many others? Kine wondered in her dazed state. *How many deaths in childbirth have these men overseen? How many murdered babies?*

The midwife had half-risen to argue with the doctor, confusion and anger on her face, but he gave her no time. An open hand caught her across the cheek and sent the woman sprawling over Kine. The weight of her made Kine shriek, the shock and fear in the midwife's lined face lending her strength.

She took a heaving breath and the room came into greater focus. The taller doctor advanced on the midwife, threatening another blow as she half cowered and half shielded Kine from his sudden wrath. The round-faced man, a tangled bundle in his hands, dispassionately watching the scene play out. The tiny limbs that twitched, the hand of her child upraised with fingers splayed in final, desperate appeal to the Gods.

Something caught in Kine's throat. The way he held her child, carelessly and without interest. It was a girl – an heir would be cradled like the Emperor's crown itself.

My daughter, Kine tried to say as the realisation cut her to the bone more effectively than any murderous doctor might.

'Please,' she whispered, causing the doctor to pause in his remonstration of the midwife. 'Please let me see her – just once. Before … see my daughter once.'

The doctor spoke in a quick, clipped tone as he glanced at his colleague. 'Quickly then.'

Incredulity crossed the face of the other, but the taller man just frowned and waved him forward.

God-Empress – grant me her life Kine prayed, half-delirious as the bundle was shoved forward. *I offer my own, but save my child! Lady Chance, name your price and I will pay.*

It took her a moment to take it all in, but then the pain and fear was washed away as she stared at the face of her daughter. Thin and pale against the darker hands of the doctor, a cruel flicker of hope appeared in Kine's heart. Wrinkled eyelids were crumpled against the weak light, rounded cheeks squashed by the grip on her, but the girl was a Wyvern still. Skin no lighter than Kine's husband, the girl's face betrayed nothing of her mixed heritage. In that moment Kine knew she could be accepted as her husband's child – loved and protected all the days of her life.

But she would not be. Forever a reminder he had been cuckolded, her husband would never suffer a girl to live. A son he could accept; an heir to carry his name on whether or not he chose to look the boy in the face, but never a girl.

'Leave us,' the doctor said to the midwife and wet-nurse.

The look on his face was empty, just another dull task to perform, but both women cringed away as he pointed towards the door. The wet-nurse scampered towards it and jerked the door open, then gave a small cry and fell back. Kine turned at the sound, the taller doctor did too, but neither saw in time what was in the darkened corridor beyond.

The doctor's head snapped back, causing Kine to flinch and moan with pain at the movement. A gutteral 'gah' escaped the doctor's lips as he staggered back then stood dumb and wavering as he faced the door.

In a blur of movement, someone entered and kicked the door shut with a flick of the heel. The other doctor shouted, the wet-nurse screamed, but Kine could make out nothing through the fog in her mind. Then the taller doctor crumpled unceremoniously, head flopping backwards with a short arrow protruding from one eye. Kine gasped as a dark figure stormed into the centre of the room, blue-braided hair flying, and her heart filled with relief and hope once more. The Gods had sent their emissary – a mortal Avatar of their mercy.

'Myken,' Kine said, delighting in the name though she barely had the strength to say it.

The woman's stern brown face had been a rare sight here in recent weeks – invented tasks keeping her well clear of her sworn duty to be at Kine's side.

Knight of the warrior caste and bodyguard to Lady Kine Vanden, Myken ignored her – if she even heard the feeble sound of Kine's voice. Her attention was focused on the doctor, the man holding that precious bundle. A knife appeared in his hand from somewhere. He held it up for all to see, not quite at the baby's throat but close enough that Kine softly wailed in new-found terror. Myken's arm was levelled, a hand-bow discarded at her feet and one of her pistols now drawn.

'Give her the child.'

'Stand down, Siresse,' the doctor said calmly, respectfully addressing her by her title as a female knight. 'Our master is the same, as well you know.'

'My master is duty,' Myken replied, 'my mistress the lady you stand over.'

'Stand down or you will die,' the man repeated. 'Fire that gun and you'll never make it out of the palazzo. You know this as well as you know why I've been ordered here today.'

'None of that matters. I am warrior caste, my service is sworn.'

'You will be shamed, your family ruined by this traitorous act – and if I fail, another will be sent. You know this. Don't throw your life away.'

'My life means nothing. Give her the baby.'

The doctor almost looked amused at that, pity and contempt sounding in his voice as he spoke. 'Nothing will dissuade you? As you wish, but I am a man of my word too. Let us put this in the hands of the Gods.'

He moved the dagger further from the baby. 'Lower your pistol, drop it on the floor and draw your knife – I will give her the baby and the Gods may choose which path is taken.'

Myken did not move at first. Kine wanted to cry out a warning. Every syllable of the doctor's words declared him to be a skilled knife-fighter, but she was transfixed by the scene. Her bodyguard was warrior caste, trained to kill with every weapon, but guns were only permitted to those of the higher castes and it was there the power of the warrior caste lay. Long blades and guns were her trade, but some sort of street-fight with knives? She couldn't win, but nor could a warrior back down.

'Agreed,' Myken said abruptly and lowered her pistol.

The doctor nodded and took a careful step back, a small smile of delight on his face. Kine had seen the look before, even in the course of her sheltered noble life. She'd seen the same from a merchant-prince whose wealth eclipsed every nobleman in the House Wyvern homeland, and in the eyes of a priest as he chastised a minor Imperial caste.

It was the look of a man who had the measure of his betters and intended to enjoy himself, humanity at its worst. But still she could do nothing, the strictures of her life and caste leaving her certain she would not sway Myken from whatever course she intended now.

With grateful hands Kine took her child from the doctor, once Myken had dropped her pistol and kicked it towards the desk. With her knife drawn, Myken did not advance on the doctor but he seemed not to care and made up the ground with a cruel slit of a smile parting his lips.

They were just paces apart and Myken had yet to even raise her knife, which still hung limp in her hands. Kine cast around desperately, hugging her daughter to her chest as she looked at the pistol on the floor, but it was hopelessly out of her reach. She would have to throw herself from the sofa to reach it and risk crushing her daughter in the process.

I will do it. If Myken buys me that chance, if the Gods offer this and this alone.

Kine looked down at the tiny face in her arms and felt a sudden intoxicating rush of love for her helpless, unnamed daughter.

'Her name is Dov,' she said in a croaking voice, just loud enough to make the pair hesitate.

Myken nodded briefly. 'Lady Chance's own name,' she said. 'It is fitting.'

Before the doctor could speak, Myken let the knife fall from her hands. In a practised movement she whipped her second pistol from its sheath across her belly and fired it at almost point-blank range. The bang was deafening in the small space as smoke erupted from the muzzle of the pistol and blood burst from the doctor's back. The man crashed back, dead before he hit the ground, and Myken was already moving to the door.

As Kine watched she realised the Siresse wore dull, dark clothes except for her red caste collar and a shapeless pack sat high on her back. Hardly the formal wear she normally wore at Kine's side, just enough to ensure she was not stopped re-entering the palazzo. Without a moment's hesitation, Myken turned the key in the lock and dragged the table beside it across.

'In,' she ordered the aghast midwife and wet-nurse, pointing toward the dressing room that stood off to the left. They jumped to obey and she locked that behind them too before heading towards the window with brisk purpose. Kine could only feebly watch her go and admire the determination in everything she did. It occurred to her then she knew so little about her saviour, the years she had been her protector never eroding the boundaries of caste between them.

The woman stopped at the desk and bent down at the big lower drawer. The desk was an old one that had been in her family for generations – a solid block of dark polished wood from the homeland. Kine loved it for the family it reminded her of.

'It's no use, I've lost the key,' Kine whispered, unheeded, just as Myken jerked it open and pulled out a velvet pouch that clinked with metal inside. She pocketed that and then withdrew a coiled rope, looping it around the foot of the heavy desk and tugging hard to ensure it was secure.

'Come,' Myken said, leaving the rope on the desk. 'We must go. The guards will have heard that shot.'

'I … I cannot,' Kine protested as Myken scooped Dov from her arms. 'What are you doing?'

Myken didn't answer as she tugged her jacket open to reveal a sling bound around her chest. With as much care as she could manage Myken put the child into the sling and nestled her between her modest breasts, tugging the edge over Dov so she was securely held.

'Come,' Myken repeated and pulled on Kine's arm. Ignoring Kine's enfeebled protests and cries of pain she hauled her up and wrapped a long robe around Kine's body. This she roughly pinned before pulling a plain cape around her mistress and bringing her towards the window. Pushing it open, she slipped the rope around Kine's chest and pulled it tight. The cold, quiet city was unveiled in the light of the Gods, thin wisps of mist curling seductively round the great houses of Dragon District ahead of them.

'No, I must fall,' Kine mumbled, 'I promised the Goddess …'

'Damn the Goddess,' Myken growled, hauling Kine up and over the windowsill, 'no Goddess had a part in this plan so just do what you're told, my Lady, and for Pity's sake do it quietly. Bite your lip right through if you have to, but be quiet here until you're on the ground.'

Even in her feverish and agonised state, Kine felt a flicker of astonishment at Myken's brusque tone – so out of character from the model of restraint and respect.

'Plan?' she mumbled.

'There's a plan,' Myken confirmed. 'A slim chance, but better than none.'

She tipped Kine over the edge, one loop of the rope wrapped around her arm to take the strain, though the jolt itself was enough to make Kine draw blood from her tongue as she fought the urge to howl.

Myken began to play out the rope as soft cries began to emerge from the sling at her chest. Her grunts of effort swiftly became tinged with pain as she stood side on to the window and took Kine's full weight. Kine began to descend in the dark night and the cold of winter surrounded her.

Before long Kine found her feet touching the ground. Only when she was half-lying on the icy gravel path did she take in her surroundings and recognise the jungle-like garden to the rear of the palazzo. She stifled a cry as a guard, musket slung over one shoulder, hurried over and without speaking untied the rope from around Kine's shoulders.

She let it happen as though this was all a dream, the absence of respect and genuflection from the liveried man just another aspect of this surreal night. The garden was dark and still, the light of the Gods casting deep shadows as they edged the tallest trees in silver. At this time of year the garden was barely used and no lanterns were lit there, as the palazzo's windows were shut up against the cold. She lay in the dark, dazed and shivering, for less than a minute before Myken scampered down the rope and stood over her.

'Thank you,' she said to the guard, who ducked his head in response.

Kine saw he was a young man when he tilted his head back up and caught the starlight. *A lover, or a love-struck youth? Is that the turn of a coin which decides whether I live or die?*

'Myken, go,' Kine whispered. 'I don't have the strength. Take Dov and leave me here.'

'My oath is to you,' Myken said with a shake of the head. 'If I have to carry you, you are coming.' She slipped a pistol from its sheath and spun it in her hand. 'Ready?' she asked the young guard.

He nodded and Myken wasted no time. She struck him a crisp blow on the side of the head and he staggered. Against his dark skin, Kine just made out a thin trail of blood running down his cheek as the guard sank to his hands and knees. Myken helped him to the floor but didn't stop to check his wound, slipping an arm under Kine's shoulder and helping her up.

'My baby?' Kine gasped.

Myken opened the fold of the sling enough to expose Dov's tiny wrinkled face to the cold night air. She opened her mouth to bawl and Myken quickly slipped a finger in to try and stave off the cry. It worked well enough and the two women stumbled together towards the street door, finding it unlocked. The cobbled street beyond was empty and only a cold wind howled up to greet them.

Myken hissed with irritation, but didn't speak as she helped Kine across and into the shadows of a neighbouring building. From there they cut through to another shadow and crossed a small square. On the far side of that was an archway decorated with snarling wyverns, the extent of House Wyvern's nominal corner of Dragon District. Beyond that was a bigger street and a handful of people walking hunched and hurried through the chilly night air. Just as Kine's legs were ready to fold beneath her, Myken brought her to a handcart station where two carts stood waiting under a sloped roof.

A pair of men broke away from the fire burning to one side and hurried to help them into a cart, the sight of Myken's ornate pistol-sheath enough demonstration of her rank that they complied without question. Kine was gently lifted up into the seat and Myken squeezed in beside her, peeking at Dov while the labourers, both black-skinned Dragons, were occupied with manoeuvring the handcart out into the street.

'Coldcliffs,' Myken ordered, picking a location that took them in the right direction without announcing the destination. 'Go fast and I'll pay double.'

This time she did get a raised eyebrow, Coldcliffs being no fitting destination for a high caste, even if it had been summer, but Myken's expression showed she wasn't to be questioned. After that moment's hesitation they set off down the empty street and the night swallowed them. When shouts rang out around the palazzo and lantern-wielding guards raced out into the street beyond, they were clear of it all.

CHAPTER 4

'Lawbringer Narin. Just the man I was looking for.'

Narin didn't move, lost in his own thoughts as he stared out across the rooftops. Ahead of him the morning mist slowly faded to reveal the southern districts of the Imperial City, but there was only one small part he noticed. East of the sharp towers in Dragon District lay the streets given over to House Wyvern.

Caught in that nest of vipers were the woman he loved and the child she carried. So close to term now. He would not have dared leave her there for so long, were it not for her husband's warrior retinue, which had only recently left with him for the Wyvern homeland.

'Lawbringer,' repeated the voice, right in his ear.

Narin jumped and whirled around to see the stern face of the Lawbringer Rhe – his mentor and now his colleague. They both wore the white trousers and jacket of the Lawbringers, the Emperor's sun and sword device on their breasts currently hidden by heavy white coats that reached their knees. They would have matched perfectly but for the fact that Narin wore a sword on his hip and Rhe had a nobleman's pistol-sheath across his stomach. The black leather was subtly stitched to combine the emblems of House Brightlance and Rhe's noble family – a forest eagle grasping a leaf-blade spear.

'Lawbringer Rhe, my apologies,' Narin exclaimed, awkwardly bowing. 'I was miles away.'

The renowned Lawbringer was a tall man who stood a good few inches above Narin. More heavily built than most of the pale rangy warriors of Brightlance, the characteristic blue-grey tint to his pale complexion gave him a cold air that was enhanced by his high-born reserve. Compared to Narin's tanned skin and dark hair Rhe would have looked permanently ill, but for the calm strength he exuded.

Narin had often wondered if, in return, he looked oddly twitchy and nervous to everyone he met in Rhe's company.

'I noticed as much. It seems to happen more and more these days – has the Emperor's blessing gone to your head so much?'

Narin blinked. *Please let that be a joke.* 'No, I … I'm sorry – I'm just tired and distracted.'

It was true he had been mentioned at court after the goshe scandal and rewarded with elevation to the rank of Lawbringer, but these days Narin was more wary than most about any sort of patronage. The day he'd earned the favour of a certain House Wyvern nobleman had been the turning point in his life, but the price attached had thrown his life into turmoil.

Narin had spent roughly a decade as an Investigator now, apprenticed to various Lawbringers as was custom. Rhe had been the last of those; just a few years older than Narin but the shining star of the Lawbringers, and as much a final test as teacher for the sheltered local boy.

'Distracted and anxious, I would say,' Rhe said after a moment's scrutiny of his protégé. 'But still you will not tell me why.'

Narin ducked his head. 'It would be a burden on your honour,' he said honestly, 'and you already keep enough secrets on my behalf.'

'The secrets I keep are not yours,' Rhe pointed out. 'Yet I would have thought doing so had earned me a little more trust from you.'

'This is, ah, different. I … I've done something I think'll soon come back to haunt me. I wouldn't want you tainted by scandal any more than I'd want to put you in a difficult position.'

'You believe I would condemn you?'

Narin winced and his eyes lowered to the pistol-sheath at Rhe's stomach. He carried only a sword himself because he was craftsman caste, and gunpowder was prohibited to the lower castes – landowner, merchant, craftsman, servant and peasant. Ownership of a gun would mean a death sentence for Narin, Lawbringer or not, but for Rhe it was also a symbol of a specific code instilled into every high caste. *Would I trust our half-friendship over your sense of honour?*

'You'd disapprove of my foolishness. I prefer not to test how greatly.'

Rhe's expression was typically inscrutable, but at last the taller man nodded. 'As you wish – come, there is a crime we've been called to.'

Without realising it, Narin grimaced. His reputation within the Lawbringers was a strange one after the goshe affair and apparently everything unnatural was his purview now. Thus far that mostly amounted to inspecting the chewed-on corpses of drunks to verify if demons had killed them or if there had been a murder committed by a human.

'No need for that face,' Rhe said, 'you will not be fishing the Crescent for human remains today. There is something else requiring your expertise.'

'Expertise?' Narin sighed, instinctively checking around to ensure there was no one to overhear them. The room was busy enough, being a large communal office used by two-dozen Lawbringers. No one paid them any attention, but still he lowered his voice.

'You know I've no real expertise. Unless you can persuade Enchei or Irato to become an Investigator, I know as little as any novice. If it's a real crime, we're doing the victim a disservice by claiming otherwise.'

'You have greater experience of the unnatural than any other Lawbringer I know,' Rhe countered. 'Any scrap of familiarity means you will see past any horror better than the rest – and you have your friends as a resource. That is as good as the Lawbringers currently have and so the crimes are ours to investigate. This is your calling; accept it and serve the Emperor to the best of your ability.'

Narin's shoulder's sagged. *Guess I deserved that.*

'You're right, of course. I'm a Lawbringer and I serve wherever I can. So, where are we going?'

The where for Narin and Rhe turned out to be an unimpressive tavern in the Harbour Warranty, tucked into an unlovely corner at the eastern end of the district. It was a run-down area of semi-derelict warehouses and slum houses where the cold of night still reigned. The shadow of Coldcliffs loomed large over this part of the city, a huge structure older than recorded history and made of the same unnatural white material as the Imperial Palace.

Narin suppressed a shiver when they found themselves in the shadow of that cliff-born slum; less affected by the frost hidden from a pale morning sun than the memory of trying to shake off the pursuit of goshe assassins there. Staying back to buy others time to escape, he'd been captured and tortured by the goshe's elite. Months later he still found the unearthly presence of that place reawakened old hurts.

'The Lost Feathers,' Rhe read as they turned into a side-street and saw the tavern at the far end.

'Heard of it before?'

Rhe shook his head as he paused and looked around before entering the street. The cobbles were poorly maintained, with furrows gouged in the ground and torn-up cobbles scattered down the street. The walls bore the marks of water damage and age, while directly opposite the side-street stood a broad soot-stain of some type of fire damage.

A handful of people stood outside the tavern, half a dozen locals fresh from their beds, and a single Lawbringer called Olsir. She was a striking woman from the far south, long plaits of grey hair declaring her to be House Iron or some country within its hegemony. Narin felt a knot in his stomach as he recognised relief in her face at their approach.

She's not one to hand over a case gladly, he realised glumly. *Don't think I'm going to like what we find here.*

'Lawbringers,' she called out, 'either of you eaten yet?'

The onlookers parted readily and retreated to a respectful distance as Narin and Rhe reached her. The tavern door was slightly open, the interior dark, but the stink of loosed bowels was enough to tell Narin what lay inside. To one side was a freshly-broken shutter, swinging loose with the wood around its latch burst and splintered.

'Who reported it?' Rhe asked.

'The maid,' Olsir said, pointing towards a young girl almost entirely hidden by a thick blanket draped around her. Her face was white with cold and terror, her hands jerking and twitching as they gripped the blanket. 'She heard the commotion from her attic room. Claims there was something pacing beneath the hatch after it went quiet again, some demon sniffing after her, but the ladder was pulled up and it couldn't get to her.'

'Do we believe the story?'

Olsir scowled. 'She didn't kill the landlord or his wife, that's for sure. Yes, I believe her.'

'A demon broke in through a window, making a neat job of it too, and killed two people, but only the maid heard?' Rhe asked, pointing at the damaged shutter.

'That was a neighbour. Once the sun came up the maid screamed for help and they broke the shutter to get in – both doors were still bolted from the inside and the maid wouldn't go downstairs.'

'That's why you believe the demon part of her story?' Narin asked, almost not wanting to know the answer.

Olsir shook her head. 'Gives it some credence, but …' She pointed inside the tavern. 'Go see for yourself and tell me if a maid did this.'

Narin grimaced as Rhe did just that, pushing open the door and heading inside. He had two fingers perched on a pistol butt as he did so, but Narin had learned that was not nerves. The pose was something of an affectation by noblemen from House Eagle's lands – an ingrained habit of readiness taught to young men and women trained for battle.

Following Rhe in, Narin resisted the urge to slide his hands around the grip of his sword. The air had a greasy foetid feel to it that went beyond the stink of spilled guts. He couldn't see much at first, his eyes adjusting slowly to the gloom, but the scattered tables and chairs told him there'd been a sizeable struggle.

Rhe stopped short and looked down just three paces inside the door. Narin instinctively moved to the side and felt a chill of foreboding as he heard the squelch of something underfoot. Rhe didn't look back; his attention was on the ground at his feet as he spoke.

'I believe you've just trodden on the evidence, Lawbringer.'

Narin blinked as the room came into focus, recoiling with disgust as he saw the dark smear of insides under his feet.

'Jester's folly! It's—' he exclaimed before bile rose in his throat and he had to swallow hard. 'It's everywhere,' Narin continued in a subdued voice.

'He,' Rhe corrected, pointing to the centre of the room. 'He's everywhere. Lady Pity, comfort his soul.'

It took an immense effort for Narin not to spew his guts up as he followed Rhe's finger. Amid a pile of torn flesh and dark stains of blood, there was most of a head – almost untouched except for a torn cheek, and damage to the eyes. The unreal distortion of brutal death meant Narin didn't quite recognise it for what it was at first, but then he saw stubble on one fleshy cheek and short hair matted with blood.

'Stars in heaven,' Narin breathed as he composed himself and looked past the head.

There were pieces of flesh scattered across the bar, dark sprays of blood on the ceiling and fireplace, more down the corridor leading away from the barroom. Most of the gruesome remains were unidentifiable, just shapeless lumps of meat sheathed in tattered scraps of clothing, but at Rhe's feet was a four-fingered hand. A boot with gristle trailing from the top rested at a tilt against the bar.

Rhe looked back at Narin, his expression as unreadable as ever, then the Lawbringer picked his way across the room to the nearest unbroken window and opened the latch. Narin did the same with a second and the weak morning light of winter spread over the horrific scene. It only worsened with the addition of colour and detail, but Narin forced himself to focus on the details rather than think about the brutality of the landlord's death. A small voice at the back of his mind howled at the horror, but the Lawbringer in him overruled it.

'He was dragged from the corridor?' Narin asked in a choked voice, pointing towards the blood-sprayed corridor on the far side.

Rhe shook his head and pointed to the fireplace. 'This is the spray of a killing blow,' he said, indicating the path of blood up the brickwork, 'as is that in the corridor.'

'So he was killed here, his wife came to investigate the noise,' Narin concluded, moving to the boot at the bar and crouching to look at it. 'But this was no cut,' he said, looking at the ruin of flesh from which a jagged stump of bone protruded like some awful maggot.

'No, no sword did this. Look at the floor.'

Narin did so, for a moment seeing nothing but half-dry patches of blood and gristle. 'Grooves in the floorboards,' he said at last, 'fresh ones mostly, but there's blood in some.'

'Claw marks, perhaps a meat hook or some monstrous weapon,' Rhe said, 'but then there is the hearth stone.'

Across the front of the open fireplace were four large flagstones, worn and soot-stained through years of use. At one end however there was another mark – a blackened smear that Narin could all too easily imagine was a footprint of some hound, except it looked as big as his own hand with fingers splayed. With a sense of dread he checked it to confirm that and realised his estimate had been very close.

He licked a finger and glanced up at Rhe who nodded to him. Rubbing his finger down one side, Narin confirmed it was not just a random soot-stain but something more permanent on the stone.

'Claw-marks, stones scorched underfoot, no obvious point of entry.'

Rhe straightened. 'I will go and confirm it is the same with the wife. You tell Olsir to let no one in and then question the neighbours, find out what sort of man the landlord was.'

'You think this was deliberate? Hard to imagine a landlord would have the sort of enemies that might be able to set, ah … to set hell-hounds on him.' Narin hesitated. 'That *is* what you're thinking, right?'

Rhe nodded, his expression stony. 'It may be this was random, but from what little I know of such folklore, hellhounds come as super-natural punishment or are bound to service by some mage. Neither seems likely, but perhaps a line of investigation will suggest itself. More likely, this was staged in some way and he was involved in something else entirely.'

'So where do you want me?'

'We have to allow for the possibility this is exactly what it seems – or it has been staged by persons with the means to enter locked rooms.' Rhe gave him a cold smile, made more chilling by the rarity of such an expression on the man's face. 'In either case, you must go and see a man about a hound.'

CHAPTER 5

Kesh edged around the door jamb and peered into the dim dining room. Cold winter light slipped through the window shutters, cutting white through the shadows. The man faced away from her in front of the empty fire. She crept forward, sliding her body gently through the half-open doorway, and assessed the room between them. Her path was partly blocked by the heavy oak table, but its surface was clear, its chairs tucked neatly under.

I've got you now.

Kesh tightened her grip on the long knife and burst forward, two steps taking her to the table. She vaulted it with ease, right foot leading the way to kick the man into the fire mantel. Just as she reached him, the man twisted with improbable speed. One arm deflected her kick as he turned away from the blade that followed it.

The air was driven from her lungs by the punch that followed, a blow that sent her sprawling back and sliding back down the length of the table.

'That's how you want it?' the man growled, drawing his own knives. 'Fine with me.'

He stalked forward as Kesh scrambled over the far edge of the table, somehow managing to land on her feet and keep her grip on the weapon. She staggered back a step before catching her balance again and setting her feet. Shoulders hunched, knife held out before her, she slipped her free hand under her jacket and withdrew a wickedly curved hatchet.

The man hesitated. 'Just happened to have that on you?' he asked, not waiting for a reply before lurching forward on the attack.

His blows fell short and Kesh gave a step of ground, well clear of the slashing blades. Seeing an opportunity she darted forward, knife-tip surging towards the man's arm. He turned and deflected it, then dodged the hatchet swing that followed. Before she could strike again the man pivoted and drove a heavy boot into her midriff.

The impact lifted her off her feet, throwing Kesh several yards back to slam into a sideboard. Stars burst before her eyes, her back screaming with pain, as her weapons were jerked from her hands. She forced herself to roll sideways in a bid to get away, but felt a hand close around her ankle. As she was hauled along the ground she twisted and kicked into the side of his knee with her free foot, slipping his grip and eliciting a grunt from her attacker.

Instead of fleeing she swung up on the offensive, using his arm to haul herself upright and slam her left hand into his face. A flash of light exploded from her palm and the man reeled, cursing, with hands to his face. Kesh scooped up her fallen knife and threw herself on him, driving the man back against a wall and putting the blade to his throat.

'Yield?' she snarled into his face.

Still pawing at his eyes and grimacing, the man nodded. 'Ah, fuck – aye, I yield! Bastard spirits o' the deep, when did you start carrying that around with you?'

Kesh released him and stepped back, sheathing her knife before fetching the hatchet.

'These past few weeks now,' she said, flexing her fingers. 'Ever since it was clear one of my damn fool friends was likely to get me into a fight soon. That's why we're training, remember?'

There were leather loops around her middle and index fingers, a small pad laced with slippery grey threads hanging from them. Enchei had made it for her once the goshe scandal had died down, having cut the threads from the flesh of a goshe elite he'd killed. What they were made of she couldn't tell, certainly not sinew but not metal either. Enchei had said the goshe's mages had inserted a piece into the man's hand and caused it to grow like a parasite under the flesh.

'Call that training?' he growled, 'I can barely see now, but I can smell burned flesh. That spark-pad ain't a fucking toy.'

'You were hardly holding back, Irato,' she snapped in response, her anger close to the surface, as it always was when they sparred. 'What about the bloody kick? You do remember you're stronger than natural men, right?'

'I held back,' he said casually. 'Your ribs ain't broken, are they?'

'Cripple's teeth,' Kesh hissed, pressing a hand to her side. 'You came damn close, just be more careful next time. You might be a soulless

41

bastard, but you're not careless. *I was the one Enchei told to give it everything, remember?'*

'Merciful light of the divine!' cried a third voice. Kesh turned to see the outraged face of her mother, Teike, at the doorway, a pair of empty baskets in her hands. 'What do you think you're doing?'

Kesh's heart sank as she realised another argument was brewing. 'Training,' she said with a wince. 'We can't be far off trouble coming our way and I mean to be better prepared this time.'

'Training be damned, my girl! You do that in your own time and in your own space – you don't do your best to demolish the dining room in the process. What if a guest had come in?'

'No ships will have finished docking yet,' she argued, 'and our two guests are still abed on the far side of the house.' She pointed past her mother to where the rear section of the guesthouse was situated, connected to this part by a corridor only. 'This isn't our old house, remember?'

She saw her mistake at once, the bristling anger she'd inherited from her mother once more appearing between them.

'I hardly need reminding,' Teike said, 'given *that* man now lives here in your sister's place – to say nothing of the fact he's the reason our home burned down and your sister's dead.'

'Don't start that again,' Kesh replied hotly, 'he pays his way and you know that.' *And this goshe training house might not have the views of our old one, but we've more rooms to earn off while our home's being rebuilt. And you've got a labourer thrown in for free.*

Her mother sniffed. 'Payment like that I'll live without. I don't know what it is between you, but I've seen your training sessions. Most of the time I'm surprised they don't end with one of you being killed. Don't pretend this one was any different; you two are a hair's breadth from stabbing each other when your blood's up.'

Kesh took a long breath, knowing how close she was to getting into a screaming match. What made things worse was that Teike spoke only the truth. Half a year after Emari's death, Irato could still kindle a rage inside her like little else. Pardoned by decree for his involvement in the Moon's Artifice affair, they were all aware that neither woman would ever fully forgive him.

'I'll leave you two alone, Mistress Teike,' Irato muttered, eyes downcast again now the violence was over. Brutal and thoughtless though he was with a knife in his hand, the effect of Moon's Artifice on his mind was permanent and Irato remained subservient to both women the rest of the time. Only part of it was instinctive; Kesh knew he still felt guilt at crimes he couldn't recall. Irato knew his part in their loss and his deference was some form of penance.

'You stay there,' Teike said, 'I may not like it, but Kesh's made it damn clear you're some strange part of what family I've got left. Half my friends think the pair of you are sleeping together anyway,' she added – Kesh's widened eyes showed the barb had hit home – 'but of course they haven't seen the murder in Kesh's eyes when she takes a knife to you. Sometimes I wonder if it isn't true myself, but whatever's going on – whether you play weapons-tutor or guard dog to Kesh – you're here now. If there's going to be an argument you'll be part of it.'

Kesh sighed, knowing the burly fighter wouldn't take part in any such thing. With his past erased by Moon's Artifice, he rarely had an opinion to express on any subject and was frequently lost without direction from her. Guard dog was a better description than perhaps her mother realised.

'What goes on when we train is my choice, not yours,' Kesh said. 'Gods, I'm sounding like a whining child now! But no, we're not sleeping together. It's nothing like that, and yes sometimes maybe I don't hold anything back, but he can take it and it's his choice.'

'Is it now?' Teike cocked her head at Irato. 'The way you and your friends described it, his goshe poison made some things not about choice. Enchei was the one who described him as your guard dog first. Now, I might not like having him around, but I don't like the sight of my daughter owning a slave and sometimes you come perilously close.'

'Mistress,' Irato broke in hesitantly, 'a slave would want to leave. I choose to stay.'

'You don't choose bloody anything,' Teike snapped, 'that's the problem!'

'Yet I would be lost without Kesh.' He paused, frowning as he tried to frame his thoughts. 'I trust her – maybe not to avoid giving me a few extra scars, but when it's important I trust her as I can't trust myself.'

'What the buggery is that meant to mean?'

'Thief's sticky fingers!' Kesh exclaimed. 'How many times do I need to explain it? The man's only got half a soul left. He forgets to care about things, about how people are more important than rocks. Without me telling him he forgets what right and wrong are, he just does what others tell him to.'

43

'There's only one thing I'm sure of in this life,' Irato said with rare assertiveness, 'and that is that I was a murderer and a thief of souls, and I don't wish to be that man again. I may not remember my crimes, but I know I could do more harm to the world without a guiding light I can trust.'

'That's another thing, young lady,' Teike said, ignoring most of what they had said, 'no more of this cursing when you're under my roof. You used to be a pious girl, remember? Now you only mention the Gods when you're cursing.'

Kesh scowled. 'I wasn't exactly won over when I met one, remember? These days I think I'd prefer to trust the demons that visit Irato more than any Ascendant god.'

'Don't even get me started on bloody demons possessing him any hour of the night,' Teike said, pointing an accusing finger at Irato. 'Dragging him out into the dark to do Gods know what. Do they follow your moral guidance too? Last month one came during dinner, remember? Soon it'll start costing us paying customers!'

'I will go and earn a wage if you would prefer me to keep clear of your guests,' Irato joined, but then shrank back from the furious looks he received from both women.

'I'm sure you could command a good fee yes, given how good you seem to be at killing folk,' Teike snapped.

'That's really not helping! Irato,' Kesh said, 'get out, will you?'

This time her mother made no objection and the big man slunk outside, closing the door behind him.

'How can you treat the man like a guard dog,' Teike said as she watched the door shut, 'and still keep him here out of some strange sympathy? Don't you dare tell me the sight of him doesn't sometimes sicken you, I see it in your face as clearly as I feel it in my heart. '

'It's my memories that hurt, not the sight of him,' Kesh said in a subdued voice. 'Might be I'd remember Emari less without him around, but I'm not ready to leave go of her memory yet. I don't know if this is forever, but it is what it is for the moment.'

Teike took her daughter's hands in her own. 'But it's a burden you don't need to take on. Oh my beautiful girl, you've always been strong, but that doesn't mean you need to assume the burdens of others. I'm not talking about Irato here, either. I may like Narin and Enchei more than your guard dog, but they're men who attract trouble. Without them, you wouldn't need to practise knife work.'

To Teike's surprise, Kesh gave a small laugh and hugged her. 'Honestly, Mother, you disapprove of my friends? Can I not go out and play once I've done all my chores?'

'You're not so grown up I can't put you over my knee, young lady,' Teike replied, a sad smile on her face. 'But seriously, Kesh – you've been through so much this last year. Not just losing a sister, but being beaten and almost killed several times, then those inquiries by the Imperial Court, interrogations from House Dragon. And all the work you did here. It hardly seems as though life has returned to normal, because when you're not here working you're over at the Crowsnest overseeing the rebuilding.'

'What else can I do? It's tiring, yes, but we need to get everything done.' She gestured around at the house they stood in. 'This Shure the Imperial inquiry loaned us was in no fit state to rent to anyone and winter's only going to make it worse.'

'Exactly, my girl! There's more work to do than I can reasonably ask of you, but you make time to train at street-fighting with Irato and now you might be away from home for a few days?'

Kesh ducked her head in acknowledgement. 'I know, but I can't just pretend my friends don't need my help. We've got money to hire in someone to help you here while I'm away. Spend it, please – labourers, a maid, whatever we need to keep the guests happy over winter.'

'Away doing *what*, though?' Teike insisted. 'Why won't you tell me that? "Enchei will be calling me away soon" isn't much of an explanation!'

'It's best you don't know any more. In case things get nasty. I don't want you anywhere near it.'

'Is that why you're brawling with Irato these days? You're getting ready for the nastiness to catch up with you?'

'If it happens, I'm going to be ready for it, that's all,' Kesh said firmly. 'I'm leaving the violence to others, I'm no fool, but if someone grabs me in the street like that bastard goshe did in the summer, I want to be ready for whatever gets thrown my way.' She took a long breath and forced a smile. 'You have to trust me, this isn't like the summer. There's no Empire-wide conspiracy, unnatural soldiers or demons involved – at least, not on their side! This is simply a friend in a jam and we're taking no chances.' She hesitated, her face falling. 'Mother, I have to do this. Not just because Enchei or Narin asks it, but … well, it's not just them involved.'

'What do you mean?'

Kesh bit her lip before replying. 'There's a little girl whose life is also at stake – a little girl, younger than Emari, who's caught up in all this. It might not make sense, but I can't stand aside. I can't avoid getting involved if I can help at all. It might be playing nursemaid's all I'm needed for, but whatever needs to be done, I *must* do it.'

In her gut Kesh felt a bitter heat at the half-lie. It was told far more to explain the impossibility of her changing her mind than to sway her mother, but the voice of a cynic at the back of her mind chastised her for just that. She had no idea whether Kine would be giving birth to a boy or a girl, but in her heart she knew it didn't matter.

A baby in need was enough – it should be enough to anyone, and would certainly be for her mother, but in the privacy of her own head Kesh had been thinking of the child as a little girl. Lady Kine was a Wyvern so any child of hers and Narin's would be little darker than Kesh's adopted sister, Emari. The combination of the two was such a powerful compulsion, Kesh hadn't even had to think when Enchei outlined his plan to her.

Before Teike could respond, Irato ducked his head back through the door. 'Kesh, there's some kid here with a message.'

'From Enchei?'

'Some weird old man is what she says. "The egg's hatched and she's learned to fly."'

Kesh nodded, a nervous lurch in her stomach for all she'd been expecting this moment. She steeled herself and looked up at her mother. Teike managed to give her a smile and kissed her daughter on the cheek.

'Go. Do everything a big sister would.'

There were tears in both their eyes as Kesh ran to fetch her bag and coat, but with the anger between them diffused the burden on her heart was a fraction lighter.

CHAPTER 6

From the Harbour Warranty it was a short journey to the tavern in neighbouring Tale where Narin's closest friend, Enchei Jen, lived. The aging veteran-turned-tattooist proved to not be at home, according to the maid who answered the door and gave Narin her prettiest smile as she invited him in to wait. Just that small moment of flirtation was enough to send Narin's mood spiralling down and he gave a gruff refusal before heading up to the waters of the Crescent in search of a boat to take him across.

Elevation to the rank of Lawbringer had brought Narin more than just authority and some of it he could do without. Women who knew him in some small way were suddenly interested in him, more than a year after the day Narin stopped trying to bring such a thing about. Even ambitious minor officials attempted to cultivate his friendship now the Emperor himself had learned, however briefly, Narin's name and deeds during the summer.

A brisk breeze skipped off the Crescent as he reached its shore and found a boat to take him across. Narin pulled the collar of his white jacket as high as he could against the chill and watched the other traffic on the wide body of water that surrounded the Imperial Island.

The high prows of House Dragon barges surrounded him, starkly red and black against the dull colours of winter, while a handful of merchant ships were dotted amongst the main traffic of Crescent boatmen who transported most of the city's goods. On every berth post the constellations of Lady Sailor or Lady Navigator were carved, the largest hung with offerings of broken oars and worn-out tools.

Narin's thoughts returned to Kine and the knot of anxiety behind his eyes tightened a fraction further. She was so close to her due time – it could be any day, Enchei had told him – but still they'd been unable to extract her from the palazzo that had become a prison for her in recent months.

I know he's as good as his word, Narin reminded himself privately, while the young boatman behind him sang out disjointed bursts of prayers and songs that they all used to warn each other of their presence. He hardly noticed the babble of voices, having lived in the city all his life, but still found it hard to concentrate on either of his problems for any length of time.

Enchei's as good as his word, Narin repeated over the cacophony of fears and questions in his mind. *He promised he would do this and he's as good as his word.*

It was hard to doubt anything Enchei said nowadays. Narin remained in awe of his grey-haired friend, who'd proved his Astaren background as he repeatedly saved Narin from the goshe. The old warrior had promised he would effect Kine's escape from the Vanden family palazzo, but nothing had been possible until Lord Cail Vanden had retired for the winter to his estate with the bulk of his warrior caste attendants.

As they arrived on the far bank, Narin tossed the boatman a coin and was on his way before the man had caught it. One benefit of his elevation had been the increase in pay, of course – Lawbringers often needed to be able to support a family, and bribery or corruption among public officials was a capital offence. Like many Investigators and Lawbringers, Narin had found little time for interests beyond his work, however, let alone vices, so barely knew where to spend the money.

In the end, Enchei had done that for him – helping himself to a large chunk of what Narin had managed to save with only a few vague promises in explanation. Narin's only objection had been that he wasn't party to Enchei's plans, but the tattooist was determined to insulate his friend from whatever was going to happen.

Perhaps was happening tonight Narin realised with a jolt – his heart lightening at the idea even as he felt a pang of fear at what might go wrong. *Lord Vanden left the city two days ago – Enchei must be about to put his plans into motion.*

He crossed the Strandway that skirted the island shore, studded with great blackened lamp-posts that loomed threateningly in the grey morning light, and headed in to the interior. Up ahead the vast unreal walls of the Imperial Palace dominated the entire island – situated on a low hill and far bigger than the varied palazzos and towers that skirted it.

Narin wound his way towards the palace, cutting confidently through the narrow streets of the low-caste areas that sat like a tangle of threads on the fringe of the more ordered streets. Within a hundred yards his surroundings had graduated from servant housing to merchant dwellings, with the homes of the nobility visible behind. Before long, he found himself at a sprawling network of workshops and offices where much of the city's administration was housed, one corner of which was occupied by the Imperial tattooists.

Here the carvings on posts became the quill constellation of Lord Scholar, adornments subtly added to gates and flagpoles bearing the Emperor's sun device. It was an ancient practice, co-opted from their pagan past if Enchei was to be believed, with trades invoking their patron Ascendants. Narin knew it was frowned upon at the Palace of Law, but the novices did it all the same and he instinctively tapped the symbol as he entered the tattooists' courtyard.

Before he could reach the door, the principal administrator had spotted Narin's approach and emerged to greet him in typical fawning fashion. The man was of the religious caste, a black collarless robe hanging from his shoulders, but he still bowed low to Narin, who returned the greeting in similar fashion. Perhaps ten years older than Narin, the administrator was a paunchy local who waddled like a lord around his small domain.

'Lawbringer Narin, am I correct?'

'You are. Administrator Serril, is it?' He received another bow at that and continued. 'My friend Enchei has spoken of you often.' *Albeit never in favourable tones.*

'And a fine tattooist he is, despite his eccentricities.'

Narin smiled at that. 'Well, he cannot help being a damned heathen I suppose – is he here?'

'I'm afraid not,' Serril said, with a shake of his near-hairless head. 'He was scheduled to work today, but has not seen fit to make an appearance.'

That brought Narin up short, words catching in his throat for a moment. 'Not appeared?' he said with a cough. 'Then that might be my fault, I'm afraid. I'd asked a favour of him and it may be he's already engaged on the task at hand.'

'I understand, Lawbringer, but he fails to show due consideration for his duties,' Serril chided. 'If he is out on business of yours, you might remind him he is not employed by the Lawbringers.'

Narin had already known that Serril was a humourless man, but hearing his tone now it was clear Enchei would never be too encumbered by duty shifts. He could barely muster the required deference for the legendary Lawbringer Rhe himself – a self-important minor official would be beyond his powers.

'I will instruct him to be more mindful,' Narin said smoothly, recently-learned habits of diplomacy serving him in good stead as his mind raced down another path. 'Thank you for your time, Administrator.'

He bowed low and turned his back, as desperate to be away as he was not to watch Serril preen at the respect he'd offered. Narin was only craftsman caste, but now he was a Lawbringer he carried some ghost of the Emperor's own authority in his wake. It was a strange combination – he was expected to be servile, but officials treated such due deference as a currency all of its own.

Today, however, Narin didn't care. Not with the news that Enchei was absent from work. As disrespectful as the man was, he wouldn't offer Serril an easy opportunity to exert his modest authority – not without good reason anyway.

Is it today? Has it happened already? Where should I go, home? No, the Palace of Law – if Enchei is looking for me he'll leave a message there. Stars in Heaven, all this time and still I'm not prepared for what's coming.

As the north wind blew hard over the city and the morning continued grey and cold, Narin forced himself not to run down the handful of streets that took him to Lawbringer Square. Over the whistle of wind a temple bell tolled distant and dismal – a deep rolling tone that gave Narin some idea of the hour as he crossed the busy paved expanse and raced up the steps to the Palace of Law.

As he entered, he caught sight of a grave-looking Investigator loitering near the front. The young woman jerked as she saw him and started forward, but not before a broad figure detached from the shadows to one side and approached Narin. In his keyed-up state Narin almost drew his sword – his hand was on the hilt before he recognised the man looming forward and realised this wasn't some poorly-timed vengeance, but a killer with a message.

'Irato!' Narin gasped, releasing his sword. 'Are you looking for me?'

Behind the former goshe, the Investigator stiffened and Narin made a placating gesture. He didn't know her well, but she was a highly-strung warrior caste who wouldn't have taken kindly to one such as Irato loitering.

'Thank you, Investigator, he's with me. You can go now.'

'As you wish, Lawbringer Narin.' She gave a curt bow and, with one final look of suspicion at Irato, left them alone.

The palace's enormous entrance hall was bustling now the morning was well advanced, so despite his desperation to hear what Irato had to say Narin hustled the man back out into the chill air of the square. While there were still plenty of people around, they were all intent on their destination and it was simple enough to find space to talk.

'Enchei sent you,' Narin stated, seeing Irato's poise of readiness and focus.

The former goshe was rarely animated without a set task to perform. The fact that he looked ready for a fight, his brawler's build accentuated by a thick fur coat that hung down to his knees, meant something had happened.

Irato nodded. 'She's out.'

'Out? She's safe? Where is she?'

'I'll take you.'

Narin nodded. 'Wait, is she with Enchei? Rhe's expecting me to find him this morning and report back.'

'Was there when I left, tending to Dov.'

'Dov? Who in Pity's name is Dov?'

Irato cocked his head at Narin as though he was an idiot. 'The baby.'

The man's words stuck Narin like a punch. 'The baby?' he gasped. 'She's given birth?'

'He was going to grab her last night – got it all set up – but the baby started coming before he could move.'

'Monk's mercy! Is she all right? Are they both all right?'

'S'pose so, they're alive at any rate.'

Narin fought the urge to grab Irato round the throat and shake him. It wasn't his fault, Narin knew that as well as anyone, but at times such as this his lack of interest in the world around him was infuriating. It wasn't self-absorption, just a disconnect in his mind after the accident. The man he'd once been was gone – and good riddance by all accounts, including those of some goshe they'd interrogated – but there wasn't quite a complete one left in his place.

'Where are they?'

'Harbour Warranty – I'll take you.'

Irato didn't wait for a response from Narin, he simply went around the Lawbringer and started walking toward the south end of the square. Narin stood there, gaping and dumbstruck for a long moment at Irato's careless delivery of the news.

A voice inside told Narin he should be shouting for joy, but all he felt was disbelief at the news, that the day had finally come and he was so far behind the times. He stared after Irato, the former goshe entirely oblivious as he strode off, and at last Narin trotted after him.

Narin gave the almost-man an askance look. Kesh's dog indeed. Narin had been careful not to get involved in that tense relationship. In the half year since the goshe affair, Kesh had become the sister Narin had never had, but she knew her own mind and had made it clear the situation was theirs to sort out. Given what else had been on Narin's mind those last three celestial months, he'd been happy to let others sort it out.

Dov's a girl's name, Narin realised suddenly, almost tripping as the thought struck him. He got a curious look from Irato but barely noticed as the full weight of understanding settled on him.

Gods on high, I'm a father, he thought drunkenly. *A little girl? I have a daughter? Is this really happening?*

His gut seemed to clamp with terror at the notion that something so fragile might now be dependent on him – that his one act of fatherhood had been to put his daughter in the most terrible danger, one that would likely hang over her head for much of her life. Bands of shame and guilt seemed to close around his chest, squeezing the air from his lungs – piling on to those he carried every day over the lies that had won him his position at Rhe's side and appointment as Lawbringer.

But through those clouds shone a single ray of light and, despite it all, a disbelieving smile crept across Narin's face. That shaft of light pierced his chest and filled his heart, branding a name into his very being.

A daughter. Dov.

CHAPTER 7

Grey slabs of cloud hung overhead as they crossed the wind-swept central path of the Tier Bridge. Half a mile in length, it was one of the three most obvious ancient structures in the city, a relic of the time before human domains. Two sprays of white arcs interwove through each other as they crossed to reach the opposite bank, their smooth organic lines like some tree of the Gods tamed to purpose.

Irato led Narin up the long greyish ramp of the upper tier, preferring the longer path to struggling through the crowds filling the lower. Merchants of all kinds had premises lining the road of the lower tier, taking advantage of the fact most traffic to the Imperial district had to pass that way. As they entered Dragon District Narin couldn't help but feel a sense of being watched by hostile eyes, though they kept clear of the streets belonging to House Wyvern.

Every brown-skinned Wyvern he saw among the darker Dragons gave him a jolt of fear, high and low castes alike. On the wide Public Thoroughfare that led down to the harbour, Narin kept the pace high and his head low, not meeting anyone's gaze until they were out of the district and into the Harbour Warranty. There, Irato directed him into the very centre of the warranty to a tight warren of narrow residential streets and weathered, old, brick houses.

He quickly saw that Enchei had chosen well – short streets that linked tiny squares barely ten yards across where children ran in all directions and the squall of babies was audible at every third window. Irato and Narin both earned brief suspicious looks from those they passed, showing this part saw little through-traffic. Without warning, they arrived at the correct address and Irato thumped his fist on a doorway no different to all the rest. Narin had almost walked past it, heading through to the next dim archway on the other side, before he realised Irato was no longer beside him.

'Who is it?' asked a voice from the other side, after a moment of quiet.

'Me,' Irato replied simply, recognising Kesh's voice before Narin did.

The door jerked open and Kesh's young features appeared. 'You took your bloody time,' she snapped. 'Well, get inside then.'

Without waiting, she dragged Narin forward, obvious on the street in his Lawbringer white. He found himself in a cramped room that contained just a single chair and a pair of hooked iron bars bolted to the newly-whitewashed brick wall on either side of the door. It took Narin a moment to work out what they were for, before realising Enchei had most likely added them himself. As Kesh then demonstrated, the bars could be slotted into hoops on the door – anyone trying to kick it down would have to be strong enough to rip the bolts out of solid brick.

'Get up there,' Kesh said impatiently, pointing towards a narrow stairway that stood just before an open kitchen door. Bizarrely, there was the rich smell of recently-fried steak in the air, but again Narin put that down to Enchei's presence.

'Enchei's found time to cook?' he muttered as he headed for the stairs.

'Kine's weak, she's lost blood and is exhausted,' Kesh snapped. 'We're trying to get her strength up.'

Narin didn't have time to respond as he hopped up the stairs and almost collided with a dark-skinned figure with long loose hair. He gave a yelp, heart in his mouth, and was going for his sword even as he recognised Myken, Kine's sworn bodyguard. It was a struggle to stop himself drawing his weapon in the face of a Wyvern warrior caste, but he realised belatedly that she would have had to be in on any plot for it to have a chance of success.

For once Wyvern honour works in my favour, Narin realised as he lowered his hand, feeling foolish. *She's sworn to protect Kine – Gods, she's gone renegade from her entire nation to do it! Another life I've managed to mess up.*

'Siresse,' he said with a small bow, using her formal title to try and make up for the disrespect. As always, her expression was inscrutable. Not once had the woman given any indication that she thought little of him or considered him a fool, but he was painfully aware there were plenty of times he'd given her just cause to.

'Thank you,' he added awkwardly. 'For all you've done.'

'My honour demanded nothing less,' she said plainly. Without the trappings of her caste – blue braids pulled loose, red collar abandoned – he saw she was a striking woman in her own right, something he'd never really noticed in all the time he'd known her. Tall and muscular, she lacked Kine's radiance but had a strength and assurance that was beauty of its own.

'Still,' he said, abashed, 'I know what it's cost you.'

Myken regarded him a moment longer then inclined her head to accept his thanks. 'My Lady is in here.'

She turned and opened a narrow doorway at the top of the stairs through which yellow lamplight flooded. Narin followed as quickly as he could and felt a burst of wonder when he glimpsed Kine's face on the other side. She occupied a bed that took up much of the room, with a battered table to the right and a raised wicker cot on the left.

Propped up by a pile of assorted cushions, Kine's face lit up at the sight of him. It was enough to send a flush of warmth into his face. Before Narin could get inside a hand caught him by the shoulder and hauled him into a bearhug. Despite being smaller than Narin, Enchei's strength was impossible to resist and the Lawbringer was so stunned he was unable to try.

'Congratulations, my friend,' the older man laughed in his ear. 'She's a beauty, they both are!'

Enchei released him and waved Myken away, back down the stairs. 'You three need some time together, we'll leave you to it.'

Before Narin could say anything he'd been shoved out of the way and the door was closing behind Enchei. He half-opened his mouth to speak, but then met Kine's gaze again and saw the tiny bundle in her arms. That was enough to wash his mind clean and for a moment he just stood there dumbly and gaped at the pair.

'My love,' Kine whispered, her usual musical tones strained and weak. 'I've missed you.'

He found himself at her side, moving as though in a dream, hands slipping over her cheeks as he kissed her. That touch seemed to burst a dam inside him and tears spilled down both their cheeks – the pent-up emotion of months rushing out in one go. He'd seen her only three times since she'd told him she was pregnant; precious evenings spent in a teahouse a few dozen streets away. The last of those, she'd been clearly pregnant but they had been unable to risk any more meetings since for fear of exposure.

'How are you?' Narin croaked. 'Her name's Dov?'

Fresh tears spilled from Kine's dark eyes as she nodded. Once, she had hidden her smiles from him, taught to conceal such things from birth, but now her face shone with delight as she tugged the folds of her bundle back to show Narin his daughter's face.

'Her name is Dov – Lady Chance had to have been smiling down on us.'

'You'll get no complaints from me!' Narin gasped, beaming even as he wept. 'She's well?'

Kine nodded weakly. 'She's well, our daughter's strong. Stronger than me, I think. I don't think right now I could cry as loudly as she has been!'

On cue the soft brown cheeks in her arms crinkled and Dov opened her mouth to cry. Narin hopped back, almost panicked by the realisation that he didn't know what to do, but Kine caught his hand and brought him back to his seat on the edge of the bed.

'Hold her,' she whispered.

Narin slipped trembling hands underneath his daughter, the tiny bundle weighing so little in his hands.

'She's hungry.' Kine's eyes lowered. 'I promised myself I would feel no embarrassment here, but I can't help it.'

Narin frowned with incomprehension but, to explain, Kine opened her robe and exposed one rounded breast. 'Your friend has had to teach me,' she admitted, lip trembling. 'He, ah … there's so much I don't know. I have hardly dared to dream of this day and now I find myself just a stupid little girl, lost in a grown-ups' world.'

An ache of sympathy erupted in Narin's heart as Kine reached for her daughter and together they settled Dov at her breast. Few noble-women in the Empire would feed their own child – certainly no House Narin had ever heard of considered it usual. It took them a while to settle her, the baby seemingly unwilling to take Kine's nipple in her mouth. After a few minutes of muffled squawks she finally lurched forward and latched on, Kine gasping at the pressure but dismissing Narin's anxiety with a shake of the head.

'Enchei says it will hurt to begin with,' she explained, 'but we cannot find a wet-nurse. I must manage myself. I must learn to care for her now I'm no longer a noblewoman.'

This last was said in such a fearful voice that Narin could say nothing in response, only slip his arms around the woman he loved and hold her for a long while. The moment was only broken when the door opened again and Enchei bustled in, giving the three of them an approving smile.

'Enchei!' Narin exclaimed, only to have the older man snort at him.
'Oh shut up, nothing I've not seen before.'

'And when did you become such an expert in babies?'

Enchei's grin wavered a moment. 'Had a family once,' he admitted. 'Missed enough of their childhood but I was around when they were tiny, at least. Might have been more'n twenty years ago now, but fashions change, babies don't.'

He went to the other side of the bed and put a hand to Kine's forehead, then pushed aside a fold of cloth to look at Dov. To Narin it looked like his daughter had a look of angry determination as she worked at the nipple, but he had no idea if that was good or not.

'How long do you have?' Enchei said abruptly.

Narin jerked as though only just waking and looked blankly at the man.

'Until you need to be back at your duties? Can't really ask your friend Rhe for the day off now!'

'I, ah, actually I was coming to see you anyway. I can stay an hour or two I think.'

Enchei frowned. 'See me? That don't sound good.'

'It isn't,' Narin admitted, pinching the bridge of his nose as the events of earlier intruded once more. 'I need to ask you what you know about hellhounds.'

'Hellhounds?' Kine said with a gasp. 'Narin, what sort of investigation is this?'

'A murder. Two, in fact.'

'Killed by hellhounds?' Enchei said, sucking on his teeth in disapproval. 'That's nasty shit right there. Never come across the damn things myself, but I know something of 'em I s'pose. In the field of evil horrors at least, I got a pretty good education. They're not good things to mess with. I take it there's no chance of you dropping this investigation?'

Narin shook his head. 'All the unpleasant and supernatural crime now gets put firmly in my lap, Lord Sorote's seen to that. What can you tell me?'

'Well, let me think.' Enchei scratched his cheek with one ink-stained finger. 'Hard to explain half of it in terms that'll mean a damn to you. They're demons – not like the things that lurk in the Crescent's waters, more like the fox-spirits that play around in Irato's head from time to time. In fact ...'

Enchei rose and went to the door, calling for Irato to join them. Narin caught sight of Myken on the stairs, still on guard, and wondered for a moment what she would do now. Before he could think of anything, Dov made a tiny sound that dragged his attention away. He reminded himself they just needed to survive the week before any sort of plans needed to be made.

Irato appeared at the door and Enchei beckoned him in, the big fighter standing awkwardly at the end of the bed. He looked from one face to another, his expression not flickering as he saw Dov feeding at Kine's breast, prompting Narin to again wonder just how human he was these days. For her part, Kine showed there was still much of the noblewoman inside her as she adopted the guarded, near-expressionless look high castes wore in public.

'Got any guests these days?' Enchei asked him. 'In your head?'

'Foxes?' Irato shook his head. 'No.'

'Likely to see them soon?' The fox-spirits were minor demons, beings without physical form that rode the minds of certain animals – an ability the goshe had twisted to try and create a god inside the mind of their followers using the poison Moon's Artifice. Irato had been dosed with his own poison when Narin first encountered him and his mind was now an ideal refuge for the fox-spirits.

Irato shrugged. 'Can't say when, but yes. Even the white fox is barely enough for their pack-leader so it's with me often.'

'Ask it about hellhounds, next time whitey comes home to roost. Might be they've picked up a scent or encountered 'em in the past.'

'Hellhounds? Another type of demon?'

Enchei nodded towards Narin. 'Our friend's on the trail of one, or so he thinks.'

'Two people got torn apart in a Darch sailor's tavern,' Narin said defensively. 'The maid survived to tell a tale of shadow-hounds, because there's only a ladder to her attic room. Claw marks on the floor and in the street outside, what looks like a scorch-mark on the hearth that isn't just soot.'

The two men stared at him, neither speaking as he finished. At last Enchei nodded. 'Okay, mebbe you're right this time. Sounds like a hellhound sure enough. Where was this?'

'Towards Tale Warranty – tavern called the Lost Feathers.'

Enchei's face darkened. 'Lost Feathers?' he repeated in a growl. 'Damn. Brodin's dead?'

'The landlord? I think so, yes, his wife too. Did you know them?'

'Aye.' He ducked his head for a moment, mouthing something that could have been a prayer if he had been the praying type. 'Not a man likely to get ripped apart by hellhounds – they're not your typical sort of demon and Brodin's never been caught up in anything like that, so far's I know.'

'What are they, then?'

Enchei sighed. 'Hard to explain to you. Calling 'em shadow-demons is right enough. Remember the fox-spirits when they were outside a body? Looked like the ghosts of wolves surrounding the creature whose mind they were riding, but their claws were made of more'n just light?'

Narin nodded hesitantly. He'd not seen as much of the fox-spirits as the others during the spring, but it had been enough to follow what Enchei was describing.

'Well, think of 'em as actually *being* the light of their outline as much as the soul that sits in the mind of whatever vermin it's riding, Irato or otherwise.'

Enchei's attempt at a joke was half-hearted and it showed in his face, a feeble attempt to dismiss the anxiety he was struggling to control.

'And the hellhounds?'

'Well the good news, maybe, is that they're not so comfortable in this world. Unlike fox-spirits, they're from some shadow of our world. Can cross over for a short time, but where the foxes are in essence light incarnate, hellhounds are no more than an idea until they're dragged here.'

'And the bad news?' Kine asked in a small voice, eyes wide and hugging her daughter close as she spoke the words Narin didn't want to.

Enchei scowled. 'The bad news is once they're here – like the foxes are light, the hellhounds are darkness incarnate. Plus someone has to bring 'em here. That tavern wasn't built over some cursed crypt, it's just a pub. So someone's using the hellhounds as a weapon and this is going to happen again.'

Narin felt a familiar tingle of apprehension. 'Why? What could the landlord have done?'

'Nothing,' Enchei spat. 'Not a damn thing. He wasn't the target – he was just some unlucky sod who got in the way. You use a knife if you want to kill someone, you use a hound if you want to track someone down.'

It was Kine who asked the question first as Narin hesitated, wary of the answer. 'And what sort of someone do you track with a hellhound?'

The grey-haired man gave a heavy sigh.

'Me.'

CHAPTER 8

The next hour passed in a blur for Narin. Lost in every twitch and cry of his daughter, basking in every precious moment of Kine's presence, it felt mere minutes before he felt Enchei shake his shoulder and pull him away. Kine was almost asleep before the door had shut behind him, desperately in need of rest but refusing to sleep for as long as Narin was there.

Heading down the stairs to join the others, Narin lurched like a drunk and had to steady himself on the door jamb once he reached the lower floor. There he found Myken standing guard at the bottom of the stair, weapons close at hand, while Irato and Kesh waited in the room behind. Perched on the table, Kesh gave Narin a sly grin as he came in.

'Feeling pretty pleased with yourself, then?'

Narin blinked at her. 'What do you mean?'

'I mean, that's one beautiful baby,' she said with a widening smile. 'I've seen a few newborns in my time and that little girl's gonna grow up lovely.'

Narin hung his head, embarrassed, ashamed and inordinately pleased all in one go.

'Thank you,' he mumbled. Before he could say anything more, Enchei smacked him round the back of the head hard enough to thump him into the wall.

'What was that for?' he snapped, rubbing his head and glaring at the sour-faced veteran.

'To wake you up,' Enchei said. 'You've not got time to stand there and be smug, not by a long shot.'

'Pretty sure you didn't have to hit me. You're stronger than most, remember?'

That prompted a cold smile on Enchei's face and Narin realised the old man hadn't forgotten his supernatural strength for a moment.

'Fine, point made,' Narin said. 'What now?'

'Now you go shaman hunting, you and Lord Coldheart Bastard.'

Narin frowned. 'You mean Rhe? Why? All of a sudden you're not so sure about that hellhound being after you?'

'I'm pretty certain, but that makes no difference. Firstly, you ain't telling Rhe that bit unless you have to. He's far from a fan o' mine already. Secondly I need you to find some things out for me. Plus,' he added nastily, 'Lord Coldheart don't like it when he ain't busy. Even if it's a raven chase, it'll keep the pair o' you busy. That's your job this afternoon, then you've got a man to call on tonight.'

'Man?'

'Your new patron, remember?'

'The Imperial?' Kesh broke in. 'That'll be fun, I'm sure he won't make you squirm too much before he agrees to negotiate with Kine's husband.'

'Negotiate?' Myken said sharply. 'What makes you think Lord Vanden will negotiate?'

'Well, he can't just tell a member of the royal family to go jump in the Crescent,' Kesh said, 'and Prince Sorote already knows about Narin and Kine's relationship. We've been waiting for a while to hear the blackmail demands, but thus far he's asked for nothing beyond keeping abreast of Narin's investigations.'

'You can trust him?'

'Trust him? He's a bloody Imperial caste! Course we can't trust him, but he'll be useful and we're out of options here.'

The knight paused a moment, looking around at the four other faces in the room before focusing back on the young girl. 'You are not their maid?'

'Me?' Kesh bristled while Enchei chuckled. 'No I'm bloody well not! I'm … well, I'm a friend o' Narin's.'

'Privy to his closest secrets?' Myken help up a hand. 'How many friends, Lawbringer Narin, are aware of all this? My Lady remains in danger and I have sworn to protect her with my life, but I see you're more careless with your secrets. How many others know of this? How far does this risk to her go?'

Narin shook his head. 'Kesh's not just some girl I know,' he explained. 'That goshe business in the spring? The ones involved were me, Enchei, Kesh and Irato – they're not acquaintances, they're family. They've all shed blood for my sake and to do what's right. I've trusted them with my life and I'll continue to.'

'And Prince Sorote?'

'A powerbroker of some sort, a dealer in secrets. He found out mine and he didn't reveal it. Whatever he wants, he's got leverage enough that he'll get it or I'll resign in disgrace, but until then there's not a lot I can do about it. More importantly, if I send some friend to negotiate for Kine's life, they'll just be killed. Why would a noble caste give a damn what we could offer when his honour is at stake?'

Myken nodded slowly. 'But an Imperial caste must be listened to,' she said. 'I understand, but your secrets are spread too widely. If you put my Lady in danger, you will have me to answer to.'

'That's rather the point, ain't it?' Enchei interrupted. 'You damn Wyverns and your honour? Vanden don't have an heir to celebrate, he's got a wife who's run off with a daughter he's little use for. Whatever tale he tells others, she's betrayed him and he'll want her dead. If we're to get the assassins called off, we need to negotiate and an Imperial caste friend might be the best prize we could offer anyway.'

The room fell into silence after that. Eventually Myken bowed her head to acknowledge Enchei's words. She pointed towards Irato. 'You – you are a fighter, correct?'

Irato nodded.

'Watch over the Lawbringer, then, ensure he is not followed. Lord Vanden may well have guessed the truth already.'

'You don't give the orders here,' Kesh pointed out. 'High caste or not, you're outcast now so you're as low as the rest of us.'

That brought Myken up short, but it was only a moment before she recovered.

'Spend as long as you like coming to the same conclusion,' she said as she turned and headed up the stairs. 'A baby's life is nothing compared to your pride, I'm sure.'

Enchei winked at Kesh as she wrinkled her nose and looked away. 'She's going to be fun to have around, this one,' he said. 'Now hop it, the pair of you, there's work to be done. Narin, tell Rhe the people of House Moon like their shadow demons, as do Raven and Salamander if memory serves.'

'That means visiting districts to the north, west and east,' Narin pointed out as Irato jumped up to fetch his weapons and coat.

'Funny that, I hadn't noticed. Just as well you like walking eh?'

Sat in the middle of a boat on the Crescent, Narin watched tiny snowflakes drift past the immovable statue of Lawbringer Rhe ahead. He pulled his winter coat tighter around him and tried to let the moment of relative quiet clear his mind. Behind him the boatman rowed in silence, straining slightly against the incoming tide that swept around the Imperial Island. As much as Narin tried, however, it wasn't the soothing sight of Kine and Dov that intruded on his thoughts – rather, it was the calculating smile of Prince Sorote of the Imperial House and some vague impression of a shadow-hound stalking the city streets.

'Why Raven District first?' Narin said eventually, giving up on the effort. 'Don't stories of shadow-demons mostly come from House Moon's lands?'

Rhe didn't turn, his head hidden by a hood raised against the cold air. 'The Detenii?' There was no emotion in his voice, though Rhe had led many Lawbringers to their deaths against the goshe's elite, but Narin felt his own hand tighten at the word. He'd had precious little chance to fight back when they had been torturing him and the memory still made him feel sick.

'The only shadow-demons I can remember hearing about. Though the goshe used the name for their elite, the stories are older than that.'

'True.'

'So why?'

'Both hegemonies stand on the edge of the known world,' Rhe began, 'Moon to the west, Raven to the east. But Moon's furthest edge is a coastline – beyond that they have found only ocean, and explorers who try to cross it never return.'

'And Raven's eastern border is Shadowrain Forest.'

Rhe inclined his head. 'Vast and uninhabitable to men, home to monsters and demons. But there is no clear border, no thousand-mile wall to keep the forest at bay. Imperial strictures have only ever rested lightly on the people there. Even on the better streets you can see fetishes and charms on plain show.'

Narin nodded. 'So finding a shaman there might not be so hard, or getting one to talk to us. That makes the Underways of Raven our best bet.'

The crossing was swift and soon the Lawbringers found themselves disembarking at a small jetty in Eagle district. Narin hopped out of the boat and started up a wooden stairway that clung to the side of the abrupt cliff which occupied much of the district's Crescent shore.

He'd never liked Eagle District much. It wasn't so much the rounded eyrie palazzos perched on the cliffs thirty yards above his head,

64

forbidding though they were, but more the racial purity not on show elsewhere in the city. The natives of the central Imperial isles, original base of the House of the Sun, had tanned skin and dark hair so people such as Narin could be seen all over the Imperial City, mingling freely. In Eagle district however, there were few natives and the vast majority were from the Eagle hegemony. To a man more used to the chaotic mix of the city's inhabitants, to be presented with a sea of only pale faces was disconcerting – all the more so when a good number looked like Lawbringer Rhe, eyes, hair and skin all as cold as ice.

They crossed Eagle as quickly as they could, negotiating a range of gifts, salutes, bows and invitations offered to the famous son of House Brightlance before they arrived at the Raven border. The change was immediate – tall buildings and pale banners replaced by layered sets of black-tiled roofs and fluttering black flags. The emblems of Raven and its lesser houses were painted everywhere – ornate and stylised devices of Raven, Crow and Bat in flight, while legions of Threehorns, Rattletails and Greyfangs tramped along the bottom of buildings.

Towards the centre of the district the buildings became rather more restrained, aiming for elegance of construction and design rather than frenetic decoration, but walking through the high-caste core to the poorer edge of the city itself saw the intricate returned to madcap. The Underways themselves were a series of narrow sunken lanes running parallel to each other with a number of tunnels between and a spiderweb of supports and makeshift bridges spanning them. Stinking gutters ran like streams down the centre of each and cramped frontages lined the lower levels, dug into the ground as far as would support the weight of the buildings above.

Rhe and Narin stood at the end of the first Underway they reached and surveyed their task. Many of the frontages were shops or taverns of some sort, Narin guessed from the range of signs rattling in the breeze. Few used the Imperial script, however, and his knowledge of Raven's language was limited. By Rhe's hesitation, Narin assumed he was faced with a similar problem, but they hadn't had time to find a native of Raven to accompany them.

'Should we go back to the local station?' Narin asked Rhe quietly.

'Not yet.'

Narin took the hint and went back to inspecting the Underway. The locals were a flamboyant lot, now they'd left Eagle district, hair ranging from black to reddish gold but almost every one had some sort of adornment in it – feathers, scarves, fetishes and constellation haircombs, all on show in one glance. All but the very poorest wore a necklace of some sort, many sporting half a dozen pieces all set with coloured stones or semi-precious gems.

'Where do we start, then?' he wondered under his breath, but in the next moment his gaze alighted on a wooden sign that jutted out above a doorway almost directly ahead of them. 'Wait, look at that,' he said, pointing.

Rhe turned. 'A crescent moon. What of it?'

'Often a pagan symbol,' Narin explained, 'because the moon plays no part in the divine astrologies – but mostly, the bones around it. I've seen those before.'

At the top of the crescent moon the sign depicted a triangle of bones, bound with red twine at the corners. In addition, strings of small bones hung from the pole and base of the hanging sign – all with their upper halves painted black and linked together by fine copper wire.

'Where?'

'Enchei's always hiding spirit-traps and warding symbols – round his home, round mine, Kesh's too now. I don't know what they're all about, but most likely whatever that place is, they'll know more about the world of demons and spirits than we do. Might be they can point us in the right direction if we ask in the right way.'

Rhe gave him a sideways look. 'Do I detect a note of admonishment?'

'Admonishment, Lawbringer?' *Damn right there was. You storm in and make demands in your posh accent, they'll clam up.*

'Perhaps not, then,' Rhe said, observing Narin carefully. 'Either way, a lower-caste Lawbringer might elicit more answers. If you would take the lead?'

Narin lowered his head in acknowledgement and slipped ahead of Rhe, crossing the street to duck beneath a low overhang and push open the door. He blinked at the dim interior, trying to make it out before blundering forward. It was as cold inside as out, his breath a ghostly cloud that was swallowed up by the darkness. Slowly he made out a room barely four yards in either direction with a low arched exit at the back. The left-hand wall was a mass of cupboards and drawers – mismatched furniture bolted together to create a solid structure. The rest of the room was covered with shelves and tables; all laden with glass jars and fragments of metal Narin couldn't identify.

A shuffle of feet came from beyond the arch, then a wizened old woman appeared with a lamp. As its warm orange light spread out over the room he realised every drawer and handle in the room had been scrupulously polished to a brassy shine, while from the ceiling dozens of chunks of crystal were suspended on thin chains.

'Good morning, Mistress,' Narin ventured.

'Mistress, is it?' she replied, the croak of her accent difficult to penetrate. 'Hah. What do you want, Lawbringer?'

She had once been Narin's height, he realised, but a stoop now dragged her down. Over ragged trails of thinning hair she wore some sort of net cap threaded with scraps of gold and silver jewellery, while from her neck hung a dozen necklaces of gemstones and bones carved with symbols.

'Well?' the woman demanded, pale green eyes squinting up at him. Narin flinched and realised he'd been staring at the pendants, rings and other jewellery she was bedecked in.

'We, ah, we're looking for information, Mistress.'

'Yer come to the wrong place then,' she snapped. 'I got nothing for your kind.'

Narin paused, wondering how best to handle her. Lots of people disliked servants of the law for a variety of reasons and he'd get nowhere if he took the wrong tack. 'Well, how about you just listen to me a moment then?'

'There's nothin' I want ta hear from the likes of you.'

'Well, you're going to anyway,' he persisted. 'We're not here to cause trouble for you and it might be you like what you hear.'

'I won't.'

'You're going to hear me out either way,' he growled, 'so maybe you lose the chip on your shoulder and do your community a favour, eh?'

'Community?' She cackled and with a clatter of bangles brandished a hand towards the street. 'Piss on the lot of 'em.'

'I wasn't talking about your neighbours. I've seen the symbols on your sign before, the bone fetishes and the rest. I may not know if you're a shaman, witch or something else entirely, but I'm not the one who's going to have to deal with how wrong my guesses are, you get me?'

'Threatening an old woman are you, eh?' she said scornfully and spat at his feet. 'Oh, very brave.'

'When you get threats, you won't need to check 'em,' Narin snapped back. 'I'm pointing out how the world is and the city's going to soon get pretty unfriendly towards anyone who deals with the unnatural side of life. Hard to live quietly when it gets out we're investigating some brutal murders with occult links and the rest of the city's feeling twitchy. Either we find out where we want to look or we have to go after everyone and see what shakes loose.' He paused then added, 'I'm sure the priests'd have a few ideas where we should be starting.'

The old woman scowled, gaze nervously darting from Narin to Rhe as she considered his words. 'I hear you,' she said reluctantly, 'say yer piece then.'

'Who round here – no, wait. Let me make this clear, I'm not looking to blame or arrest anyone here. I want an expert who'll tell me what I'm looking for, understand? Good. So, who round here do I talk to about demons?'

She snorted. 'Any kid in the street, they know their folklore round here.'

'I'm talking about dealing with demons.'

'Damn Imperials, you don't know nothing. There's no making friends with a demon, no magical covenant or soul ta sell.'

'That's a start, then. What else do you have?'

She gave him a disgusted look. 'All sorts, but why'd you want ta know about demons?'

'Because a couple just got killed inside their own home by one and I don't think that's the end of it. If it happens again folk are going to start looking for someone to blame.'

'Demon did it, you just said that. Nothing ta do with me.'

Narin scowled. 'Fancy telling that to an angry mob?'

The woman's tone lost its edge almost immediately as she appreciated his point. 'And what're you looking for, lawman?'

'The right person to blame.'

'Was a demon did that, you said so yourself.'

'And some demons get summoned. This was no fox-spirit.'

'Summoned? No one round here's mad enough ta try stuff like that; worst you'll find is curses that tangle a demon round yer soul. Summoners – that's not just playin' wi' foxes, that's draggin' evil from the lower hells.'

Narin leaned forward, hearing the edge of horror to her voice. 'So it's hard and it's dangerous, right? So what would someone need to do it without getting killed? Supplies for the rituals? Who'd stock that sort of thing?'

'I don't know, ya don't get old playing with horrors.'

'So who do we ask about hellhounds? Who'd know the answers or be part of the circles we need to talk to?'

'Pah, who knows? More'n a few fancy themselves as dark mages but none'd be dumb enough to summon anything strong enough ta kill like that. You sure about this?'

'I saw what was left,' Narin said.

His stomach tightened at the memory and she saw enough in his face to cut off any further disbelief.

'No Raven'd do such a thing,' she said, almost in a whisper, 'it's madness ta even try. If ya see the true face of a hellhound, it burns yer eyes from yer head. No human can endure such a sight. But I only know my district. Might be someone elsewhere in the city's got the answers ya need – who knows what madness Leviathans or Salamanders will try? Ya might speak ta Samaleen. If anyone knows she'll be the one.'

'Who's Samaleen?'

'No friend o' the Lawbringers, that's fer sure. Think o' her as a different sort o' religious caste and yer halfway there. Be respectful, mind, she may look not much ta Imperial eyes but don't let that fool ya. Of any arcane in this district, there's none with more respect and she's mistress o' the district's waters. If anyone knows where ya should be looking, it's Samaleen.'

'And how do we find her?'

The old woman scowled. 'She ain't one fer being found by Lawbringers. Might be I can get a message to her and she'll decide if she wants ta get involved.'

'Tell us where she is,' Rhe broke in abruptly. 'Shadow games and mysticism don't interest me. There is no one in this city bar the Emperor himself who is above the law, no one who is permitted to insulate themselves from the Lawbringers. We shall remain respectful of all citizens who do not impede our investigations, but be aware how that may turn.'

'So we're back ta threats, eh?' she said in a subdued tone.

Narin's anger she had taken in her stride – he was low born like her, after all – but Rhe's aristocratic certainty was far more unfamiliar and chilling. It had taken Narin a year before he heard more than just the high-born dispassionate view; a cold and unyielding tone towards those below him.

'We prefer to act with the cooperation of the citizenry,' Rhe replied, 'but there has been murder done and we are guardians of the law. If I must overturn this entire district to secure answers, I shall do so.'

She ducked her head and turned back towards the rear room, dragging a heavy coat off a nearby chair.

'I'll take you to her,' she mumbled, well aware of the effect the full scrutiny of the Lawbringers might have on practitioners who were publicly condemned by the various temples. 'But don't think she's so easily swayed. Yours ain't the law she answers to.'

'All answer to our law,' Rhe declared. 'One way or another, the law remains.'

CHAPTER 9

The old woman, whose name Narin belatedly learned was Thanan Draig, led them back across the Underway to an arched tunnel on the other side. It resembled some sort of ancient burial place with huge, rough-hewn stones framing the opening, but smelled like any other alley in the city. Doorways and shuttered windows led off on either side, with one narrow passage outlined by the yellow glow of a lamp.

The tunnel opened out on a rounded hollow that served as some form of marketplace. More doors and ancient tunnels led off its twenty-foot-high walls, above which loomed rickety-looking buildings that seemed to crowd out the grey sky above. More snow was falling and starting to settle on lintels and awnings, turning the ground underfoot to mud. They attracted more than a few curious and hostile looks, not just from local gang members easily identified by the bone fetishes studding their noses and cheeks. None went further than glares, though; the sight of the pistol holster across Rhe's belly was enough to ensure unimpeded passage.

A large doorway built out into the hollow proved to be their destination and at Thanan's direction Narin hauled the protesting door open and peered inside. The only light was a fire in the centre of the room, burning beneath a brick chimney that doubled as a supporting pillar. The room was some sort of ante-chamber that contained half a dozen benches and a massively fat man whose pale green eyes flashed angrily in the firelight.

'You're not welcome here,' he rumbled as he hauled himself to his feet.

'That doesn't interest me,' Rhe replied, walking inside. 'We're looking for Samaleen.'

'Been shooting yer mouth off, Thanan?' the fat man snapped. 'Yer'll regret that.'

'No she won't,' Narin said, walking right up to the fat man and looking him in the eye. They were of a similar height, though Narin had no doubt the other was much stronger than he. 'You want to know why?'

'No – get out.'

'She won't,' Narin persisted, 'because I'll be back to check on her. We gave her the choice of bringing us here or having Lawbringers crawl all over the Underways until we found out what we wanted. If I find some ignorant scum has tried to punish her for that, you'll find out we're not all such sticklers for protocol as Lawbringer Rhe here.'

The fat man's eyes narrowed, as much at Rhe's name as anything else. 'Yer still not wanted here.'

'And I don't give a shit what you want. We're not here to cause trouble for Samaleen, but we've got a murder to investigate and she's most likely able to tell us what direction we should be looking.'

'She's killed no one,' the fat man insisted.

'If we thought she had any part in it, we'd be past you now and arresting her. It's her knowledge we want, that's all.'

If the fat man had anything more to say, Rhe didn't wait to hear it. The pale Lawbringer crossed the room, heading for the only other doorway, and ushered Thanan with him. The old woman did so with her head bowed, avoiding the fat man's expression, but Narin saw his threat had hit home anyway. With one final look he turned his back and joined the other two as Rhe opened the door to a stairway leading deeper underground.

Narin followed Rhe and Thanan down to a lower level where a handful of lamps illuminated an expansive vaulted cellar that he guessed dated back to the Greater Empire. Fat pools of shadow lurked at every corner, enough to hide a multitude of dangers, but Rhe strode on without seeming to even glance around. Narin took a more wary approach, knowing his own reactions weren't as honed as his battle-trained noble colleague. Faint sounds of movement came from all directions but they reached a squarish opening in the floor without seeing anyone and Thanan led the way down a wooden flight of stairs into a chamber altogether more natural.

'What is this place?' Narin couldn't help but ask as the sound of rushing water echoed up towards them. He could smell water too, some sort of underground river most likely, given that there were several running this way and tumbling out of the cliffs beyond.

'A nexus of power,' Thanan hissed. 'The ignorant would call it a temple, but it's no such thing.'

'And Samaleen is the priestess of this not-a-temple?'

The old woman didn't answer, merely pressed on to the bottom of the stair and stepped aside for Rhe and Narin to pass her. There were no lamps, just a gloomy mass of shadows that gradually began to fade as Narin's eyes adjusted. A faint definition began to emerge, putting Narin in mind of Irato's description of the Starsight Blessing the goshe elite had possessed. He began to make out the lines of a dozen more steps nearby that led down to an uneven floor and the glassy surface of water beyond.

With a jolt he realised they were in a massive cavern, thirty or forty yards in each direction, with enormous columns and stalactites spread all around. The uneven walls were coated in what must have been some sort of glowing lichen, from what he could tell, casting a light that was barely perceptible but just enough to give a sense of shape and outline to obstacles.

'Samaleen,' Rhe called out, heading towards the water, a still pool at the heart of the room.

Sitting at its edge were figures draped in long frayed robes, heads covered by shapeless cloth hoods that hung low over their faces. Narin's attention was grabbed more by the faint mist that hung over the water – from the stairs he could look down on the surface of it and see that the mist was not spread evenly over the pool but traced distinct paths across it.

'For what reason do you come here?' intoned a woman's voice, though from which of the figures Narin couldn't say.

'We hunt a murderer,' Rhe replied, 'a summoner of demons.'

'You will find none here. You are not welcome.'

Abruptly, one of the figures stood up and uncovered her head; Samaleen, Narin assumed. She was young, no older than Narin, and as pale and proud as any Eagle noblewoman, but with far darker eyes. Unlike most they'd seen in the district, she wore no jewellery of any kind. Her head was bald and bore pale markings Narin couldn't identify – some sort of arcane script, but whether it was a tattoo, scarring or paint was impossible to make out.

'You disturb the balance of my sanctuary, you must leave it. Thanan – you willingly led them to this place?'

'We gave her no choice,' Narin said. 'We've already had that conversation with your guard dog up there, but somehow I doubt you're so stupid as to need me to spell things out.'

'You are a long way from your law,' Samaleen replied, far from intimidated. 'Here in the deep there are older laws.'

Her voice was measured and calm, but a shade slower than normal, which made Narin suspect her meditations were drug-assisted. Whatever state she was in, however, Samaleen would be far from willing to incur the scrutiny of the Lawbringers. Hers was an unpopular sub-culture within the city, that much Narin did know, and any confrontation would go badly for them.

'The law extends wherever the servants of the Emperor walk,' Rhe declared. 'If you want us gone from this place quickly, listen to what we have to say. We need your knowledge. Innocents were killed, we believe by a hellhound.'

On the water the paths of mist seemed to flicker uneasily, but if Samaleen felt any concern she showed none.

'I commune with the spirits of the deep, not the hunters of the other plane. I do not endanger others, I know nothing of this crime.'

'And your spirits have told you nothing of a summoner in this city?' Narin asked. 'Surely you know at least of places such people might keep to. It can't be something so easily achieved – aren't there rituals required, rituals that might need supplies of some sort?'

She shook her head slowly. 'Such people are outcasts wherever they go, they would trust no stranger. But summoning is not a Raven way – our concerns lie with the beings of Shadowrain Forest. We have no need of searching out horrors on the other plane when there are enough on our nation's borders.'

'Who then? Where should we look?'

'The Houses of the southern continent,' she said after a long pause. 'The other plane is one of wilderness and desert – where burning creatures roam and shadows hunt.'

'The Wyverns have desert lands, and others too,' Narin argued, 'why not them?'

'The rulers of Dragon and all its lesser houses are faithful to the younger Gods. What few enlightened exist there prefer to commune with the beasts of the wild and guard against the voices of the deserts.'

As she spoke, Narin repeated her words back in his mind. The price of his promotion had been the understanding that the supernatural would be his purview. The Lawbringers had always been deficient in that respect and the Lord Martial of the Lawbringers was determined they would not again be proved so ignorant as they had been during the Moon's Artifice incident.

As a result, Narin had determined to commit any such information to paper, to establish some sort of body of knowledge for himself and his comrades. Enchei had naturally provided a framework for it, but his was an expert level of knowledge. What the common folk believed, what the seers and magicians thought, might actually be more useful to the Lawbringers, given that Astaren almost acted on a separate plane to the rest of the Empire.

There was no contempt in Samaleen's voice, Narin noted with a touch of surprise. The Empire's established cults worshipped only the once-human Ascendant Gods and cursed all dealings with the supernatural realm beyond the Gods. Persecutions were rare, but not unknown. Samaleen harbouring a particular hatred of the more zealous Gods such Lord Ranger and Lady Pilgrim would be easily understood.

'Redearth then, Iron and Wolf. Salamander too? Good, we've narrowed things down to just forty-odd nations.'

'All I can tell you is that the spirits of the water have not been disturbed by any hunters of the other plane. The waters of the city are untouched by this summoner. I do not treat with the denizens of the other plane; I have no contact with those who do so unless they stray beyond their usual places. Of those I have crossed paths with in my years, one was a Redearth woman – so powerful I suspect she was Astaren – the other pair a Diresong and Scarab who died as they attempted to enslave spirits of the hidden waters.'

Those last two are both Wolf subordinate houses, Narin thought to himself. *A starting point there?*

'The Emperor thanks you,' Rhe announced, recognising there was nothing more they would learn from her.

'Does he?' Samaleen asked, an edge to her voice. 'I hear of his edicts even in this dark place. It is not thanks he offers in those.'

'Nor does he pass laws against you and your kind,' Rhe said pointedly. 'The priests bay for your blood, but I have no such charge to bring here.'

'Just as well.' Samaleen hesitated, lifting her head like a dog catching a scent. 'What else have you brought here?' she demanded angrily. 'The spirits are disturbed – something is here that has no place in the deep dark.'

Rhe and Narin exchanged looks.

'What do you mean?' Narin asked hesitantly, hand on his sword.

75

Now there was contempt in her face. 'I mean you have brought something unwelcome here,' Samaleen snapped. 'Go – get out. Pollute this place no longer and take whatever tainted thing has come with you.'

With that she turned her back on them and retook her seat around the edge of the water, shrouding her head and settling herself with one last shake of the head.

'Have we brought anything with us?' Rhe said, looking fixedly at Narin.

Behind him Thanan looked panicked at the thought, casting anxious looks at the now-still Samaleen. One of the woman's companions raised his head to look her in the eye and she shrank under the gaze, but the man only nodded to one side. Thanan's shoulder's sank at the gesture, but she obeyed without hesitation and went to sit where he had indicated – doubtlessly awaiting more private words from Samaleen once the Lawbringers were gone.

'Not that I'm …' He paused. 'Perhaps Irato? He might be following us, watching our backs, though I saw nothing of him all the way here.'

'Your former goshe friend? Why would you need a proficient killer to watch your back?'

'It's, ah, it's a long story. I can't say why he'd have followed us inside.'

'But it will not be good,' Rhe concluded, drawing a pistol as he headed back towards the stair. 'Trouble follows in your wake, Narin. I had hoped you'd left such things behind when you became a Lawbringer.'

Narin followed him up the stairs. 'I'd hoped so too,' he said weakly, not believing his own defence.

Rhe stopped and turned to face him. 'The Lord Martial feared as much,' he said, in a cold tone that was as close to furious as Narin had ever heard from Rhe, 'but I argued in your favour. Do not make me regret doing so.'

Narin fought the urge to shrink away, aware that a Lawbringer should stand tall and certain even in the face of a man so recently his superior.

'My life's not so easy to control,' he replied stiffly. 'Some things were set before I was made a Lawbringer.'

'What awaits us?'

'I don't know.' Seeing Rhe's pale face tighten, Narin quickly continued. 'If I had to guess and the Gods were against me, House Wyvern warrior-caste assassins.'

Rhe grunted, but whether it was from surprise or a lack of it, Narin couldn't tell, and in the next moment the big Lawbringer resumed walking, but this time he moved more cautiously – like a man ready for violence.

'First we deal with whatever Irato's found,' he said softly. 'The reasons will wait for later.'

Not seeing anyone on the stairs, the pair cautiously crept up them. The wooden steps were old but solid and made mercifully little noise as they ascended. Despite that, Narin knew they would be painfully exposed as they emerged through the hole in the cellar floor. Exposed on three sides and with the many pillars casting long shadows, there was no real advantage to be had there so Rhe did not stop. Drawing his pistols, he carried one in each hand and walked calmly up the last stretch, extending the guns in either direction as he went.

To Narin's relief no gunshots rang out and he followed the fearless Lawbringer up and into the cellar, both making for the lee of a stone pillar just as a voice rang out.

'Stay where you are.'

'Who are you to give instructions to a Lawbringer?' Rhe replied. They both searched around the darkened cellar but could make out no one in the gloom. 'Who are you to hide in the shadows like a coward?'

'This is not your fight,' said the voice as a dark-skinned man stepped out from behind a pillar ten yards ahead of them. 'Step back, Lawbringer Rhe, our quarrel is with your colleague – not you, not the Emperor's law.'

Narin could see immediately the man was a Wyvern and his accent confirmed it. Tall and lithe, his red collar marked him as warrior caste but the rest of his clothing was remarkably plain. The understated clothing of a man with a mind to kill rather than impress.

'Narin, do you know this man?'

He shook his head.

'You sound like you're fresh off the boat,' Narin ventured as the Wyvern's fingers twitched, pistol as yet untouched in the holster at his waist though he had no doubt other guns were already trained on them. 'We've never met before.'

'This is a matter of honour,' the Wyvern said scornfully. 'I had expected better of a Lawbringer, even one of low caste. Your cowardice disgusts me. Bring out the other one.'

From behind another pillar, Irato emerged under the none-too-gentle urging of another Wyvern. The man was calm despite the fact a pistol muzzle was pressed to the side of his head and his sheepskin coat hung open, showing he had been stripped of his weapons. A tall woman stood just behind him, one hand gripping his collar as she pushed the gun into his skin. Long blue braids of hair hung down over her shoulders, large white eyes shone out through the gloom.

'I wouldn't do that if I were you,' Narin warned.

'We do not take orders from a coward. At least you do not deny what you have done – for that I would have shot you where you stood. Step forward, Lawbringer Narin, meet your death with what bravery a low born can muster. You will tell us where my cousin hides. Do so willingly and I will let you die with sword in hand. Continue to hide her and you will choke on your balls as you're dragged through the streets.'

'This is a matter of honour?' Rhe interrupted in a level voice.

'It is. Even an Eagle nobleman should understand that. You will stand back, Lawbringer. You know what must happen when a low caste spits on the honour of a warrior family.'

'Oh, I understand honour, but there are many kinds. With regret, I cannot yield.'

'This man has dishonoured my family, and he must die for it,' the Wyvern snarled. 'Do you deny my rights?'

Rhe turned so his gun was pointing at the man. 'I deny nothing, but still I cannot yield. He is a Lawbringer and entitled to my presence at his side. You have not declared your name, have not issued challenge, so this is no formal duel where he stands alone.'

'He is low caste!' the Wyvern roared. 'He will hear my name as his life drains from his body, I need offer no formality.'

Rhe cocked his head to one side and looked past the leader to the woman with the gun at Irato's head. 'Narin is right, though, I really wouldn't do that if I were you.'

The Wyvern glanced back at his comrade – most likely a sister or cousin, given that this was a matter of family honour. 'This man was following us. He's lucky we have not broken his legs already.'

'Still, I reckon you're making a mistake there,' Narin said, taking a step forward and slowly drawing his sword.

'He will not be harmed if you tell me where she is; upon my honour.'

'Honour,' Rhe echoed, 'but not formality. Irato, Narin – allow me to educate you on the form that is to be observed here.'

'There is no form to be observed,' the Wyvern snarled, drawing his own sword. It was a long straight blade that tapered to a short point – a two-handed weapon that had reach over Narin's.

'Indeed not,' Rhe said as he shot the man through the eye.

The gunshot was deafening in the enclosed space and Narin still saw the muzzle-flash despite closing his eyes just in time. By the time he opened them Irato had already moved. The grip his captor had on him seemed not to make any difference as he jerked around with unnatural speed and broke her arm. The gun went off as he did so, but Irato was out of the way by then. In the next moment he slammed a forearm into her face as he dragged her second gun from her waist. The woman staggered backwards and he followed her, using her body as a shield as he fired the pistol at some hidden figure.

Narin rounded the pillar ahead with sword leading, cutting down at the gun he assumed was waiting for him. His blade sliced flesh before he saw the man in the darkness. The flash of the pistol half-blinded Narin, but he swung up at the man's face without hesitation and felt his weapon bite before the Wyvern fell away.

More gunshots echoed around him. Half-dazed, he reeled from the bright flashes coming from left and right. From nowhere a massive figure appeared in front of him, pistols in hand. Narin saw the guns come up and felt a moment of pure terror before the Wyvern hesitated then continued the movement and hurled his spent weapons away.

Narin ducked, but felt one of the weapons smack against the side of his head. As stars burst blackly in his vision, he watched the Wyvern draw his own sword. Narin backed away but found himself with his back to a pillar. Before the Wyvern could close Irato barrelled into the man's side and the pair went sprawling. The sword was lost on the ground but the Wyvern barely paused. Despite his size the man was quick. He hauled himself on top of his attacker and punched Irato first in the shoulder then in the gut with his ham-sized fists. The former goshe lay on his back and could only swat at the descending fists with palms that crackled with tiny threads of lightning.

The Wyvern pressed his advantage and punched down into Irato's face. The impact rocked his head back and cracked it against the floor, but as Narin moved to help, the light around Irato's hands became a spitting corona. His own wild blow was enough to startle the Wyvern and Irato jumped up as the man scrabbled sideways.

With brutal efficiency he slapped a lightning-wreathed palm against the man's ear and followed it up with a knee to the face that snapped the man's head back. He fell, limp before he hit the ground, but Irato was taking no chances and slammed his knuckles down into the man's throat. There was an audible crack as a bone snapped under the force of impact.

Panting, Irato looked down at the man for a moment then turned and cocked his head at Narin.

'Reckon they know, then?'

Narin winced as he checked around and realised that it had all gone quiet in the ancient cellar. The peppery stink of gunpowder filled his nose, a haze of smoke lingering in the chill air.

'I preferred you when you were mindless,' he growled and extended an arm to the former goshe.

Irato took it and stood. 'You made me this way,' he pointed out. 'Only got yourself to blame.'

'Yes,' said a voice behind him. 'Let us discuss blame.'

Narin didn't need to turn to know it was Rhe behind him and his heart sank.

'Please, not now,' he said wearily as he turned to face the aristocratic Lawbringer.

'Really? Men have just tried to kill me and it's not convenient for you?'

Narin felt a growl of anger in his stomach. 'They tried to kill me first,' he snapped, 'and that wasn't the bit you objected to, was it?'

'Hey now,' Irato warned, 'let's not do this here.'

'You have a point, Lawbringer?' Rhe said coldly, ignoring Irato.

'They want to kill me for honour, aye. I'll take some blame in this, but let's not piss around. It's not my fucking caste system that made 'em want to kill me. Might be I've done some things I'm not proud of, but life ain't perfect and that doesn't give those bastards the right to hunt me down like a dog. But you'd likely have done the same in their place – and you'd have stepped aside if I'd not been a Lawbringer. A commoner like me doesn't actually mean shit to you, does it?'

Rhe didn't speak for a long moment, all emotion hidden in his pale face.

'You believed everything I said to that man?' he asked quietly. 'Narin, I had thought better of you.'

Narin snorted and turned his back, sheathing his sword as he stalked towards the exit. 'It's your damn caste system, not mine. Those are the rules that say I can be killed by these men and breaking them isn't something I'm going to apologise for.'

'Did I ask you to?' Rhe called.

Narin stopped and hesitated before turning. His time in training under Rhe had taught him enough about losing his temper. He pinched

80

the bridge of his nose and took a long breath, realising his hand was trembling slightly with the elation and panic of the day.

'No,' he admitted as he swallowed the fear-born anger inside him. 'Sorry. But what slights these men consider worth killing for aren't on me. I'm not high caste. I'm sorry you were dragged into the mess I created, but don't blame me for these men trying to kill you today.'

To Narin's astonishment, Rhe inclined his head to him. 'Then I shall not. I believe I deserve an explanation, though. I was proposing to stand beside you again over the next few days, so it is reasonable to ask what I'm dealing with, no?'

'I ... I suppose so. Ah, well, this is mostly it. There'll be Wyverns trying to kill me. If they fail, there'll probably be some official complaint against me at court which will lead to my disgrace and expulsion from the Lawbringers.'

'Lord Vanden of House Wyvern?' Rhe inquired.

'Aye, he'll be the one.'

'Is there news I've not heard yet?'

Narin ignored the sound of Irato snorting in the shadows as he went about fetching his weapons, and no doubt helping himself to the purses of the dead warrior castes. 'I doubt it's yet common knowledge. His wife fled his palazzo in the night, left him.'

'The Lady Kine Vanden Wyvern,' Rhe said slowly. 'A most beautiful woman, as I recall.'

Narin flushed and said nothing.

'She was pregnant, if memory serves?'

'She was.'

'Close to giving birth?'

'She had a little girl in the night.'

'And she was not quite the colour Lord Vanden expected?'

'Lord Vanden's out of the city, has been this last week.'

'It seems I am still missing a detail then,' Rhe said after a moment's thought.

Narin winced. 'He wouldn't have needed to see the baby, not after that attack Enchei and I saved him from.'

'I see. Do you have a plan to get out of this alive?' Rhe made a disapproving sound. 'Does one of your more unusual friends have a plan to get you out of this?'

'Of a fashion.'

Rhe sighed. 'I recall how many died last time you cooked up such a plan.'

'That won't happen this time.'

'But in the meantime Lord Vanden is returning to the city and will ruin you when he arrives, assuming you're not dead of course.' Rhe shrugged and began to reload one of his pistols, hands moving through the motions almost as though unbidden. 'We'd best be quick, then.'

'How do you mean?'

'I need you and your friends to stop this summoner, remember?' There was a trace of humour in Rhe's voice as he spoke – as much as ever came from the aloof aristocrat – but Narin heard the chilly overtones all the same. 'We should get this case solved before you're dead or disgraced.'

'I, ah, I suppose so.'

'Good. Well then, I believe congratulations are in order.'

Narin's surprised laughter echoed through the room.

CHAPTER 10

A brief wail broke through the fog of sleep that filled Kine's mind. She opened her eyes and blinked at the unfamiliar room, dimmed by the closed shutters of the window. The best that could be said for it was that it was clean. Narin's aging friend had seen to that. Whitewashed walls and mis-matched rugs on the floor diminished the house's shabby air, but it remained a dismal and cramped sight to a woman so used to a palazzo.

Beside her, Dov squinted up at the ceiling and gave another stuttering cry. With weary hands Kine leaned over and cradled her daughter. Instead of being soothed, Dov's cries increased and Kine felt a now-familiar sense of panic at the anguished sound. She fumbled at the robe she wore, opening it up to expose one breast and nudging her daughter towards the nipple.

A hot sense of shame washed over Kine as she tried to get Dov to feed. Her success had been mixed and what had come had been a result of Enchei's assistance. The old man had manhandled child and breast in a manner Kine would have considered unthinkable just a day previously, but she'd silently endured it and seen some form of reward at the end.

Doing her best to copy what she'd seen, Kine ignored the ache in her back and gently teased her daughter's mouth open. The ache was nothing compared to her pain elsewhere, pain she was scarcely able to admit to in a man's presence, but she bore them both with a mantra of sorts running through her head.

Dov is all that matters. Whatever the price, I will pay it.

Kine blinked back the tears, her discomfort nothing compared to her fear for her daughter – gifted with an uncertain and dangerous life. She looked down and adjusted Dov's head, the wrinkled little face working hard to feed but half turned away from her goal.

There came a knock at the door and Kine flinched. As she tried to drag her robe across her naked breast and belly, Dov slipped a little and began to bawl.

Dov is all that matters she said again and again in her mind as the tears spilled down her cheeks. In a small, choked voice, Kine called 'come', to whoever was behind the door before hunching low over the baby.

Myken appeared around the door and stood half in the room, blocking the view from behind her. The woman had cut her hair short, Kine realised with shock – long braids hacked away until it was as short as a boy's, off the shoulder and tied up at the back in a small topknot.

'Your hair,' she croaked, but couldn't find the words to continue. Myken's red warrior caste collar remained, but all other signs of their House had been removed from her person.

'It is what I am now,' Myken stated, her face a mask against the world. 'There are many Wyvern sell-swords in the city; there is no sense in pretending I am still a House knight.'

'I'm sorry.'

Myken hesitated, her usual implacable calm wavering slightly. Just the sight of that made Kine hate herself for what she'd done to the woman. However much she knew that knights were taught not to be self-serving, that as a noblewoman's bodyguard Myken had accepted all it might entail, Kine's actions had still put Myken in disgrace.

Most likely she would be disowned from her family, struck out of the records and never spoken of again. Before that could happen, Myken had herself cut away the ties of her past – removed the House symbols she'd bled for and the marks of tradition and honour that had been part of her entire life.

'I serve you until death,' Myken said finally. 'No true warrior fears a harder life and those who matter will not curse me. It remains my honour to stand here. Had I abandoned or turned on you my cadre siblings would have rightly hunted me down as a traitor and coward.'

Kine closed her eyes, unable to reply in the face of such conviction and strength. Myken had always been a woman she'd admired and now Kine realised the depth of that feeling.

'Enchei has brought you soup,' Myken added after a moment. 'You should eat.'

Kine swallowed and nodded. Just the mention of food was enough to make her realise how exhausted and drained she felt. She had barely eaten since getting here, but for Dov's sake she would force something down.

Myken opened the door further and stepped aside to admit Enchei. The greying man carried in a thick clay bowl and set it to one side, seeing Dov was feeding.

'How is she doing?'

Kine looked away and let her robe slip. Enchei gave an assessing grunt and adjusted Kine's arm before restoring the fold of cloth.

'Hurts?'

She shook her head, still unable to meet his eye.

'Good. When it does, tell me and I'll give you something for it.'

To Kine's astonishment, Enchei then pulled out a handful of large iron nails and headed to the window. Belatedly she noticed a hammer hanging from his belt and with swift efficiency the old man drove five nails in regular spaces around the window. That done he fixed one end of a coil of copper wire to the topmost and wound it all the way round the five nails, creating an uneven circle before using the rest of the wire to form a five-pointed star-shape that covered the window.

'Sorry about the noise,' he commented, nodding to the nails, 'just a precaution.'

'Who will that stop?' Myken asked, assessing the man's work. 'The wire's too thin to do more than trip any intruder.'

'Don't you worry about it,' Enchei said with a shrug and a smile, 'the window frames are strong enough to stop people. Would you indulge a superstitious old man, though?'

From another pocket he retrieved a small leather pouch cinched tight and hung it off the top nail.

'A hex bag?'

Enchei stiffened at the tone of Myken's voice. 'Like I said, indulge an old man.'

Myken made an angry sound in her throat that Kine recognised and she raised a hand to ward off any argument.

'Please, Myken, let him be. There can be no harm.'

'As you wish, my Lady.' Myken bowed. 'We should let you rest now.'

The warrior gestured for Enchei to leave with her but instead Enchei sat on the side of the bed, ignoring her entirely. Kine gave such a start at his abruptness she almost jerked Dov off the breast. Such familiarity had never happened in her life, but Enchei seemed unaware of even basic politeness, let alone caste protocol. She gaped for a moment, but caught Myken's eye as her bodyguard started forward. With a tilt of the head she asked the woman to leave and Myken, face tight with disapproval, nodded and backed out again.

Once they were alone Kine took a moment to scrutinise the veteran to whom Narin had entrusted her life. She knew there was more to him than was obvious at first sight, but still Enchei seemed an unlikely protector and his pagan beliefs were hardly encouraging. From his face she guessed he was from some House like Raven or Ghost, but even a man born on the edges of civilisation would surely have learned something of custom in the Imperial City?

Enchei's eyes were sharp and bright, but crow's feet surrounded them and the grey of age was in cheek and hair alike. Shorter than the tall Wyvern warriors, he had a spry, wiry look to him rather than thick slabs of muscle. To a woman brought up within the Dragon hegemony, where physical power was so prized, it was an effort of will to accept he was Myken's equal.

'Thank you,' Kine said at last, realising they had been inspecting each other in a rather unseemly manner. She tried not to wonder what he saw; a noblewoman helpless without her servants, a betrayer of her husband, or just an exhausted mess. 'I had not thought this would be so hard. I had hoped my body would know what to do.'

'You'd have figured it out,' Enchei said with a smile. 'Best way to learn something is to be given no choice but get it done. Think my father said that once. You've had one hell of a night, rest a few days before expecting to be able to think straight. Just don't be too noble-caste about it, hear me? Won't do this little one any good if you get all reserved or proper when you need help.'

Kine lowered her eyes, knowing full well what he meant. Having a strange, low-caste man show her how to breastfeed had strained against every rule of her rigid upbringing and she was already steeling herself to ask a favour of Kesh, who was at least female in a way her stern, muscular bodyguard somehow wasn't.

'How is it a man can make me look such a novice at motherhood?'

Enchei nodded and scratched his cheek. 'Funny the things you remember,' he agreed. 'Damn, guess it's been a few decades now! But my memory's better'n most and I was around for the birth of my girls. Didn't know a damn thing o'course, but I stored away every piece of advice the midwives and old women gave.'

'When did you last see them, your girls?' Kine asked. She saw it then, the flicker of pain in his eyes as Enchei stiffened.

'Too long,' came the gruff response. 'Life ain't always fair. Guess you're finding that out yourself, but don't let pride make it worse. That's all I wanted to say. Honour's the easiest thing to give away when you're in a tight spot. Only a fool sacrifices at the altar of pride.' He stood and pointed towards the bowl. 'Remember to keep your strength up.'

'I'm sorry, I didn't mean to pry,' Kine said, but he waved it away.

'Not your fault it's a touchy subject.'

'It is why … are they why you're helping me?'

Enchei looked startled at that. 'A man's ghosts can make him do most things,' he said after a pause, 'but if they're the only reason he can think of to help someone in need, he's no right calling himself a man.'

'But I've put you all in so much danger.'

Strangely he laughed. 'Danger? Pah, Lord Vanden don't scare me.'

'He will summon my brothers, my cousins and their bannermen. He will demand they correct this insult to his name – not that they will need any urging once they hear of it.'

'A few aggrieved arseholes trying to protect their family honour,' Enchei said scornfully. 'That's not danger, not in my book. Narin's done worse to me and you kids ain't got nothing on the shit I've landed myself in.'

'They are skilled warriors,' Kine insisted, 'I don't want anyone to be hurt because of what I've done.'

Enchei smiled nastily. 'They get hurt, that's their own fault. Too many folk care about the honour of others – the world can always use another lesson there.'

'They will not heed any lesson. Honour is all they have. My family is not rich, we have only our honour and the prowess of our warriors.'

'Then we'll kill 'em all,' Enchai said, standing. 'Won't be the first time.'

For a moment he looked past her as though staring into the distance and Kine felt a slight chill at the sight. It wasn't the face of an old man who'd spent the day making soup, but of a veteran who had marched grimly through death and ruin. She could almost hear the screams on the wind. From the faintest of twitches in his cheek, Kine realised Enchei could too. Those ghosts would always be with him.

As they emerged back into the daylight, Narin, Rhe and Irato found themselves in a changed city. Peering out of the main entrance, Narin saw no waiting Wyverns or anyone else obviously not of Raven District under their cloaks and sheepskins. The snow had continued to fall while they were underground and now it was not frost that paled the streets but an increasing layer of snow.

At last Narin realised he couldn't wait any longer and led them out into the open, squinting up at the fat white flakes drifting down around them as the three men headed across the sunken marketplace. The snow crunched noisily under their boots as they walked, buttoning their thick coats up to the neck against the cold.

'The temperature's dropping,' Irato commented as he watched the locals hurry past. No one spared them a look now, suspicious or otherwise. As the snowfall became heavier, folk were intent only on finishing up their day's tasks. 'Think we've had the day's warmth, tonight's going to be bastard cold.'

Narin nodded and suppressed a shiver. 'Good thing Wolf District is so close, not sure we'll have the Gods to light our way after nightfall.'

Instinctively, he turned to face south, where Wolf lay. The great pines on its major streets would normally be visible over the rooftops on a normal street, but with the snow falling heavily Narin realised he couldn't even tell whether that would be the case here.

Without waiting, Rhe led the way to the nearest tunnel out of the marketplace and only once they were safely in the shadows there did he stop to talk. His pistols were reloaded and ready to be drawn at a moment's notice, the brass butts poking out through his specially adapted coat.

'As you pointed out underground,' Rhe said, looking at Narin, 'I have better insight into the minds of aggrieved noblemen than you. They waited for you at the Palace of Law and followed you, hoping you would lead them to Lady Kine.'

'Then why try to kill me?'

'Their first goal is to punish Lady Kine, you're a lesser consideration. But off the street and out of public view, they could question you as much as they liked to discover where you've hidden her. Killing you would be an afterthought – the Lord Martial would no doubt object, but not vociferously once the circumstances became known. The Lawbringers are already too egalitarian for some noble families and you've not made this a situation to test those boundaries on.'

'Well, that's reassuring,' Narin said with glum acceptance. 'Looks like I'm avoiding the Palace of Law for the time being.'

'You still have a job to do,' Rhe reminded him, 'risk to your life or no. But greater precautions are required, certainly, even more so with this snow. Sound does not travel far and folk keep off the streets. That might embolden however many are left of Lady Kine's cousins.'

'Looks like you'll be seeing a lot of me and Enchei then,' Irato said. 'Or rather, we'll be seeing a lot of you. Not much point if you can see us.'

Narin shrugged and forced a smile. With the memory of Dov's tiny hands warming his skin, it took little effort. 'Always the fool in the middle it seems. I suppose I've only got myself to blame.'

'As long as we're all agreed there.' Irato nodded towards the far end of the tunnel. 'Go on then, get moving. This weather's only going to get worse and your day's a long way from over, remember?'

'This would be the plan to get you out of this mess?' Rhe asked. 'A full day's work indeed, given the size of the problem. Come on.'

Crossing through another two Underways, they headed straight for the Raven-Wolf border. The two Lawbringers walked quickly, the locals keeping well out of their way, but Narin didn't bother checking behind for Irato. He knew the former goshe would keep up without difficulty, trailing them as he watched for anyone else doing so.

Despite the savage iconography and all-too-real hunting dogs that padded alongside high and low castes alike, Narin was not alone in finding Wolf District a restful place. At its heart were two of the largest parks inside the city wall, and the higher-caste housing was mostly based around tree-enclosed squares. With the falling snow it took on a more mysterious air – close and ghostly.

As they walked, the numbers out on the street dwindled, the population no doubt taking shelter to see if they could wait out the blizzard. It showed little sign of lessening, however, as the pair stopped for a moment to greet two of their comrades on patrol from the local station and pick their brains.

As luck would have, the Lawbringer was a native Wolf; a burly woman of middle years with rusty-brown eyes and an easy smile despite foul weather. At her side lurked a gangly youth almost enveloped in his grey Investigator's coat, a shock of red hair marking him as House Forest, first among the major Houses of Wolf.

'The afternoon takes an unexpected turn, the renowned Lawbringer Rhe in my modest district! My name is Shom,' the Lawbringer introduced herself with surprisingly jovial courtesy. She gestured to her companion, 'my Investigator, Tooren. You I don't know, however.'

'Lawbringer Narin,' Narin supplied with a small bow.

'Your timing is excellent, Lawbringer,' Rhe said. 'We have need of some local advice.'

'Oh?'

'We are looking for the shamans and magicians of Wolf,' Rhe said, 'and a little direction would be appreciated.'

'Magicians?' Lawbringer Shom echoed, glancing at her Investigator. 'Not many of them that I've heard of. Tooren?'

The young man cleared his throat, no doubt as intimidated by the famous presence of Rhe. 'None, but I have not been here long,' he said in precise, but accented, Imperial. By custom he would not be wearing an indication of caste on his Investigator's robes, however it was clear he was high caste and not long off the boat from the Wolf homelands. 'Back home it would have been more simple.'

Shom gave him an appraising look, one that suggested House prejudices more than anything else to Narin. 'Maybe it would. Even round here folk say there's a dark heart to every Forest. Can you be more specific about what you're looking for Lawbringer?'

'Not your typical witch-doctor or shaman,' Rhe said, 'but rogue elements among those who deal with the unnatural world. We hunt a summoner of demons.'

At that Tooren flinched slightly.

'Anything you want to add, Investigator?' Narin asked.

Tooren shook his head, eyes lowered. 'Nothing, sir,' he muttered almost as an afterthought.

Shom rolled her eyes. 'I do know one thing, Lawbringer. Mine are a closed people. Even renegades may receive some measure of protection round here – the instinct not to speak to outsiders is bone deep. Might I suggest you return tomorrow morning? This weather looks relentless; you will have a hard time of it in what hours of light remain. I may also be able to accomplish more as a local.'

Rhe nodded and cast a look at Narin. 'A sensible course of action. We've been directed to several districts – this would cover the ground much more quickly.'

'It would be an honour,' Shom said, 'and the district is quiet anyway – always is in the cold and I could do with something rather more interesting than drunks getting into a fight.'

'I wish I could say the same, but our day has been sufficiently eventful already,' Rhe replied. 'I will go to the District Posts of Redearth, Salamander and Iron to submit similar requests.'

Narin blinked at him. 'And I should go to Moon District?' he hazarded, that being the only other Great House mentioned by either Enchei or Samaleen.

'You have other business, I thought? The situation caused by your own stupidity?'

Narin ducked his head. 'Ah, yes.'

Lawbringer Shom laughed at the exchange. 'Easy to look foolish in the company of Lawbringer Rhe then?'

'Yes,' Narin admitted, 'but sadly that's not even the half of it.'

'Hah! Well at least you can laugh at yourself, that's a good start. The trick is to make sure he's laughing with you.' Shom indicated Rhe.

'He will have to work on his wit in that case,' Rhe said gravely. 'It's somewhat lacking at the moment.'

CHAPTER 11

Administrator Serril dropped the note as though it was a turd and frowned at it for a long while. Eventually he looked up towards the door, as though expecting the young man who'd delivered it to still be there. He wasn't, though – was never likely to be, given he wasn't a messenger by trade, just a grocer's boy who'd been given a coin to deliver it by a customer.

The empty doorway deepened Serril's frown. So astonished and perplexed was he that he needed someone to rail at, but he was alone and the absence seemed to compound his irritation.

'That man …'

Serril tailed off. He was not one to curse or even raise his voice. That was not the way of the religious caste and whatever opinions he might privately hold about Enchei Jen, he would not permit the man to add to the burdens on his soul.

He picked up the note again with thumb and forefinger – a sniff of distaste his only comment as he read it through again.

'Not be available for work,' Serril repeated in his mind, 'nursing a friend to health.' No indication of when he might grace us with his presence again. Does that man think his employment a mere convenience?

The tattoo rooms past his office were unusually quiet, but somehow that only made the note more galling. The weather had ensured many of their customers had not come as expected so those tattooists who'd bothered to come to work had little to do. But the principle remained and none of them would have dared send such a perfunctory missive to announce their indefinite absence.

Serril re-read the note then tore it up in a fit of pique and threw the fragments into the small iron stove behind his desk. The scraps were consumed immediately – he'd filled the stove with as much coal as it would take, knowing how pervasive the cold could be. An angry voice at the back of his mind wanted to hurl the remaining papers in too, but they were never in danger.

The paperwork of a tattooist administrator was a solemn duty; lives could be ruined by a moment of carelessness on his part. In an Empire where a life history was sketched out on a person's skin, the tattoos on their right shoulder were more binding than any legal document. Fraud and corruption were punishable by death – for while the complex House symbols could not be adapted to become another's and a caste sign could only ever be downgraded by adding details, those were not the only marks recorded.

Military ranks, titles and honours could lie alongside certified trades, promotions, marriage records, or criminal convictions. Anything of importance was recorded there and there were plenty of stories of war heroes with symbols running all the way to their wrists, just as some criminals would flaunt their own markings. Serril's small fiefdom generally did not deal with criminals – the courts at the Palace of Law had their own tattooists – but several times they had borrowed his staff to assist.

'Administrator?' inquired a voice at the once empty doorway.

Serril jumped in his seat, rudely shaken from his musings. He half rose before catching himself and for a moment was frozen in the act, hunched forward over his desk, before he allowed himself to sink back down.

'I am Administrator Serril,' he said, wrinkling his nose at a bearded man brushing a layer of snow off his coat and onto the rush mats underfoot. 'Do you have an appointment?'

'May I?' the man asked, ignoring the question as he indicated the seat on the other side of the desk.

Slim and faintly aristocratic of bearing, the man's blue collar declared him to be a merchant. The presumption was not entirely outrageous, but Serril was a man used to having his authority rather better respected.

'If you have an appointment, give me your name and wait in the hall,' Serril said frostily.

'Alas, I do not,' said the man. 'I am here on another matter.'

He was a man in his early middle years, with an easy assurance in the way he carried himself. *A man who's found success*, Serril guessed from the stranger's clothes and manner. There was nothing ostentatious about either, but both spoke of quality and position nonetheless. He tugged his own black robe straight, almost austere in its plainness but that was the custom in his caste.

After an appropriate pause Serril indicated for the man to sit and he did so after shrugging off his heavy coat, which dripped with melting snow. A lower caste he might be, but merchants were a significant presence in the Imperial City and a little graciousness never went amiss around the wealthy and powerful.

'Which matter is that?'

'I am looking for someone.' The stranger gave him a disarmingly apologetic smile. 'A delicate matter, a shade embarrassing I'm afraid.'

'I am sorry, Master, ah …'

'Avineil,' the stranger supplied, 'Jest Avineil.'

'A House Eagle name?' Serril hazarded. 'Perhaps a northern domain?'

Again that diffident little smile. 'House Hornet, yes. Of course you would guess that, you must be something of an expert in the Empire's peoples.'

'I would prove a poor servant of the Empire if I merely shuffled these papers without properly taking note of them,' Serril said, indicating the certified letters on his desk informing him of what tattoos were to be given to whom.

'Indeed – would that your contemporaries back home were so assiduous in their work! I myself once had to correct a notation in progress because the wretch could not read properly.'

Serril nodded sympathetically, relaxing back in his chair with his fingers steepled over his round belly.

'I have heard such stories from across the Empire,' he admitted, 'but the standards in the Imperial City are rather higher than certain provinces – the speed and accuracy required of my tattooists ensures only the best are employed here.'

'I can well imagine.' Avineil brushed his fingers over his right arm. 'One of these was done by some decrepit drunk given the job by his nephew I suspect, a backwater town where few needed his services anyway.' He shrugged carelessly. 'Still, I am told by some that a less-than-perfect hand adds a certain authenticity to military honours.'

'So some believe,' Serril said through pursed lips, 'but quality and accuracy remain our watchwords here.'

'Of that I have no doubt – nothing less would properly serve his radiant majesty.'

'Quite right, but you did not come here to discuss the quality of our work.'

Avineil inclined his head. 'As I said, I am looking for someone. I, ah, I do not know his name however, I have a description only.'

'Has there been some sort of trouble?'

'No, no!' Avineil said quickly, raising his hands to emphasise his point. 'Quite the opposite, in fact, he prevented trouble. My, ah, my cousin is a young man and something of a fool when he drinks, it pains me to admit. He is a good lad at heart, I assure you, but reckless and when drunk quite unable to separate private thoughts from things that should be said out loud.

'Several days ago he managed to provoke some sort of fight – or what would have been a fight had a tattooist wearing an Imperial Sun not intervened. A grey-haired man of average height, past fifty years old my cousin tells me. He wasn't sober enough to thank the man at the time but tells me this tattooist saved his life; that he surely would have been killed by the thugs he had chosen to quarrel with.'

'A local man?'

'No, paler than a native of this place – perhaps Eagle or Raven by birth? Doubtless a former soldier, given his calmness in the face of drawn weapons.'

Serril lips tightened. 'I think I know the man you are speaking of.' In his memory he recalled the last line of Enchei's note – *should anyone come asking for me, please do not keep anything from them on my account.*

Avineil seemed to brighten at the news. 'Is he here?'

'No – he ...' Serril hesitated as he considered what to say.

Master Jen was just the sort to wade into a bar fight, his arrogance knew no bounds. It was galling enough to receive such a perfunctory note from one of his staff, now he was to pass on messages and information for the man too? No, Enchei Jen deserved no special treatment at all – indeed, he would be punished for his failure to report for duty. Serril certainly would not assist him in receiving any form of reward.

'He is not. I'm afraid if he does return I am likely to terminate his employment here for unreliability.'

'Oh really? Such a shame, I hope it is not on account of my fool cousin. Might you know where I can find him? I would like to thank him still; this latest incident has perhaps woken the boy up to his recklessness.'

'I regret I cannot do that. There are strict rules over the names and home addresses of tattooists. I cannot give out information to a stranger without proper authorisation.'

Avineil inclined his head in acceptance. 'I understand, protocols must still be followed. Might he be returning here ever? I could leave a note if he is likely to be here to collect such a thing.'

'That I cannot say. I know he will not be around these next few days – whether he will show his face here after that remains uncertain. As I said, he is unreliable, but not a fool. I'm sure he is aware of the likely consequences of his absences.'

'I understand,' Avineil said as he stood and retrieved his coat. 'Thank you for your time, Administrator.'

'Do you wish to leave a note for the man anyway?'

The stranger looked at him for a long time, long enough to make Serril feel strangely wary. At last he blinked and the cold look vanished from his face as he shook his head with a small smile.

'I had thought to offer him a post within the trading house, but from what you say I might regret doing so. The loss is his – I have at least attempted to fulfil my duty towards him, but I cannot spend too long dealing with his own failings.'

He paused and cocked his head at Serril. 'I have my hounds to deal with today also. Do you like hounds, Administrator?'

Serril blinked at him. 'Hounds? No, I … no, I have never much cared for beasts of any sort. They are messy and chaotic.'

'Indeed, mine do bite rather,' Avineil sighed, 'but when one hunts, what else will do? Good day, Administrator – may the blessings of the Gods be with you.'

Narin trudged across a ghost-haunted city. The trepidation he felt was as heavy as his snow-laden coat, as draining as the miles walking through fresh fallen snow. The fat flakes continued to fall with silent, stolid persistence, creating a thick curtain through which the boatmen of the Crescent refused to row. For Narin that more than doubled the distance he had to walk, but this was one errand he could not put off. After nearly two hours he finally stood underneath the grand tower-like entrance to the Imperial Palace; a massive stone structure supported by a hundred pillars, which was in turn dwarfed by the gigantic buildings behind.

As he'd reached the palace, Narin hadn't been able to resist stopping at a raised walkway that looked down over the Imperial Canal running for over a mile down its southern flank. Just below where Narin had stood was a small island, barely ten yards across, around which the Imperial barge could be turned before being berthed under an overhang.

At the centre of the island stood a statue – an Ascendant God from the Order of Emperor, Lady Navigator. The Goddess stood tall and proud, twice the height of a normal woman and raised further up by a pedestal of waves and the arched tails of whales. With flashes of silver embedded in the white marble statue, it was an arresting sight through the falling snow, the canal and towpaths all deserted around it.

With a blanket of white on the city this corner of the Imperial City looked ever more otherworldly and alien. The palace itself had been built in an age before human civilisation; one of several relics of a mysterious and long-dead race that survived untouched by the passing millennia. It was built on a scale no architect could comprehend, of a white stone no mason could work and for all the many hundreds who lived there it defied the imposition of human domain.

For Narin it also highlighted the difference between himself and the high castes who lived in such places. He came here only reluctantly and was glad to turn his back on the tined crown of the Great Court – even if it was only to enter the sprawl of normal streets that clustered around castle-sized towers projecting from the Great Court like ranks of flying buttresses. The towers stood in three rows of four, each one three hundred feet tall and connected by covered bridges that spanned the gaps high above the rooftops of the lesser buildings.

It remained a dizzying sight to walk through, the towers looming and oppressive, but as with the rest of the city the streets had been largely abandoned to the snowstorm. That afforded Narin a much quicker journey through the narrow streets where the merchant houses of the Empire did their business and before long he was thumping a weary fist against the unassuming door of a small building in the heart of it all.

To his irritation, nothing happened at first. Feeling something of a fool, out in the cold, Narin hammered harder on the door this time, fighting the urge to check around himself for any curious faces. At last there came a noise from within the building, a small structure with little to characterise it which stood all alone at the end of a street. It was not a place Narin would have given a second glance to had he passed it, no markings at all beyond a small engraving of its name in the lintel above the door – The Office of the Catacombs.

Without ceremony the door was jerked open and Narin found himself staring into the open muzzle of a pistol. It took a moment of panic before he recognised the polished walnut stock and ornate brass decoration on the barrel, but by then he had stepped back and half-drawn his sword. From the other side of the door there came a chuckle.

'My apologies, Lawbringer. How are you?'

Narin growled as he sheathed his sword again. 'How am I? Frozen stiff with a gun stuck in my face, Prince Kashte.'

The door opened further and Narin saw the young Imperial holster his gun before gesturing inside. 'Still brimming with respect for your betters I see, Master Narin,' came the cheerful reply.

'That's Lawbringer Narin to you, my Lord Sun,' he replied, forcing himself to rise to the challenge of being gently insulting to a man so far above his station it was dizzying. Kashte had proved a valuable ally to the Lawbringers as they assaulted the goshe on Confessor's Island and beyond the veneer of formality he was surprisingly welcoming to Narin.

Without Kashte and his small cadre of young Imperials, many more of Narin's comrades would be dead and the group had extended their strange sense of comradeship to Narin. He couldn't fathom whether they considered him one of them or were just under the thumb of the same man. Narin remained unsure which idea he preferred, but he was painfully aware of his need for allies, the way his life was going.

He followed Prince Kashte and almost groaned with pleasure at the warmth within as the door was shut behind him. The building was a two-storey square block with too many exposed walls, but a large iron stove stood in the centre of the room with what looked like half a wagon's worth of coal in tall baskets beside the door. A mezzanine covered half of the interior while below that was an iron-bound cellar door at a steep angle to the floor, currently closed.

'I wasn't sure you'd be here, Prince Kashte,' Narin said hesitantly as he looked at who else was there.

There were three large desks on the lower floor, two in use with the third enough of a mess to be clear Kashte had been working there. The other two people at the desks were also Imperials – a man and a woman he didn't recognise, gold on their collars and the intricacies of current fashion obvious in their clothes. Exactly what they were doing he couldn't tell, but each one had a stack of massive leather-bound books on their desk alongside a mass of scrolls and papers. Narin took a step to get a closer look but Kashte neatly manoeuvred himself into the way before he could see anything.

'History is a relentless master,' Kashte said with a small smile, 'it cares nothing for the weather outside.'

'Your master, eh?' Narin mused, 'I hadn't realised your devotion was so complete.'

Not wanting to make himself unwelcome, Narin gave up on the strange sight of Imperial castes hard at work like common scribes and instead struggled out of his greatcoat, which was fast creating puddles on the flagstone floor.

'They are assisting me,' called a voice as one heavy cellar door began to open.

It moved only slowly because it was six inches thick and reinforced with iron rods, but at last the thin face of Prince Ayel Sorote appeared from behind it.

'I am writing a history of the Empire, but the sheer weight of source material is too great for one man alone.'

Not much older than Narin, Prince Sorote affected the air of a middle-aged academic, dressing far more conservatively than his younger assistants. He still wore the gold collar of his caste, but forwent most of the detailing on their clothes and glittering jewellery. Even now Narin was reminded of their first meeting; the unassuming man waiting for him at his home who interrupted a day of murder and violence with veiled threats of his own. Narin was still unsure what to make of Prince Sorote more than half a year later, but for a man who held Narin's life in the palm of his hand, the Imperial had been remarkably helpful in the aftermath of the goshe affair.

'So you ask members of your own caste to assist you?' Narin asked, astonished at the idea. Imperials were hardly known for putting in a hard day's work and much of the labour, he assumed, would be monstrously dull.

'The religious caste have a rather narrow outlook on the world,' Sorote replied, 'they lack ambition and understanding. By contrast, the education of any Imperial caste must be of the highest order. We can hardly deal with the intricacies of the Empire and all the various nations within it without a rounded knowledge and the sophistication of thought to apply it fully.'

Narin, whose own education was far more limited than that of the religious caste, wasn't sure what to say in response, but Prince Sorote didn't seem to be expecting one as he reached Narin.

'Now, my friend, how are you?'

The Lawbringer gave a sour laugh. 'Well, this morning I was picking through the torn-apart remains of a man, which took me to an underground pagan temple and an ambush outside it.'

Prince Sorote blinked. 'So this is not a social call?'

'Not exactly.'

'In that case, Suner, Verrey – might you give us some privacy?'

Sorote half-turned to the Imperials Narin didn't know as they looked up from their work and nodded. Narin watched the pair stow their pens on polished inkstands and rise without a word – no emotion on their faces that the Lawbringer could discern, but that spoke enough of their relationship.

While Sorote might well be a higher-ranked member of the sprawling Imperial family, to almost dismiss them in that way spoke of something greater than age or rank. One hoisted up a large book from his pile and together they headed to the cellar door from which Sorote had come.

Narin had never been down there himself, but he'd seen enough to know it wasn't just a storeroom through those reinforced doors. That the bolts were on the outside was curious enough, but he had no intention of giving Sorote the satisfaction of ignoring his questions on the subject.

Before long the door was shut behind them and the three were alone in the small building. Narin pointedly looked at Kashte, but Sorote just directed him up the mezzanine stair to where his own desk was situated.

'A drink, Lawbringer? I for one believe a toast is in order. You may speak freely in front of Prince Kashte – he is my deputy here in the Office of the Catacombs and proving himself a most able historian.'

Narin looked at the polished guns holstered at Kashte's waist and remembered what Rhe had told him of the attack on Confessor's Island. Not only was the young man a highly-trained fighter, he wasn't some duellist. He had the hard manner of a veteran soldier – something that prompted only more questions, given that Imperials never went into battle. Exactly what it was in the historical records or Sorote's catacombs that required such honed skills remained a mystery.

'A toast?'

'Indeed. We've not heard any happy news from across the Crescent, but in this case I choose to interpret that as a good thing. If the city was told an heir to a Wyvern lord had been born, one might fear for any news of the mother that followed. If you are here and there is no news, well, it might be events took an unexpected turn. Scandal travels more slowly in the cold, I have found.'

A beautifully-cut glass tumbler was pushed into Narin's hands and a healthy measure of some golden spirit poured in. The two Imperials raised their own glasses, the curl of a smirk on Prince Kashte's lips as Sorote spoke.

'To fatherhood – a child new to the world.'

Narin remained too stunned to move or speak as the other men drank.

'You will not drink with us?' Kashte asked quietly after a moment of Narin staring at them.

'I, ah – I mean no disrespect,' Narin said, 'but to hear you state it so plainly …' His words failed him but Sorote nodded with understanding.

'My friend – forget it all for the moment.' He clinked his glass against Narin's and nodded towards it. 'Forget the danger, forget the scandal and anything else that's to come. I know your secret, Kashte also. Before anything else, any bargaining or manipulation, let us just first take a moment to be men.'

'I … what?' Narin remembered only too well Sorote's pleasure that not only did he have an affair with a married high caste to hold over Narin, but there would be a child to serve as evidence too.

Sorote smiled. 'The child, a boy or a girl?'

'Girl.'

'Her name?'

'Dov.'

That prompted a snort from Kashte. 'Lady Chance's given name? I like that. Are you hoping for the Ascendant's favour?'

'Kine chose it, but it's fitting I think. Her life will be uncertain from the start – chance brought Kine and I together, chance'll determine whether any of us survive.'

'I suppose so. To little Dov then – Lawbringer Narin, I congratulate you.'

This time Narin did drink with them, swallowing down half the smooth, faintly sweet spirit. It was like none he'd ever tasted, no doubt nothing most Lawbringers could ever afford.

'Thank you,' Narin forced himself to say. 'I suppose you've guessed why I've come, then?'

'It wasn't to give your friends the happy news in person? I'm saddened.'

'Today's been a bit too busy for that, I'm afraid.'

'Oh, really?'

Narin nodded. 'I know I'm in your debt and that's not the best way to come asking for another favour, but there's other news you might be interested in too.'

Sorote raised an eyebrow at Kashte and gestured to the armchairs arranged before his desk. 'By all means sit, then, tell us the tale of your day.'

Narin did so and took another mouthful of his drink before continuing, feeling a flood of warmth enter his belly and drive out the chill of the failing day.

'You've had a hold over me for a while now,' he began with a slight hesitancy. It was true Prince Sorote had known of Narin's affair with Kine and held it over him, but still Narin was uncomfortable baldly stating how much he was in the power of another man.

'One that may have evaporated now,' Sorote commented, 'but let it be noted that I never exerted or abused said hold.'

Narin raised a hand. 'I know – I wasn't accusing you there, it is what it is. Or was, maybe. The Gods above know I've no cause to complain about what you've done with the information. I might not understand why but right now … well, what's the phrase – I'm counting Jester's blessings? However, you'd said that you would be willing to assist me. I know it puts me back in your debt, but given what little you've asked of me these past few months that's a price worth paying.'

'I am prepared to offer assistance,' Sorote said slowly, putting down his drink. 'However, what I'd asked of you has been less than fruitful, if you remember. A brief essay on the fox-spirits and the varying orders of demons is all I have to show for my benevolence. History is not an easy master, remember? And while it may be patient, it has limits.'

'I understand, and I have other news. You asked to be kept informed of unusual crimes within the city – if I was a betting man I'd say you were the one who suggested such crimes fell under my and Rhe's purview.'

Kashte leaned forward. 'My advice, you don't become a betting man,' he said with a cold smile, 'your luck might've held out thus far, but I don't think you're cut out for going toe-to-toe with Lady Chance.'

Despite everything, Narin laughed. 'Don't worry, gambling's the last thing on my mind! You're not the only one surprised my luck hasn't got me killed yet.'

'You were about to keep me informed of something?' Sorote interjected.

'Yes – it's too early to give you much more than an idea of what's involved, but you'll be interested for sure. At worst I think you'll get a sense of the shamans in the city and how that hidden side of life fits between ours and that of the demons.'

'And at best?'

Narin scowled. 'Not sure entirely, but we're investigating a murder, two in fact.'

'Murderers are not that unusual, despite the efforts of your brethren.'

'I know, but the victims were killed by a hellhound. From what I can tell, those don't just crawl out of the Crescent at night – they're summoned from a realm of demons, and that means there's someone in the city doing the summoning.'

Sorote leaned forward. 'You have my attention, Lawbringer.'

'Now, I don't know what your interest is exactly, but I'm guessing whoever's behind this you'd be happy to kill, kidnap or steal from. We've only just started looking for whoever did it, but given the mess that was made I don't think we'll find Astaren at the end of this path. The victims were innocents so far as we can see. If you're the ones to punish what went on instead of the Lawbringers, that's a betrayal small enough for me to live with.'

'Perhaps it would be best if you didn't try to guess my motives,' Sorote said gravely. 'Your expertise is dealing with criminals, after all. I would not wish you to think me petty or self-serving.'

'My apologies, I hadn't meant that – I just wanted to be clear that, given the information you've asked me to gather, there's still some value in protecting me.'

'And protect you I will, my friend, in so far as I am able. The Imperial caste is trained to mediate and negotiate – once Lord Vanden returns to the city, something I expect to happen very soon, I will approach him on your behalf. As I intimated previously, I believe I have a solution to his concerns.'

'What about Kine's family?' Narin asked with a grimace. 'A group of them already tried to kill Rhe and myself earlier today.'

'They have come over from House Wyvern's lands even before the birth?' Sorote frowned. 'I hadn't expected Lord Vanden to have the balls – ahem, so to speak – to demand their involvement. Wyvern custom gives him that right, of course, being the higher-ranked party, but it is surprising. Warriors on a blood feud I cannot negotiate with, but perhaps Kashte would be willing to watch your back? Even when honour demands your blood, they will hesitate to draw on a gold collar.'

Narin shook his head before the minor prince could comment. 'Don't worry, I've already got Irato doing that. The man might not be subtle, but I should probably try to limit the chaos I've caused. I don't think getting an Imperial caste caught up in fighting on the streets is the way to do that.'

'It seems there is still hope for your political acumen,' Sorote said. 'So, Master Lawbringer – I would offer you another drink, but I suspect there is someone you would like to get back to.'

'You're right. Tomorrow's going to be a long day. Are you … are you sure Vanden will be willing to negotiate?'

'Of course,' Sorote said with a smile. 'He's a nobleman and a relatively minor one at that. A Wyvern such as Vanden considers his influence, wealth and honour in all things. It will simply be a case of listening to his bluster and offering him something of greater worth than the bride he has lost. Lady Kine will never be able to show her face in polite society of course, she will have to enter the House of the Sun with a black mark on her caste tattoo, but neither of you are fools. You know the consequences of staying in the city and you've made no suggestion that you might flee.'

Narin stood stiffly. 'We're aware of what it means.'

'Then so long as you can keep a measure of discretion, the situation can be managed with none of you dying. Her patronage in the Imperial House will be dependent upon you however, am I clear?'

'I understand.'

'Good.' Sorote beamed at him. 'Lawbringer Rhe continues in good health, I trust?'

Narin was startled at that. *Rhe? Is he still what you're interested in? I'm certain you're the one who suggested anything involving demons and the unnatural was given to me to investigate. If that's what you're after, why does Rhe still matter to you?*

'He is unhappy with people trying to kill me, but that's a tune I've heard before,' Narin said.

'You have confessed your sins to him?'

'Of a fashion.'

'And his opinion?'

'You can never tell with Rhe. Even after all this time with him I'm never certain. I know he doesn't approve, but exactly what he'll do about it I can't say. He's no typical nobleman so if he chooses to speak out for me, nothing will stop him, but I suspect he thinks I've failed him.'

'From what I hear, he is not a man to fully comprehend the lengths one will go to for love.'

104

Narin blinked at Prince Sorote – as calculating and cold-blooded as any nobleman he'd ever met. 'I suppose not.'

But Rhe only doesn't understand, he added privately as he made his goodbyes. *You do, you're just not someone who'd care. I'm not sure which is worse.*

CHAPTER 12

The daylight had long since faded by the time the bells rang for Smith's Zenith. Administrator Serril looked up from his work and noticed the quiet for the first time. It was well into the evening, four hours till midnight and almost as many since sundown. From outside came the soft whisper of falling snow while behind him was the comforting hiss of his stove as the coals burned low.

Even before nightfall the cold of day had deepened to a harsh bite. With few people bothering to meet their appointments, Serril had sent half of his tattooists – the ones who'd arrived, anyway – home early and the rest had finished up not long afterwards. He turned to face the stove and pulled the black iron door open to let the remaining warmth escape into the room. He would be heading home soon and had left the stove to die down in anticipation. His lodgings was a pleasant house on the edge of the merchant streets of the Imperial District, but better for the long, hot summers than bitter, brief winters.

'With luck the fires will all be lit,' he muttered as he set about ordering his desk ready for the morning. 'A good thing it's not far. The snow must be deep by now.'

To confirm his suspicion he went to the doorway and opened it on to the darkened corridor beyond. It ran to three sides of a square around a central courtyard typical of the Imperial District, the shutters that lined it all closed and barred. The difference in temperature was like a slap to the face and Serril physically recoiled before he crossed the corridor and unlatched the nearest shutter. Pulling it open invited in a blast of freezing air and for a moment he could see nothing through watering eyes.

At last he blinked the tears away and looked out at the blackness beyond, trying to gauge how deep the snow was. It glowed bright on the ground, lent a lambent shine by the gas lamps of the major streets and the arcane illumination of ancient buildings. Little enough to see with on a normal day, but the pristine covering of snow that lay like gently rolling hills gathered every last glimmer.

'More than a foot,' Serril noted, mournfully. 'Almost two. I suppose I should be glad it's eased, at least.'

What fell now were tiny glinting motes that sailed through the air on a faint breath of wind. Serril watched them a while, captivated by their serene progress, before the cold numbed his cheeks and drove him back inside. He closed the shutter and latched it again, but before he could reach the warm sanctuary of his office, a creak came from down the end of the corridor.

On instinct he turned and looked, but he was the last person in the building and it was pitch black.

'Is anyone there?' he called, to no avail.

Outside came the distant, haunting howl of some sort of dog – faint, but enough to make him flinch in the gloom. Serril glanced back at the now-fastened window. The breeze was weak, but coming from the east. With the city silent under the snow's assault, it was perhaps those great wolf-like beasts the nobles of House Wolf kept as hunting dogs – their howls carried for miles, Serril knew.

He reached for his office door when the sound came again, the creak of wood under a foot. For a moment he was frozen, but at a third faint creak Serril whirled around. Now the corridor was not entirely black. There was some sort of light in the darkness at the far end; a pair of red flames. As he watched they moved slowly, drifting forward like eyes as the wooden floor groaned under the weight of their owner.

Behind them a second set appeared and a deep panting sound cut through the air. Cold dread filled Serril's gut as he watched the lights draw closer, then his wits returned and he bolted through the door into his office. Inside, the lamps had dimmed, the stove's orange light flickering uncertainly. Serril hauled the door closed behind him, just as a grey figure appeared behind it.

Serril stumbled backwards into the end of his desk as the thin, insubstantial figure crept closer, hands clawed and reaching. Serril howled in fear and scrambled back, falling to the floor in his panic to avoid being touched. Long, emaciated features blurred faintly as it moved, hanging robes drifting in a breeze that didn't touch Serril's skin. Ghost or demon, every movement was deliberate and painstakingly slow – its pale eyes blank and blind as it sought him in the air ahead of it.

Serril scrabbled well out of its way, but the grey figure found something else instead. A slit-like smile stole across its face as its talons found the edge of the door. It scraped at the wood for a moment, Serril's horror mounting, before catching hold of it and dragging the door open again. Beyond there was darkness – darkness and two burning eyes.

He tried to cry out, to shriek in fear or call for help, but the breath caught in his throat as a deep growl cut through the air. The darkness came closer and terror eclipsed everything.

'Tell me about your children?'

The words spilled out before Kine knew what she was saying. Before she'd finished the sentence she knew it was a mistake, but in her exhausted state could do nothing but watch the cascade of emotions tumble over Enchei's face. He trembled as though physically struck by what she'd just said, eyes low and hands tight in his lap.

'My children?' he said reluctantly. 'All in the past, they are.'

'I'm sorry – I didn't mean to upset you.' Kine turned to check on Dov. The little girl lay peacefully in the crib beside her bed, sated at last by an awkward, uncomfortable feed. 'I should have known better.'

'No, it's not your fault. Just not talked about 'em in a while.'

'Please, ignore me. I'm just tired.'

Enchei shook his head. 'Not much to tell,' he said in a hollow voice, eyes staring down at the ground as though lost in another time. 'I'm a renegade. Abandoned them, I did, along with all the others I walked away from.'

He looked up and she saw the pain in his eyes.

'I had my reasons, good ones too, but that don't make it feel any better. Never did. Left 'em fatherless when they were young. Of all the stains on my soul, that's one of the worst.'

'Only one?' Kine said before she could stop herself.

'I was a soldier. My girls might've meant the world to me, might've been the ones who deserved all I had to give 'em, but I was a soldier. You fail your family, it's a cruelty but it's not the end of their lives. You fail the men who serve with you, they die and you shatter more families than your own.'

'What were their names?'

He shook his head. 'Can't tell you. I've not spoken 'em to another person since I left, I'll not start now. The danger'll never go away. Slim as any risk might be I'll not speak their names again.'

Kine stared at him a long while, feeling the cold fingers of foreboding on her neck as she saw her future – or Narin's, perhaps.

'How do you live with such fear?' she whispered. 'The shame and humiliation I will bear. It is my fear for Dov I can barely fathom, let alone control. How do you do it?'

'As best you can,' Enchei said with a frown.

'We're not so different really, despite everything,' Kine said in a small voice. 'Dov will always be under threat, won't she? I must live with what I've done to her, the danger I've forced on her.'

Enchei forced out a smile for her. 'It's not as bad as all that. She's a baby; she'll never feel the threat. By the time she's old enough to know it, it'll be long gone.'

'My family will never forgive me,' Kine insisted, 'their honour demands my blood.'

'Sure it does, you noble castes do like to make life difficult for yourselves. But you're not alone and no one expects the likes of us.'

'What do you mean?'

'Your brothers or cousins, they're high caste so they think like high castes. There are rules and traditions; ways of going about everything, including satisfying wounded honour. Of those of us involved, save the Siresse, Narin's the closest we've got to honourable and that boy won't think twice when it comes to doing anything he can to protect you. Kesh, Irato and me, we don't come close to playing fair and we know exactly how they'll act before they've even done it. That gives us an advantage and soon enough your family will get the message that forgetting you's the easier course.'

'They'll die before they leave me alive here.'

Enchei gave her a wolfish grin. 'Aye, I'm sure some of 'em will, but I'm comfortable with other people dying instead of my friends. Always useful to have both parties with the same end in mind.'

Kine sank back on her pillow as a wave of exhaustion rolled through her body. 'Narin said you had a cavalier attitude to life.'

'Me? No, just to the lives of folk I don't care about. I was a good soldier in my day and there's already plenty for a man to worry about in this world. What happens to folk intent on hurting others has never figured much for me. Don't get me wrong, I've got a whole host of ghosts in my shadow and I feel their presence every day, but few of 'em are that type.'

'You are unlike any man I've ever met, Master Enchei,' Kine said sleepily.

'Aye I know, just don't tell Narin that. He'll get jealous.'

She ignored the barrack-room banter. Even in her fugitive and exhausted state, Kine could not help but keep to the customs of her House and caste. A lady would never even acknowledge such a comment, be it idle joke or something more inflammatory.

'I am glad Narin has a friend like you,' she murmured. 'I hope one day we can repay your kindness.'

With her eyes half-closed she still noticed Enchei stiffen and stand. 'Just bring that girl up happy,' he said with a strange tone to his voice, 'that'll be enough for me. Sleep now, she'll be hungry again soon.'

'I should gut you where you stand!'

Sharish's green-brown eyes flashed with anger as she advanced on Kebrai, a curved dagger in her hand. The Leviathan backed smartly away around the table, empty hands held out in front of him as the snarling woman reached for him.

'Fucking fish-feeders, you and your damn schemes!'

'What happened, Sharish?' Sorpan demanded from his seat opposite Kebrai. 'Didn't you find him?'

The woman's scarred brown cheek crinkled into a scowl as she turned the knife in Sorpan's direction. He ignored the gleaming edge drifting dangerously close to his face.

'I found him – found more than him!' Again she turned to the Leviathan. 'Kebrai, you pond-swilling worm, why didn't you tell me Priest was going to be there too?'

In her frustration Sharish kicked the chair Kebrai had recently been occupying and sent it crashing into the wall behind before brandishing her dagger over the table at the big Leviathan again.

'I didn't know!' Kebrai protested, sounding calm but clearly familiar enough with Sharish to treat her anger seriously. 'Do you think my master bothers to keep me so closely informed?'

'You get enough,' she snarled, 'don't fucking deny it.'

'What happened?' Sorpan demanded. 'Sharish – put the knife down and tell me what you learned!'

'Who're you to give me orders?' she snapped, the blade waving back in his direction. 'You're not one of us.'

Before she could do anything more Sorpan had grabbed her wrist. In one neat movement he pulled himself up from his chair and twisted her hand back – not far enough to break anything, but her grip was sufficiently weakened that she couldn't stop him plucking the knife from her fingers and tossing it away.

'I'm not giving you orders,' Sorpan said calmly as he released her, 'but Priest isn't going to like you carving Kebrai open when we're in the middle of an operation. Tell me what happened and when you saw Priest. I hadn't realised the ship had reached the city yet.'

'It's here – here or close anyways. My hounds were closing on that administrator's scent and Priest had a phantom in the room already! Bastard knows how dangerous it is – you too, Kebrai!'

Sorpan frowned. 'This phantom can harm hellhounds?'

'No, but they could've turned on me,' Sharish snarled. 'The phantom carries Priest's scent and if those demons think I've guided them into a trap they'll claw my soul to shreds. They're not tame and they're not slaves.'

'But they're frightened of Priest, these famed predators of the other plane?'

Scorn blossomed on Sharish's face and she shoved him away from her. 'You've no idea, have you? Think you were top dog here? Did you reckon all your little tricks were enough to scare us? Priest …'

'Does not like to share secrets,' Kebrai interrupted loudly, 'so that should be enough on the subject. To answer your accusations, Sharish: I did not know they were so close to the city, no. Priest does not answer to me and does not always give warning, but are you really so surprised? This is not the first time we've been watched from afar.'

'More to the point,' Sorpan said, interrupting before Sharish could reply, 'Priest's close to the city. It might be we should have some leads by the time the ship docks so, again – what did you learn?'

That seemed to temper the fierce woman's anger a little. She nodded and went to fetch her blade – her manner calm enough to make it clear she would not be threatening them with it any longer.

'I got what we need – more'n that, in fact.'

'An address?'

She shook her head. 'Doesn't work that way, but I got a sight of the tavern he lodges in. I don't know it, but I got enough of a sense that it'll be no trouble to find.'

'Anything else? I doubt we'll find him sitting quietly at home if he's heard about the tavern owner.'

'Aye, a fresh memory got dragged up with it. A Lawbringer – not hunting him, a friend, I reckon. Also a sense of absence, but I couldn't

111

tell if it was recent or impending. Another face came along in the wake of that, one I reckon I did recognise.'

'Who?'

She scowled. 'Lawbringer Rhe himself. Priest won't be happy about that, I'll bet. That's a name sure to draw attention to our hunt if he gets caught up in it.'

'You're getting ahead of yourself,' Kebrai warned, 'if we move quickly – tonight, even – we might take our quarry.'

'The lodgings?' Sorpan asked. 'Don't be such a fool. You want to run straight there and kick down the door? We've no idea what we'd be getting into and most likely he's already heard about yesterday. Your methods aren't as subtle as I would have hoped, so we've lost the element of surprise.'

Kebrai gave a dismissive wave of the hand. 'Your faith in the Lawbringers is misplaced. They deal with thieves and runaways – not demons. They're unlikely to recognise the signs of Sharish's hounds, let alone spread panic by letting it become common knowledge. Would you like to be the one to tell my master you ignored such a detail as the location of his home?'

'Better than being the one to walk up to the door,' Sorpan said darkly. 'I'll gladly leave that pleasure and all the glory that goes with it to you.'

'We have others we can send – expendable types – to draw out anything like that.'

'And hand over any final shred of surprise we might have? Please tell me, Sharish, you were a little more restrained this time? An Imperial administrator dying in his office will serve as fine fodder for the city's gossips without a clear link to last night's murders.'

The woman nodded. 'The phantom helped there at least, diminished their hunger, but they'll roam the city tonight until they've fed.'

'At least the victims will be unrelated to our tattooist,' Sorpan mused, before turning back to Kebrai. 'That helps our cause, muddy the waters for anyone trying to work out what we're up to.'

'He's one man alone,' Kebrai said, faint colour appearing in his bloodless cheeks. 'I can summon more than enough support to ensure our net is tight.'

'You don't need to,' Sharish interjected. 'I'm not risking tonight happening again. Those Smoke mercenaries of yours, how many do you have?'

'Six.'

'Then I'm taking them for the hounds.'

Kebrai blinked. 'Are you sure?' he said quietly. 'Is that not rather drastic?'

'Not if Priest's going to be watching me work,' she insisted. 'I can't keep hounds on the hunt with a … with one of *them* nearby. I need to bind each one to a body – it'll drive the men insane, but not immediately and the hounds can hunt independently that way. We can have them spread out across the city and search for our prey's scent – I'll need to be somewhere secure and quiet if you want them under control, but it speeds up the hunt.'

'What about this Lawbringer?' Sorpan pressed. 'If the two are friends, he might know where our quarry is. This absence could be a result of last night or something else entirely, but we should assume he's gone into hiding. He and I are a cautious breed – he won't run straight off, but he'll have a back-up plan ready.'

'You want to take a Lawbringer and strip his mind?' Kebrai demanded. 'You believe that's the more cautious approach?'

'I want to know more about who this Lawbringer is and where he fits into the picture. I want his identity and skilled watchers in his shadow. I want our tattooist found and something more considered than a mad scrambling chase to take him.'

Kebrai was silent for several long moments. 'I will have to call in additional people for the work. What Priest will say about increased exposure I cannot tell you.'

'Make your arrangements,' Sorpan said with a sniff. 'I'll take the first shift tomorrow. Sharish, how long before we have your hunters deployed on the city?'

'The following morning, assuming I can find the supplies I need.'

Sorpan nodded. 'Then with luck we'll have something to show Priest. Or the city will be in uproar and all the Astaren and Lawbringers out hunting us. Either way, what we'll have managed won't be boring.'

CHAPTER 13

It was well into the night by the time Narin returned to the house. The snow had stopped and an eerie silence now coated the city. The inverted twilight of a world under snow left him feeling feverish and disorientated – never more so than when he crossed the Tier Bridge heading into Dragon District. The dark drifting water and dull gleam of shore were illuminated by a fractured heaven of clouds, pierced by the bright stars of the Gods above.

Even the lower tier of the bridge was twenty or thirty yards above the Crescent at its peak, while the sparsely occupied upper level was a wasteland of half-derelict houses looking down at the towers of Dragon District beyond. With a foot of wind-sculpted snow on the bridge, it proved a long and treacherous walk before Narin reached the clumps of rough houses that sheltered within the petrified forest of its many struts.

The bridge was a dangerous place at night, footpads haunting the cramped alleys around the buildings that lined the bridge. That late, Narin had the road to himself. He was forced to trust in the Sun-and-Sword emblem on his coat to dissuade those desperate enough to be out in such bitter weather.

Slowed by the depth of the snow, numbed by the cold and soaked from the knee down, it was a shivering figure that banged awkwardly on the door of the house and pressed close to the viewing port so his identity was clear. When the door was finally opened Narin almost pitched forward into the blessed warmth of the room beyond, lurching toward the kitchen door until dragged to a halt by Kesh.

'Wait, damn you,' she hissed, closing and barring the door behind him before she turned to help him struggle out of his coat.

Though it was wax-treated, the wet had still managed to permeate it and his clothes were now soaked to the bone.

114

'How did it go?' Kesh asked once the more sodden clothing was removed and hung up.

'Bad,' he said through chattering teeth as Kesh ushered him into the kitchen. His fingers prickled and stung as he neared the stove there and fumbled at a pan sitting on top.

'Oh just sit down,' Kesh ordered as she watched his feeble efforts.

She nudged him towards one of four chairs at a battered table and fetched him a bowl of stew. It took Narin a while before he could grip a spoon properly, but desperation won out and he was soon shovelling food into his mouth, moaning with pleasure at the warmth.

'Now – tell me how bad.'

'Wyverns,' he said between mouthfuls, 'tried to kill me. Kine's cousins.'

'They followed you?'

'From Palace o' Law. Dead now, but others out there.'

Kesh paled and her hand went instinctively to the hooked hatchet on her belt.

'Damn, we thought we had at least a week or two before that happened.'

'Where's Enchei?'

'Getting some sleep along with Myken.' Kesh hesitated. 'Narin, he's been looking spooked all day. I've never seen that before, it's making me worried.' She frowned. 'Make that *more* worried, given what you've just said.'

Before he could reply there came the muffled thump of a fist against the door. Narin jumped at the sound, spilling stew over the table as Kesh rose to answer it. It took him a moment to remember that Irato had been following him all day – so skilled at shadowing that Narin hadn't seen the former goshe once.

Irato didn't stop to talk as he peeled off his snow-sodden coat and stamped into the kitchen. With barely a glance at Narin the burly man headed over to the remaining stew and doled out a bowlful for himself – apparently unhindered by his hours outside.

'Trouble, then?' Kesh said, sitting between the two men.

'Pissant nobles,' Irato grunted between mouthfuls. 'Nothing Rhe and I couldn't handle.' He looked up at Narin. 'You were a big help too, o' course.'

Narin said nothing, too weary and overwhelmed to respond. He finished the last of his bowl and sat with his mind blank, staring down

115

at the table as the warmth of the room continued to permeate through his body.

'Emperor's light!' Kesh exclaimed. 'Cheer up, why don't you?'

'What?' Narin shook his head. 'I'm tired is all. Today could have gone better.'

'Well, it ends on a high so smile, you miserable sod.'

He frowned. 'What do you mean?'

'What do I mean?' Kesh sighed. 'A year ago, if someone had asked you how, if you could choose anything, you'd want to be ending each day, what would you say?'

'I, ah … with—' Narin sat upright. 'Piper's lament, how could I be so stupid?'

He stood so quickly he lurched backwards and had to steady himself on the wall while Kesh and Irato exchanged looks.

'Aye,' Kesh said with a laugh. 'So maybe you should stop staring into nothing and go sleep beside your two loves.'

Despite everything a stupid grin washed over Narin's face. 'Thank you,' he said rather uselessly as he rounded the table.

If either of them replied, he didn't hear as he headed up the stairs as fast as he could. At the top he slowed, realising how much noise he was making, and eased the door open to poke his head around it.

Kine's bedroom was dark, just lit by the glow of the small fire.

'Narin.'

He saw the dark face in the bed turn slightly as Kine whispered his name. She shifted weakly in a rustle of linen until she could lift her head and look at him, the brief white flash of a smile warming his heart in a way the stew hadn't managed.

'Aren't you coming in?'

'You don't mind?'

There came a weary laugh. 'Don't be so foolish, my love.'

Narin crept in and closed the door with all the care his shaky hands could muster. That done he edged towards the small wicker cot where he could see the tiny cheek of his daughter twitch as she huffed gently in her sleep.

'Come to bed,' Kine urged.

He bent over her to kiss her on the lips. 'I won't disturb you?'

Kine smiled and fumbled at the blankets until she had freed a hand and taken a hold of his. 'We will be the ones to disturb you,' she said, 'she needs to feed every few hours. Narin, your hand is freezing!'

'The snow's been falling all day. If you'd held out another night ...'
Narin winced at the thought.

'Then Lady Chance has been good to us, and I thank her for it in my prayers. Come, take off those damp clothes. Come to bed.'

Narin stared dumbly at her for a moment longer, then his senses returned and he hauled off his boots. Stripping off his tunic and trousers, he was halfway into the bed as he yanked his shirt over his head, but the jolt of his arrival provoked a moan of discomfort from Kine.

'What is it?'

Kine blinked and pursed her lips. 'Childbirth,' she explained in a whisper. 'Take care.'

Narin ducked his head, feeling foolish, and gently slipped the rest of the way under the blanket. Aware of how cold he was still, he kept his distance from Kine until the woman reached out and tugged at his pale waist.

'Come closer.'

'I need to warm up first.'

'And I will warm you,' she said firmly, 'but I want you here right beside me. This night will be over quickly enough and I've dreamed of it for too long.'

Narin eased himself over, hardly daring to touch her dark skin but eventually unable to resist. As his fingers came to rest on her arm he watched with fascination the goose bumps raise on her shoulder. There came a sigh from Kine, both of pleasure and shock at his cold skin, as he fitted his body against the line of her hip.

'My love,' she murmured as he slid his arm across her ribs and held her as gently as he could.

The moment stretched out for Narin, a culmination of so much hope and fear he could scarcely believe it had even come, but before he could say anything more a cough from the cot sent a frisson through his body. Excitement and panic too as he realised how little he knew about babies. He eased himself up to look at her as another choked noise came from the cot, but just as his alarm flourished Dov opened her mouth and began to wail.

Kine patted him on the arm. 'I'll show you what to do,' she said with a smile.

In the second bedroom, over the kitchen, Enchei lay staring at the ceiling in the dark. Without a lamp or fire in there it was almost

117

pitch black, warmed only by the chimney from the stove below and the bodies of its two occupants. A grunt came from the other bed and Enchei turned to look at the bundled shape of Myken. The Wyvern warrior had gone to bed with as little ceremony as any person Enchei had ever met in his long years of soldiering.

Shown the narrow beds that stood on either side of the small room, she stripped down to her long cotton underwear without a word, draped her clothes over the end of the bed and wrapped the blanket tightly around her muscular frame. Within a minute, her breathing had told Enchei that she was asleep and he was left with his thoughts in the quiet of night.

Tell me about your children.

Enchei felt a chill run through his bones, an in-built fear reaction that was anathema to the soldier he had once been. It wasn't just the subject, the shame he felt at leaving them, but the very real danger his twin girls would always be under.

The ice and snow of the Imperial City forgotten, Enchei felt a spring breeze on his cheek as his memory dragged him back to that final morning. The scents of spring on the wind, patches of purple crocus and yellow daffodils dotting the valley they called home – the warm touch of the sun on his face and the wriggling bundle of two young girls in his arms.

They had taken a last walk down to the paddock where his horses were waiting. One girl in the crook of each arm, he'd put aside his doubts and shame to spend a last few minutes with the pair. Enay's arms were looped tight around his neck, knowing he was leaving, while Maiss was content to be cradled, her fingers brushing the stubble of his newly shorn head.

They stopped at the river as they'd done so many times before, watching the tiny fish dart through the clear, shallow water or rooting out the green-clawed crayfish from the stony bed. This time they just sat at the water's edge and watched a leaf sweep down the sun-kissed water while the horses whickered gently on the far bank.

'I have to go away,' he had said eventually, fighting his tears as he spoke. 'I have to leave.'

'We know,' Maiss had replied with an equanimous tilt of the head. 'You have to go and fight the bad people.'

Enchei's head had dropped at that. This last mission was not to fight bad people, it was to be the bad people, but how did a man tell his daughters that as he abandoned them? His mission would take him beyond the borders of the Empire, to the minor nations that existed beyond the mountains and forests that held even the Empire of a Hundred Houses at bay. A place beyond the Empire, something that was rarely acknowledged at all by those within. There he would foment civil war and overturn a dynasty five hundred years in the making – all for the chance to investigate a single, unique house that lay at the heart of it.

'That's not what I mean,' he said haltingly. 'I have to go away and not come back. I did something foolish and if I stay you'll be in danger.'

'You're not coming back?' Enay asked with a tremulous voice. Of the pair, she'd been the one plagued with dreams of him not returning, tormented from an early age by such fears. Now they were coming true.

'I'm sorry, I can't. I … I've left a message for each of you, in your heads.' He touched them each on the forehead as he spoke. Normally such a mention of his unnatural skills would bring grins from both, but now they could only fight back the tears. 'You cannot tell anyone about this, not even your mother, do you understand me?'

Of course they didn't, how could they?

Enchei shifted in his bed as the faces in his memory wavered and cracked briefly, tears spilling down the cheeks of both while he hugged them close.

'I will make you forget what I've said, for a time. I'm sorry but I have to.'

'Why?'

'Because people will notice if you're so upset about me leaving. I must make it so you don't remember this conversation until someone comes to tell you I'm dead. You will know it's not true, but you can tell no one, it's too dangerous. When that time comes, you will find the message in your heads – my last words for you.'

He hated himself for doing it, but there was no other way and with a small effort he dulled that moment in their minds – shifted it to the back of their memories until the day it was allowed out again.

I'm sorry, girls, Enchei said in his mind from two decades later. *I hope you managed to forgive me.*

He rolled over and tried to pretend tears weren't threatening in his own eyes. The memories cut like a knife – worse even, for this he could not block out or ignore. This pain cut too deep for him to bury as he had dozens of times with battlefield wounds. Not even Ivytail could drown this personal a loss and he didn't try. Instead, Enchei lay in the dark and listened to the once-familiar sound of a woman sleeping close to him.

And there he found more loss, the touch and scent of the wife he'd left behind – the woman he'd loved and lied to as he abandoned her. A tight embrace, a fierce kiss and the memory of a sleepless morning together before their girls had woken. It had not been enough, could never have been enough, but he could leave her nothing more of himself that morning. So he had simply ridden away, rifle on his back and sparing only one final look at the gate of their estate. She had waved to him then as she always did, putting on a brave face for her girls who clung miserably to her skirt.

The shame of that morning lived with him, undiminished. The betrayal of his House and deception of his comrades was something long forgotten in Enchei's mind, a footnote to be acknowledged and nothing more. Of all the ghosts in his mind, those three figures at the door to their home remained the vanguard, and against them he would always be helpless.

CHAPTER 14

Narin woke early after a fractured night; mingled bursts of exhausted sleep and anxious wakefulness. Dov's cries were born of need and, for the main, were easily calmed, but not long before dawn they became frantic and insistent for no reason Kine or Narin could fathom. Eventually, Narin had half-dressed and carried the baby around the bed again and again, almost drifting off to sleep himself as his daughter was slowly soothed.

Still he refused to sleep elsewhere, whatever the day might bring. Foolish or not, Narin had longed for that night and would not be moved until the first scrap of dawn's light lined the shutter outside their window. Only then did he prod the fire back into wakefulness and reluctantly haul on his stiff leather boots, but it was with a glow of happiness he kissed them both goodbye and headed downstairs.

Enchei was waiting for him in the kitchen, Kesh having long since gone to bed.

'Good night, then?' the old man asked.

Narin smiled wearily. 'As good as promised,' he agreed, accepting a black mug of coffee. 'Gods I hate this stuff,' Narin commented as he took a tentative mouthful.

'Aye, but most likely someone'll try to kill you today,' Enchei grunted, pushing forward a board on which he'd cut a few slabs of bread. 'So let's not have you so tired you're ready to fall over.'

'What about you?' Narin said. 'You're hardly your irritating and alert self this morning.'

Enchei scowled and took a large swallow of his own coffee. 'Aye well, you get old and ya don't sleep so well.'

'Why not? You didn't get any at all the previous night – even an old wreck like you should've been tired out after all that.'

'Tired yes, asleep no. Sometimes a man's thoughts don't allow for it.'

'Conscience keeping you up?' Narin had meant it to be a joke, but from the way Enchei tensed he realised it was far closer to the bone than he'd realised. 'Sorry,' he added. 'Want to talk about it?'

That elicited a snort from Enchei and restored his more usual manner. 'Not a bloody chance. You've got enough on your plate anyway.'

'I'm not a child, Enchei,' Narin pointed out, 'I'm your friend and you're helping me enough with my problems. Is it about these hounds?'

Enchei looked up, eyes wary for a moment. 'I, I suppose so.'

'Right then,' Narin said. 'Today, Rhe and I are going to be trawling districts for summoners – Wolf, Redearth, Salamander and Iron. That's a lot of ground, a lot of Lawbringers we could be wasting the time of. Now I know how this goes, I can't claim some knowledge without telling others how I came by it, but tell me now if we're going to be wasting the day. I'm walking round with a target on my back here. In the absence of being able to do bloody anything about it, I'm fine with that, but it'd help knowing if these investigations are going to get us anywhere.'

'I ain't the fount of all demon wisdom you think I am,' Enchei snapped. 'Don't know a whole lot about hellhounds and lots of others besides. Truth be told I can't really say if you're wasting your time.'

'What can you say?'

Enchei shrugged. 'That you might not be, for what that's worth. I ain't certain of anything here, I just don't like coincidences.'

'Coincidences like you knowing the barman who was killed.'

'And the night he was killed,' the veteran said darkly, 'that's part of it too. Was a special night for me. If I'd not been paranoid, I'd have been drinking there till closing that night.' Enchei sighed and knocked back the rest of his coffee. 'Right, here it is then. Last year, that night, I was drowning my ghosts in that pub like I do every year. A man came in and we recognised each other – not who we were, but what, if you get my drift. Now, my people aren't much fans of renegades and you don't get to retire anywhere but on the family farm.'

'And you think he's now hunting you?'

'Could be him, could be someone else. My lot never used hellhounds or contracted out to those who do, but a lot could've changed in twenty years. It don't make sense, but it's one hell of a coincidence – the sort that gets a man killed if he ain't careful.'

Narin forced himself to eat while he thought. 'And if they catch you, then what?'

'You know what,' Enchei said. 'No one's taking me alive.'

As though to make his point he grabbed his long leather coat and tugged it on. Narin remembered the quilted interior to it, the powder or earth that Enchei had sewn into the coat himself.

It had seemed a quirk until their conflict with the goshe, where Narin had seen the firepowder used by Irato's former colleagues, both as weapons and to burn their own casualties beyond recognition. Their crossbow bolts had exploded on impact, lighting up the night with blinding white-hot flames – and the goshe's weapons had been crude compared to Enchei's. Whatever the old man had in store for his suicide, Narin knew he had taken pains to ensure there would be nothing left at all.

'Is it really as bad as that?'

'Aye – the man I was officially died a long time ago. They find out different, my family's in danger and I won't allow that. He didn't know my name and there won't be enough left of me to identify if it comes to the pinch.'

'So how do I investigate that?' Narin asked, almost laughing at the task he saw ahead of him.

'I'm no Lawbringer, you know your craft better'n me. All I can tell you is I don't think it's my lot playing with hellhounds. For Astaren things don't change quickly – methods, approach, commanders, whatever. Twenty-odd years ain't long enough to go from nothing to using weapons like that in one of the most observed cities in the Empire. Some renegade ain't worth revealing a new toy to the rest o' the Empire.'

'Even if you've a traitor to hunt down? Someone who faked his own death and could now be working with the enemy?'

That made Enchei hesitate, but at last the older man shook his head. 'No – there'd be no need if they knew *who* I was. You'll have to take me at my word there. I'm right, but you don't get to know why, okay? No, what's more likely is someone's looking for a feather in their cap and is doing it on the side.'

'On the side? How could that work?'

'Simple – demons were here before the Empire. Shamans and the like have existed as long as humans have. As much as the Astaren might like to pretend so, they don't hold all the cards even if theirs is a winning hand. There are others out there – some keeping to their own, others willing to use their unique skills for the right price.'

'Astaren mercenaries?'

'Freelance agents,' Enchei corrected. 'We could be talking about a teenage girl or a wizened old man who never served any House a day of their life. Don't just be looking for soldiers out there. My point is they might be working for Astaren whether or not they know it. The great merchant houses, banking consortiums or militant temples, not least criminal organisations – none are above hiring special mercenaries like that. We called 'em Gealann back home, they're as different to sellswords as Astaren are to warrior castes.'

'Would the Astaren employing them step in if I made an arrest?' Narin asked as he slowly took in the information.

'Unlikely, they're doing it at a remove for a reason. If it doesn't expose them, it's possible, but you don't want your masters noticing what you've been up to for the wrong reason. Certainly not when you've been doing it in a Dragon-controlled city and are risking a wider conflict if those buggers catch you. They tend to disapprove of things like that, so more likely they'll write it off as a roll of the dice that didn't come off. So long as they don't lose Astaren or artefact-weapons, everything else is expendable and they'll walk away with no more'n a moment's regret.'

Before Narin could ask anything more, Enchei rapped his knuckles on the tabletop and took a last bite of bread. 'Come on, the morning's a wasting.'

'Come on?'

'Aye, I'm your shadow today. No doubt Lawbringer Rhe's waiting at the Palace of Law so best we don't keep him too long. Remember when you leave to use the exits we agreed in order, don't need you slipping your own protection now.'

Enchei reached into a bag that was sitting on one of the vacant chairs and extracted a pair of gauntlets made of some sort of flexible mesh metal. Narin had only seen them twice before, but he recognised them easily enough, part of Enchei's Astaren armour and likely more was hidden underneath his clothes. That he intended to wear it during the daytime showed how seriously he took the threat to his life.

'I suppose winter's a safer time for you,' Narin commented as he pulled on his jacket and buckled his sword belt around it. 'Everyone's bundled up under layers of clothes.'

'Also keeps an old man's bones warm when by rights he'd be freezing his tits off,' Enchei said with a forced smile. 'So if you've got your head on straight, let's be off.'

Outside, the city was clean and bright. A weak sun peeked through the ribboned clouds and the breeze had lessened so, while the air was crisp and cold, Narin found his heart lifting as he left the narrow, snowdrift-cluttered sprawl and reached the Public Thoroughfare. Few people were up and about this early so the snow remained thick on the ground, rooftops heavy with slabs of white. He ignored the Tier Bridge, eerie and shining in the morning light, as a likely place for Kine's relatives to watch, instead crossing by boat so he had a clear view of those crossing behind him.

Once he was satisfied, Narin took an oblique route to the Palace of Law. The inhabitants of the Imperial District seemed reluctant to wake this morning, lulled by the soft blanket that covered it. Here and there were pockets of children and adults out to play in the first fall of winter, but by usual standards the streets were deserted when the bells of Smith's temple rang the waking hour.

The Palace of Law was equally quiet and there was a rare, relaxed air about the place as Narin entered through the training courtyards. He smiled as he spotted a group of young novices engaged in a rather less formal battle than would normally take place there – using them as an excuse to pause and watch the gate he'd entered by. If there was anyone following him, they remained outside and at last he dragged himself away in search of Rhe. The senior Lawbringers, of whom Rhe remained the youngest, occupied a long, curved hallway on the second floor that looked east over the city.

Narin wove his way through the tall oak partitions that extended halfway to the ceiling until he reached Rhe's spartan corner – just a bare desk that looked abandoned beside the two neat stations next to it. To Narin's surprise Rhe was standing waiting for him when he arrived and the look on the Lawbringer's face spoke volumes.

'Come.'

Narin turned as Rhe marched past him and followed in the man's lee, only catching up alongside as Rhe turned the corner and set off down the stairs.

'What's happened?'

Rhe stopped walking, an unusual abruptness to his manner. 'Murder and foolishness.'

Narin frowned. That Rhe might be angry with him was hardly a surprise, but it seemed that his ire had increased since yesterday and the Lawbringer was a man with ice in his veins. Brooding on a slight was not his way at all.

'What are you talking about?'

'Come.'

Rhe led him down the stairs to where the remaining Lawbringers had their communal offices. At the foot of the stair stood a piece of black slate – ten feet high and twenty wide. It was where all the serious crimes reported in the city were posted, divided by district and overseen by a scowling Lawbringer who was a legend in her own right.

Badly injured early in her career, Talash Cailer had walked with a cane for over forty years now and had overseen the slate for most of that. It was her domain absolute and her formidable memory was as much an institution of the Lawbringers as the crack of her cane on the calves of careless novices.

'Lawbringer Cailer,' Narin called with a bow.

'Back so soon, Rhe?' she replied, merely nodding in response to Narin's greeting. 'Surely you've not forgotten anything?'

'I merely intend Narin to see the news for himself.'

Narin felt a sinking feeling as he scanned the slate; it took him only a moment to realise what was wrong, but that was enough. The least-used corner of the slate was reserved for the Imperial District and there were only two crimes recorded there – one outstanding from two days previously, and one new.

'Civil tattoo rooms,' Narin read, mouth as dry as ashes. 'Imperial administrator, violent murder.'

'Friend of yours?' Cailer asked, peering hard at Narin's expression.

He shook his head. 'Not really, but I saw him recently if it's the man I think it is. Did they say how bad?'

'Bad?' she echoed. 'Worse than murder? Ah, but your tavern one yesterday – that's what you mean. They only said violent, but the doors were locked and no mention of theft. Means the killer came in over the roof and through a window – a lot of trouble for a middle-ranked administrator.' Cailer gave him a nasty smile. 'Judging from the look on Lawbringer Rhe's face, I think I know who got volunteered to work through all the writs to see what's missing or changed.'

Narin glanced towards the man and felt something similar.

But it's not the boring job Rhe's got in mind for me; at best it's one of the lesser hells. Even without everything that happened yesterday, it'd have been a stretch to get him to believe this is a coincidence. Only question now is whether I've got enough of a career left to see this all through to the end.

'Shall we head to the scene?' Rhe said coldly. 'You can perhaps fill me in on the way.'

Narin ducked his head as Rhe swept imperiously past. This time he didn't try and catch the man up but kept in his wake while Lawbringer Cailer cackled in the background.

Outside, Rhe set a pace that seemed not to account for the fact there was close to a foot of snow on the ground. Narin struggled to keep up with the taller man's strides, but was more concerned by the fact they had left the palace by the main entrance. Whether deliberate on Rhe's part or not, any one of the twenty-odd anonymously bundled figures in Lawbringer's Square could have been there to watch for him.

What Narin did know from his years working with Rhe was that the Lawbringer wouldn't listen to requests to go another way – not now. In Rhe's eyes, his trust had been betrayed and whether or not it put Rhe himself in danger, they would go the way he chose or Narin's authority and position would be stripped from him before noon.

All he could do was hope Enchei had found a vantage point that allowed him to see the square as well. At the first crossroad they came to he slipped his hood off his head and turned right to stare off down the street in the direction Enchei was likely to be. He stood for a moment out in the open, looking in vain for his friend, before replacing the concealing hood and hurrying after Rhe.

The pair fought through the snow in silence. Narin felt a strange gladness as he reached the civil tattoo offices and saw the Investigator standing guard at the gate of the central yard. The young woman bowed and stepped aside without a word, opening the gate for Rhe to continue on through.

The yard was predictably empty and they headed on to the main door, which listed unnaturally. It took a small effort to shove the damaged door open – one hinge had been bent as the lock had been broken, presumably by whoever discovered the murder – but soon they were inside and restoring the door to retain as much heat as they could.

An oblong ante-room with stools lining two of the walls greeted them, empty again, while voices echoed down the dim corridor with closed shutters down the left-hand side. They headed along and discovered three grey-faced locals huddled around a shared fire in one of the tattoo rooms. They all looked up nervously as Rhe looked in, but said nothing as he inspected them for a moment and moved on to the next room.

There, at last, he found a Lawbringer and a second man in the sober black and white of the Imperial administration.

'Lawbringer Phein,' Rhe said as he entered, 'I hope you don't mind if we intrude on your investigation?'

Phein, an aging House Moon, dismissed the notion with a wave of his dusty ebony hand and introduced them to his companion, a tall local as sternly thin as Narin expected from all religious castes. 'This is Second Custodian Drejen, here to gather and take custody of the Administrator's writs.'

'Lawbringers, at your service,' Drejen said. He bowed to them both despite his relatively high status and caste. Custom required great deference to the Lawbringers from officials when, by long-standing Imperial decree, public corruption was ruthlessly dealt with.

'Second Custodian,' Rhe acknowledged as Narin bowed. 'Have you found anything amiss here?'

Drejen shook his head. 'Nothing obviously so, but it will be a while before I can confirm that. Given the murder, I do not expect to. Anyone trying to manipulate records like this would know the lengths we must go to in the event of a crime. A murder only defeats their purpose.'

'So if they were disturbed by the Administrator,' Lawbringer Phein continued, 'most likely they never bothered manipulating any writs – it only invites their arrest. But might I ask your interest here, Lawbringers?'

'We were informed it's an unusual sort of murder,' Narin said. 'We had another odd killing yesterday and would like to check whether there is a link.'

'By all means – the next office. I have finished cataloguing the scene, the Second Custodian here was about to proceed with his duties, but I'm sure he will wait a moment longer.'

Drejen gave a deferential bow of assent and they moved on to the next office to inspect the scene. Before they even reached it, Narin felt a flicker of dread. The floor had fresh splinters scattered all around and the wooden door itself was a mess of deep scratches, such as might be made by a huge hound battling to get in. Once inside the office, however, things were a different matter.

'Did they not get through the door?' Narin wondered as he walked carefully around the desk. He glanced back at the door and saw that the clasp had indeed been broken open, but if it was hounds of any sort they hadn't caused the same chaos as in the tavern.

Rhe didn't comment as he peered down at the corpse wedged between a cabinet and the fireplace. Narin joined him and spent a long moment staring at the terror-stricken face of Administrator Serril. He felt a strange quiver as he did so, though he barely knew the man. It remained a strange, unearthly sight to see the corpse of someone he knew – someone he'd seen in life going about their business.

The paunchy, balding administrator had hardly been his favourite person, but it seemed a sick joke to see him caught up in the violence of a side of life he had no place near. While this had not been the brutal destruction of life in the tavern, there was no question of this being a natural death. Five small wounds were obvious over Serril's heart, formed not quite into a circle, while the skin around his eyes appeared to be scorched, red and blistered.

'Lady Pilgrim, walk with him,' Rhe muttered quietly, 'Lord Monk speak for him.'

Narin grunted in response, the prayers for the dead not so automatic to one of his caste. Before the age of ten, Rhe would have had the prayers memorised along with dozens of other forms and traditions, but the obligations of the low born were more mundane. Instead, he reached out his hand and held it over the wounds on Serril's chest. Whether or not it meant anything, the uneven circle certainly corresponded to his four fingers and thumb, as though Serril had been killed by stiletto-like claws.

'No hound kills that way,' Rhe pointed out softly. 'Is this something else?'

Narin shrugged. 'The eyes remind me of something. Remember the fox-demons? I'm sure someone mentioned them stealing souls through a victim's eyes. What if that means memories too?'

'I must trust your knowledge there,' Rhe said in a curt voice, clearly aware he wouldn't get much of an explanation from Narin if he pressed him. 'You think this is still hellhounds?'

'Unless someone brought a wolf to the door,' Narin said, nodding towards the damaged door. 'Obviously there's a piece or two we're missing still, but my thinking is a hellhound might not use scent like a real dog. What if they use memories or thoughts instead? They use that to follow a trail, led to the next victim by images they stole from the mind of the last? Something happened to his eyes and it wasn't needed to kill him. What if the stories of their prey going blind at the sight of them is simply an explanation for that?'

'A hunting hound follows the trail, its master tells it what scent to follow. There is still someone guiding this hunt – directing the hounds.' Rhe's tone became more pointed. 'And we know whose scent they follow, don't we?'

Narin glanced up guiltily. 'I know nothing, but you're right; this is a coincidence too far.'

'Were you planning on telling me?'

'I didn't know what there was to tell you!' Narin took a breath, determined not to foolishly snap at his superior just because his temper was frayed that week. 'A friend of mine occasionally drank at the tavern we saw yesterday, that's all I knew. That he's a shaman doesn't make him unique in this city – there are all sorts here, you know that.'

'But you suspected.'

Narin sighed and nodded. 'I asked him about hounds. He didn't have much to tell me, but he did say that you used hellhounds to track someone like him. What the barman knew about him I can't say, but most likely his profession at least. It'd only be sensible to assume it was enough to lead them here.'

'And where will the scent take them after this? Those who know your friend know that he does not have many. Are you the next link in this chain?'

Sorpan struck a match and leaned into the overhang of the arch he was sheltering under. He took his time about lighting his cigar as he watched the two Wyverns walk slowly past the civil tattoo office for the second time. They were both tall even for Wyverns, braids threaded with red and blue hanging down to the pistol butts peeking out of their heavy black coats.

'Not the most surreptitious, are you, boys?' Sorpan mused. 'So what's your interest here?'

The Wyverns were heading his way, doing their best not to directly stare at the Investigator standing guard on the gate as they passed. Either they wanted to be noticed or were blithely ignorant of how to follow someone, but either way the Investigator had one hand on her stave as she returned the look, for all the good it would do her against armed warrior castes.

Sorpan turned to rest his back against the archway and puffed appreciatively at the cigar. Some assignments took a man to the distant corners of the Empire, and as exotic as such places sounded, they often weren't known for their luxuries. There was little that wasn't available in the Imperial City, however, and whether or not the cigar was just a plausible excuse to stop and stand, he intended to enjoy it.

The Wyverns came closer, muttering in low, angry voices to each other. Sorpan had been waiting at the Palace of Law for Lawbringer Rhe to emerge and discovered he wasn't the only one interested. Most likely the Lawbringer's colleague was the one he was looking for, but these Wyverns were a mystery Sorpan intended to solve before he let this hunt progress any further.

'The last thing we need's you two attracting attention,' he muttered as they came closer. One of the Wyverns glanced up, hearing him speak, and scowled. Sorpan gave him a cheery smile – one far from the deference a warrior would expect – and tossed his cigar in the snow before ducking back around the corner.

The voices conferred again, their anger increased as Sorpan had expected. Their blood was up, that much he could see, and the warriors of any House were easy to predict at the best of times. The archway had led to a short alley with two exits. One opened on to steps leading up so he took that, his sharp ears detecting the crunch of snow underfoot as the Wyverns strode after him to take offence at the perceived disrespect.

Sorpan padded up the steps and ducked around a wooden dovecote. The Wyverns entered the alley not far behind and while they tried to decide which exit he had taken, Sorpan dropped noiselessly down behind them. He stubbed his middle fingers against the base of each one's skull with a practised motion. The blow would have just mildly irritated the pair under normal circumstances, but Sorpan felt the needles drive home and the Wyverns staggered forward instead. They each managed a single step before dropping to their knees, grunting as one then the other fell face down.

'Excellent,' Sorpan commented to the world at large as he reached into his jacket and extracted a slim leather case. 'Now let's have you as docile as little lambs. My friends and I have some questions for you.'

He glanced back towards the archway, through which he could just see the corner of the tattoo office building.

'Lawbringer Rhe, you and your friend may need to wait a while, but don't worry. We'll get to you soon enough. That I promise.'

CHAPTER 15

It didn't take Sorpan long to work his arts on the two Wyvern warriors. When he revived them it was in a rather more muted state, one simple instruction occluding their thoughts. Once he released them the pair set off without a word, intent only on heading to the upper level of the Tier Bridge.

Sorpan hung back for a while after they'd left, preferring to tail them as though they were not slaves to his orders. With House Dragon being the dominant force in the Empire, there were always high-caste Wyverns in the Imperial District. The risk they might encounter and ignore someone they knew was too great to travel with the pair, but he couldn't ignore their involvement any more than he could interrogate them out in the open.

Snow lay thick on the ground so the numbers out on the streets remained thinned. There were no litters or carts for the oblivious warriors to impede and they walked without problem all the way to the bridge. Their faces and clothes made them unmistakable Wyverns, their weapons and collars declared their caste, so folk naturally parted for them. It was only when a second pair of Wyverns hailed them at the bridge that their deficiencies became apparent.

Sorpan winced as the two newcomers, a man and a woman, repeated their hails and his new pets stuttered to a halt. There was nothing he could do in public, but his crude workings had suppressed their thoughts and for a few long moments his Wyverns just stared blankly at, so Sorpan supposed, their friends. Unable to comprehend the greeting, they eventually just continued on their way – brushing past the others without a word and pushing on up the long, shallow slope to the upper tier.

Sorpan could only curse under his breath and hurry after them as the bewildered newcomers stared after them before following. Again they called out, but only once and Sorpan was almost spotted in his haste as the Wyverns nervously checked for curious onlookers.

They're all engaged on the same mission, he realised as the pair started in their comrades' wake up the slope.

A small smile, quickly smothered, crept on to Sorpan's lips. *They don't want to draw too much attention so they're just following along. It seems I've hooked a few more fish – let's hope they prove useful after all.*

The pairs of warriors made slow, wavering progress up the icy slope. Rather than follow them quite so obviously, Sorpan wove his way across the broad lower road and trotted up the right-hand slope instead. The spray of twisting white pillars that descended around each afforded him a measure of cover and he was sufficiently sure of foot to reach the top ahead of the Wyverns.

The slaved pair drifted to a halt once the road levelled out underfoot again. There were few people on the upper tier, it being a longer, harder route across even without inclement weather, so they merely stood in the centre of the street and stared forward at the assortment of houses lining it. The second pair were naturally cautious, but their attention was fixed on what was ahead, so Sorpan was able to make his way to a door on the city side before anyone else moved.

As he opened the door and slipped inside, the slaved pair recognised him and lurched to follow just as their comrades caught up. It was a small, two-storey building in the lee of a larger one – little space to move in, but Sorpan had no time for anything elaborate.

The slaved pair entered and followed Sorpan's pointing finger to the back room, affording him enough space to slip behind the door, pull a short baton from inside his coat and watch the other two into the room. Again their attention was taken up by their comrades, but each had their hands on their pistols, ready to draw. In one movement Sorpan barged the door closed behind them and aimed his baton at the nearer of the Wyverns. They turned together and Sorpan squeezed the handle of his baton before either could react. A strip of air shuddered and wrenched between them, catching the nearer Wyvern full in the face. Her eyes rolled up and she simply folded up without a sound, collapsing to the ground.

Her comrade fared little better as Sorpan swiped down at the man's hand before he could slip a finger on to the trigger of his gun. Another flick of the wrist brought the baton up into his face just hard enough to rock him backwards before Sorpan could fire it again at point blank range. The man dropped like a puppet whose strings had been cut, leaving Sorpan standing over their bodies – the two slaved Wyverns watching him with unblinking eyes.

'Right then,' Sorpan began, more to himself than anyone else, but before he could say anything more there came a splutter of anger from the staircase in the far corner of the room.

'What in Navigator's name is going on here?'

'Ah, Kebrai, good – help me, will you?'

'What have you done?' the big Leviathan asked, aghast. 'You bring warrior castes here then attack them? What madness is this?'

'Just a little improvisation, no need for hysterics.'

Kebrai swallowed hard and continued in a more level tone. 'Sorpan, there are armed soldiers in the house. Do you have any idea how Priest will react to that?'

'I imagine Priest will be less of a timid little child about such things,' Sorpan snapped. 'Now if you've finished, take their guns and any other weapons.'

Grumbling, Kebrai did as he was told. He received no resistance at all from the conscious warriors, which seemed to embolden him, and before long had pistol-sheaths and sword-belts over both shoulders.

'Where's Sharish?' Sorpan asked as he retrieved some cord and bound the hands of the unconscious pair. 'Still out?'

'No, she's upstairs getting ready.'

'Excellent.' He waved a hand at the two slaved Wyverns. 'Take these two to her, she can use them instead of your mercenaries. These ones too, once I've interrogated them.'

'Them? High castes? Why? What's going on?'

Sorpan took a long breath and suppressed the urge to turn his baton on the Leviathan. He was beginning to see why Priest would soon be arriving in the city. Kebrai might be a useful servant, but he was no leader and far from adaptable.

'I will tell you later. First I need to find that out myself exactly. I found Lawbringer Rhe, his friend too, but those two were following Rhe. Before we go ahead with any snatch of a dangerous subject, we need to know what they're doing and why. This second pair we just picked up at the bridge – they were stationed to watch passers-by so I doubt we're just limited to four. They're not experienced in surveillance, though – most likely this is politics or some sort of blood feud, but anyone with guns getting involved poses us problems.'

Kebrai stared at him blankly for a moment, then a hiss from Sorpan jerked him into movement. 'Sharish, right. Ah, you two, follow me.'

It took Kebrai a while and a flurry of pantomimed gestures, but eventually he urged the warriors to follow him up the stairs and through the false panel that led to the house next door. Sorpan left him to it and hauled the incapacitated warriors to the small, unused kitchen at the back, dumping them in chairs. The man and woman were still out cold, minds temporarily overwhelmed by the baton weapon, but it wasn't a long-lasting effect. Sorpan gagged the man, knowing he'd likely be out longest, and pulled up a chair of his own to wait.

He withdrew another cigar and lit it, then placed his baton on a side table along with a pair of knives. To add to the effect he dug a rusting cleaver from a drawer along with a meat tenderiser and a handful of nails.

'I'll leave your imaginations to do the rest,' he advised the slumped Wyverns, 'but let's hope you're easily persuaded. I'd prefer there was something left for Sharish to work with.'

The stage set, Sorpan got comfortable and started his brief vigil.

At the Civil Tattoo Office, Narin and Rhe were finishing off when the clatter of feet heralded a new arrival. Before long a breathless novice of the Lawbringers appeared in the room. The girl goggled at the corpse now laid out flat on his desk while she recovered herself, but wasted little time in relaying her message to them in short, abrupt gasps. She had dark hair cut above the shoulder that would have given her a boyish air, but for her defined, delicate features.

'Message from Lawbringer Cailer, sir. Two murders for you. Merchant in Eagle district, Veneis Street. Pair of servants in Fett, Hymber Lane.'

'Were any details given?' Narin asked with a sinking feeling, knowing the answer already.

'Brutal.'

Rhe grunted. 'Time we split up. Narin, you take Fett. After that, you have an expert to consult.'

'What about the district posts? We were going to check on progress there later today, no? Should we divide them up?'

Rhe shook his head and turned to the novice instead. 'What's your name, girl?'

'Tesk, sir. Avrin Tesk.'

'I have a job for you, Tesk. Return to the Palace of Law and find some young Investigators able to spare the day for me, make sure they

135

can all write. I want one at each of the district posts of Wolf, Redearth, Iron and Salamander. They may have a wait on their hands, but I want a report as soon as possible – Lawbringers at each are collecting information for me, they are to receive and record that information before bringing it to me or Narin at the Palace of Law. Do you understand?'

'Yes sir,' Tesk said after a pause.

Rhe's cold grey eyes narrowed. 'Novice Tesk, we are hunting a savage murderer. Better I repeat my instructions than an error is made.'

The young woman wilted. Less than fourteen years old, Narin judged, she was a slip of a thing and more than a foot shorter than the famous aristocrat. But even as Narin's heart went out to her, Tesk straightened and looked Rhe directly in the eye.

'Yes, sir,' she said rather more clearly than before. 'Wolf, Redearth, Iron and Salamander – Investigators to wait at each district post for your reports, record them and return to one of you with all haste.'

Rhe nodded approvingly. 'Good, be off with you then.'

The novice turned and ran back the way she'd come.

'Cailer's eye for talent remains as strong as ever,' Rhe commented as they took one last look around the murder scene. 'Remember that one's name.'

With nothing else required of them, they left the body in the charge of Second Custodian Drejen, who was compiling painstaking lists in the next room. A message had been sent to the temple of the God-Empress, whose devotees performed most death rites, so their priority was now the new murders.

Under a crisp white sky they crossed the Crescent together, Fett and Eagle District being neighbours, with Rhe staring up at the high palazzos of Eagle without speaking the whole journey. Once the boatman had left them, however, Rhe caught Narin's arm before he could head off in search of Hymber Lane.

'The child is well?'

Narin blinked a few moments before a tired smile crept across his face. 'I, ah, yes, so far as I can tell. Kine too.'

'What's your plan about Lord Vanden?'

'My plan's to keep as far away from him as possible. I've got someone else to negotiate on my behalf, someone he's got to listen to.'

'And how will you satisfy his honour?'

'Still working on that.' Narin shook his head. 'All about honour, isn't it? Not even the right and wrong of what I've done, but the perceived slight or shame. Where's the sense in that?'

'Honour is a cornerstone of the Empire; you would do well not to underestimate its strength.'

'Reckon I'm getting a lesson in those respects,' Narin sighed. 'In any case, my negotiator understands it well enough and he reckons there's a way out. I don't know how much I'll like it, but beggars can't be choosers.'

'And who is this negotiator?' Rhe asked pointedly. 'Who have you trusted your secrets to?'

Narin cocked his head at the man before smiling. 'You think it's Enchei? Gods no, I don't want to start a war. I can't tell you who, but they can do the job.'

'At what price?' Rhe's expression hadn't changed. 'Who will you owe this favour to?'

'Let's be honest here,' Narin said with a scowl, 'it doesn't look like I'll have much of a career in the Lawbringers after this is over. Either I'm dead, disgraced or something else that'll mean I'm not much use to a power-broker. I'm good with that – if I have Kine and Dov at the end of it I'll gladly say a prayer of thanks at Lawbringer's shrine as I'm being kicked out.'

'You say that now. You may feel differently when you are penniless and ostracised.'

'I know. I'm not so stupid as to deny it's possible, but Enchei managed it,' Narin insisted. 'After all this time I still don't know what he's running from, what horrors are in his past – let alone all he's lost. I do know he's accepted it, though. That was the price he needed to pay and while his ghosts might follow him, they don't rule him.'

Rhe looked at him a long while, but at last he inclined his head a shade and, without a further word, turned away to head into Eagle District. Narin watched him head down the street, wondering how Rhe himself would act in the same situation – wondering too whether what he'd said was even the truth.

I've wanted to be a Lawbringer my whole life; can I really walk away so easily?

On new-found instinct he checked around him, realising he was now alone in the street and vulnerable. The cold air seemed to gather round him, a sudden sharpening of the chill he'd been trying to ignore in his bones. Even as he looked at the figures walking past and the meagre traffic on the Crescent, one of which he assumed would be Enchei, the answer to his question came easily.

In his mind appeared the warm memory of Kine's touch, of Dov's squinting eyes and tiny, jerking fingers.

With them, aye, I reckon I can. The novice-masters always said pride held me back – caring too much what others think of me, how much of a fool I might look. Now's the time to let all that go. If I have to crawl through shit and kiss Lord Vanden's feet, I'll do it with a smile on my face. The high castes can keep their honour; I've no use for it and my pride can go with it.

He set off at a brisk pace, heading in the opposite direction to the one Rhe had taken. Honour he had little use for, but the lives of others were worth more. He owed it to Enchei to find this summoner and to the city to save any lives while he still could. If that was his parting gift for the Lawbringers, it'd be enough.

Enchei sat in the front of the small boat as he was rowed across the Crescent by a long-haired, long-limbed boy young enough to be his grandson. Whether the youth had heard his grandfather mutter such a stream of curses before was another matter, but the alarm on his face told a story.

'Old, I'm getting too damn old,' Enchei hissed, gaze fixed on the Lawbringers on the far bank as they spoke on the shore. 'Bastard was right there, should've cut his fucking head off and worried about the rest later. Stupid indecisive old fool.'

He'd been following the two Wyverns at a distance, only to discover they weren't the only ones in the wake of his Lawbringer charges. There had been a third man, one Enchei recognised only too easily.

How in the lower hells did they latch on to Narin so fast? Or was it Rhe somehow? What do these bastards know? Did they get so much out of Serril they were set the next morning?

Narin's destination that morning had been a kick to the gut, though he'd feared it would happen.

I bet that puffed up cockerel Serril ignored me. I had half a mind to demand he refused to admit anything about me – tempt him into spilling everything out of spite, but I thought they'd go in with threats and he'd realise he was out of his depth.

Enchei lowered his head, wanting to say a prayer for the man who didn't deserve the horrible death he'd have received. He had despised the man, but it was a petty, mundane unpleasantness Serril had possessed, nothing more. A paper-pushing bully could become a monster, Enchei had seen that before, but Serril hadn't been one – just a fool living in a sheltered world.

'Should've followed him, tracked him back to his nest,' Enchei growled, spitting in disgust at himself into the water. 'Burned them out while I had the chance, even if it meant Narin was left alone.'

But even as he said the words, his stomach clenched and a memory came flooding back to him. It came fractured and disjointed; distorted images and sensations as much as anything else. A flash of grey skin and red eyes, of falling and a blinding pain, of grief and guilt piled high upon his shoulders.

Vague and insubstantial as it was, it stood with the last memories of his daughters in the vanguard of his ghosts and hurt him just as bad. Once before he'd done something similar – left the comrades he'd been shadowing on a calculated risk – and the price haunted him to this very day. Everything traced back to that decision, that failure of judgement that had left two brothers – and a sister-in-arms, dead in a distant field.

A rare luxury, he reflected once the memories had lessened their grip on him. *Few men can trace so much of their life all back to one moment, one rash decision. But every turn of the cards for me has come from that single hand. Thirty years and more laid out in the divination of my actions.*

'Never again,' he whispered to the heedless waters of the Crescent. 'A failure I'll not be scarred with twice.'

They reached the other side and Enchei tossed a coin over his shoulder to the boatman. The youth had to juggle to catch it, but the aging warrior's attention was elsewhere, snagged on a more recent memory. The sight of a man he'd met briefly in a tavern, followed into a secluded corner by two Wyvern warriors. Enchei knew the likely outcome of such an encounter and what he'd do in the same situation.

So will two enemies become one? How'll that change things? And who's really in charge? Is this Sorpan a go-between, or something else?

Enchei nodded to himself, a grim look on his face as he began to hurry through the streets to catch up with a sight of Narin.

Looks like I'll be taking a walk through the home district soon, see if any familiar faces are in town. He grimaced. *Hard not to see my ghosts on those streets. This week's shaping up to be a real barrel of laughs.*

CHAPTER 16

The attic of the stone house on the bridge was shuttered and dark when Sorpan made it up there. He paused halfway up the steep steps, looking around for Sharish and her charges before intruding further.

'You got the other two?' came Sharish's voice from behind the brick chimney stack in the centre. 'Bring them up.'

Sorpan nodded as he looked around at the attic room. It lacked any sort of furnishings, though a pair of small braziers flanked the chimney. Four figures sat toward the sides with their heads tilted uncomfortably forward by the slope of the roof – two of the House Smoke mercenaries and the Wyverns he'd sent over with Kebrai. All were tightly bound, the mercenaries glaring murderously at him as though he was their betrayer, while the Wyvern warrior castes just stared, dull-eyed and empty.

'You've not started? Good.'

Sorpan ducked down briefly to attract the attention of the two now-docile Wyverns who stood at the foot of the steps. At his command they followed him up into the attic, the taller of the two thumping his head against the sloped ceiling in the dark.

'Desert's breath!' Sharish exclaimed. 'Keep them from touching anything!'

Sorpan looked up at the ceiling and blinked once, twice. 'Gods above,' he said, with the hint of a smile on his face.

Across the entire four panels of roof were symbols and wardings, painted on the wood in something that didn't show up to normal eyes. Arcane shapes and scripts interspersed by a full set of divine constellations. Even Sorpan, who could see clearly in any light, had not spotted them at first and needed an old invocation woven into his eyes to read them.

'Crouch down, careful of the roof,' Sorpan instructed the two as Sharish re-checked the symbols.

'There are shackles there,' she said distractedly, running a finger over the surface to ensure there was no dent or damage.

Sorpan was relieved to see the wild shamaness was all business now. What she'd proposed to do sounded, to his informed ear, perilous and complicated, so Sorpan had already resolved to be well clear if she wasn't taking due care. Reassured, he set about bringing the docile Wyverns to the shackles indicated and securing them alongside their fellows.

'Now what?' he said once Sharish had returned to her workings around the chimney stack.

She raised an eyebrow at him. 'Here to learn a new trick?'

'Would it be safe?'

The tanned woman gave him a lupine grin, all white teeth and intent. 'Compared to what?' she laughed. 'Cinnamon tea and pastries with Priest? Another bottle of Ivytail with your friend the tattooist?'

'Sure, compared to them.'

She nodded. 'Long as you don't do anything stupid, you'll be fine. This house has so many wardings it's a surprise any of us can find the damn place!'

Sorpan nodded and sat on the floor, taking a moment to arrange his long coat around him and ensure his personal defences were just as secure. Sharish fetched a tarnished brass bowl from the floor and continued with her work, using her finger to paint an invocation on the side of the square chimney stack above the unlit brazier.

Sorpan checked the other side and realised she'd already done one there; a star of protection with a complex character in the centre that Sorpan guessed was the word for *hellhound* in some demon script.

'Sit here, legs under you,' she instructed as she drew a small brass-bladed knife and went to the first of her bound captives. The mercenary strained at his shackles and tried to kick out at Sharish, but he was securely fastened and a few hefty kicks to his midriff drove the fight from him.

'I'm not going to kill you,' she said firmly to the man, 'just take a little blood for the bowl. The more you fight, the bigger the cut needs to be before I get any in the bowl. I can kick seven shades out o' you first if you prefer. Unconscious is fine, but dead's no use.'

If the man gave any sort of response, Sorpan didn't see it, but Sharish seemed satisfied that her message had got through and bent with her knife. Good to her word, she made a small nick at his throat and held the bowl underneath it until a small trickle had run in. She repeated the job with all their prisoners, calling over her shoulder to Sorpan as she did the last.

'Light the braziers.'

He obeyed, pinching a few twigs from each until they burst into flame and dropping them back onto the rest. He could smell an oil of some sort on the kindling, faintly infused with lemon grass, so it quickly caught and the light of their orange flames began to dance around the attic.

Sharish fetched the pale twisted-tines staff she used to summon the hounds and set the head on the top of the burning braziers, pouring some of the bloodied mixture from the bowl over it. The liquid spat and crackled over the wire twisted all around the head, sparks flaring up all around it, and this she touched to the invocation sigils above the flames. They burst into life and Sharish hurried around the chimney to do the same on that side before the oil burned out.

Once both were lit she took her place on the far side from Sorpan, where he assumed there was another star of protection, and stuttering bursts of light immediately began to illuminate the room. Sorpan found himself holding his breath both in fascination and alarm as he watched the light flicker around the room, taking on a life of its own. The flashes intensified without warning, a searing staccato flurry that made him flinch as though the light cut right through him.

A second great burst of light came, then another and another – six in all, interspersed with the frantic flames from the braziers and lesser flutters from the summoning staff. Alongside distant thunder Sorpan heard faint, mournful howls that seemed to circle the room, slowly growing in intensity as they came closer, but just as it seemed the monstrous beasts were about to crash through the roof and into the attic room, the braziers gave one final stutter of light and extinguished.

There was a moment of complete darkness that even Sorpan's eyes couldn't penetrate before normality reasserted itself and he watched the nearest of the Wyverns – once docile and empty – peer forward at him with predatory intent. A growl of throaty menace cut through the air, not quite human in tone, and Sharish chuckled from the other side of the chimney. Sorpan heard her grunt and push herself up from the ground.

'Good boys,' she whispered to the straining sextet as they tested the strength of their bonds and their growls mingled to one unearthly sound. 'Now let's see how you hunt.'

Narin returned to the Palace of Law with a heavy heart. It had been a morning of murder and Narin was not so old and jaded he didn't feel the weight of it on his soul. While the death of Administrator Serril hadn't been quite what he'd expected, the servants murdered in the Fett Warrant matched the tavern exactly. It had happened deep into the night, according to an Investigator who'd been standing guard over the carnage until dawn. The victims were presumed to be a local couple whose home opened on to the alley – their door was ajar and the bloodied footprints of a huge hound led inside, only to vanish in the middle of the room. Actual identification was predictably hard, for if anything the attack had been more frenzied than that in the tavern, but the neighbours were certain – as they were of hearing distant howls echoing around the surrounding streets.

Rumour was already spreading about the crimes, the locals whispering that it was the work of some secret blood cult from House Wolf, for who else would have such monstrous dogs to hand? Narin did his best to dampen down the stories as he interviewed the neighbours, but found it difficult when the most plausible alternative was demons creeping from the river. A search of the property unearthed nothing to suggest any involvement in the supernatural or criminal activities – it was an entirely typical low-caste household of modest size and even more modest possessions.

With the next of kin just one street away, Narin went to pay his respects, though of course they had already been fetched out by the fearful neighbours. Again he could offer no real assurances or explanations and while he had managed to stop himself from being sick at the scene, a sour taste filled his mouth the entire journey back. All the way, his stomach had lurched repeatedly as the scents of the midday trade began to emanate from the many eateries on his route.

Once inside the Palace of Law Narin went to Rhe's desk and slumped into a chair. Rhe was not back yet from the other murder scene and Narin was glad to have a few minutes of quiet before they compared notes.

'Why those servants?' he wondered aloud, all alone in the partitioned section. 'Were the hounds sent there by design? Did they go on a rampage or is this some sort of distraction?'

He leaned back and closed his eyes, head throbbing with fatigue.

'If I were doing this, how would it play out?' he muttered to himself, forcing himself to stay awake. 'If I had a reason to kill the tavern owner, no doubt anyone else there is also going to be considered fair prey.

'That leads me to the tattoo administrator and no doubt he leads me to someone else – but if this is about Enchei, how do the servants and an Eagle merchant figure? He doesn't know them – I might not know all his friends, but I'd have heard mention of one I'm sure. So why? They follow a clear path and then deviate from it, but why?'

'To disguise the path,' Rhe broke in from somewhere ahead.

Narin jumped like he'd been stung, up on his feet and staring blearily for a while until he managed to focus on the Lawbringer standing before him.

'Sorry, just resting my eyes,' he muttered guiltily.

'But thinking clearly,' Rhe said. 'You're following the train of my own thoughts, so the choice of eyes open or closed is your own. With murders so obvious and brutal, our summoner is perhaps attempting to throw us off the scent by committing random killings to muddy the water. It's the only explanation that satisfies me at present, as distasteful as it might be.'

Distasteful? Narin wondered as he tried to order his thoughts. *Tragic and entirely unsurprising, I'd have thought.*

'How long were you standing there?' he asked.

'Not long enough to hear anything I did not already know,' Rhe said, at which Narin remembered the Lawbringer had already guessed Enchei was the likely quarry of these hellhounds.

'Now what?'

Rhe looked Narin up and down. 'Now you go home,' he said without criticism. 'You are no use to me half-dead and I'm sure it will be a few hours before our reports are gathered, so you might as well sleep.'

'Home's further away these days,' Narin said. 'I'll go find a corner to crawl into here instead. Best I don't run the risk of being followed back any more than I have to, anyway.'

The pale Lawbringer nodded and gestured back the way he'd come. 'Follow me, I know somewhere nearby we can eat lunch in a private room. With luck today's escort will find a way to join us, he and I can talk while you sleep.'

After a morning of walking Narin found himself physically unable to argue with the prospect. The most he could manage was to direct their path so, after leaving word of where they would be with Lawbringer

Cailer, the pair headed out past the magnificent temple-like courtrooms that abutted the Palace of Law.

As it was they walked only a few dozen yards out of the Palace of Law's defined grounds, Rhe taking him to the sprawl of inns that had been unofficially annexed by the corps of lawyers who served at the neighbouring Imperial courts.

While they stood out amid lawyers drawn predominantly from the black-coated religious caste, there was the advantage of a private guard for the whole complex and a number of rooms available for hire. Narin had never worked out the exact nature of power and control over those inns, knowing only that the buildings within the perimeter wall had been adapted and consolidated into four main premises, a cabal of prominent high-caste lawyers ruling each. He half expected to see Prince Sorote as they ascended the steps of the largest inn, but instead an aging clerk, stood behind what had once been a bar, welcomed them with all ceremony.

'Lawbringers, how may I assist you?' the man declared in polished tones. 'Are you looking for someone?'

Behind him was a series of brass plaques and small wooden shutters that announced the presence of their permanent residents, with chalk boards at the furthest end for less permanent guests. Lurking in the shadows beyond the bar were a pair of young men also dressed like clerks but with cudgels hanging from their belts. One was a local youth, the other a dark-skinned Dragon, but they both had the same wary expression, which Narin recognised as one worn by most young brawlers raised on the streets of the Imperial City.

'A private room and food for the rest of the day. Our names to remain off that chalk board, our presence to be denied unless it is to a female novice called Tesk who will be running errands for us.'

Narin blinked at the clerk as the man nodded with assent. 'Or a bad-tempered old sod who you'll know by his attitude.'

The clerk gave a nervous half-laugh. 'So long as he's not dressed as a lawyer, sir, that should be simple enough to work out.'

His fingers hovered for a moment, poised in indecision, then he pulled a key from under the bar and turned to the younger clerks. 'Oniren, take the esteemed Lawbringers to the thief's room.' Again he inclined his head to Rhe. 'If you'll permit, sir, but that's not a joke on my part. The room has a barred window and a strong door in case you want it. Oniren, after you've taken them fetch a plate from the kitchens.'

Oniren turned out to be the Dragon of the pair and after fetching up a candle he led them without speaking up two flights of stairs and to the end of a corridor. Narin noticed all the doors had locks with a grille-covered viewing shutter at eye level, but the door Oniren stopped at had the addition of heavy bolts on the outside. The room itself was as plain as might be expected; whitewashed walls making the best of the winter light that crept through the window, a desk below that and a table on the other side of a small fireplace.

As Oniren left for the kitchens, Narin employed the candle to light a pair of oil lamps and the already-laid fire, keen to drive out the winter chill that had permeated the room. Rhe stood to one side of the window as Narin worked, taking careful note of the faces turned in their direction. Only when Narin had finished with the fire, shucked off his heavy coat and unbuckled his sword, did Rhe glance back.

'What?' Narin asked irritably. 'You see anyone out there?'

'Only your friend, circling the block.'

'That's good, isn't it?'

'Perhaps. It occurs to me, however, that if there's a second faction searching for you, we do not know what we're looking out for. Wyvern soldiers are easy to notice, unknown Astaren less so.'

Narin grunted. 'If it helps, Enchei doesn't reckon they'll be Astaren.'

'He's sure?'

'Seems to be. He says they're more likely to be mercenaries in the pay of one – shamans hiring their skills out rather than elite soldiers on a mission. Gealann, he called them.'

'At last some good news, then.'

'Really?' Narin said with a puzzled face. 'How?'

'The world of the Astaren is closed to the likes of us, but we've already met someone akin to a shaman during our investigation. Their world is not so insulated from the normal course of things, they are not untouchable. Our district posts may yet provide a useful thread to follow through this maze.'

Narin nodded, finally understanding. 'So nothing for it but to wait, for our new favourite novice or Enchei.'

He looked down at the fire and gave a weak smile before laying his heavy coat on the floor in front of it.

'In that case, I'm going to sleep like a dog. Wake me when there's someone to bite.'

Hands clasped within the warm sleeves of his silvery fur coat, Kebrai watched the ship ease into dock. His characteristic lilac eyes sought one figure amongst those on board, but all on deck were hidden from the cold in heavy woollen robes or luxurious white furs. Kebrai knew just from the ship's lines that it was House Leviathan in origin, but the stylised whale shape at the prow made that clear to the whole Empire. The ship was an ocean-going trader of the Etrage merchant House, one of several that operated from the Ren archipelago off House Moon's southern coast.

A line of three triangular flags down its mast declared its home port while the purple sails, when raised, bore the cask and bottle emblem of Etrage — echoed on the bronze brooch Kebrai currently wore. He pictured the port, Ren Jir, in his mind — a far cry from the great city he stood in now, but a sight that lived long in the memory. Modest in size, Ren Jir was an over-sized town built on ground hard-won from the island's forests, surrounded by giant trees that stood close to five hundred feet tall. Some rose out of the sea itself up to a mile off-shore, creating channels their ships were forced to keep to, while those on land loomed to create a daytime twilight filtered green and red.

Preventing the jungle from reclaiming the city was a constant struggle for the inhabitants, but there was gold of a sort all around that kept the effort worthwhile. Wealth hung from those very trees besieging Ren Jir in the form of the rusty fronds of a parasitic plant. Jirrin was the spice that underpinned the wealth of the House of Etrage and the ship's hold would be full of tightly-packed linen bundles of dried Jirrin, ready to be ground to powder.

Its hot, earthy flavour had paid for labourers from House Moon to wage war against the jungle in Ren Jir — just as it had paid for the polar bear furs worn by the disembarking merchant and his associates, and the intricate gold filigree on the lapels of each that declared their position within the merchant house.

To Kebrai's surprise, there was an outsider among them — pale enough to be mistaken for a Leviathan perhaps, but as soon as the woman set off down the gangway ahead of the rest he saw she was not. The high collar of her coat and hat half hid her face, but she glanced in his direction and he recognised the sharp features of House Eagle along with the purple collar of the noble caste.

A potential employer, or something else? Kebrai wondered, blinking in surprise at the sight. *Jester's Cold Heart – they're just who we don't want involved here. Bastards or fanatics they are, usually both. It's not often I'm rooting for House Dragon, but the sooner those two go to war the better – and the better for us if Dragon come out on top. Damn House Eagle to the lower hells with its Mindwalkers and Storm Paladins. This life's fickle enough without getting knifed by some mind-stolen friend or the like.*

Before he could fathom what her presence indicated, the Eagle noblewoman headed off in the other direction and the main group reached him. The principal among them was a man of mixed descent, a beguiling combination of Leviathan's greyish hair and purple eyes, and the dusty-dark skin of House Moon. Tall and elegant, he had all the poise of an Imperial, though his blue collar showed he was indeed merchant caste.

Around him were four clerks in anonymous dark woollens from varying minor Houses under Leviathan, while a knot of brutal-looking House Shadow mercenaries followed. Rather more notable was the bodyguard standing in the merchant's lee, her red hair flying loose in the breeze. Though she wore a white fur too, it was open at the front to reveal a scarlet and white tunic with polished silver clasps as well as ornate pistols and sword. Kebrai gasped inwardly as he realised she was a Banshee – a member of House Siren's renowned elite warrior cadre.

The merchant approached Kebrai, seeing he wore the mark of the House of Etrage, who bowed respectfully.

'A cold day for a vigil,' the man said. 'Is demand for Jirrin so high that you would wait here for us to arrive?'

'Business, I regret, is somewhat slowed by the weather,' Kebrai replied. 'My vigil was not for Jirrin however.'

He grunted. 'Not here for me? Very well, I expected as much. Ainai, I will wait to hear from you – Frasin, you will oversee the unloading.'

Kebrai bowed as one of the clerks scuttled back to the ship, waving over the harbour porters who were waiting nearby. Kebrai had already secured their services so the valuable cargo would not be waiting out on the dock and a dozen handcarts stood behind the porters to transport the Jirrin bundles to their warehouse.

Without a further word the merchant swept past Kebrai, clearly familiar with the route to the offices they maintained in the Imperial City. The Banshee gave Kebrai a hard look as she followed and the rest were quick to fall in behind, all except one.

148

The clerk called Ainai was as tall as any of them, but stood with head bowed as though trying to hide that fact. Without speaking the woman looked up and fixed Kebrai with a small smile – one that chilled his blood, though it was familiar enough. She was striking to look at – fine cheekbones and delicate features – but unearthly for it.

Only a fool would call her beautiful. Her looks could strike a room silent but it was through wonder or terror, not desire. For desire there needed to be a spark of life and Priest at rest looked as vital as a perfectly-embalmed corpse – ageless and soulless.

'A chilly welcome, Kebrai,' Priest said, 'I hope your news will warm my heart instead.'

'Priest,' Kebrai acknowledged, resisting the urge to kneel. 'I have news at least. I am uncertain of how far progressed you would like events to be by now.'

Like everything about his master, her name was a mystery even to Kebrai. Even the title of Priest was something of a misnomer. It was an obscure designation from her past rather than a comment on her caste, informing only an exclusive few as to what Priest had once been.

'Ready to be concluded,' Priest said with a twitch of her lip. Behind her, almost half the crew of sailors paused in their unloading and all looked up as one – staring for a moment at Kebrai before returning to their duties as though nothing had happened.

Kebrai stifled a shudder. *Sea Snake Devotees,* he realised. *Here to take the prey.*

He couldn't help but stare at the nearest; dead white face and pale blue eyes. His mouth was a cruel reptilian slit, almost lipless with a black tongue inside.

Our own warrior cult, but without the honour or dignity of the Banshees. How many has she brought? Twenty? I don't think I've ever seen so many employed at one time. She must be as hopeful as Sorpan about what this renegade could tell us.

'We are not yet ready,' Kebrai said, his mouth dry, 'Sorpan demands caution at every step, but there is progress. Sharish has the scent and houndsmen will be walking the streets this evening.'

'I sense there is something more,' Priest said. 'You have more than the usual look of a mouse about you.'

Kebrai ducked his head. 'Sorpan has discovered a complication, perhaps two.'

149

'And they are?'

'The proximity of a well-known Lawbringer to the prey, and an overlapping hunt.'

'Hunt?' Priest said, one eyebrow faintly raised. 'We have competitors?'

He shook his head. 'They are hunting a friend of the prey; Wyvern warriors on a mission of honour. Sorpan has suborned four and they now serve Sharish as houndsmen, but there are others and they have the backing of a nobleman.'

To his surprise, Priest smiled at that.

'House Wyvern, you say? What a curious turn of events.'

She drew her heavy woollen cloak tight around her body and nodded towards the direction the merchant was walking in, still visible through the diminished numbers on the Harbour Walk.

'Come – tell me everything on the way.'

CHAPTER 17

Narin awoke in the afternoon to find Enchei come and gone, Novice Tesk arrived and his own wits somewhat restored after those precious hours of sleep. Tesk had brought the reports they had been waiting for and shown the presence of mind to question each Investigator as she did. As a result, Narin found himself hurriedly swallowing a few mouthfuls of food while Rhe read aloud the report on shamanism and old religions of the lands of House Iron – most particularly the high plateau region shared by Houses Redeve and Gold.

Aware the daylight was against them, longest night a mere Ascendancy away, Rhe and Narin set out for the north of the city, leaving Tesk in the rented room to check the remaining reports before returning to her duties. In his paranoid state Narin felt the girl's calculating gaze watch him all the way out of the door – ambitious novices were often more than willing to jockey for the attention of a Lawbringer like Rhe – but once out on the snowy streets his more real concerns took over once more.

They crossed the Imperial District and headed for the Mason's Bridge that wove a stepping-stone path across the narrower north-western edge of the Crescent. As luck would have it, the lesser bridge across the Crescent led straight into House Iron District and little more than half an hour after waking, Narin found himself on the mainland side looking back at those following. The dark stone bridge was narrow and old, its shoulder-high parapet crested with snow. Just five yards across at any point, it afforded a good view of all those crossing in their wake and, despite their investigation, Narin found himself anxiously lingering as he watched for Wyvern faces above the heads of the locals.

'Enchei didn't say where he was going?'

At his side, Rhe shook his head. 'Only that he had urgent business and was fetching Irato to watch over you.'

'Did it look like he had a lead?'

'More the opposite,' Rhe said. 'He looked like a man haunted, driven to desperate measures.'

'It's affected him this much? I'm surprised. He's lived as a hunted man for almost two decades now.'

'And now the hunt is closing in. Whether or not he was sure before, the death of Administrator Serril's far too much of a coincidence to ignore. If his former paymasters are behind this, they know exactly what he's capable of – and what they need to do to take him.'

'So they hire in outsiders, mercenaries, for the hunt itself, to avoid risking conflict with House Dragon?'

'It would be a logical move,' Rhe said. 'The goshe affair was a distraction, it postponed the war between Houses Dragon and Eagle, but the tensions remain and the Imperial City is technically a Dragon protectorate.'

Narin scowled, lifting his head slightly as he caught sight of a dark face on the bridge, only to realise they wore a white servant-caste scarf, not the red of a warrior. While their sullied honour might be the reason they wanted to kill him, no warrior caste would stoop to such a demeaning subterfuge.

'Aye, wouldn't want them to cancel plans for a brutal war now, would we? Only a fool'd hope the distraction was enough, that they might take the opportunity to step back and not bother with the slaughter.'

Rhe inclined his head. 'Hope does not make one a fool, but certainty of belief will give him a jester's crown. They are great powers with a history of enmity and a shared border – one preeminent in the Empire, the other determined to be. Neither will rush into war, but it will happen and the other Houses are cautious of provoking Dragon in the Imperial City. No one wants to be on the receiving end of House Dragon asserting its authority, not when they were denied the chance to make an example of the goshe.'

'So what makes these Gealann so ignorant?' Narin asked 'Or so greedy that they're willing to take such risks? Or do House Dragon only care about the actions of other Houses right now?'

'Perhaps Enchei angered his former masters so greatly they'd be willing to offer him as a prize? They punish the deserter and send a brutal message to their own ranks, but how far could revenge go? Far enough to reward the mercenaries with whatever secrets they can pry from Enchei's mind and body?'

With a gesture Rhe indicated they had waited enough and the pair set off down the Public Thoroughfare running through the heart of Iron District. The cold had barely impacted business on the busy street – shops of every kind lined the wide avenue all the way to the wedge-shaped fortress that split it in two, left and right towards the districts flanking Iron.

'It's quite a risk.' Narin admitted hesitantly, 'but Enchei's in no doubt what'll happen when he dies, he's warned me of it several times. What if his former masters could be reasonably certain of that? Maybe not so great a risk when they made him the man he is before training him how to think and act.'

'An informed calculation,' Rhe said, nodding in agreement. 'A far more satisfactory interpretation – but it means there might yet be an agent monitoring events, ready to step in should the mercenaries fail entirely.'

'Oh, thanks for that happy little aside,' Narin said with a snort and a shake of the head. *Want to piss on my mood a bit more?*

He bit the comment back, reminding himself their ranks were only technically equal now. Rhe remained a senior Lawbringer and wouldn't appreciate being spoken to the way Narin would to Enchei.

Passing the brutal, iron-flanked walls where Iron District's noble ruler presided, they pushed on to the further reaches of the district towards the old city wall that stood like broken teeth above what had once been a huge defensive ditch. As they walked, Narin noticed that they were heading away from the water that occupied two sides of the district – a river defining the western border while the Crescent marked the south.

Noble palazzos studded the shores of both; the largest were built parasitically around six white columns as ancient as the Imperial Palace. Ranging from a hundred feet high to almost three hundred, the pointed spires jutted out from the roofs of each palazzo like the spear-tips of the warriors within. Each one displayed the wealth of Iron's ruling families; recessed friezes decorated in gold and obsidian, ornate stonework cresting each of the round palazzo levels and gas lamps studding the walls to illuminate their opulence.

'Far from Samaleen's domains,' he pointed out, indicating that they were moving uphill towards the foundries and furnaces of Iron's industrial heart. This part of the district was chaotic with smoke stacks belching to the clatter of metal and voices.

'Far indeed,' Rhe agreed. 'A place of flame rather than water.'

The report had said exactly that, Narin remembered. The mountains and lakes that skirted the Veylesh plateau each had their own enclosed cultures, separate from the rest of the House Iron hegemony, and the high summer on the plateau was a scorching, relentless few months where the afternoon sun would kill.

During this time, so the report claimed, the boundary between planes blurred and the shadow demons of the otherworld could cross into the real. The tribes relied on shamans to protect them, as did the miners in the gold mines of the crater valleys flanking the plateau, and there were many old legends of renegade shamans co-opting their demon enemies as assassins.

Following the directions they had been given, the Lawbringers wove a path through narrow and grimy streets, the snow trodden to grey slush, until they reached what had to be their destination; the Minerild. A curved perimeter wall rose up before them, dotted with forges and foundries, while open archways led inside to a warren of twisting paths and dark tunnels. It was a huge circular building like a gigantic broken tower – almost a hundred yards across and without a single roof to cover it. Instead there were linked buildings inside the perimeter, all made of the same dirty grey brick, and one raised section of wall a hundred yards long that Narin suspected was to deflect the sea breeze.

Trusting their information, they headed in past flapping, bedraggled banners bearing the sigils of all nine subordinate Houses under the House Iron hegemony, along with half a dozen more symbols Narin didn't recognise. The crowd of locals within were mostly grey-haired Irons, which made identifying the sandy shades of Gold and Redeve an easier task, but their goal was on the higher floor where a strange network of shrine-like edifices rose up from the patchwork of roofs within the perimeter.

Brick stairways led up the side of several buildings so once they had barged through to the interior of the Minerild, it was an easy task to ascend into the open air again. The shrines themselves were composed of slabs of pale slate, bound together by twists of verdigrised wire and shaped into squat cones and columns. So far as Narin could see, the placement of them was random, owing more to available space than any obvious pattern.

There were few people up there in contrast to the ground below, the weather making it treacherous, but a half-dozen figures had braved

154

the cold and shuffled around the flat rooftops and narrow walkways between – all so heavily wrapped up it was impossible to tell the sex or descent of any. Just as they were assessing the sight, the nearest figure caught them looking around and angrily jabbed a finger in the direction of one of their kin before pointedly turning away.

They followed the direction and negotiated the three precarious bridges – each one little more than a plank securely fixed – until they came to a circular sort of shrine connected to those around it by sagging lengths of chain, each link adorned with a fluttering cloth that bore a symbol or character Narin had never seen. Before he could investigate them closer, the figure attending it slipped back a heavy hood to reveal the bronze skin and tattooed face of a man in middle years, long blond hair pulled back from his face by a spray of copper mesh.

'More Lawbringers,' the man announced wearily. 'And there I was hoping cooperation might mean you didn't bother coming back.'

'It might have,' Rhe replied sternly, 'were it not apparent that there's a killer in your midst.'

To Narin's surprise the man laughed at the accusation and turned, whistling to attract the attention of another figure nearby. 'Father, over here.'

'You are Kobelt Ulesh Hoke?' Rhe pressed. 'I am Lawbringer Rhe, this is Lawbringer Narin.'

'Aye, that's me,' the man said, amber eyes flashing in the pale daylight, 'and I can tell you there's no chance there's a murderer here. That Investigator who came here, the Iron-born one, he could tell you that.'

'We might need more assurances than that,' Narin said, 'given the fact that hellhounds have killed at least five people in the last few days.'

'It was no one here,' Ulesh asserted as his father joined them, almost the image of his son bar the lines on his face. 'My father, Geret Hoke – Senior Kobelt of the Minerild. Tell them, Father, no one here would send demons on a hunt.'

'Here? Only a handful have the power for such a thing,' the older man said in heavily-accented Imperial, gesturing at the rooftops around them. 'None are so stupid. We teach rituals of protection only, that is what this is all for. Perhaps if they had the knowledge, one or two of our most gifted Kobelen could draw a hunter into this realm, but no more than once.'

'They could not control them?'

155

'Them?' The pair scoffed as one man. 'Only I,' continued Geret, 'could control more than one, this thing is beyond Ulesh even. It will be years before he is strong enough. No other Kobelt here could summon more than one; no other Kobelt here would survive to try twice.'

Rhe adjusted his coat fractionally, just enough to make it clear his pistols were within easy reach. 'You declare yourself our principal suspect then?'

'Are you mad?' the man gaped, as his son bristled with barely-restrained anger.

'I am not, but I shall impress upon you my seriousness. I hunt a murderer and if this power's so rare, you may know who possesses it – or at least can help us find them.'

'And you choose threats to achieve this?'

Rhe shook his head. 'I choose to believe you will help us, but you narrow my options by making such a statement. Are you protecting another? Taunting my authority? Simply mistaken or misguided?'

'This is foolishness,' Ulesh broke in, 'even the priests of Lady Pilgrim know and trust us. Go ask them yourselves.'

'What *do* you know of summoners then, what can you tell us?' Rhe said. 'The report I have tells me your kind are respected members of the community, so that is why I came with one Lawbringer beside me rather than a hundred.'

'Most considerate,' Geret growled. 'Yet all we know of summoners is rumour. When they are exposed, they are hunted down.'

'Your son follows in your footsteps,' Narin said, keen to calm the conversation a touch. 'Does the ability pass down through families?'

Ulesh nodded. 'Often, but the last reported summoner was decades ago. I remember grandmother telling me the story.'

'That man and his acolytes were all put to death,' Geret declared. 'I do not remember any mention of family. As for rumours, they are hearsay, no more. A tale from the Ren islands five or six years past, a power struggle between merchant houses, I believe, also the assassination of a House Rain general two summers ago – Ulesh, can you remember more?'

'That massacre on Shols – House Storm's lands. Was that not said to be a shadow demon? A dozen villagers killed when a trading ship from Ren was forced to beach there, all those who helped make repairs. The ship had sailed by the time of the massacre, though, and no one among the survivors could agree on the ship's designation so it was never traced.'

156

Narin nodded, committing the details to memory rather than attempting to scribble them down in the freezing wind.

'What about these shrines of protection? They're wards against the demons? If you can protect against them, can you find them?'

'The shrines disrupt energies; they exist to make it harder for the demons to cross into this realm. But a summoner tears at the veil – they cannot prevent that.'

'Can they tell you if it has happened? Where it might be happening?'

Ulesh shook his head, glancing at his father to confirm his agreement.

'Do you know how it is done?' Narin persisted. 'How it might be done?'

'I do, but I will not attempt such a thing.'

'But is there equipment you might need? Ingredients for a potion? Certain conditions?' He gestured around at the snow-laden roofs. 'Clearly this isn't a case of the city becoming so hot the border between realms blurs.'

'Equipment? No. A staff to channel energies, certainly, but nothing exotic they would need to purchase. As for conditions – height is good, a tower with air all around would be best. As far from earth, stone or water as possible, for their realms are shadow and flame.'

'Anything more?'

Geret shook his head. 'I must meditate on this, consider the ritual. You are Rhe? I will send word if I think of more.'

Rhe inclined his head. 'Lawbringer Cailer at the Palace of Law will know of our whereabouts. I thank you for your time.'

As the pair returned to ground level, Narin waited until they were on the stairs and out of sight of anyone who might hear them. 'You've a plan, then?'

'A next step,' Rhe said with a small shake of the head. 'We have a trading ship and a merchant house mentioned there – the Ren archipelago appears to be at the heart of their rumours. It is thin, but what else presents itself for investigation?'

'These people needed to get to the city somehow,' Narin agreed, 'so why not use one of your own trading ships when sneaking in someone you wouldn't want noticed? It's winter, the arrivals at the docks cannot be so great that we can't narrow down a list of trading houses based in the Ren archipelago. It's not close, so there shouldn't much traffic at this time of year.'

'Which gives us one or two names, while the city records will list holdings of those trading houses and their affiliates. Safe-houses that might be employed by mercenaries using the trading house as the front. A reported power struggle backs up the theory; control of a minor trading house would be simple to arrange with such unnatural means at your disposal.'

Narin forced a smile as he pulled his coat tighter around him. 'Indoor work at least, it could be worse.'

'And then you remember you are a hunted man.'

That wiped the smile from his face. 'Aye, then there's that. Thank you, Lawbringer. Just what I needed to hear right now.'

'You are welcome. Come.'

In Ghost District, a vigil began. For all that House Ghost's lands were more than a thousand miles from the Imperial City, their sovereign territory in the city was a bustling affair thanks to the long, arch-festooned avenues that led through the district and out of the city. Sat on high ground above the shore surrounding the Crescent, Ghost District harkened back to the mist-wreathed mountains and valleys of its home thanks to an uneven range of nine half-natural edifices punctuating the landscape.

Channels had been dug around natural rises and rocky outcrops to enhance their height, then spiral paths had been carved around them and the interior carefully excavated to produce both exclusive markets and grand eccentric palaces for Ghost's nobility. Walkways, aqueducts, decorative arches and twisting stairways connected the five largest – producing a strange treetop community for the lower classes while the high castes enjoyed all manner of delights on two separate tors, all adorned with a garish variety of lanterns, banners and signs. The last two structures were the linked stronghold of the local triumvirate, millennia of Ghost tradition dictating that coop-erating factions governed their people.

To a man such as Enchei, long apart from a land he barely called home any more, it was a powerful reminder of all he'd left behind – of the nation he had once loved and the family that had meant more to him than life. Despite the marshalled force of memories, he skirted the grand view and found himself a vantage point of a modest, high-end importation house well away from the jewels of Ghost District. It was a quieter corner, as it had been decades before when he'd once walked freely into the four-storey house he now watched from a distance.

Little about it had changed – a fresh coat of black paint on the doors and shutters perhaps, but the invisible wardings laced into the brickwork and humming through the lead muntins in the windows were as strong as they had ever been. Enchei kept well clear, knowing what would happen should he stray closer than a dozen paces, and instead talked his way into a lodging house three doors along from it.

Drugging his bemused, unwilling host ensured he would be left alone and from a darkened upper room, through shutters that had seen better days, he settled down to watch faces and gaits, fashions and attitudes, for as many hours as might be required. Barely moving – barely awake, by some measures of the word – the few remaining hours of daylight dragged past his window like a procession of the condemned. Fragments of memory occasionally drifted to the surface of his mind as he waited, prompted by some tiny detail or the idle wandering of thoughts.

The exploits of his only real career, now decades past, rose to scrape at ill-healed scabs of memory. The taste of the smoke-spiced air of Sight's End as he followed a minor target through that city's madcap tangle of alleys, and once-divine screams that ripped both earth and sky asunder in what became known as the Fields of the Broken. Then the soft slimy kiss of mould and moss on his skin as he lay for hours in a pagan temple – his cracked skull ringing with the screams of comrades dying because of his impetuousness.

That last was stronger and had been for days now – the turning point, the moment where his blunder could have brought ruin down upon the entire Empire. The thought still chilled Enchei. Quite beyond the fact his daughters would have been the first casualties in any such war, there was the sheer horror of what might have been unleashed on the world, had some ambitious Astaren doctor discovered what had happened to Enchei in that temple.

Old and young went into the house. Craftsmen caste standing aside for nobles at the tall black door, occasional porters carrying boxes wrapped in bands of white silk and under guard from Ghost warrior castes hired to protect their wares. Some were entirely innocent to Enchei's practised eye – others appeared innocuous yet were screaming *Astaren* for the quiet, lethal grace they avoided others with, or all-too-brief glances that most likely inspected the streets and houses around them in unnatural detail. He saw everything and nothing from his darkened room, surmising what he could from the numbers he saw and the legitimate trade pursued by the house.

What he hoped for, however, was akin to what the religious might consider a sign from their favoured god. And it didn't come. Night arrived in its place, swift and sharp, as the temperature plunged and the fleeting light of the Gods illuminated the hard sparkle of frost on every edge. Before long the darkness deepened, heavy cloud rolling in and covering the sky.

Away to the left, had he craned to see them, were the many hundred lanterns of the nine tors that shone with fierce defiance of winter, but there were only two sights he craved – the opening of shutters on the upper floor ahead of him, or an older figure who walked with the assurance of a king through that night-sky doorway.

Still, neither came. No face he recognised, no man or woman who might command here. With so little having changed in this place, Ghost's Astaren maintaining a modest presence in the city, Enchei could picture close enough the sort he was looking for – the sort he had once reported to – but no close candidate revealed themselves and as dusk became a cold memory, he was about to abandon his post for the day when something quite unexpected happened.

Without warning, his head was filled with voices. First one, then two, three and four – calls, warnings, commands, he had no idea. The words were garbled and unintelligible, beyond his power to understand, but they told enough of a story that he was preparing to flee with his weapons ready when a far bigger surprise came.

Another voice, this time a man's and not garbled in any way, as though the man was standing right beside Enchei and using his natural voice. No elliptical code or uncertainty, no measures of precaution such as any Astaren might use as a matter of course. Just a few brief words, bursting through the night air like a hasty songbird's call.

But even more than that, it was a voice he knew. A voice not heard for twenty years, a voice he had never thought to hear again. Even with the chilling words it carried, Enchei felt a flush of warmth at the crisp tones of a man he had once loved as a brother.

Then sense reasserted itself and he reacted to the words that, given they were sent without code or artifice, could only be offered to him out of some similar brotherly affection.

'Hellhounds have tripped our outer wardings. You know what you must do.'

CHAPTER 18

Enchei bolted. Confusion and surprise filled his mind, but the old instincts were stronger. Away from the window, one step and reaching for the door. Weapons ready and every nerve singing, he pushed on through to the darkened corridor beyond.

At the back of his mind he heard a jangle of voices, disguised and incomprehensible. The Ghost Astaren calling orders, summoning their defences. Then, at last, distant howls – lingering, lupine voices that shuddered between worlds as they cut through air and stone alike. One, then a second, then he could not tell how many. It didn't matter, Enchei realised. He was hunted – they had his scent and were closing in.

He paused at the stairs, light flickering in his eyes as his mage sight searched for traces of his hunters. He sensed nothing, nothing out of place and the air still on his skin. From outside there came a faint rumble of thunder and wind shuddered against a window pane. He looked out at the night beyond and saw sleet falling, heard the faint drum of sleet on the building's roof.

Through the slashed air he made out a slanted roof, bowed with age and layered with broken snow. Beside it a grander building – a covered terrace looking out over the roof between them. He opened the window to clear a path for himself and looked out, down at the ground. All seemed clear, the streets emptying as the slushy downpour grew.

Why was I warned? What game's being played here?

Enchei let the questions hang unanswered at the back of his mind, focusing on the jump ahead of him. A short run-up and he was through the window, landing heavily on the roof below. He punched down as he struck, driving an armoured fist through the slates to anchor himself on the slippery slope. A gust of wind whipped across his face, soaking his grey-seamed hair to the darker shade of decades past.

Four steps to the neighbouring building, one short hop to grab the ornate iron rail and haul himself up. Enchei barely broke stride as he crossed the terrace and put his shoulder to the narrow door on the far side. Bolts burst under the impact and he barely made out the shape of the room before he was through it and down a stairway to the room beyond. A woman's cut-off cry accompanied him across the room to the long drape-covered balcony door.

He hauled it open, ignoring the panicked movements from the bed behind him, and dropped over the rail into an alley beyond. It was fenced ahead of him, seven feet high, but Enchei never slowed – planting one boot hard on the neighbouring wall as he scrambled over. Then he was in the street, the red-tinted glow of the triumvirate tors shining in the distance. There were no gas lamps on the streets of Ghost District and only a handful of bronze door lanterns illuminated a street crisscrossed with arches.

Up above there was the stutter of lightning sheeting across the sky, one great flash followed by two others. In its light he saw a figure clearly defined against the sky, crouched on an archway and watching him. A long coat flapped madly in the lesser flashes that followed; grey like an Investigator's, grey like a Ghost noble caste. Just as he was about to turn and flee, more howls cut through the dulled rumble of thunder – this time behind him.

Enchei bolted left, away from both dangers and sprinting down the street. A sense of the district unfolded in his mind, the narrow maze of streets that might lead him to safety. There were sanctuaries he could cross, tangled streets through which they would struggle to track him. Whatever scent they had, temples or waterways would interfere with it – places sacred to other beings whose power eclipsed Enchei's own and would mask him.

He jinked down a short set of steps and into a narrow side-street. The rain continued to fall as he skidded around one corner, vaulting a wall and crossing a deserted garden to get on to a tree-lined avenue. Empty branches in the gusty wind waved him madly on, but Enchei sprinted only a short way down it before cutting through once more. The river lay ahead, a natural destination but a choke point too. An old shrine to Lord Monk, Ghost's favourite son, might provide a hidden place to turn and, if not, he would find good ground to fight on – anything that might provide him with an advantage.

'You have him, sister?'
'I do.'

162

'And the others?'
'Following close.'
'Show me.'

An image appeared, a frozen glimpse – a man, fire-lit and fleeing down a street – accompanied by a sense of movement, a vertiginous lurch compelling travel south-east.

'I have it.'
'Be ready for when I strike.'

The howls came unexpected and louder – closing in as Enchei reached the shrine. Six pillars supported a dome open to the elements on all sides – but every direct approach to the kneeling stone statue in the centre was blocked by an array of short, slanted walls inside and outside the shrine. The entire array was thirty yards across, but would involve double that to wind a path through. Enchei ran within and headed south, skirting round the outside rather than head straight. He emerged a quarter-way round the circular shrine, darting between carved monuments to the God-Empress and into a cramped side passage between houses.

Out the other side he sensed movement and instinctively slew away. Something flew forward at him from the other direction, a figure edged in boiling shadow and flame, and he turned his weapons towards it before it crashed home. Silvery darts were swallowed by the darkness and barely slowed it. A lance of distorted air slashed across it and cut the flame. Still it came and Enchei was forced to kick out. The figure slammed into his boot and Enchei felt ribs crunch under the impact.

Possessed by a hellhound? Oh screaming fuck.

The impact drove them apart, Enchei fighting to keep his balance as he turned his baton towards the first movement. Before he could fire, another figure of shadow and flame pounced with a monstrous snarl, slamming Enchei back against a wall. For a moment they were face to face – the contorted features of a Wyvern warrior caste with huge canine teeth straining to reach Enchei. He brought his knee up into its ribs with all the strength he could muster and again felt bone break under the impact, but the twisted parody of a man barely shuddered.

Blood-red threads of light exploded from the Wyvern's eyes and for one long moment Enchei stared straight into the glowing eyes of a hell-hound as it prepared to strike. The pressure on his arms was immense – at the back of his mind Enchei realised the possessed man's muscles must be tearing apart – but he had other concerns. Mantras sang at the back of his mind in a crazed cacophony – magics buried there by the mage-priests of Ghost. A bitter-tasting fluid filled his mouth and Enchei wasted no time in spitting it into the Wyvern's eyes. The light twisted and writhed as the acid struck and now the possessed man screamed, the hellhound's control wavering as his eyes began to burn.

It was all Enchei needed to break the grip holding him and he raked forward with his left hand – steel-clad fingers ripping through the Wyvern's exposed throat while darts erupted into his open mouth. As blood poured from the man's wounds the aura of fire seemed to intensify, the darkness surrounding them deepening to chilling howls from all directions.

He twisted the man around and threw him back in the direction of the other, the body of the possessed man collapsing backwards while his aura of shadow remained – grew even. Enchei looked for the other and felt a spark of panic as he couldn't find it. Before he could do anything the street suddenly exploded into blinding white light – a pure burst that seemed to cut through the smoky mess coalescing ahead of him.

Under the assault the hellhound was ripped asunder and cast back into whatever realm it came from, leaving Enchei panting and blinking alone in the street. He moved on instinct, keeping himself from becoming a stationary target even as he tried to wipe the afterglow from his mage-sight and fathom what had happened.

The sleet continued to fall, but beyond that curtain there was sudden stillness in the street. No voices or howls, no threads of light or shadowy trails. He was alone and where the second possessed man had gone, Enchei couldn't fathom.

'But who cares?' The aging warrior growled. 'Ain't staying to find out.' He broke into a sprint down the street, ready to defend himself but covering the ground as fast as he could. The street remained empty long after he was gone and only the brutalised figure of a Wyvern nobleman remained.

A crackling collar of light seared the second warrior's throat as she silently writhed and snapped at the leash holding her. Blackened blisters appeared on her dark skin, her red caste collar already torn and ruined, but she paid them no heed. Her contorted, deformed jaw worked furiously, but to no avail, as the leash held her securely out of reach of her captors.

Both wore long grey sleeved cloaks against the rain, sheltering their faces from the Wyvern at their feet. After a moment of consideration, the shorter of the two crouched and reached out a hand towards the Wyvern.

'You're going to banish it?'

'You've another suggestion?'

'Not yet.' The taller figure cocked its head a moment, considering. 'Send it back with a message?'

'What message will they listen to?'

'Perhaps none, but you cannot tell for certain.'

'What it can report isn't worth the slim chance they'll listen.'

'I suppose so. Kill her then.'

The deed done, the shorter figure straightened and looked its companion straight in the eye. 'And the old man? What do we do there?'

'There's nothing to do there – yet. We continue to watch.'

'Caution,' the shorter sniffed scornfully. 'Always bloody caution.'

'Always,' the other confirmed. 'That is our life. Don't worry, when the time for reckless abandon comes, the lead is yours – that I promise.'

Kesh idled in the doorway, watching the Wyvern knight, Myken, do press-ups on the empty bedroom floor. Along with her long dreadlocks, Myken had shed her tight-fitting tunic and trousers. Despite the chill in the air, she wore only her small-things as she exercised and a thread of sweat beaded the line of her spine.

'What do you want?' Myken said at last, not breaking off from her efforts.

'Just trying to work out what you're doing,' Kesh replied. 'Is this how the warrior caste relax? Kill time?'

'A true warrior maintains their every weapon, of which the body is one.' Myken paused. 'But in truth – I'm bored. This inaction does not suit me.'

Kesh snorted. 'Was life so exciting as bodyguard to a noblewoman?'

'No, but there was purpose. My role wasn't to merely stand beside her. The best bodyguards anticipate danger – root out threats before they reach the principal.'

'Did you ever find any?'

Myken slowly stood and Kesh became very aware of the woman's height and muscles. That her guns were on the floor to one side, out of reach, was little reassurance. 'You have a point to make, *servant* caste?'

Kesh touched the white scarf around her neck, such a ubiquitous item of dress for all people in the Empire she'd put it on that morning without even thinking – unnecessary as it was unless she left the house. 'Oh, don't take the warrior caste with me, woman,' she sighed. 'Right now we're equals and you're relying on me. You want to risk going outside later, be my guest.'

'Insolence towards a high caste remains punishable, even within the Imperial House.'

'Not in this house,' Kesh said. 'You could shoot me in the head if you like, but you wouldn't live long to enjoy it. Narin you might be able to take, but once Irato or Enchei got home you'd be as good as dead.'

The two women stood facing each other for a moment before Kesh shook her head. 'Come on, let's make some tea. You're not in the barracks any more, no place for pissing contests here.'

She turned and headed down the stairs towards the kitchen, not leaving Myken time to reply, but before she had set the kettle on their small stove, Kesh sensed the woman at the door.

'The strictures of our society are not a pissing contest,' Myken said at last. 'These strange circumstances are no reason to give them up.'

'As good a reason as any,' Kesh countered. 'Come on, take a seat and just talk to me like a woman, not a warrior.'

The suggestion seemed to startle Myken into silence, but eventually she did just that and sat straight-backed in one of the chairs. Kesh fetched a battered porcelain pot and spooned grey flakes of tea into it before taking a seat herself.

'How did you stand it?' she asked quietly, looking up at the taller woman.

'What?'

'The boredom. The years of nothing but watching a woman live in a gilded cage.'

'It is – was – my lot in life, the Lady Kine's too.'

'But Lord Vanden's hardly a powerful man or a threat to the other noble families in the city. She can't have ever been in much danger.'

Myken's lip twitched. 'She is a beautiful, passionate woman. There were other dangers.'

'Ones you failed to stop,' Kesh pointed out. 'Or didn't it look like Narin would count?'

'Lawbringer Narin,' Myken began hesitantly, 'was a man entranced by her. He was not the first and will not be the last. I can identify an assassin in a crowd, but my training failed to include identifying my principal falling in love too. Their friendship was good for her and it is not my place to interfere – and then it was too late to interfere. She was in love and her heart was set. The choice was hers, and I am her servant.'

'So now what? Where do you go from here?'

'Wherever she wishes,' said a voice from around the door jamb.

Kesh and Myken both jumped up, but in the next moment Kine's drawn face appeared in the doorway.

'Wherever you wish, Siresse Myken,' Kine repeated, walking gingerly in. 'I owe you that much at least. I hope the jewellery you had the presence of mind to rescue with me will be put to good use there.'

'My Lady,' said Myken, reaching for Kine's arm, 'you should sit and rest.'

'I will stand. I have been abed long enough that a few minutes on my feet will be a blessing.'

'And Dov?'

'Is well and asleep upstairs.' With her hands firmly gripping the back of the chair Kine smiled weakly at the pair of them. 'She's fine, we will hear her when she wakes.'

'Want any food? Tea?'

'Tea would be welcome, thank you. I can feel my appetite returning at last.'

Kine looked down and patted her belly. 'Strange, I had thought I would not look quite so ... well, pregnant, once I had had the baby. I could be months-gone by the look of me now. Even after all this I can hear the voices of my aunts, telling me I must become presentable soon. That I must be desirable for my husband by Order's turn – I think that's what they always said.

'It was never clear if they cared how far into the month we were, Order's turn was always the line drawn. When I draw up a list of things to be glad of, never hearing those bitter voices will be close to the top.'

'Don't worry,' Kesh said as she fetched the hot water, 'there are shrill bitches everywhere you look in these parts too. We'll soon get you feeling right at home.'

Kine lowered her eyes, a narrow set to her lips. 'I do not consider this a holiday,' she said quietly, 'or an amusing step away from the strictures of my birth.'

'Aye, well – might be that came out nastier than I intended. Just all this talk of assassins and hellhounds making me a mite snappish.'

Kesh opened her mouth to say more but then closed it with a snap. The Wyvern noblewoman raised an eyebrow but Kesh shook her head. 'Never mind, none o' this is my place to ask.'

'Ask all the same,' Kine said gently. 'You've done me a great service as a favour to a friend. Such a service I could have only asked Myken to perform, or Narin. To do it for someone you've never met – I owe you whatever answers you wish for your kindness.'

'Do you really know what you're doing?' Kesh blurted out, before blushing faintly at her own abruptness. 'I don't mean to pick a fight there, but you want to live as Narin's wife? Take a servant caste tattoo? Cook and clean the rest of your life? With a face like yours, there's a lot o' men going to notice you. You slap a warrior caste's face now and a punch is the best you can hope for. Do you really know how you're going to live?'

'No,' Kine replied, unabashed. 'I've tried to imagine it, I really have, but you see how helpless I feel as a mother without servants. You're right – I do not know, I *cannot* know how I will live, but I chose to live. Perhaps there were other ways I might have saved my life, but there is one thing this pregnancy has taught me: I wish to be a mother.

'Not a woman who watches her children be raised from afar. Not a jewelled pet on her husband's arm, not a tool to be used for manipulating others or the secret power inside my husband's palazzo. A mother who is the full order of stars to her child; who feeds and clothes her, who is the one she runs to and the one she laughs with. I had time enough to think about what I would lose and what I might gain. The choice may be made in necessity, ignorance even, but I am glad to make it.'

From upstairs there came a stuttered cry. Before Kine could move, however, Myken headed towards the door.

'It may be you're not alone there,' Myken said, pausing. 'Gentleness does not come easily to one brought up as a warrior. It's time I also learned something new.'

CHAPTER 19

Deep into the night, while fitful bursts of rain clattered on the roof, Narin and the others sat around the small kitchen table and debated the day's events over a supper so many hours late it could hardly be called such. It was a fractured conversation where one person's sentence was regularly finished by another, steaming bowls of rice and beans proving a greater draw for those chasing the chill from their bones, and took a long time before it was done.

To add to the distraction, Dov fussed in her mother's arms and every other sentence Narin spoke went unfinished until prompted by one of his companions. As strong as his need to shovel food into his mouth was, he found himself unable to resist the small, angry sounds and it took until he was most of the way down his bowl before his news was out. The reports of fresh murders and Enchei's confirmed suspicions had cast a pall over the table, but the meagre thread from the shamans of Iron District proved a hope they gladly grasped.

'How long can we last this way?' Kine said in a hesitant voice, a moment of hush having fallen over the table. 'Hunted in two directions? Enchei, it sounds like you were lucky to escape those hellhounds at all.'

He scowled and stared down at his food. 'Aye, might be getting older than I'd thought, to let 'em get ahead of me like that. Still not sure how I got away in the end. Almost like someone was playing with me.'

'Perhaps they were,' Myken spoke up. 'You said you were given a warning, by magical means. They intended for you to run, to make a game of it.'

He shook his head. 'Man I got that warning from, he was like a brother to me. If he had to kill me, fair enough, we went our separate ways and he was as good at it as anyone, but to play a game with me? To enjoy himself here? No, I don't believe it.'

'It has been twenty years, people do change.'

169

'Not that much. If he'd got that messed up in the head, he wouldn't be allowed out of the home valleys, let alone to come here where trouble's so easy to find. No, it was a true warning and one I reckon we've got to have a chat about.'

Kesh gave a snort. 'In that case, I second Kine. How long can we go on like this? This is more'n we ever expected to take on. I'm not walking away here but, Gods above, how do we come through this alive looking ahead and back at the same time?'

Narin scraped the last of his food out of the bowl and swallowed it hurriedly. 'Got something better in mind?'

'Aye, mebbe. How about we pick a fight?'

'With who?'

'The Wyverns.' She nodded towards Kine. 'Her family aren't going to stop, it doesn't matter how soon Lord Vanden gets here or what your Imperial friend can use to buy him off. They're out for blood and we don't need to keep on looking over both shoulders, do we? The four of us, we've a good record for holing up and killing anyone who tries to break in. Let's do that again – make a mistake and let the Wyverns follow you home, Narin.'

'And if they're ones working for this summoner, eh?' Enchei growled, 'what then? Those two who came for me, one was a woman and I didn't see Sorpan take a woman off the street. He must have found others; maybe they're all taken.'

'Well bloody make sure on the way,' Kesh said scornfully, 'you're meant to be good at this sort of thing, old man. Use those shamans Narin met or something else, it doesn't matter. All I'm saying is, sort out one problem then focus on the other.'

'Glad it's so simple for you,' Enchei snapped. 'Meanwhile, those of us at the sharp end find it a little more complex.'

'You miserable old sod,' she replied, 'I'm staying behind because you asked me to – no other reason. I know someone's got to be here so I've not bitched about the women being left safe at home, but don't you fucking dare throw it in my face!'

Enchei hesitated then his shoulders slumped. 'Aye, you're right. That wasn't fair, wasn't true. I'm just … unsettled right now. Too many of my ghosts walking these streets and it's got me on edge. I didn't mean to take it out on you.'

An uneasy silence settled over the table. Narin looked around at the faces, trying to work out if there was a real problem there, but all he saw was tired sullenness from both Enchei and Kesh. Myken and Irato maintained a stony reserve and Narin realised they had both accepted Kesh's idea with alarming fatalism.

Only Kine betrayed any anxiety at the suggestion and Narin slipped his arm around her. 'Don't worry, love. Kesh's not planning on putting you in danger, certainly not Dov.'

'Dov?' Kesh looked up, alarmed. 'Seven hells no!' She reached over and slid a fond finger down the baby's brown cheek. 'Don't you worry there. She, my sister …' Kesh bit her lip. 'You know about my adopted sister?'

Kine nodded.

'She came to us when she was a few years old. I never saw her as a baby, but Emari's skin was not so different to Dov's. She was a Greenscale by birth, still such a little thing when the goshe killed her. When I look at her face, it's too easy to see Emari as a babe. I'd never let anyone hurt her.'

'House Greenscale,' Kine echoed in a choked voice, placing a delicate kiss on Dov's head. 'I've visited their lands several times.'

'Emari never did,' Kesh said sadly. 'Never got a chance to see her homeland. We dreamed about going there once, when I became a ship's captain and Emari my first mate.'

Shyly, Kine offered over the swaddled baby who had fallen silent and lay staring up at the lines of shadow cast over the ceiling. Kesh took her gratefully and cradled Dov with awkward, but painstaking care, while a tear slid down her face and onto the baby's cotton wrappings.

'So when do we kill 'em?' Irato piped up after a moment of silence, face falling slightly at the glares he roundly received. 'What?'

Kesh glared at him. 'Remember we talked about you saying things when the conversation's tailed off?'

Irato nodded. 'Something about not doing it.'

'Exactly.'

'But I didn't ask anything personal this time and the argument was over. You looked happy.'

'Let's call it a general rule, since you can't work out tact by yourself.'

'Fine.' Irato shrugged. 'Conversation's going now though, so when do we do this?'

Despite himself, Enchei laughed. 'It depends on whether Lord Vanden's returned to the city yet. Kesh, you up for a trip in the morning?'

On cue the rain began to hammer down harder. 'Where?' Kesh said with a small laugh, glancing up towards the roof.

'Imperial District, before you visit my old rooms in Tale. I need some things from the strongroom, more wardings to put up and mess with those hellhounds. I've got to assume they caught my scent on the street and if it happens once, it can happen again. Here I'm hidden, I made sure of that, but I could do with some patches of fog to hide in when I'm outside.'

'I'm going to play with royal family? Better start practising my bowing and grovelling.'

'Please do better than earlier,' Kine said with a smile. 'Your efforts with Siresse Myken might not please a prince of royal blood.'

Kesh snorted and nodded. 'Aye, guess you could be right there. Prince Sorote sounds like something of a true bastard.'

'Just remember he doesn't need to know the whole story,' Enchei said. 'He doesn't know about me and I'm damned if he finds out today. Narin promised him a summoner and Sorote's welcome to them, but I don't fancy swapping pursuers, understand?'

'He knows nothing about you?' she asked, surprised. 'How did you keep that out of your reports, Narin?'

Narin shrugged. 'No need to mention it. Enchei's a former soldier, Sorote knows that. Nothing I said to Prince Sorote suggested he was more noticeable than that. Man's got enough hanging over my head.'

'And too many people know my history already,' Enchei snapped. 'My life's hanging on the thread of Wyvern loyalty oaths,' he added, pointing at Myken, 'and bloody Lawbringer Rhe's lack of ambition. Not a whole lot needs to change before I'm as good as dead. I'm damn sure I don't need some Imperial power broker deciding how he could best profit from the situation. Don't even get me started on the conversation I need to try and have tomorrow, that's a whole new level of suicidal foolishness right there.'

'I suppose that means, for once, I'll be having a better day than most,' Narin said brightly. 'A day of trawling shipping records and merchant holdings; it'll feel like luxury after these days past.'

Enchei smiled nastily at him. 'Aye, well, you'll be taking double precautions to help Irato spot any tail you might pick up. They know what you and Rhe look like and they might make a move next time, rather than wait for their hellhounds to catch my scent again. Make sure you tell Lord Cheerful what could be coming, I know he'll thank you for the added complications to your investigation.'

'Oh yes,' Narin said as he rose and took hold of Dov, ready to turn in for the remaining hours of darkness. 'You're a true friend, Enchei.'

'Hey, we're all in this together. My day goes to shit and I'm dragging yours down too. Sleep well, my friend.'

In the dead dark of night, with the light of the Gods hidden by cloud and the sound of her passing masked by rain, the Banshee walked the Underways of Raven District. The streets and passages of that place were deserted; not even the cutpurses were out to steer clear of the woman adorned in blood and snow.

The long coppery tresses of her hair were tied back and hidden beneath a scarlet hood, the seams and silver buckles of her bone-white leather coat picked out in red. Her coat was loosely fastened, revealing the red collar of her caste and leaving her guns within easy reach. The coat bulged on one side, a flap of cloth that covered the hilts of her narrow duelling blades, one long, the other short. A tiny stitched sigil of House Siren was visible there and a second lay just below her collar, a sop to convention for all that the warrior cult needed nothing more than their coat and looks to announce them.

She walked with fierce purpose, never pausing to check her surroundings or ponder her path. Driven by some unseen force, she wove an efficient path through the Underways until she reached a sunken marketplace, the doors and windows leading off it all shuttered and dark.

The Banshee went to a jutting doorway and brought her fist down against the wood, a single blow that echoed around the high walls of the marketplace. She waited, near-motionless, until the door was yanked open and a fat man peered out.

'What the f—' As he realised what she was, the angry words died in his throat. 'Ah, didn't mean no offence, Siresse, you woke me.' Awkwardly he bowed to the high-caste woman and waited for her to speak.

'I have a message for the mistress of this place,' the Banshee rasped. Her voice sounded strange, a mechanism operated by unfamiliar hands.

The man paled and shrank back, gaze dropping nervously to where her weapons distorted the line of her coat. 'She's not here, I swear it.'

'Who is here?'

'Just, ah, just a couple o' others.'

She took a step towards him. 'Nagai? Novices?'

'Nagai!' the man said frantically. 'Performing the night rituals, the appeasements and such!'

She cocked her head at him as though listening to a distant voice. 'Appeasements? We cannot have that now, can we?'

With a practised movement she flicked up the side flap of her coat and plucked out the straight-bladed parrying dagger that nestled over the hilt of her rapier. Not bothering to draw the longer weapon, she advanced on the fat man who whimpered in fear.

'You will give a message to your mistress,' she said.

The man sagged momentarily, relief flooding across his face, but then she darted forward and drove the tip of the dagger into his chest, piercing the lung in one smooth movement. In a flash she withdrew and thrust it into the other with such speed and precision the man had barely time to look astonished. He gave a strangled cry and stumbled back, falling to the ground as much in surprise as under the force of the blow. The blade slipped silently back out, now tipped in red.

The Banshee stared down at the man as he scrabbled and wheezed on the floor, watching him like a beetle crawling past.

She raised the blade again and jabbed once, twice, while the man convulsed and screamed, hands now clutching his ruined eyes. Panic and horror took him over, but the wounds in his chest made every attempt to scream a paralysing agony and all he could manage was a broken, muted gurgle. He writhed and kicked, heels scuffing uselessly on the dirt ground.

'Let her read this message and carry it far,' the Banshee whispered. 'Let her bring the rage of demons out on to the streets. Let this frozen city be consumed by the fire of Dragons as they scrabble for control.'

For Kesh the morning came almost as soon as her head had touched a pillow. One moment she was lying in darkness tucking the folds of blanket under herself, then Enchei was shaking her awake. Once she dragged herself outside, the biting cold jolted her fully awake and at the Tier Bridge she spent a while looking out over the city as it sparkled under a pale morning sun. The rain of night had washed away much of the snow, but in its place was a thick coating of hoar-frost that glistened in the freezing air.

She made good time across the Imperial District and soon found herself at the door Narin had described, the small building that seemed to house Prince Sorote's personal fiefdom of the Office of the Catacombs. From the Lawbringer's description, they had surmised the cellar door led elsewhere – but neither the city natives nor Enchei had heard of catacombs beneath the district.

'Remember, Kesh,' she said to herself as she approached the door, 'they're worse than nobles.'

Before she could reach out and knock, the door jerked abruptly open and Kesh found herself staring, open-mouthed, at a handsome, gold-collared young man wearing a pristine black-spotted fur and gold-chased pistols across his belly.

'Who in the name of Sailor's hairy crotch are you?' the Imperial demanded.

At last Kesh shook off her surprise and knelt, ignoring the damp touch of the cobbled ground as she bowed her head and folded her hands over her chest.

'A friend of Lawbringer Narin's,' she blurted out. 'My Lord Sun, my apologies, I hadn't expected you to open the door before I knocked.'

'Narin, eh?' The man's immediate outrage lessened and Kesh guessed this was Prince Kashte, Prince Sorote's preferred weapon. 'What's your name?'

'Kesh, my Lord Sun.'

'Ah, the sister.'

She felt a jolt at being described that way, but reminded herself that Narin had been compelled to relate most of what had happened during the Moon's Artifice affair. Emari's poisoning and death at the hands of the goshe weren't the raw wounds they had once been, but to have some stranger casually reference it left a bitter taste in her mouth.

'You are Prince Kashte, sir?'

'Excellent, we're acquainted already,' Kashte drawled sarcastically. 'Stand up then, no need for a scene here.'

Kesh did so, careful not to look him directly in the eyes and more focused on the fantastically detailed decoration on his pistol grips and sword hilt. 'I was sent in search of Prince Sorote.'

'I'm sure you were, but he's busy right now.'

Kashte hesitated a moment, half turning back towards the door behind him before apparently changing his mind. He pulled the door completely closed and beckoned Kesh to accompany him as he walked off down the street. At the first corner he turned left, heading north towards the barren shore of the Imperial Island. It took Kesh a moment to remember there was a single barge station there, one used solely by high castes.

'Narin grows impatient for news, does he?'

'We have a complication,' Kesh said cautiously, not knowing what Narin had already told them. 'We were hoping to cut our list of problems.'

'Our list?' Kashte gave her a sideways glance. 'You're in this all the way? You bear him an obligation?'

'He's a friend who needs help, my Lord Sun,' she said firmly. 'One who helped me when I needed it.'

'That may not have been his primary concern.'

Kesh shook her head. 'Doesn't matter, they're family as far as I'm concerned. Weird annoying cousins, mebbe, but still family.'

'Certainly I shall not be one to deny a duty to family.'

I'm sure you won't, not when the Emperor is some sort of distant cousin and the blood of Gods sits in your veins.

'Narin asks if a certain nobleman has returned to the city.'

'No need to be coy, girl,' Kashte said with a small smile. 'I know about his problems and their names too. As it happens, I'm hoping our Wyvern might be fluttering towards his roost this very day.'

'And you can talk him down? Kine doesn't think her family will give up the chase, whatever Lord Vanden tells them.'

The prince smiled. 'Ah, the Lady Kine! I do so look forward to meeting this troublesome beauty in due course. As for her opinion, I suspect she's correct. Vanden bears no direct authority over her family and his rank isn't so great he can order them to desist – unless he brings the Lady Kine back into his household, which remains unlikely. The Vanden family's influence is limited even here, more so back in the homeland.'

He paused and turned to face Kesh. 'Cut down your list of problems? Do you intend to murder your betters?'

'Of course not, my Lord Sun,' Kesh replied demurely, 'but if they try and murder us, we can hardly be blamed for defending ourselves.'

'Indeed not. However these will not just be goshe apprentices carrying knives. Your friends may have a few advantages in a straight fight, but so far as I've discovered, a bullet to the face is the best advantage of all.'

'We'll make sure it doesn't get to that – if we can lure them into a trap, we can stack the odds in our favour.'

'But first you wish to ensure the Lord Wyvern is mollified, that your problem will not grow beyond a few dead warrior castes failing to protect their family honour?'

'Exactly.'

'Lawbringer Narin should have greater faith,' Kashte said sternly, picking up the pace. 'When Prince Sorote assures him of a result, he need only have patience.'

'Ah, my Lord Sun, I think it was more a question of Narin feeling cut-off from the rest o' the Empire right now. We're in hiding half the day, might not be hearing everything that's going on in the city. We've got bigger problems than Lady Kine's family now.'

There was a pause. 'What sort of problems? Narin's investigation has taken a dramatic turn? Please don't tell me he's blundered into another Empire-spanning conspiracy. We could do with not repeating the events of the summer. Prevailing wisdom is that House Dragon will not be so friendly this time in the face of any threats to their authority in the city.'

Kesh coughed to cover a smile. 'Blundered's such a specific word.'

'Oh merciful Stars of Heaven, what has he done now?'

'Just his job, but this ain't so much of a coincidence. He said he told you about the hounds?'

'He did – my sources tell of several more murders two nights past. Will I be hearing of more later this morning?'

'I don't know about that, but it's a complicated story. Not sure it's all mine to be telling you, but the short of it is: we know who the hounds are after.'

'Let me think, what would be the most foolish thing to do in this situation? Ah, yes. Has Narin given them shelter, as he once did you?'

'That's about the size of it.'

'So in effect you have a hellhound after you as well.'

'Don't be silly – ah, my Lord Sun.' Kashte inclined his head to acknowledge the effort, not bothering to keep the small smile from his face, so Kesh hurriedly continued. 'What's one hellhound, after all?'

'*More* than one?'

She coughed. 'It might be there's a pack of 'em. Possessing the bodies of warrior castes, too.'

'Wyvern warrior castes?' Kashte asked with a sigh.

'Among others.'

Unexpectedly, the Imperial laughed loudly. 'Tell Master Narin he is either the unluckiest man in the Empire, or he really should choose his friends more carefully.'

Kesh bit back her first thought there, half-joking though it would have been. She'd already got away with more familiarity than was safe.

'I will tell him, my Lord Sun.'

'Good.' He pointed towards a street entrance ahead. 'Come, it's this way. Try to look presentable, it will already be scandalous I'm bringing a servant with me.'

'Yes, my Lord Sun. Ah, where, might I ask?'

'The Failkeep, if you must know. If Lord Vanden is indeed returning today, as our information suggests, that's where he will enter the city.'

'You're going to suggest Prince Sorote's compromise today?'

Kashte gave her a strange look. 'One does not simply blurt such a thing out in the street. A negotiation involving lords is a delicate affair; there are forms to be adhered to and conventions to be obeyed.' He sniffed. 'It should go without saying that if you speak during any of it, unless directly addressed, I will break your jaw for your insolence. Do you understand me?'

'Yes, my Lord Sun.'

'Excellent.'

Narin crossed the threshold of the Palace of Law and felt a now-familiar sense of easing. The streets remained perilous for him, but that great doorway signified a sanctuary in his mind. Kine's family would not attack him openly, he knew that much. Most likely he was safe on the public streets where he was in plain view, but the Palace of Law was an inviolable step. Kine's younger brother, Shonray, would be leading any blood feud, she had assured Narin. Perversely, it was Shonray's obsession with honour that kept Narin safe.

They want me, my head and Dov's. You are lesser to them, a detail to be dispatched at their leisure. Shonray would be within his rights to challenge you to combat; the Lord-Martial of the Lawbringers himself could not countermand it without a direct appeal to the Emperor, but he will not. So long as he needs to find me, you are safe in public places.

'How safe I am from hellhounds remains to be seen,' Narin muttered to himself as he headed towards the stairs.

Before he'd gone a half-dozen steps he stopped, some sixth sense prickling at the back of his neck. Narin glanced around. It was mostly Lawbringers and Investigators arriving for their morning toil, but off in the wings there was a figure out of place – one stood quite still, staring straight at him.

The winter chill of fear slithered down his spine but then he made out the figure itself – wearing a long robe with a hood hung low over the face. It seemed familiar and certainly nothing a warrior caste would wear. Narin gave a start as the figure took a step towards him, but in the next moment the pieces clicked into place in his mind. He approached and bowed.

'Mistress Samaleen,' Narin said formally, 'how may I help you?'

The pagan priestess stopped short. She hesitated for a moment before sweeping back the hood to reveal the Raven heritage of her face and the tears streaking her cheeks. Even then she did not speak at once and Narin found his own voice stilled.

'You've brought death to a sacred place,' she said, in a strained voice. 'You bring death in your shadow.'

'What? What's happened?' Narin took a step forward and lowered his voice. 'Did more Wyvern warriors come to your temple?'

The scorn was immediately evident on her face. 'What does the summoner want?' she demanded.

'A … a man, we believe. They hunt a man.'

'Just one man?'

Narin faltered. 'What happened?'

'The death that walks in your shadow,' she spat. 'That's what happened. The ghosts that march at your side.'

'I don't understand.'

'Of course you don't – you have no understanding of my world. You blunder through with your Imperial badge and your sword, trusting them to keep you safe and caring nothing for those in your path. What has happened? Two of my kin were murdered last night, along with the man who guards our door. The man you threatened.'

Narin began to protest his innocence, fearing he was about to be publicly accused of murder, but she cut him off.

'They are all dead – tortured and brutalised, their eyes put out and their corpses used to pollute the sacred waters.'

Samaleen's voice took on an even harder tone. 'Their eyes put out,' she repeated. 'Burned with sticks left in them and still alight when they were found. I may not know much of hellhounds, but lore speaks of how they burn a soul out from the eyes.'

'That doesn't mean it's hellhounds,' Narin objected.

'It's a message,' she hissed, 'of that I'm sure. This was the summoner or some mortal servant of theirs. Demons could never gain easy entry to our sacred places, but it's in the nature of hounds to claim territory as they pass. We have no rivals here that might want to strike at us and divert attention elsewhere. A human killed my priests and I do not doubt it was done under orders of this summoner.'

Narin blinked. 'You think the summoner's here to stay? Claiming the city as his home territory?'

'You think they hunt a single man? To risk exposure in this place for one man alone?' She shook her head. 'These murders are a warning to the beings of the hidden waters, that much is clear to me. A warning and a challenge.'

'One you intend to rise to?' Narin asked coldly.

'And be led by the nose? Don't be foolish. I am here to tell you the summoner has made this threat and you would be best served to catch them soon.'

'And if I cannot?'

'My people cannot keep their heads down forever, the spirits of the waters will not run and hide. If there are more attacks or the summoner continues to roam free in this city, there will be a response. Perhaps that is what they want, but either they're ignorant or they over-estimate their own power.'

'What do you mean?'

'The spirits of the waters are mindful of tensions in this city; they have no intention of inflaming any human conflict.'

'But?' Narin prompted.

Samaleen cocked her head at him. 'Tell me, Lawbringer, have you ever heard of the Apkai?'

He frowned. 'I, ah, yes, in actual fact. The highest order of demons.'

'Gods by another name,' she confirmed. 'Is that a conflict you want to see on the streets of this city?'

Narin shook his head. 'But why would the summoner risk such a thing? Surely they know you serve the Apkai?'

'I am no servant,' she snapped. 'I am no priest to bow and scrape. We are seekers of understanding, walkers in the hidden realms – to do that we forge alliances and allegiances, but we are not pets. The spirits of the waters I am aligned to are, however, themselves bound to those of greater power and soon they will stir those powers to action. If your hellhounds are carving themselves a territory, they will soon incur the wrath of something far greater – beings only the Gods themselves could stop, should they choose to unveil the full majesty of their power. Do not let this escalate, Lawbringer. Do not let these fools bring destruction down upon the city.'

Without waiting to hear a response, Samaleen tugged her hood up again and stalked away, leaving Narin open-mouthed and staring after her.

'More good news, Lawbringer?' said a voice behind him once Samaleen was outside.

He sighed inwardly and turned to the familiar pale face of Lawbringer Rhe. 'Guess.'

'That bad?'

'Depends if you want hellhounds picking a fight with the native demons of the city.'

'On balance, no. At present I'm wondering how long it will take for House Dragon to take an active interest. They may ignore rumours for a certain time, but if there are more bodies on the street they will be persuaded otherwise.'

'I know,' Narin said, 'and that's not the only good news for the morning.'

Rhe paused. 'I am starting to dread hearing news from you, Lawbringer Narin.'

At that, Narin had to stop himself from bursting out in laughter. The idea that the cold, lethal former nobleman could dread anything seemed entirely impossible. The look on Rhe's face was sobering though – containing as little humour as it did dread.

'I'm afraid you might be right with that one,' Narin muttered. 'I'd like to say at least things couldn't get much worse, but not even I believe that.'

CHAPTER 20

As they reached the Failkeep, the veneer of sociability dropped away from Prince Kashte's manner with all the abruptness of a portcullis. Kesh had expected to be dismissed in some fashion, but still the shift in his manner left her startled. After sharing a boat across the Crescent with the young Imperial, they walked up through Arbold Warranty to the wide plaza that led to the city's principal gate.

The plaza was a six-sided expanse open at one end, opposite the enormous city gate, while shops and eateries occupied two tiers of arcade on the other four sides. Six great columns defined the boundaries the eateries were allowed to sprawl to – twenty feet of granite decorated with gold, atop which were statues of the six Greater Gods. The God-Emperor and God-Empress stood on the nearer edge of the plaza, their benevolent gaze cast toward the distant palace of their descendant, Emperor Sotorian.

Behind them stood the other four in their allotted positions, Lords Knight and Smith behind the God-Emperor, the Ladies Shaman and Jester behind the God-Empress. All were beautifully detailed in gold and white marble, but the plaza was still dominated by the Gate of the New Sun behind them. It was a three-quarter disc thirty feet high, sheathed entirely in polished brass and engraved with the names of every Emperor to follow the Gods themselves. The gate was a testament to the divine, just as the broken remains of a stronghold framing it reminded all passers-by of the Ten Day War that broke Imperial power forever.

In the depths of winter there were no tables set out in the open air and today was no exception, with the puddles on the ground frozen solid. However, it took no more than a look from Prince Kashte to have one brought out from the coffee house nearest the God-Emperor's statue. Kesh glimpsed dark wooden panels and staring faces through the doors as they were flung open by the house's staff, while Kashte merely sniffed and waited for a chair to be placed behind him.

Kesh moved behind the Imperial, skirting the shop-fronts until she had a view of both Kashte's face and the grand open gate. From there he would summon her like a servant if needed and she was unlikely to be disturbed. Prince Kashte had settled himself between two columns, facing the gate and seemingly oblivious to the looks he received from travellers and locals alike. She doubted an Imperial had ever likely patronised the coffee house before – despite its long-standing reputation, the highest castes had no need of visiting places of commerce outside the palace – and certainly not just appearing on foot.

It was seconds before a tall silver pot was brought out on a tray along with a selection of sweet pasties, the sight of which made Kesh's stomach groan. Kashte muttered something she couldn't catch to the waiter as he served the prince, tossing down a silver coin. The man bowed low and hurried away while Kashte ignored the drink, sitting with a studied idleness as he watched the myriad figures entering the city.

Kesh knew such dedication was hardly necessary. Lord Vanden, a nobleman of House Wyvern, would hardly slip through unnoticed, whether or not he was modestly positioned within the House. First would come a liveried beater, cracking his stick on the ground to clear a path, then low-ranked warrior castes in battle dress before the litters of retainers and family. The canopied carriage of Lord Vanden would follow those, and perhaps a pair of mounted knights before the servants and carts of luggage all followed by more soldiers. Such a parade was standard when nobles travelled between homes and it made enough noise to give ample warning to anyone expecting it.

'Ah, Mistress?'

Kesh jumped at the unexpected voice. She turned to discover a nervous-faced waiter standing at her side in a grey uniform with a white caste collar. He held a silver tray upon which was a steaming earthenware mug.

'Yes?' Kesh said, realising the man was waiting for her to respond.

'Ah, your Master has instructed we keep him supplied with coffee for as long as he remains.'

'Master? Oh, yes, the Lord Sun. Well good, he may be here a while.'

'It is the house custom to provide drink for servants too, for as long as they attend their lords and ladies.'

'Really? That's for me?'

The man inclined his head. 'Edict obligates Imperial castes to pay for all goods up front, a decree of Emperor Jakerien if memory serves. Noble and Imperial castes traditionally pay well above any likely price and your Master's largesse is particular.'

'It is?' Kesh shrugged. 'Can't complain then, can I? What's that, tea?'

'Indeed.' He offered the tray forward but Kesh made no move to take it.

'Given my Master's largesse,' she said carefully, 'how's about you bugger off with that and fetch me some warm wine instead?'

The flicker of a smile crossed the man's face. They were both servant caste and both knew perfectly well that the coffee house owner would be furious, but not in front of a prince of the royal blood.

'As you wish, Mistress. I, ah, it looks like your Master is settled in there. Best you don't overdo it, given Imperials who carry guns tend to have short tempers so far as I've heard.'

'Don't you worry about me,' she said, smiling sweetly, '*your* Master will water the wine so we'll end up even I'm sure.'

The waiter bowed to her and backed away, disappearing back into the coffee house with her request. Before long she was sipping at a delicious cup of clove-spiced wine and finally feeling ready to settle in for a long, dull morning. Protocol was far from her strong suit, but Prince Kashte had told her to go with him and the rest of the city would have to wait as a result.

Kesh knew she couldn't ignore an Imperial's wishes, whatever Narin or Enchei might need, but while patience wasn't a natural virtue of hers, the young woman had learned it well enough. She settled back into a corner of the arcade's pillars and got comfortable, scanning the crowd for Wyverns of all types while ahead of her Kashte lounged as only a prince could.

Bastard knows I can't sit down, Kesh realised, catching the man glance very slightly at her out of the corner of his eye. *That probably makes this amusing for him.*

It took two hours of standing, by which time her feet were numb and her knees aching, and two false alarms of noble castes arriving. It was a strange, disconcerting feeling for a woman able to work all day on the deck of a ship. The constant motion became part of you then, the activity and movement rolling through your body and becoming part of the work you were doing. To stand perfectly still was alien to Kesh; to keep as still as a soldier on guard rather than let Kashte see her shift and fidget was an arduous task, but she refused to give him the satisfaction of seeing her bend.

Kesh almost gasped with relief when she heard the whip-crack of a cane beat the flagstone floor of the plaza. She saw Kashte stiffen at the sound too, also unwilling to reveal his eagerness. He had a better view of the gate, though, and she realised by his manner that it must indeed be Lord Vanden heading back to discover the news of his pregnant wife. With a studied carelessness, Kashte popped a final piece of pastry into his mouth and made a show of brushing the crumbs from his fingers. Kesh moved forward a shade but, without looking at her, the young nobleman gestured for her to keep her place.

He pushed himself up and ambled forward as a tall Wyvern woman in blue passed, cracking a five-foot-long cane on the ground with crisp, practised strikes, then a quartet of warrior-caste soldiers in greatcoats. As the carriage, large enough for four passengers, reached the centre Kashte took another step forward and, with a flick of the fingers, signalled to the driver to reign in.

A bejewelled hand pushed at the carriage curtain and a round face appeared there, poised ready to bellow at the driver before he saw the impressive Imperial caste standing just before him. Forgetting her place entirely, Kesh stared in fascination at the middle-aged noble with thinning hair who was husband to the radiant Lady Kine. She knew the match had been made because Kine was born warrior caste, but the pairing remained somewhat ludicrous.

Kesh couldn't help but wonder if Lord Vanden realised how ridiculous he must have looked to the rest of his House; a man without great power, prowess or looks, with a notable beauty on his arm. Marrying a lower caste was not unheard of at all, but to Kesh this negotiated pairing smacked of a dull man with a desperate need to impress.

'My Lord Sun,' Lord Vanden stuttered, fumbling a moment with the door catch before finally managing to scramble out and bow. 'Might I assist you in something?'

From behind the carriage a large warrior caste with greying hair stepped forward, weapons on show, as the armed Imperial neared his lord. Vanden stopped his bodyguard with a gesture and the man eventually bowed to Kashte, receiving not even a look in return. Both were so intent on the prince they didn't notice Kesh edge as close as she dared without intruding.

Prince Kashte inclined his head cordially to the nobleman. 'My Lord Vanden Wyvern, it is a pleasure to make your acquaintance. I am Prince Kashte.'

'I, ah, you honour me, Prince Kashte.'

'Please?' Kashte gestured for Lord Vanden to come closer so they were not speaking at a formal distance. 'I bring a message from a relation who would be keen to make your acquaintance.'

Lord Vanden's brown cheeks flushed. 'Ah, relation?' he croaked, barely loud enough for Kesh to hear.

Kashte's welcoming smile turned patronising to Kesh's eye. 'Not my most illustrious of relations,' he assured Vanden, 'but a man of standing nonetheless. He begs you attend on him this afternoon, at the Glass Tower.'

'This afternoon?' Vanden coughed. 'Prince Kashte, I am yet to reach my own home, where my wife just a few days past gave birth. Might the matter not wait?'

'I'm afraid it is somewhat pressing. It involves some business your wife's family are engaged in. My relation has been asked to intervene in a business transaction and does urgently need to speak to you.'

'My wife's family,' Vanden stammered, paling. 'I was, ah, unaware any of her relations were in the city. I cannot imagine what involvement of mine there could be.'

'I am ignorant of the details, my Lord Wyvern,' Kashte said apologetically. 'However I had gathered the impression you were a wronged party and deserving of redress. I can say no more on the matter, but my relation was most eager you might spare him your time today rather than let matters worsen.'

'Worsen?'

'I am afraid so. I believe the situation is coming to a head soon unless we can prevent it.'

Lord Vanden did not speak for a few moments, lips pursed as he tried to puzzle through the involvement of an Imperial broker, as would be obvious by Kashte's presence.

'The Glass Tower?' Vanden croaked at last.

'Indeed, my Lord Wyvern. The furthest of the palace towers I realise, but one that does ensure privacy for delicate matters.'

'I will be there.' He coughed. 'I mean, I shall be honoured to attend upon a member of the House of the Sun.'

'I thank you,' Kashte said, with a small bow that would do much for Vanden's reputation among those watching. 'Now, I would not wish to delay you further. As you said, there is great excitement awaiting you at your palazzo.'

The rather-stunned Lord Vanden allowed himself to be ushered back to the carriage, his bodyguard stepping forward to assist his master up the step, and the procession carried on as soon as Kashte had withdrawn. Kesh was glad to see the young prince kept his expression entirely level until the last soldiers had left the plaza, only then nodding back towards the way they had come earlier. With a sigh Kesh fell in behind him and they started the walk back across the district towards the nearest ferry station.

It was a while before Kashte broke the silence and dismissed her, leaving Kesh to her own boat and the longer journey around the Imperial Island towards the Tale Warrant. Given she had to accurately remember Enchei's instructions on how to access his secret rooms or risk a swift and unpleasant death, the lack of distraction was a welcome thing.

From the relative anonymity of an upper walkway on the bustling Dawn Tor, Enchei considered his problem. Just half a day before, he had effectively been chased from this part of the city by hellhound-possessed soldiers. He remained unsure exactly how he'd escaped them, that second one just vanishing when it had a perfect opportunity to attack, but he doubted he'd get so lucky again.

Now he had to expect there would be more possessed sniffing every lamp-post in the district, in addition to a wide net of Astaren agents watching for the intruders. Somehow he would have to slip past both threats and get close enough for a conversation with a man he hoped wasn't actively trying to kill him.

But one of us has to take that first risky step, Enchei reflected. 'And by one of us, I mean me,' he added under his breath. *Let's go get a sight of the house then, see if he's put out the welcome mat.*

He descended and skirted the streets until he found a dark corner with a view of the importation house. The upper floor remained closed up, a long bank of shutters covering the windows all along the front, but now the door below was also firmly closed. Even at that distance Enchei could read the short announcement that urgent repairs required all business to use the rear door. Following the instructions – in a fashion – left Enchei with limited options. The rear door led onto an alley, only one end of which was open. Enchei knew the layout of streets well enough to not need to see it for himself, but if the notice was in fact a message for him that alley would be just a signpost.

It didn't take him long to discover he was correct. There was a single good vantage point from which to observe the alley, one that he knew already, so his concern was watching for traps both arcane and mundane before heading there. Despite his old instincts screaming a warning with every beat of his heart, Enchei could find nothing to indicate danger despite half an hour of searching.

Instead, he sensed a whole range of makeshift demon wards scattered liberally around the neighbouring streets and recognised that if any possessed had done the same, the patrolling Astaren would know about it immediately. With a once-familiar frisson of nerves running down his spine, Enchei walked up a short flight of steps to a narrow section of walkway that would command the only hidden vantage point.

He glanced towards the rear door to confirm his location then cast around for the next breadcrumb. It appeared in the form of a scrap of parchment wedged into a gap in the beam directly above his head. With one final check around he opened it and forced himself to stifle a laugh. In a neat copperplate script were a few nonsensical lines, but they were enough to ease the fears in his aging heart. The handwriting he recognised from decades past and the words echoed through his memory in the same clear voice he'd heard the previous night.

The offer of Lady Healer's greatest gift, Lord Shapeshifter's blessing on your greatest disguise, Lady Chance guide you through, Lord Monk greet you.

It was directions of a sort, Enchei realised. He cast his mind back to the friend he'd once served alongside, the man who had composed the words. With a nod of understanding, Enchei walked back down the way he'd come, remembering there was a high-end tavern facing it.

You always called whisky Lady Healer's greatest gift, Enchei thought, *so that's an offer of friendship. Now where's my greatest disguise?*

The tavern had an alley running down the side and with a jolt Enchei saw a washhouse with workers outside. *There we are. Wasn't quite the finest disguise we ever managed, but you almost pissed yourself laughing at the idea of pretending to be washerwomen back from the river.*

He set off, avoiding the traffic on the street and walking briskly down the narrow alley. 'Lady Chance guide you' was a common refrain among soldiers when a risk was unavoidable. One man of violence simply saying to another 'here you must trust me' – a gesture of sympathy more than anything else, but one Enchei appreciated still. Lord Monk referred simply to the fact the Ascendant God had once been a religious caste of House Ghost. Within the pantheon, his would be the most familiar face to Enchei.

CHAPTER 21

'Weapons,' growled a man standing in the dim back room of the washhouse.

'How about you fuck off?' Enchei advised him, scanning the room as he spoke.

'Drop your weapons, *now*,' said the man as he slipped his hands out of the pockets of his dark greatcoat. His hands were empty, but that was little reassurance to Enchei.

The room contained a pair of stools, stacked rectangular boxes with linens spilling out of the topmost, and a pair of doorways leading off left and right. The veteran paused, ready to kill in a heartbeat, and each stared at the other. The young man from Ghost was in his middle-twenties, Enchei gauged, with long dark hair that spilled down over his stiffened collar. He was dressed as a merchant caste in expensive and well-fitted clothes, a rapier on his hip.

Astaren would pick whichever caste was most convenient for the time and Enchei noted that his friend's bodyguard was deliberately not warrior caste – or any that would allow him to carry a pistol. That tended to be a pretence worth using, so if they weren't it spoke volumes for how much the bodyguard had been altered by the mage-priests of Ghost.

Enchei took a breath. *No point pretending this wasn't a gamble already.*

'How about you,' he said slowly and deliberately, 'fuck off and fetch me a drink?'

'Dak!' called a voice from behind the left-hand door, 'you can retire.'

The bodyguard's face tightened and he headed for the other door. Grainy daylight spilled through when he opened it, illuminating a look of grim dislike for Enchei, and then he was gone, with the door closing noiselessly behind him.

'Got yourself a pet, then,' Enchei said as the other door opened. 'Stars above! You got fat too.'

The other man chuckled and brushed down his jacket with an affected self-consciousness. 'I am a man of import now; one must maintain the correct image.'

His landowner-caste clothes were the height of fashion and beautifully tailored; a grey double-breasted jacket with a dozen gold buttons. While he was larger than Enchei, he was hardly fat by the standards of most men their age, but quite a difference to the lean young men of war they'd been.

'What image is that?'

The Astaren shrugged. 'Would you ever trust a whip-thin lord who looks like he lives on bread and water alone? If you ask me that's the sign of a fanatic who should be shot in the head first chance you get.'

'I suppose so,' Enchei said in a neutral voice. 'So – here we are.'

'Here we are,' his former comrade confirmed, 'and before we get down to reminiscing, I should make a few things clear.'

Enchei's hand tightened. 'Oh?'

'We're not equals, not any more,' the other said. 'We've taken separate paths and mine involves not having my real name spoken aloud. Understand?'

'Aye. I'd prefer the same here too. Anything more?'

'Yes, in fact.' He cocked his head at Enchei. 'Best we acknowledge this early – we go way back and I know all about you. *All* about you. I'm here as a friend who owes you, but let's not act like children. You're in my power and were before you stepped into this room.'

'Might be that's the case.'

The man broke into a welcoming smile. 'Good. So when I embrace you as a brother and offer you that drink, let's dispense with the excessive caution, eh? There's nothing I can put in your drink that gives me greater hold over you than I've already got. I deal with half-truths and agendas every damn day of my life so when I share a drink with a brother I'd like not to dance around needlessly. Frankly, if I gave the order you'd likely kill yourself right here in front of me.'

'Do we have to test the theory?' Enchei said, fighting to keep his hands from clenching into fists even as he realised the truth in the man's words.

'Not at all.' The Astaren stepped forward and embraced Enchei with a near-bone-crushing force. 'It's good to see you, brother.'

It took Enchei a moment longer, but at last he relaxed and pulled the man close. 'Aye, you too. It's been too damn long.'

191

The Astaren stepped back. 'Too damn long? Is that all you've got to say for yourself?'

'Eh? Well, ah,' Enchei coughed. 'Sure, sorry about the whole faking-my-own-death thing. Can't say it was a choice I enjoyed.'

'You had reason enough.'

Enchei hesitated. 'You know about that?'

'We were brothers,' the Astaren said gently, 'I was never going to abandon my brother's family now, was I? Quite aside from letting anyone try and recruit those girls through memories of their father, I made it clear they were as good as my own and that's kept the jackals clear.'

'How ... how are they?'

The man's smile fell. 'Your girls are good, last time I saw them. Both grown up strong and beautiful. No children of their own, but they were never likely to live the most normal lives now, were they?'

'And ...' Enchei couldn't finish the sentence but his friend sighed all the same.

'I'm sorry, my friend.'

'How?'

'A tumour. There would've been nothing we could do even if ... well. You know the rules.'

Enchei nodded. 'When?' he asked, throat suddenly dry and tight.

He felt stupid but couldn't fight the hollow sense of loss at the words. He had abandoned his wife decades ago, he had been dead to her, but to hear she was truly gone remained a blow. Some small spark in him had hoped she'd found happiness, living with grandchildren to cluck over and a man to treat her right. Treat her better than he had anyway – Enchei had loved his wife, but he'd spend months or years away and then he'd made her believe he was dead.

A poor excuse for a man he seemed, in that light. Any Astaren knew how to kill and dominate others. Enchei had no notions of martial manliness, not when the mage-priests could make anyone super-human. Whatever the cause, he'd failed in his duty of simply being there for Salay. Hearing of her death, though he had half-expected it, twisted and withered something inside him.

'Almost a decade now. She went peacefully, that I promise you. There was no pain.'

Enchei bowed his head. 'Thank you. Did she ever know?'

'About the girls? No, they didn't want to burden her with it. She worried enough about them, with you dead. Never gave up and she

192

kept on the estate so they were always well-looked-after, but she worried all the same.'

'Aye, well, she would have.' Enchei sighed and bowed his head. 'Strange. I knew I could never go home again, but I always felt something like a thread, running straight the way back there. A ley line pointing that way – pointing towards her. Some days we walked in opposite directions and I felt it tug on my heart, on others we were in step like we were arm in arm again, walking through the woods back home.'

'You were,' his friend said quietly. 'Every dawn she'd walk those hounds of yours round the woods. It gave her time to be with you, she said.'

That brought a small smile to Enchei's face, but it faded like a whisper on the breeze. 'And now you're here,' he stated, 'with power over my life. Think I'll be needing that drink now.'

The Astaren reached into the half-open box and pulled a clear glass bottle from it. As he unstoppered it, Enchei caught the sweet smoky scent of the finest whisky.

'This should chase the cold away,' his friend announced, drinking before he offered it to Enchei.

'Thanks.' Enchei took a swallow, savouring the taste as he stared at the bottle in his hand. 'Been a while since we've done this,' he commented eventually. He looked up. 'Still can't quite believe we are. How long have you known?'

'About the girls? Since before their mother died, maybe five years after you left?'

'And you were never tempted?'

The Astaren snorted. 'Tempted? No.'

'Why not?'

His friend gestured toward the other door where his bodyguard had gone. 'He's here because he's bound to me. Of all those in the city he's the only one I can trust, because his mind will fold in on itself before he betrays me. You'd be surprised how many volunteers there are for that – more than I realised, men and women who work out they're never going to reach the top based on their own merits.'

'I realised it myself,' Enchei said. 'Doesn't mean I ever wanted my mind bound to another.'

'But power never meant much to you. Even with your promotions, you only ever saw power as a burden.'

'Is that your answer?' Enchei asked. 'You were so confident of reaching the top on your own merits you ignored such a huge windfall?'

'I *am* one of the Five,' his friend replied with a hint of reproach. 'Is it arrogance if you turn out to be right? As for the girls – when I found out, I was marked for command already. I knew the path I had ahead and ...' He shrugged. 'Well. If you're the sort who's willing to betray family, you're not the sort to be chosen in the first place. Before anything else though, before all loyalty and anything else you might hear with a cynical heart, I don't want to die knowing I'm the bastard who maybe started the biggest war in history.'

He shook his head and reached for a drink. 'Even if your girls were treated right rather than just as brood mares, I suspect the others of the Five would agree with me. There's a balance of power in the Empire and we like it that way. Children inheriting Astaren abilities from their parents? That way chaos lies – chaos and millions of dead. Best thing you could've done is hide it from us all those years. You did a good job there and I for one am glad to be duped.'

'Hide it?' Enchei spluttered. 'I didn't know anything had been done to me for years. Not until I heard my daughters talking to each other in my mind!'

That brought the man up short. 'Honestly?' he said, an eyebrow raised sceptically. 'You didn't know?'

'Not a damn clue. I guess you know when it happened? Or worked it out, at least?'

The grim look on his friend's face told Enchei the man knew it all too well, and remembered the reports of Enchei's impetuousness leading to the death of his comrades.

'Aye, that's it, the Lady of Mists. When I fell in that temple vault and cracked my skull, I only knew *she* healed me. She ... she and her kin left me to carry a warning back across the mountains. Didn't occur to me she'd changed something inside me. I found that bit out the hard way.'

The Astaren snorted, some sort of cold amusement at the absurdity of all they had lived through. 'You led a charmed life, my friend. Most of us never meet a god or high demon once in our lives, but you ...'

'And look what it's brought me,' Enchei scowled, gesturing at the difference between his own worn clothes and those of his friend. 'A dead wife and strangers for daughters. It wouldn't have been worth it even if I'd gone down in history as a hero.'

'To some you did,' the Astaren said quietly, 'remember that at least, my friend. There's no power or passing of time that's likely to make me forget the Fields of the Broken and those who come after me will know it too. I owe my life to few men and women, but in that place I was more scared than I've ever been in my life.

'We don't get spotless records in this life. You don't get to trek to the other side of the world and bring everyone back. Not me, not any of the Five or those under our command. So whatever happened in the years beforehand, the Fields of the Broken is what we'll remember you for. The lives you saved; the godthing you stopped.'

Enchei looked away. 'Hard to feel like a hero there,' he said, after a long pause. 'We almost went mad with fear, even with what we are and how we're trained.' He took the bottle again. 'And now because of it, I'm hunted by hellhounds. Is it one of the Five doing it?'

His friend shook his head. 'I'm here alone because, well, because there ain't many survivors of the Fields around. A man came to see me in the spring and asked how many of us there were. He claimed to have met another survivor in the Imperial City. A cagey old man with some brittle edges who said he was retired.'

'And you confirmed it?'

'Of course not, but if a man believes something it's hard to persuade him otherwise. I was all set to have Dak murder him before he reached his next mission – he was never going to go far anyway – but he's a man with contacts, so I decided to use him if he proved not to be completely loyal to the House.'

'Use him? Contacts?' Enchei hissed as he realised what the man was saying. 'He's a Gealann liaison? You've got plans for one of the groups he has links to and don't want it traced back so easily?'

His friend put a hand on Enchei's shoulder and looked him straight in the eye. 'My friend, you were never good at this game, so here's a little help. There will always be layer upon layer in what we do – the decisions of the Five and our equivalents in the other Houses too. Be they Dragons, Ghosts, Eagles or any other Great House; to just read one goal in any action would be foolish and dangerous for you.'

'I see. So what's my part in this?'

'With tensions as they are, now's not a good time for us to run an operation in the Imperial City. We've no interest in antagonising House Dragon.'

Enchei frowned. 'So ... what? You want me to kill him for you?'

'In a nutshell. That's the price of keeping your family safe – it's not been easy and I've taken more than a few risks in the process. It's time to repay my benevolence.'

'There's a handful of hellhound-possessed soldiers out there, a summoner, a Ghost Astaren and who knows what else – all after me, and you want me to just turn it around like that?'

'You're resourceful and a survivor,' his friend said simply. 'I have faith in you.' He gave an apologetic cough. 'There is, ah, there's probably also a Benthic Knight leading them.'

'Oh Gods above!'

'That's the one I want, if it's at all possible. Killing everyone will suffice, but if you can secure that one or trap one of its ghost-slaves for me, you would do the rest of the Empire a great service. No one trusts House Leviathan so we could do with knowing better what weapons they possess.'

'And I'm going to do that how exactly?'

'Oh, you don't have to do the killing yourself,' his friend said with a cold smile. 'I informed House Dragon what's going on several weeks ago. There are two detachments of Stone Dragons and a unit of Firewinds ready in the city. I get the impression they're somewhat itching for a fight. Their pride was wounded by the goshe and Lawbringer Rhe facing them down.'

Enchei gaped. With those three battlefield units, House Dragon could carve through a small army. On the goshe island there had been one unit of Stone Dragons and their losses had mostly been a result of arrogance and ignorance. 'Stacking the deck in my favour, eh?' he croaked.

'They've agreed no House Ghost will be harmed or taken. I was very specific about that point and they *will* honour it. Just as I don't wish to provoke them, they'll not make enemies they don't need to when they may end up in all-out war with Eagle.'

'Just Ghosts, eh?'

'I can't secure promises for those not of my nation,' his friend said unapologetically, 'they're on their own if they get involved.'

'Let me thank you on their behalf.'

'I think it best you don't discuss this with them.'

'Aye, I know.' Enchei took another swallow of whisky then handed it back and wiped his mouth with two fingers. 'Well, this week just got a whole lot more fun.'

'I'm sorry it's come to this, but that's the way of the world. I'm sure you wouldn't have preferred me to assign a specialist team to the matter instead. What assistance I have been able to muster will be waiting.'

196

Enchei nodded. 'Aye, it's the way o' the world.' He was quiet a moment, feeling the weight of the world on his shoulders, but he knew there was nothing he could do. He ran a hand over his face as though trying to wipe the weariness and worry away, then forced a smile and embraced his friend once more. 'I may not like this much, but I can hardly whine I'm ill-used now, can I? It's what they made me for, after all. One final task is a smaller price than any other of the Five would've asked. One thing I do know is I'm damn sure not going to part the wrong way a second time, not with the choice being my own this time.'

'Thank you, my friend.' The Astaren smiled. 'We will be watching for your signal. Good luck.'

CHAPTER 22

It was a fact pointedly unacknowledged that the single – albeit vast and extended – family that comprised the Imperial caste was dependent on both the industry and wealth of their lesser citizens. For all the magnificence of the huge Great Court, the Emperor's residence or the branching sprawl of linked palazzos inhabited by the Imperial caste, the greatest concentration of wealth in the Imperial Palace lay on the books of the merchant quarter.

A strange symbiotic relationship had grown up between the distant strata of society as they met within business consortiums, each one needing the other to prosper. The human-built streets of the merchant quarter teemed with life as much as with the invisible, intangible tang of wealth – a hive of commerce constructed around the twelve great towers that punctuated it.

Those towers, as with all ancient structures within the sprawling complex called the Imperial Palace, were the property of the Emperor and administered for him by a bureaucracy of the religious caste. Each one was a square, flat-topped tower of smooth white stone found nowhere in nature; three hundred feet high and identical from the outside but all named for the peculiarities of their interior. The strange, shifting acoustics of the Whisperspire provided privacy that was said to confound even Astaren spies, while the Star Tower numbered among its varied astronomical wonders an orrery of near-perfect accuracy, four storeys tall.

The Glass Tower, where Prince Sorote waited for his guest, had every internal wall and floor made of some unknown form of glass – hardened to the strength of steel, but appearing fractured so that it was nearly opaque with millions of flaws and fissures within the glass itself. Nowhere in the entire tower was there a clear piece larger than a baby's palm, yet the surface was smooth and every corner gently rounded.

Despite millennia of use, none of the fractures had lengthened, failed or sliced the skin of anyone within. A diffuse light shone through the entire building, a dull white glow that echoed the sky above. In high summer it was blinding and uninhabitable, but for much of the year it was a warm and bright place that had five over-sized storeys given to the copyists of the Imperial House.

One corner of the tower, as with many others, comprised an over-sized staircase that wound around an open shaft running most of the tower's height. Within that shaft, human artificers had installed a pulley system so that only servants were forced to ascend the many hundreds of uncomfortably high steps. Two thirds of the way up the tower, Prince Sorote now had an entire floor to himself – Kashte had been careful to secure that and post Imperial caste sentries on the stair as guarantee.

The room he had chosen was typical of the Glass Tower – empty but for a pair of *somethings* best described as oversized wing chairs that faced each other in the centre of the room. They were ten feet high at the back and not just made of the same fracture-pattern glass as the floor, ceiling and walls, but a part of it too, with no discernible seam between any of them. Curves and indentations in the design, however, ensured a man could climb into the seat without sacrificing grace, and once there sit comfortably enough for any length of meeting.

The only human addition to the room, aside from a pair of black-lacquered doors, was a long polished table that seemed small and out of place compared to the rest of the room. Prince Sorote watched the city through a tall window set into the glass wall – comprised of small, diamond-shaped panes that, instead of muntins dividing the panes, had bands of fractures, echoing the rest of the tower. When he heard the rattle of the ascending cage he left the snow-swept view and went to stand beside the table, ready to respectfully greet his guest. The black double doors whispered open and Prince Kashte entered before making way for the dark-skinned nobleman behind him.

'Cousin, may I present to you Lord Cail Vanden Wyvern?'

Sorote inclined his head to the portly nobleman dressed in his finest silks – formal House robes of blue and white, threaded with the purple of his caste. 'Lord Vanden, I thank you for joining me – especially at such short notice.'

As the doors were shut behind him, Vanden bowed low to Sorote, lips pinched pale as he tried to fathom the full implication of the prince's involvement. He managed to murmur the prescribed thanks for an Imperial's invitation, but looked stunned by the whole situation and more than a little terrified. In any other setting his bodyguard would have remained at his side, but in the domain of the Emperor his safety was guaranteed and a paucity of witnesses would serve them all.

Sorote indicated the strange armchairs and the Wyvern allowed himself to be gently herded towards them.

'A drink, my Lord Wyvern?'

I ... thank you, My Lord Sun,' Vanden said, struggling to raise his voice. It was as if the wind had been driven from his lungs so Kashte, serving wine to the both of them in lieu of keeping a servant present, poured him a generous amount. Almost as soon as it was handed over, Vanden had slurped half of it down and at last he seemed to gather his senses.

'I must confess, My Lord Sun,' Vanden said hesitantly, 'I am surprised at your involvement in matters of a Wyvern family.'

As he spoke Lord Vanden glanced at Kashte, watching to see if he would leave, but the minor Imperial merely stepped back to afford them a measure of respect.

'Please, address me as Prince Sorote. Prince Kashte there is my aide – he will attend us as necessary, but you may be assured of his complete discretion in all matters. He is fully abreast of the situation, but will not be party to this discussion. Should you wish him to leave, no offence will be taken I assure you.'

Sorote sipped his wine and spent a moment regarding the man opposite him, aware he could not rush the discussion to come. When Vanden failed to voice any objection to Kashte's presence, Sorote nodded his appreciation to the Wyvern and continued.

'First of all, may I express my condolences for this regretful situation as it has been laid out for me. You have been robbed of a wife and heir in a manner no man of your station should have forced upon him.'

Vanden's lips twitched at that. 'What do you know, Prince Sorote?'

'Enough. Kashte is also aware, but such details are not for us to discuss.'

'Then what do you want?'

'An end to the disagreement,' Sorote said plainly, 'to mediate a resolution that ensures what damage done is lessened or compensated for, without further bloodshed.'

'I have shed no blood,' Vanden said, drinking quickly again, 'yet I fail to see how your involvement can erase the harm done to my reputation.'

Sorote motioned for Kashte to fill the man's wine again. 'The harm is done,' he conceded, 'but perhaps it can be mitigated. That is why I am here, why *we* are here, without retinues or witnesses. You may speak freely in this matter.'

'Freely?' Vanden spat. 'The words I have to speak are not for you but that whore of a bride – no, I have nothing for her. I would not piss on her burning corpse. My honour demands that she die, you know this and there is nothing to discuss. The only words I have are for the one I thought was my friend.' He tailed off, hands visibly shaking and Sorote allowed the quiet to descend once more and dissipate the anger crackling inside Lord Vanden.

'If you will permit me,' he began slowly, 'such satisfaction of honour would be fleeting, my Lord. Vengeance is your right, but it would not serve you for long.'

'What do you mean?'

'You are without an heir; the child was a girl, so her return serves no purpose under Wyvern law and the death of an innocent would be a stain on all our souls. Furthermore, there is shame cast upon you for the manner of Lady Kine's flight. This I cannot prevent. It is a fact, and will not disappear.'

'What can you prevent, then? Why are you here, Prince Sorote? Does my wife pay your fee with jewels stolen from my palazzo? I could petition to strip her of such assets, you know this. How did you become involved here? How did this become an Imperial concern?'

'My acquaintance is with the other party.'

Despite the fact he didn't speak Narin's name, Sorote could see the inference strike Vanden like a physical blow. 'How?' he croaked.

'He is useful to me,' Sorote said elliptically, 'and thus I have an interest in preserving his continued existence when such a thing remains possible.'

'Over the laws of my House?' Vanden snapped. 'Over the traditions of this Empire?'

'I am Imperial caste,' Sorote said coldly. 'Do not think to lecture me about the traditions that preserve this Empire, Lord Vanden. I come to you to seek a resolution that you will accept, not flout our laws or history.'

His words blunted the Wyvern's anger and Vanden drained his glass again. 'What is it you suggest, my Lord Sun?'

'An improvement in your situation,' Sorote said simply. 'One that might leave you better off in the coming year than you are at present. I'm not ignorant of the pressures on you, the diminishing you will experience when Lady Kine's flight becomes common knowledge. What I offer is an alternative to brief satisfaction of honour.'

'How?'

'A new marriage in the coming year – perhaps the lady in question to publicly visit you in the next few days for you to ascertain her suitability.'

Vanden sat up, confusion and wariness writ clear on his face, but Sorote could see his words had prickled the part of every nobleman's heart that housed his honour.

'What lady?'

'Of the Imperial caste – currently out of favour at court and under my care. You would find her a most obedient and faithful wife, her caste soon proving more significant than the reasons the Emperor is unhappy with her.' Sorote leaned forward. 'I must state now that her continuing health and happiness remains of vital importance to me. She is royal family and would remain so; treat her with the care I would expect or there will be ramifications.'

'I ... I understand. Her blood is of the Gods, she would be treated as such. But who is she? Do you have her agreement?'

'She will agree as I instruct her to.' Sorote hesitated a moment, but knew he had to press on. 'Her name is Princess Kerata – she was once of the ruling council of the goshe. As with all of the goshe's declared leaders, she was in fact under the compulsion of others and the magics they worked on her have permanently left her pliable and docile. You may not have the most exciting of companions in her, but she will obey your word without question.'

'Goshe?' Vanden spluttered. 'What further stains to my reputation are you determined to inflict?'

'None,' Sorote said firmly. 'Understand me now – your reputation is stained already, nothing further can be done about that. Kerata's history will have no great impact on it, I assure you. When you are married the city's gossips will wonder if your wife wasn't put out to make room for a woman of far higher rank – Lady Kine is noble caste only by marriage, I believe? Whatever Lady Kine's actions, her rapid replacement by an Imperial caste will cast an entirely different light on which of you two truly drove this matter, and of course judicious rumour can be employed to kindle this. Princess Kerata is mixed blood, as you may know; her mother was Dragon noble caste and the offspring she will bear you will be acceptable heirs for a Wyvern nobleman, I believe.'

'Your confidence is heartening,' Vanden said sourly. 'If—'

'I am fully aware of the details of your first meeting with the Investigator,' Sorote broke in, 'and I am a man whose discretion may be trusted as surely as his ability to arrange private matters. You *will* have acceptable offspring, that I guarantee, and the Princess Kerata will grace your side at all functions where a gold collar commands the necessary respect. Marriage to an Imperial caste does not permit your own caste to be elevated, but honour would of course compel your peers to tacitly consider you so.'

Lord Vanden was quiet a long while and Sorote realised he needed to order his thoughts rather than be pressed. Honour was one of the cornerstones of the noble caste and the humiliation of this incident was grave.

A braver man might already have taken his life once he heard Kine had escaped, quietly and away from the city so it could be described an accident. The fact Vanden had been castrated by gambling house enforcers would have been reason enough for many within the Dragon hegemony, and that had happened two years ago. Vanden clearly had no interest in that avenue, so Sorote had judged he was amenable to alternatives. Anything that might salvage his reputation and allow him to walk alongside his peers without accusations of cowardice – accusations which one way or another would lead to duels – would be welcomed, albeit with a pretence of grudging resentment.

'What assurances do I have?' Vanden asked quietly.

'Of the marriage? Princess Kerata will call on you in the morning as a first step. If you are satisfied, we will immediately draw up an agreement of betrothal to be approved by the Emperor. Speed in this case will support the alternative theory.'

'And what of the child?'

'Her arm to be stained with the caste of her father. The Emperor's law is clear that the sins of the father are not to be visited upon their children. She is blameless here.'

'There are others to blame,' Vanden growled.

Prince Sorote nodded. 'Indeed. Lawbringer Narin shall have his actions reported to his superiors, with my advisement that discretion is requested to protect wronged parties, but punishment shall be theirs to decide. The Lady Kine shall have her caste mark struck out and your marriage annulled. She will enter the House of the Sun as a servant caste under instruction that she not give account of this situation to any. If the wronged parties are embarrassed by talk originating from her, she will be cast out of the House of the Sun as unworthy of its protection.'

'That is all? The whore gets to live with her lover and raise her child?'

'Would you prefer to raise the child as your own?'

Vanden flinched at that and Sorote didn't press the point, not wanting to humiliate the man further.

'The child will live with its parents and grow up as a low caste member of his House – unworthy to be noticed by you or your peers. The Lady Kine will be stripped of titles and honorifics, she shall be a commoner and live in that fashion. To a woman used to the luxuries of a palazzo, I imagine that will be a significant punishment. I would expect the Lawbringer's status to be revoked, and supporting a family solely on an Investigator's wage is difficult, I am led to understand. She will likely have to take service and cook or clean for other low castes, an ongoing humiliation to serve as punishment.'

'I want more,' Vanden rasped. He looked up from his glass with murder in his eyes. 'I want her hurt for the betrayal.'

'She is not a warrior,' Sorote pointed out. 'Physical punishments outside of your household must be restrained.'

'I don't care about that! Where was her respecting of custom when she whored herself to a man I believed my friend?'

Vanden shook his head and Sorote could see the man was working himself up to fury.

'I want to stripe the bitch's back – she's to be servant caste, let her be punished like one.'

'Lashes, my Lord Wyvern?' Sorote asked, taken aback. 'Whip her like a common criminal? Think of the precedent! Whatever the crime, to have a woman of the highest castes publicly whipped would serve to lower us in the eyes of lower castes to their level! Once her caste mark is struck, such a punishment in the future is conceivable, but when she is so recently noble by marriage? It is unthinkable; the Emperor would not permit it.'

'I want her hurt,' the man repeated. 'If not by me or in public then so be it. But I want her back striped so she will never forget the lashing she has given me. That every man who has her after me sees my mark.'

It was Sorote's turn to think now. He didn't bother looking at Kashte, knowing the combative young noble would simply shrug carelessly at the suggestion. This was not the demand of a noble caste doing business however – it was the spite of a man spurned. It was the anger of male pride that surpassed caste or nation, uncaring and uncompromising. He could not be reasoned with, Sorote realised, and history through the ages told tales of stubborn malice defeating sense.

'One stripe on her back,' Sorote said finally. 'One lasting mark there – issued by Kashte here. You may witness it if you must, but I will not permit any form of confrontation to take place.'

'To break the skin,' Vanden said with an edge of hunger in his voice. 'I will not have her bruised a week only.'

'To break the skin. You will have your blood; once the Imperial decree of betrothal is signed I will invite you back here.'

'She will agree?'

'She's in no position to negotiate with me,' Sorote said. 'For your part, you will take no action against her, the child or Lawbringer Narin – nor speak of her beyond the barest amount required to acknowledge her existence should you choose to. You will have the marriage annulled under Wyvern law and consider her gone from the face of the world. Furthermore, you will inform her family in the city that you intend nothing further to her harm and end any obligations you may have put upon them with regards to her and their honour.'

The Wyvern shook his head. 'I cannot end their blood feud. They were obliged to come at my call but not to leave.'

'I understand. You will make your position clear and ensure they know you will not support them politically, financially or in any other way. The blood feud is Narin's to deal with – I leave that to the Gods to decide.'

Vanden looked from Sorote to Kashte, staring at each of them for a long while before struggling out of his seat. 'Very well, my Lord Sun, we are agreed. I will expect the Princess Kerata to visit me at her leisure and the terms of this agreement to be delivered in writing.'

'It will be done. Good day, my Lord Wyvern.'

CHAPTER 23

A drop of water ran slowly down the new-formed icicle and settled at the bottom. Kesh found herself holding her breath as the drip trembled slightly, a frisson of breeze threatening to shake its grip. Before it could, the drop settled and froze around the icicle – the building's tears lengthening in the bitterly cold air.

'In your own time,' called a gruff voice below her. 'This isn't important, so don't worry too much.'

Kesh rubbed her half-numb fingers together and muttered a curse under her breath. 'Calm down, old man,' she replied, glancing over her shoulder at Enchei. 'It's hard to tie the damn things when it's so cold.'

She went back to her labours, using a length of string to attach a spirit-catcher to the overhanging eaves of a building. They had secreted almost a dozen around the Harbour Warrant already that afternoon, with more still to come. Frames of painted twigs bound in twine were criss-crossed in thin copper wire to create a net shape, while spider-threads of wire radiated out from the frame and tied on to anything available.

'Come on,' Enchei grumbled from below, impatiently slapping the palm of his hand against the wooden crate top Kesh was currently standing on. It jolted slightly under her feet – the load inside it kept the crate secure, but still the movement was unwelcome.

'How is that helping?' she asked as she cinched the knot tight. Knowing how wound up he was, Kesh didn't stop to give him a reproachful look. Instead she extracted another length of twine from inside her fingerless gloves and wound the next trailing line around the verdigrised tip of a nail that protruded down through the roof batten.

'Sorry,' Enchei said as she reached for the last. 'Just getting kinda jumpy down here.'

'I'm done,' she announced, clambering down from the crate as best she could while bundled up against the cold. The temperature remained low and thicker clouds were rolling in. More snow was coming, that much she was sure of, so Enchei's urging was not entirely a product of anxiety.

'Where next?' she asked as Enchei stared off down the street. 'Enchei?'

'Eh?' He glanced back. 'Did you see anyone down there?'

Kesh tilted her head to get a better view. 'I can see a few people down there,' she hazarded. 'You get a glimpse of red?'

'No, grey. A long cloak.'

'A long grey cloak? It's fucking winter, Enchei – of course people are going to be in long grey cloaks.'

'Not like this.' He hesitated. 'Looked a bit like one I saw while I was running.'

'Weren't they Wyvern warrior castes? Brown skin and a red collar's what you should be looking out for, not some plain colour half the district might own.'

Enchei shook his head. 'Maybe you're right.'

He turned his head from left to right as he sighted a path from the last spirit trap they'd hidden. They were just on the border with Dragon District now, one street away from far more Wyverns than Narin would be comfortable with. Fortunately for them, the cold had kept the crowds from the streets and no one seemed to be too interested in what the pair were up to, so they had their pick of buildings to hang the spirit traps from.

Kesh pulled the next from the bag slung crosswise around her neck and held it up. Threaded on to the copper wire were three bones describing the corners of a triangle, bones which Kesh had decided not to ask the origins of.

'I still don't see how these are going to snare a hellhound.'

'They're not,' Enchei said absentmindedly, 'not in any way you'd understand.'

'Then what?'

'Think of them like mirrors. You're trying to follow a spark through the city streets and you're carrying a storm-lantern, right? Every time you lift the covering of your lantern, the mirrors cast the light in all directions.'

Kesh nodded. 'I see. So you're keeping the mirrors close enough to reflect the light off each other and all over the street?'

'That's about the size of it.'

He pointed towards a tall warehouse with red-painted doors. Above the name of the merchant house that owned it was a stylised leopard, indicating a minor House under the Dragon hegemony.

'Let's go see if we can get one on there. That might bring us a loop to close, then we'll go see our friend Pirish, climb around on the roof of her smokehouse.'

They started off but had gone only a dozen yards when Enchei stopped. 'What is it?'

He ignored her, frowning with his head cocked to one side as though trying to dislodge water from his ear. 'Did you just hear something?'

Kesh checked around them. There was a raucous game of some sort being played by a handful of children at the far end of a side-street, a hawker announcing his wares, two men guiding a laden handcart down the rutted street and snatches of chatter drifting from the houses around them.

'You might need to narrow that down for me,' she ventured.

'You sure you weren't followed from the tavern?' he asked, giving her a suspicious look. 'When you grabbed this stuff?'

'No,' Kesh said testily, 'that's what you were there for, remember? I followed every detail exactly as you said. I don't think even the tavern owner noticed me at all, but the whole point of how we met up was that you could confirm I wasn't followed. Second-guessing yourself now, old man?'

'Aye, mebbe you're right.' Enchei shook his head. 'Just paranoia. If there was anyone following you, they were better'n me.'

'And you said you'd made it harder to catch your scent out on the street, no?'

'I hope so. This lot'll certainly cause 'em some problems, but … Ah, never mind. Let's just get the job done.'

With a shrug he set off again, but Kesh stayed a moment longer. *Maybe his paranoia's infectious,* she thought as she looked down the alleys lit with grimy winter light.

Off to her right was little more than a narrow path between houses that stretched all the way to the Public Thoroughfare, judging by the brighter glimpses of movement at the far end. That view dimmed momentarily as a figure stepped across the alley.

The wind rushed towards Kesh as she tried to focus on the figure. They wore a storm-cloud cloak, its edges dancing in the breeze while black strands of hair cut a jagged path across their eyes. Kesh's heart went cold then the slim figure wheeled away and out of sight. For a moment she didn't move, just stood and blinked away the chill on the air. Then her wits caught up with her and she jumped into movement, one hand diving into a pocket where her spark-pad rested. As she caught Enchei up she slipped on the goshe weapon he'd made for her and secured it around her wrist.

'Enchei,' she called.

He turned and caught the look on her face. 'You're jumping at shadows too?'

'I think so.' She hesitated. 'I don't know, maybe. A grey cloak.'

He nodded and checked the streets around them.

'Keep up with me,' he said, assessing their path. 'We'll find somewhere we can get a look at anyone following. If it's hellhounds we'll head toward Lord Omtoray's fortress. If they've any sense they'll keep clear of the smarter streets of Dragon District. If they don't,' he shrugged, 'they'll find a load of touchy warrior castes provide something of an obstacle.'

Late in the afternoon Narin made his way back to the Palace of Law. His eyes ached from staring at page after page of records, straining to read the small neat script of religious-caste administrators. A rolled sheet of parchment was in his hand, clutched as tightly as a sword-grip. Lawbringer Rhe had left him to his search at the harbourmaster's office – a chilly set of rooms overlooking the deepwater wharves, not far from the building-site that had once been Kesh's home.

It had long been joked that within the House of the Sun, lawyers had replaced the warrior caste in the years following the Ten Day War. That opinion had endured throughout the centuries of the Lesser Empire but Narin, as with the rest of the Lawbringers, knew the truth of the matter. When the Imperial warrior caste were banned there remained many thousands of men, women and children not of battle-age and the bulk had been admitted, by the taking of holy orders and marriage, into the religious caste.

For a few years a variety of groups of warrior-monks flourished, only to collapse under the weight of internecine conflicts commonly believed to have been orchestrated by the Great Houses. With the central cults largely collapsed, however, and the caste expanded a third by the influx, the religious caste found solace in administration instead. The Imperial House slowly became a buffer between Great Houses unable to trade with each other without it devolving into violence, and the religious caste simply wrote it all down as though attempting to create an inventory of what remained of the Empire.

It had proved an invaluable resource for the Lawbringers over the years; room after room, building after building filled with files and books while black-coated religious castes shuffled through them like a strange breed of ant. With Imperial mediators and merchants orchestrating an era of direct trade across the Empire, Narin had access to listings of every acknowledged consortium, merchant house, guild, union, trading family and fleet for at least a thousand miles in every direction. With the quiet, reverential aid of a senior administrator and his assistants, it proved a relatively simple task to secure records of the Ren archipelago and a listing of merchant houses within it.

Armed with this knowledge he had travelled to the Harbour Warrant and secured similar assistance from an identical collection of bureaucratic lay castes there. With typical attention to detail, the records of arrivals on the dock noted captain, crew, designation, affiliation, origin and cargo. Records in that building alone dated back decades, but Narin's interest lay in the short period of time when travel beyond the Inner Sea was increasingly risky.

From those records there were two possible names, but one clear front-runner. Five weeks past a schooner of the Oelest Merchant House had arrived direct from the principal island of the archipelago. Two weeks later a four-masted barque registered under the Etrage Merchant House had docked on its return voyage from Sight's End, second-largest city of the Imperial lands and a haven of criminals and spies alike. A precarious playground of intrigue the Lawbringers had never fully tamed, Sight's End overlooked a two-mile strait with House Ghost on one side, House Wolf on the other, but the Emperor's flag in the middle.

To confirm matters for Narin, there had been a second arrival under Etrage's banner in the last few days, this time from the west where the Ren archipelago was situated, off House Moon's southern shore. The clerks assured him it was not unheard of to have a spice-run appear in early winter given the cargo, but Narin could only think of one word to explain it: *reinforcements*.

He felt a surge of childish excitement as he spotted Lawbringer Rhe across a crowded room and darted like a novice around and between clusters of his peers until he'd caught the man up. His enthusiasm melted as Rhe turned and for once Narin saw emotion on the man's face. A faint flush of anger in Rhe's pale tinted cheeks told its own story and Narin faltered as he saw it.

'What's happened?'

'A meeting I knew was coming,' Rhe said quietly. 'Tell me what you've learned.'

'Me?' Narin hesitated then remembered the parchment in his hand. 'The Etrage Merchant House – the names of two ships recently docked and their captains. One's still here, arrived just a few days ago. And a list of registered Etrage holdings in the city which might serve as safe-houses. There are only four, as you might expect, and one is apart from both stone and water as the shaman suggested.'

'Good.' For a moment it looked like Rhe was going to say more, but the Lawbringer fell into abrupt silence.

'Rhe, what was the meeting?'

'An emissary, ostensibly for you. They came to me as your superior.'

Narin felt a cold slither down his spine. 'Seven hells,' he muttered, 'some House Wyvern official?'

'No. House Dragon.'

'What?'

'A woman with two attendants. She was at pains to describe herself as an emissary but declined to say who from. Warrior caste by her collar, not the usual background for an official representative of Lord Omtoray.' Rhe's jaw tightened. 'It seems they are aware of the summoner in the city and perhaps more besides. They demanded to know what progress we had made.'

Narin felt a sinking feeling. 'They're not willing to be shown up a second time, not after the goshe conspiracy unfolded right under their noses.'

'Indeed. That a son of House Brightlance was the one to refuse them, they took as significant. Had I not been a Lawbringer I might not have been insulted by that, but had I not held this position I might have called her to duel for such an insult.'

'Which would've hardly helped matters between Dragon and Eagle right now,' Narin added.

The hard stare and pent-up anger in Rhe's face showed how close the man had come. Narin knew it wasn't for the innate antagonism between the Houses of Dragon and Eagle hegemonies, though that was reason enough for most. No, for Rhe it was something more basic to his soul. His allegiance had never been to his House or their Eagle rulers, but Rhe's was a world of cold certainties. That someone could believe him so venal as to manipulate a murder investigation and the Emperor's laws for personal or political gains – now that would anger the Lawbringer in a way few things could.

'I believe,' Rhe said haltingly, 'I believe it is time I met your Imperial friend.'

'I— What? Ah, are you sure?'

Rhe nodded. 'I am no ingénu. That I choose to keep apart from the politics of the Empire does not mean I am ignorant of it.'

'Then why?'

'Because I am *not* ignorant of what it means when House Dragon wishes to involve itself and a son of Brightlance refuses them. Because your patron is expending considerable capital over a newly-raised Lawbringer and I would like to know why, just as I would like to know why Prince Kashte is not the only experienced fighter at his command. In the Empire, progress is only ever achieved when there is a balance of forces acting upon you. Only then are choices possible and, right now, I suspect we shall be swept aside unless we achieve that balance. The Lord-Martial cannot help me in this so it's time we found one who can.'

Narin stared at him a while before ducking his head. 'His name is Prince Sorote, of the Office of the Catacombs.'

Rhe blinked at him. 'We are of the noble castes, we do not casually drop in on each other. When will you see him next?'

Narin stifled a snort. 'Ah, something tells me I'll be dropping in on him this evening.'

'An excellent idea. You may leave your list with me. No warrior should go on the attack without being sure of their footing; the Etrage Merchant House will wait another day.'

Kesh and Enchei crouched together in the lee of a defunct bootmaker, watching fat flakes of snow make leisurely progress to earth in the street beyond. A steep overhang kept them in shadow while a mouldering barrel provided some form of cover as they watched for pursuers. Spike-topped walls flanked the side-street they watched; large townhouses belonging to noble castes of House Greydawn on the left, House Smoke on the right. The terraces presented a broad obstacle for anyone approaching the high-caste streets of Dragon – forcing any pursuers to sprint around and hope their quarry hadn't already vanished, or follow them into a choke-point.

Thus far, there had been nothing. After several minutes Kesh could stand it no longer and shifted further back to straighten up.

'There's no one there,' she said, nudging Enchei with her toe. 'Either they've stepped back or we really were jumping at shadows.'

Enchei didn't respond, lips pressed tight together. She left him to it and eventually the grey-haired man nodded and stood also. 'Guess you're right.'

'I'm always right, or have you forgotten?' Kesh said with a weak smile, feeling the jangle of nerves inside her slowly settle.

'What bell is it?' Enchei muttered, more to himself than Kesh. 'Dusk's coming soon. Let's head back.'

'Which way?' Kesh pointed back down the side-street. Ten-foot stone walls ran the full length on both sides and it was hardly an enticing prospect, should any grey-cloaked figures be coming the other way. 'Probably the last thing they'd expect, us to double-back like that.'

Enchei shook his head. 'I think we skirt all the way around. We don't know how many they are, might've left one to watch for just that.'

'Cross the Crescent? Take a boat just further along the bank maybe then south back into your web of mirrors?'

'Buggered if I know,' Enchei admitted at last, 'just a case o' which side guesses right now.'

'Fat lot of use you are,' Kesh said, gently elbowing him. 'Come on, shake out of it, old man. We can't have you staying spooked now.'

He nodded. 'Aye, you're right. Just feeling my age a little, but that does us no good. If we're still looking to shake pursuit we'd take a trip round the fortress. No point doing that now so let's cut east out of here and turn towards home after a couple of streets. Either they're waiting for us or they've passed already.'

He led the way and Kesh followed close behind, careful not to spend too long looking around as they went. The sad fact was Dragons didn't like women as much as some Houses and there were plenty of high castes around here. It might be suspicious if she kept checking left and right, but it'd certainly be taken as insulting were she to look a warrior caste directly in the eye while she did so.

They passed a well with an ornate canopy, a verdigrised dragon ready to leap from snow-dotted tiles, before following a warrior-escorted litter down to the Public Thoroughfare. So far as Kesh could tell, Enchei saw no one of concern as they crossed and continued south into the Harbour Warranty. They covered the ground quickly as the sky began to darken and lazy flakes of snow began to fill the air.

Before long they were on the commercial street behind the Harbour Walk where warehouses met eateries and taverns, the occupants of one side all filtering across to the other after a long, cold day's labour. Kesh felt an ache in her heart as they reached the Public Thoroughfare leading down to the harbour market.

She couldn't help glancing up it at the tarpaulins stretched like skin over timbers of her childhood home, the Crowsnest boarding house, jutting ribs against an angry sky. But as she did, she found herself staring straight at a grey-cloaked figure – just twenty yards off and watching them from under a low hood. Kesh yelped and Enchei spun, one hand on his baton and ready to fight.

The figure did nothing, merely watched them stumble to a halt. For a moment that was all either of them did, then Enchei growled a curse and turned away, heading for the fisherman's market. It took Kesh a while to work out why, fumbling for her knife as she went, but then it struck her. The market would have been finished hours ago and in winter it was only ever a handful selling there. The blue-tiled stone stalls were a winding network of paths, half covered by steep wooden awnings, through which they could run and hide or fight without bystanders getting caught up in it.

Weapons out, they ran toward the centre of the market only to stop dead. Ahead of them was a second figure in grey. Dressed in better clothes than either of them, Kesh couldn't see the figure's face or caste collar, but the cloak was open enough to show a pair of ornate daggers rather than pistols.

'Get behind me,' Enchei growled, pushing Kesh back. He looked left and right as the first grey-cloaked figure slipped silently into the market, not far behind them.

'Now isn't that fine?' the second figure announced. 'She's brought out his protective side.'

Kesh blinked. It was a young woman's voice; acid in tone, but hardly sounding like she was possessed by a demon, and nor was she a Wyvern warrior caste. Her gloved hands were empty. Kesh could just about see them bunched into fists behind her open cloak.

'And there we were wondering if he even had one,' the other added in a similar voice, 'but perhaps you can teach an old dog new tricks. Just needs the incentive of a mangy bitch.'

That one slipped off her hood and Kesh saw a pale face, short dark hair and gleaming green eyes. Of a similar age to Kesh, she was the taller of the two figures by a several inches.

'Stars in Heaven,' Enchei gasped, sounding like he'd had the wind punched from him.

'Really? Is that the best you can come up with?' said the second, pushing back her hood to reveal a face so similar they had to be sisters.

Her hair was longer and a touch darker, her eyes cobalt blue, but it was the same line of jaw, the same button nose. The woman briefly looked Kesh up and down then seemed to dismiss her and return to Enchei.

'You've had enough time to think about it, after all, or didn't you bother?'

'Maiss,' Enchei croaked. 'I'm ...'

'Lost for words, apparently.' She sniffed and stepped forward. 'So let me instead. Hello, Father. We've missed you.'

CHAPTER 24

'We can't do this here,' Enchei said. For once the man looked unsteady and dazed, speaking as though by rote – his old instincts coming to the fore while his mind reeled.

'Caught you at a bad time?' asked the green-eyed woman. 'Somewhere you need to be?'

'Enay, calm,' her sister, Maiss, called. The woman's attention never left Enchei, however. She watched him like a cat; a cold regard that could turn to affection or viciousness in a heartbeat.

'That was you following me all today? Yesterday too?'

Maiss's lips twitched. 'Someone needed to watch your back.'

Enchei was frozen in a moment of indecision. 'What's important comes first,' he muttered to himself.

Putting his weapons away, he started abruptly forward. Maiss didn't move a muscle until he'd reached her and swept his arms around the young woman, then she seemed to melt under the fierce hug.

Enchei turned them both as he held his daughter close, one hand reaching out towards Enay. The green-eyed woman held back a while, lips pursed. At last she stepped forward and allowed the man to gather her to him, though she stood stiffly and only put an arm around her sister.

'I'm so sorry,' Enchei whispered through her hair. His voice was choked and strained, as though Maiss's embrace was crushing.

'You left us,' Enay replied, sounding suddenly child-like and frightened. 'You always promised you'd return and then you went back on your promise.'

'It was the only way,' Enchei said. 'I couldn't find another way out.'

'Why did it have to be a way out?'

'You know why,' he insisted. 'I couldn't have you hunted your whole life.'

Kesh felt the urge to step back and leave them to their reunion, but they were still out in the open and, whether or not it had been the girls following them all day, Enchei remained hunted. If the hellhounds could find him once, they could do it again.

She coughed. 'Sorry to break this up, but we need to go.'

'And in what way is this any of your business?' Enay snapped.

'I'm his friend,' Kesh said carefully, 'and they still have Enchei's scent. If we get attacked, I won't last so long in a fight.' *And look how I'm rising above that mangy bitch comment, choosing to believe it's the anger talking.*

'Enchei? That's your name now?' Maiss asked, half-disengaging from her father's embrace.

'My old name's still known by some,' he said in a firm voice. 'Best it's never spoken.'

'How about ...' She tailed off as he shook his head at her and stepped back. Maiss frowned at him before turning his head around and parting his hair with her hands. Kesh knew the man had an ugly scar there, one more thing he didn't like to talk about. 'Lady Magistrate's black eyes, what happened?'

'I cut my voice out, had to.'

'Why?' she gasped.

'Cut your voice out?' Kesh broke in. 'I've heard you say that before, when you spoke to that demon in the summer.'

Enchei nodded. 'Astaren can talk to each other from miles away, but it was a power the mage-priests gave me. I realised long before I deserted that it could be turned against me. If they knew there was a traitor nearby they could send out a command my body would be forced to obey – I wouldn't be able to stop my second voice from calling them to me.

'Hells, I might not even know it was happening until I was surrounded. Jamming a red-hot blade into my skull ain't the most fun thing I ever did, but it was better than the alternative.'

'What? Better than anyone finding out who you really were? What did you do that was so bad? What danger could your family have been in?'

Enay took a step towards her. 'Enough danger – and that's all you get to know, bitch.'

Kesh flexed her fingers, the spark-pad still attached to her hand, and took a long breath.

'There's no need for that,' she said carefully. 'You're pissed off at your father, fine, but none of that's my fault, so rein it in, okay?'

'Cool it, the pair of you,' Enchei called, somewhat recovered from the shock now. 'Kesh, just trust me that they'd be in danger.'

'I always have,' she replied, 'but that was when I thought they were worth the trouble. Now I'm not so sure.'

Enay raised a hand, opening and closing it as she gave Kesh a scornful look. 'I don't give a damn what you think,' she said quietly, coming right up to Kesh so they were less than two feet apart. 'Question is, what do you know?'

'She knows enough,' Enchei supplied, 'and as my friend she's had the grace not to ask for too many details. She's not the enemy here, Enay, she's someone I trust.'

Enay pulled her glove off and closed her fist. 'Ever noticed a scar on my father's knuckles?' she asked, pointing to a thin line that ran down between the knuckles of her first and middle fingers. It was dark red and glassy in the way of a freshly healed scar.

Kesh glanced at Enchei, then remembered she had seen exactly the same thing. He'd cut his hand after their first fight with the goshe in that exact place. From the look in Enay's eyes, that realisation was clear on Kesh's face.

Without warning the fresh scarring on Enay's hand distended and split as a grey point slid out from between her knuckles – faintly serrated, like ridges of bone, but a dull, dark metallic colour. About three inches in length, it looked wickedly sharp and Kesh was suddenly very aware of how close the short blade was to her own stomach.

'Let's just say we inherited more than most from our father.'

Enay smirked and the blade darted back inside her fist, whereupon she opened her hand and waggled her fingers at Kesh before turning her back.

'If you've finished showing off?' Maiss growled at her sister. 'The woman's got a point. Kesh, is it?'

Kesh nodded.

'Don't mind my sister; she doesn't play well with others. I'm glad to meet you, but how about we head back into your maze of spirit traps before we do proper introductions?'

A grunt from Enchei sounded like agreement so Kesh gestured for them to lead on and Maiss did so without a word. Her sister darted forward to be alongside her, leaving Enchei and Kesh facing each other for a moment. He shrugged, the ghost of a smile on his face.

'Oh come on,' he said out of the corner of his mouth as they made to follow, 'how likely was it any child of mine would be all sweetness and light?'

Back at the house Narin said nothing as he stormed in, almost shoving past Myken in his haste. He ducked his head into the kitchen and then was upstairs, boots hammering on the steps until he'd reached Kine's room. Only then did he slow, reminding himself he couldn't burst straight in for fear of waking Dov. From below there were voices, Enchei and Kesh joining Myken in calling up to him, but Narin ignored them all as he edged the door open.

He peered round the corner to see Kine smile back at him, Dov in her arms. At the sight of him, Kine's face fell.

'What's happened?'

Narin scowled and went on in, shutting the door in the face of whoever was following him up the stairs. 'Your husband,' he said darkly, tugging his coat off and unbuckling his sword.

He let them both fall on the floor as Kine offered Dov forward. The sight of her tiny, wrinkled face couldn't quell the thoughts churning through his mind, but quietened them enough for him to force a smile. He sat down on the side of the bed and brought the baby up to his lips to plant a delicate kiss on her forehead.

'That's better,' Kine said, kissing him. 'That's how you come home to us, not growling like a bear.'

Narin blinked at her and realised she looked as if she'd revived since he'd slipped out that morning. It was still strange to see her without a noblewoman's full range of makeup and for a moment Narin had the sense she looked larger without it. Dark skin in the Empire was synonymous with strength after all, given House Dragon's centuries of domination. Kine was a lean and beautiful woman still, but without the edges of her face softened or hair perfectly in place, she had more of Myken about her.

And she'll need to be strong, a treacherous voice at the back of Narin's mind added. *Even before her husband's parting gift, she was going to need every ounce of strength to cope with her new life.*

'Sorry,' he muttered.

'No apology is necessary,' Kine said. 'Just don't do it again. Now tell me, what has my husband done?'

'Returned to the city. He met with Prince Sorote this afternoon.'

219

'Has he refused to release me?'

Narin shook his head. 'No, he has.'

'Then that's good news, no?' she said hesitantly.

'Yes, no, of course it is,' he said reluctantly, 'but the terms ...'

'What? Is it Dov?' she said with growing alarm. 'Surely he doesn't want her?'

'No, nothing like that. He ... he wants you whipped for betrayal.'

'Whipped?'

Narin lowered his eyes, unable to look at Kine directly as he spoke. 'That bastard Sorote agreed. I doubt he even had to think about it.'

'Whipped,' she repeated in a hollow voice. 'How many lashes?'

Narin gave a bitter laugh. 'Sorote negotiated it down to one. The noble Lord Vanden will be satisfied if you bleed, if you are left with a scar as his last gift to you.'

They sat in silence for a long while, Kine's arm around his waist as Narin held Dov as close to his chest as he could. The baby snuffled and twitched in his arms, eyes half-opening and looking up at him.

'So be it,' Kine said in a firm voice.

'What?' Narin looked up at her and saw the determined set to her face. 'No, you can't!'

'I can and I will,' she replied simply. 'I prayed when Dov was born, prayed to the God-Empress that her life would be spared. I was willing to sacrifice my own if that was the price she demanded. Whether or not this is her will, this is the price demanded for our freedom and I'll pay it.'

'There has to be another way. Let me take the lashes, a dozen if he wants! You're still weak, you have a baby to care for—'

'I have had a baby,' she said with a small smile, 'and it hurt more than anything I could have imagined. One lash will be nothing compared to that.'

'Kine, no!'

'Would you not still love me?' she asked pointedly. 'Would you not still love our child? My shame will be tattooed on my skin, the marks of caste erased to declare that shame to the whole Empire.'

'Of course I'd still love you,' he protested, 'but it's unheard of, to whip a high caste outside of the army. Vanden knows that as well as anyone.'

'Soon I will not be high caste, so I take the good with the bad.' She touched a finger to Dov's tiny brow. 'The good outweighs the bad a hundred-fold. Tell Prince Sorote I will do as he commands.'

'I—'

She raised a hand to stop him. 'You will allow me to make my own decision, you are not my lord and master, remember?' A coquettish smile crept onto her face as she added, 'Yet.'

Before Narin could gather his thoughts she prodded his shoulder. 'Come, we should go downstairs. It sounds like Master Enchei and Mistress Kesh have news of their own. Would you help me up? I'm starting to lose interest in this one room and the company would be welcome.'

Dumbly, Narin did as instructed and carried Dov slowly down, following Kine. Before she had reached the bottom, Myken was there with hands outstretched to support Kine should she need it.

'Thank you, I can manage, Siresse,' Kine said gently. 'The pain is better today.'

'Don't tell me,' Enchei called as Narin reached the door of the kitchen, 'you've got good news?'

Narin shook his head as Kesh rose to allow Kine room at the table. On the stove a large pot bubbled and Narin realised the room was full of warming scents. Judging by the wreckage on the side table beside the stove, Enchei had set about supper as soon as he returned. The veteran was in the process of kneading a large ball of dough with more force than Narin had ever seen him use before.

'My husband has agreed to give up his claim on me,' Kine announced once she'd eased herself down into a chair. 'I shall enter the House of the Sun as servant caste and bow gladly to all of you, the price of my freedom being a single lash to my back.'

'He intends to have you whipped?' Myken stood. 'In that case I will kill him.'

'You will not!' Kine exclaimed. 'I will not have you throw your life away for an insult that I brought down upon myself!'

'You are noble caste by marriage – the law does not permit him to do this,' Myken insisted, 'neither Imperial law nor Dragon.'

'But he could beat her within an inch of her life,' Enchei piped up, 'quite legally too, so long as he did it all himself. That's permitted for husbands under House Dragon law, Wyvern too. Don't even get me started on House Iron law.'

'This is not the same. He wouldn't be protected from a response by her family or bodyguard in either case.' There was a cold anger to Myken's words that told volumes about what might have happened, had Lord Vanden treated his wife that way.

'Aye, lucky for the handful who're protected that way.'

'Siresse Myken,' Kine said firmly, 'you will do nothing. My decision is made, I will accept this retribution and I will be free of blood feuds and noble castes forever.'

'While Vanden gets himself a new wife,' Narin added bitterly. 'I hadn't got around to telling you that part.'

'New wife?' echoed the entire room almost as one.

'Who?' Kesh added, faster than the rest. 'Who would marry someone shamed in the eyes of his House?'

Now Narin did manage some sort of smile. 'It turns out we know her, or I've seen her at least. Remember the goshe sent their ruling council to the Palace of Law to discuss the attack on us? Remember they brought an Imperial to show how dangerous the investigation could be?'

'Princess Kerata?' Enchei hazarded. 'She's mixed-race you said back then, right? Dragon or one of the major Houses under it. He's won himself a bloody Imperial caste as wife? He's going to be related to the Emperor by marriage?' He shook his head in disbelief. 'For that prize, most noblemen in the entire Empire would have thrown their wives at you, Narin!'

'And she's likely as docile as Irato,' Narin said. 'She'll be the perfect wife for him. Sorote as good as dammit said he'd arrange for her to get pregnant and give Vanden a legitimate heir.'

'Giving Prince Sorote control over a Wyvern nobleman,' Myken added. 'Let's hope that counts as payment enough for the service he's extended.'

'I doubt that,' Narin said. 'He's the sort who'll want to be paid by both sides of a deal – that's how Imperials work, isn't it? For all the time he kept my secret, he knows I'm still his to use. I can only hope he and Rhe come to some sort of arrangement that keeps me bloody out of things and counts as another mark on the slate.'

'Rhe?'

'Asked to meet Sorote,' Narin explained. 'Rhe got a visit from some Dragon emissary demanding to know what was going on with our investigation. He wants to find out from Sorote what sort of cover the Lawbringers can get at court if they come face to face with Dragon troops. Can't say I blame him much; when there are guns drawn you don't want to be the only House Brightlance facing a load of angry Dragons.'

'Astaren,' Enchei said quietly, pausing in his kneading. 'It won't be troops that go after that summoner, it'll be Astaren – Firewinds scouring the city free of shadows.'

Narin frowned at him, the veteran apparently lost in his thoughts for a moment, but it didn't look like Enchei was willing to share them so he carried on. 'Astaren, then. The point is, Sorote's been interested in Rhe from day one. I never found out why other than the obvious, Rhe being the most famous of Lawbringers, but bringing those two together might be all he originally intended from me.'

'So that's all to the good then,' Enchei declared. 'I can give you something for the pain, Kine, something that'll dull it but not make Lord Vanden feel cheated. I for one always rather liked a woman with scars.'

Kesh snorted and thumped the man on his arm, but that just made him grin more and before anyone could comment further there came a bang on the front door. Narin jumped at the sound, causing Dov to screw her face up and cry, but it was just Irato returning.

'Good news for all of us then,' Enchei continued as the former goshe stamped in and shook off his snow-laden coat. 'It doesn't look like our summoner is sanctioned by my former employers, so whoever's behind it they don't have a team of Astaren to back them up.'

'How did you find that out?' Narin said.

He nodded towards Kesh. 'We've been jumping at shadows all day, the pair of us, but it turns out they were friendly ones. My daughters are in the city, come to watch over their old man.'

'Your daughters?' Kine and Narin gasped together.

'Aye, all grown up and a thousand miles from home.'

'And what's more,' Kesh broke in, 'they're—'

'They're shy,' Enchei said loudly over her, 'which is why they ain't here, but they brought good news in their wake so I'm glad enough of it. They've gone back to Ghost District now, see what help their contacts there might be able to provide.'

He gave Kesh a look that told Narin there was more to the tale, but given how close the former Astaren kept his secrets among friends, the Lawbringer left it at that. There would be time enough to talk to Enchei in private later, he knew pressing the man would be counter-productive. As though to emphasise that, Enchei cleared his throat and pointedly changed the subject. 'I take it Kine's family aren't going to listen to sense?'

Narin shook his head. 'There has to be a way we can turn them back without killing them all.'

'What's wrong with killing them all, again?' Irato asked, receiving a sharp look from Kesh in response.

'They're my family,' Kine said, 'I owe them that at least. My brother, Shonrey, will never stop, nor my cousin, Vosain, but the rest will doubtless be with them out of duty and fear of Vosain. He is a very fine duellist and experienced soldier, very dangerous.'

'Could we have killed him already?'

'He is very tall, even for a Wyvern, and broad with it. He has only half an ear and a scar down his cheek after being grazed by a bullet in a battle with House Smoke raiders.'

'Shame,' Irato said with a shake of the head. 'One more to die then. Probably two. Hope you're not too attached to your brother.'

Kine shook her head gravely. 'We were never close. When I chose not to be trained as a warrior, I rarely saw him, and of course now I am dead to him. He wouldn't acknowledge my presence in a room other than to kill me.' She lowered her head a shade. 'He is family and I do not wish him harm or my parents the grief of his loss, but we were never close.'

'Fuck him then,' Irato concluded. 'When do we do it?'

'Tomorrow if we can,' Enchei said. 'Pirish won't mind me owing her another favour; we can borrow her smokehouse for the ambush. Warrior castes won't try to burn the place down, that'd be cowardly.'

'Can you not simply follow them?' Kine pleaded. 'They will have brought younger cousins with them, boys like Toher who are old enough to bear their own guns under law, but ...' She tailed off, knowing how young men were sent to battle.

He shook his head. 'Doubt it. Most likely they're based up in Dragon District, surrounded by other warrior castes. Might be Irato and I could do it quiet like, but you heard Rhe's news. If there are Dragon Astaren on alert in the city, it's not a risk I'm willing to take.'

'I will,' Myken said. 'I know both their faces and I have two guns. I can kill them both.'

'Not without dying,' Enchei pointed out. 'I know you're warrior caste and you lot are stupid about fighting, but I'm in charge of any violence that goes on here and I prefer to do things so no one on my side dies. It's a strange idea I know, but it's served me well over the years.'

'Who put you in charge?' she asked coldly.

'The Gods them-bloody-selves,' Enchei snapped. 'You're sworn to protect the caste system of this Empire. Don't deny it, it's the principal purpose of the warrior caste.'

'Your point?'

'My point is, *might is right* in this Empire you're sworn to protect, and none of you could stop me even if you all came at once. You either agree to obey me now or I'll put you down and out until it's over. So what's it to be?'

'Please, Myken,' Kine urged, putting a hand on the woman's arm. 'Don't sacrifice yourself, not for me.'

Myken's face was tight as she turned to look Kine in the eye. 'That is my duty,' she said hoarsely, 'that is all I know.'

'Well, like the rest of us, you'll learn new tricks,' Enchei growled. 'Trust me, Siresse, there'll be a place for you after all this – if nothing else then with the Lawbringers, given they're likely to need all the guns they can muster. In this life there's always enough duty to go round, enough to make you sick and break you if you let it.'

'Please?' Kine repeated.

Myken bowed her head. 'I will obey you in this.'

With an effort, Enchei brightened. 'Good. Now who's hungry?'

CHAPTER 25

Narin woke with a start from a dream about Wyvern warriors. Dark raging faces and brass-fitted pistols, blue braids flying as they pursued him through tiny endless streets. He had Dov in his hands, cradling the child as best he could while he ran. Chunks of stone exploded all around him as his pursuers shot again and again, while his hands were so tangled in Dov's swaddling he couldn't free one to grab the pistols he wore in a holster identical to Lawbringer Rhe's.

He'd heard Kine calling as he ran, but couldn't find her no matter which way he went, and as he woke he found his hands still bunched and tangled in the blankets of their bed.

'Narin?' Kine said sleepily from beside him.

He stared wildly at the dark room for a long while, gasping for breath until the dawn rays creeping through the shutters finally outlined the room enough for him to shake off the dream. 'I ... Sorry.'

'No matter,' she purred, tugging at his hand to slide it over the bump of her belly and bring his body closer. 'I have the rest of the day to sleep.'

Narin's brain caught up with reality just enough to allow him to smile then. He eased his head up a little to look at the crib beside the bed. It was totally silent and for a moment he felt a flutter of panic, but then a wheezing snort came from within. He gently settled back down, fitting his body around Kine's and planting a line of kisses down her shoulder.

Just that moment of contact seemed to wake his body and he felt himself stiffen against her skin. A flush of embarrassment and desire washed through him as Kine shifted slightly and he realised she felt it too.

'Sorry,' Narin whispered again.

'For what?' she said, bringing his fingers up to her mouth to kiss them one by one. 'For desiring me?'

'No, but I …'

'Will have to wait, yes,' Kine finished with the ghost of a laugh, 'given lying still is uncomfortable enough. But so long as you are willing to wait, I'm just glad you still feel that way.'

'Good. Something tells me it won't stop any time soon.' Narin smiled. 'Do you have to leave yet?'

'No, my love,' he murmured into her hair. 'There's no rush.'

'I'm glad. I doubt it'll be long before Dov is hungry, stay until then?'

'I promise.'

Nestled against her dark skin, Narin drifted off into something approximating sleep – his body more than willing to take any scraps of rest it could gather. A stuttered cry woke him again as Kine lifted his arm gently away.

'I'd hoped not to wake you,' she whispered. 'She didn't cry at first, I thought I had time.'

Narin pushed himself up and put a hand on Kine's shoulder. 'I'll get her, you sit up.'

She raised an eyebrow at him. 'She will need to be changed.'

'Oh.'

'But fortunately for me you are no proud warrior, fearful of her staining robes or honour.'

Narin grunted, unable to resist the look on her face. 'And given you're some idle high caste, incapable of managing a day without us commoners to wait on you, I'd better jump to it.'

Kine smile wavered. 'No longer,' she whispered. 'Soon I'll just be a woman with no skills of any use for the world she inhabits.'

Realising he'd pushed it too far, Narin went and kissed her. She quickly ushered him away with a dismissive hand and urged him back to the baby, whose cries had grown more insistent.

It took him a long while to get Dov cleaned up and settled to feeding, but eventually Narin managed to move on to dressing himself. He pulled on his still-damp jacket and headed out with one final look back at the bed, descending the stair as quietly as he could.

Irato was waiting for him in the kitchen, a misshapen pillow and blanket by the stove showing where he'd spent the night. Clearly he'd slept in his clothes, shucking off just his weapons and stiff leather armour before settling down.

He even sleeps like Kesh's dog now, Narin thought idly as he entered and headed for the big black iron kettle to one side of the stove.

'Morning,' he said as he grabbed a flatbread left over from the previous night and smeared oil over it.

'Going to be a cold day,' was Irato's response. 'Fog's come in. More snow too.'

Narin nodded, pouring himself some bitter black tea. He slumped at the table, the earthenware cup grasped like a lifeline as he worried at the bread with his teeth. They sat in silence until he was finished, Irato watching him patiently until he was almost done then rising to pull on the last of his armour. Slotting half a dozen weapons into various sheaths on his body, Irato hauled his heavy sheepskin coat over it all and headed for the main door without waiting for Narin.

The Lawbringer sat a moment longer, remembering that this was the day he'd be actively encouraging Kine's vengeful family to follow him. How they were going to stop the other, more terrifying, faction from doing the same was beyond him right now, but Enchei had it all worked out – or so he claimed.

'Come on then,' he said at last, heaving himself reluctantly up.

Irato unbarred the front door and together they headed outside into a ghostly world. For a moment Narin wondered if he'd in fact died, struck down by some assassin waiting at the door, and not even felt it. Snow coated every rooftop and open patch of ground, not thickly but with more falling. On top of that there was a thick fog hanging over the city, spreading its chilly fingers through the streets.

The sounds of the city were distant and unreal as they walked, the towers of Dragon District mere suggestions against the sky. The fog was thick enough that he was forced to take the bridge to the Imperial District, hairs prickling on his neck as he felt hostile eyes on him. The people of the city were up and about early that morning, however. Fearing another heavy snowfall, the citizens were clearly keen to be about their daily tasks while they still could and Narin had company of all castes on the streets.

He turned into Lawbringer's Square and stopped short. Lawbringer Rhe stood in a familiar pose in the centre of the square, hood raised on his long white coat but unmistakable by his stillness. His coat was closed, hiding the pistols across his waist from view, but as usual he carried an Investigator's stave, held horizontal behind his back.

While others hurried around him, Rhe looked like a vengeful spirit unaware of the living going about their lives, his terrible gaze reserved for one man. Narin felt his heart sink at the sight and trudged forward.

Only when he was up close to the Lawbringer did Rhe slip his hood back and reveal his pale, blue-dusted face. In another, that pallor would look like signs of hypothermia, but Narin knew that was just his Brightlance heritage.

'Lawbringer Narin,' Rhe said, inclining his head formally.

'Lawbringer Rhe,' he replied, feeling his trepidation deepen. 'Has something happened?'

'I'm afraid so. I spoke to your friend, Prince Sorote, last night. He informed me of the meeting he had with Lord Vanden Wyvern.'

'Oh.'

'The petitions for annulment and Imperial betrothal go to the Senior Minister today. As such I decided it was necessary to inform the Lord Martial of the situation, at your behest.'

'My behest?'

Rhe nodded. 'It would be appropriate for such information to come from you via your superior. You would not want Lord Martial ald Har to receive the news from other sources in the Imperial Court.'

'I see.' Narin felt his anger rising and bit down on it hard, knowing perfectly well he'd brought this down on himself. That Rhe hadn't told him he was going to the Lord Martial with Narin's infractions was galling, but he knew he'd received all the special treatment he could hope for already. 'You're right, of course. And now?'

'Now he waits upon your presence.'

'Do you know what he is going to do?'

The question seemed to surprise Rhe, but he didn't hesitate to reply. 'He hasn't informed me of his decision, but I am certain you will be demoted back to Investigator. Unless there's a complaint lodged by Lord Vanden, he will not wish the public scandal of expelling you entirely, and Prince Sorote's involvement is likely to have prevented that. Where you will be assigned is another matter, but you will accept it without complaint.'

Narin pursed his lips and bowed his head. 'Yes, Lawbringer.'

'Come then.'

Rhe led the way into the Palace of Law and up the echoing flights of stairs to the higher levels. The top two floors were reserved for the Law Masters of the Vanguard Council and Narin had been up there only once, when the Lord Martial had informed him he was to be elevated to the rank of Lawbringer. Much of the top floor was reserved as private apartments for Lord ald Har and his main chamber was a round room overlooking Lawbringer's Square and the city and sea beyond it.

Three tall windows stood fifteen feet high opposite a broad oak desk, while six black marble pillars were set an arm-span in from the wall to support a conical roof. From the very peak of the roof, Narin saw a beautiful framework of silver and jet, studded with cut glass or crystal – the constellation of Lord Lawbringer glittering in the room's lamplight.

Around the room were portraits of past Lords Martial – Toro Dragon and his successor flanking a larger one of the Emperor behind the desk. It depicted the young Emperor holding court as he had likely never done in his life; pronouncing judgement between two kneeling low castes. Narin could see from their clothing that one was House Dragon, the other House Eagle, and felt like laughing at the message the artist had intended.

'Lawbringer Narin,' the Lord Martial said, not looking up from his desk.

There was no greeting implied in the words but Narin still bowed and replied as formally as he could. Rehn ald Har was a white-haired man and older than Enchei, but bulky with muscle for all his age. Though by tradition he was an Imperial emissary and a stand to one side held the pistols of a warrior caste, he wore neither gold nor red. A Wolf by birth, he wore a plain white coat against the cold and the only colour on him was the disturbing red tint to his eyes.

'Do you have anything to add to Lawbringer Rhe's account from last night?'

'I, ah, I don't believe so, my Lord,' Narin said, glancing at Rhe. 'You know of my infraction and the result – and I presume also of the blood feud her family pursue?'

Ald Har nodded.

'I do not believe Lord Vanden will complain about me at court. I hope the shame I have brought upon the Lawbringers will be limited.'

'Limited?' Lord ald Har growled. 'Given what you stirred up in the spring, limited shame is hardly the reprise I had hoped from you. The both of you seem intent on uprooting the traditions and position of the Lawbringers within this Empire, whether by design or carelessness.'

The Lord Martial stood, hands flat on the desk and leaning forward towards Narin. 'What are you, Lawbringer Narin? Why are you within our ranks?'

Narin blinked in surprise. 'I, I don't understand, my Lord.'

'What House do you serve?'

'None, my Lord – ah, that is the House of the Sun, but no other.'

'Then what part of the Imperial House is that? You won the patronage and friendship of Lord Vanden Wyvern by some act of prowess and bravery – or fortune, perhaps. And when you turn that friendship to ashes, there is another to protect you elsewhere – one whose name is omitted from the petitions going before the court today. Where did you win this patron, Lawbringer Narin? Whose pay are you in?'

'I serve only the Lawbringers,' Narin said, feeling his cheeks flush at the idea. 'I am acquainted with a member of the Imperial family, it is true, but the Emperor's law remains my master.'

'And the name of this prince or princess?'

'I— I have been asked not to share it.'

'Do I look like some fucking stranger off the street?' ald Har roared. 'I do not care what you have been asked – you are in my employ and I will not brook you serving another master! You recall the punishment for corruption in public office is execution, *Lawbringer* Narin?'

'I do, my Lord,' Narin croaked, feeling a renewed flush of fear.

'Narin,' Rhe interrupted. 'Tell him.'

Narin turned to look at the tall Lawbringer for a moment, mouth half-open as though wanting to ask Rhe something, but Narin's mind was blank. At last he caught up with himself and closed it again, bowing again to Lord ald Har.

'My apologies, Lord Martial. I didn't think properly. I've been keeping secrets for too long, it's become too much of a habit. His name is Prince Sorote of the Office of the Catacombs.'

'Never heard of him,' ald Har commented.

'Nor had I,' Rhe said, 'but I have confirmed his existence. What role he is playing I do not know, but he made out he represented no party other than the interests of the House of the Sun.'

'Good for him.' The Lord Martial's face twisted into a look of disgust. 'You are demoted, Investigator Narin, and count yourself lucky at that. If I discover you acting under this prince's orders, I will not hesitate to send you to the headsman, do you understand me?'

'I do, my Lord.'

'Now get out. You are suspended from duties for a week.'

'A week?'

Narin was startled by that. Suspended without pay was a common punishment, but a week was lenient compared to the Lord Martial's evident anger. The loss of that money Narin could survive without

231

going hungry, but he'd known men forced to live without a month's wages or more and in winter that could prove dangerous.

'A week only. You have that long to see this blood feud ended, one way or another. Duelling is prohibited under Imperial law, but Dragon law allows such a thing if your prowess extends to facing a warrior caste with longsword. So long as you find justification under law I do not care how you address your problem, but if you remain encumbered by the consequences of your actions in a week's time, you will be thrown out of the Lawbringers. If you succeed in ending this feud, if you are alive and remain one of us, Lawbringer Rhe will work you harder than you ever knew possible. Your penance will be a remorseless reminder of an Investigator's duties.'

Narin bowed, knowing that would have been coming whether or not ald Har decreed it. 'Yes, my Lord.'

'Now get out.'

Just before Narin reached the door, the Lord Martial called out again. 'Wait.' He sighed, sounding like age was once more settling on his shoulders. 'There was a child.'

'Yes, my Lord. Her name is Dov.'

'She is healthy?'

'Yes, my Lord. Her mother too. I ... I intend to wed her when I can.'

'You remember at least the first Lawbringer oath?'

'Yes, my Lord – "protect the innocent". I will give my life before I allow her to be harmed, either of them.'

'Above all, we are Lawbringers,' ald Har said gravely. 'We serve the Emperor's law and the oaths we made before the Ascendant God himself. Fail mother or child and I'll kill you myself.'

'Yes, my Lord.'

CHAPTER 26

'Narin.'

He stopped on the stair, feeling strangely light-headed after the Lord Martial's words. When he turned, Rhe was at the top, stave in hand.

'Lawbringer?'

Rhe held out his hand. 'I must take your sword. You are no longer permitted it. I suggest you have a novice fetch your greys from your home. I doubt it would be safe for you to go back there, but you should not be wearing the white.'

Narin couldn't help but laugh briefly at the absurdity, but he unbuckled his sword without comment and shrugged his white coat off his shoulders. Underneath remained the white jacket of the Lawbringers, of course, but tossing the coat aside was as much of a statement as he could be bothered to make. He watched it slide rather pathetically down the remaining steps of that flight before it came to rest in an unimpressive heap at the bottom.

'You blame me,' Rhe stated.

'You?' Narin shook his head. 'You could've had a little more tact perhaps, Lawbringer, but I don't blame you. No, I know I'm the fool here and this was always going to come. I just didn't expect it today.'

'Here.' Rhe held out the stave to Narin. He wanted to refuse it, but he had no room in his life for petulance now. There were still people trying to kill him and going unarmed wouldn't stop them. He was low caste, after all; Narin had already provided sufficient reason for a warrior to cut any man down in the street.

'Thank you,' he said finally. 'What about the summoner?'

'The house is under surveillance. We will not move until we're sure what we are dealing with, but we cannot wait a week.'

Narin nodded. 'Without me you lose my friends too, I expect. I'll ask them if you want, but I doubt they'll join you unless they're making the decisions.'

'I understand.'

'You'll take more casualties without them,' Narin added, wondering if the stony-faced Rhe cared about such details. Noble and warrior castes saw death differently to the rest of the Empire.

'The Gods have willed it so. I'll endeavour to minimise our losses. I hope the surveillance will assist there, and Prince Kashte may be persuaded to join us again.'

'Good. There's lots of royal family going spare,' Narin said, too weary to put any real effort in his bitterness.

He nodded absentmindedly to himself and set off again. This time he was not called back and soon he rejoined the anonymous bustle of the lower floors. At the bottom he stopped on the stair and spent a while looking blankly at the great slate where Lawbringer Cailer oversaw the city's crimes.

The woman saw him staring and limped over, leaning heavily on her cane but determined to ascend the half-dozen steps to where Narin stood.

'So you got busted down, eh?'

Narin blinked, unable to help glancing back up the stairs. 'What? How did you hear so quickly?'

Cailer smiled. 'I hear everything.'

'Lawbringer Rhe?'

'My novices are the ones to bring me gossip; you think they're likely to get anything from him?'

'Then what—? Oh, the Imperial petitions.'

'It's not hard to put those threads together. Petition for divorce, disappeared pregnant noblewoman, your friendship with the husband – and o' course you coming down those stairs looking like a puppy just had his bits cut off with the sword you don't have no more.'

She turned and beckoned to one of her novices. 'Danshuer, come here.'

Narin flinched as a tall, dark-skinned youth darted forward, but when he looked he realised the boy was a Moon, not a Wyvern.

'Gods,' Cailer commented, noticing his reaction. 'You've really not been having a good week, have you? Danshuer, head to Narin's quarters – Lord Scholar compound, isn't it?'

Narin nodded.

'Mistress Sheti,' he said before shaking himself out of the daze. 'Find her there and she'll let you into my rooms.'

'Go fetch him a set of greys and coat. That your stave?'

Narin glanced down at the one in his hand. It was identical to his own, but it belonged to Rhe and he realised he'd be glad to hand it back. 'Stave too.'

'You heard the man, jump to it. If you're not back within the hour I'll be more than displeased.'

The novice blanched a shade, no doubt having experienced Lawbringer Cailer's displeasure before. He bobbed his head and scampered away.

'Now you go sit up in the shrine. An hour or so among the oaths might be good for you – remind you what's important and it'll keep the gossips away.'

'Bugger the gossips,' Narin replied, standing a little straighter.

'The ones who don't out-rank you, sure,' Cailer said. 'But there were some with their noses out of joint after the way you got raised, remember? The last thing you need is a confrontation to heat your blood further. I doubt the Lord Martial's well disposed towards you at the moment so don't let anyone goad you. Either you'd be expelled from the Emperor's service or restored to novice and ordered back into the dormitories as punishment.'

Narin nodded, the spark of anger in his heart not enough to cloud common sense. 'You're right, I've got a blood feud to deal with. Petty squabbles will just get in the way.'

'That they will, if you're fool enough to let them.' Cailer cocked her head at him. 'I'll tell you what, though, I'm an old woman and need for little, but I'd not object to having a woman with some learning around to help me with chores. My maid's a foolish little girl who can barely sweep the floor without breaking something. I've no children, but I'm getting old enough to think it might be good to hear a baby's cry in my house before I die.'

His mouth fell open, recognising the generosity of the gesture for what it was. 'I— Gods above. Thank you, Lawbringer Cailer; that is good of you.'

'If she's high born, might be she'll get the maid working better than I can. The girl barely speaks she's so frightened of me. I can't have her live in, though; I'll not have wailing disturb my sleep.'

'Of course.' Narin hesitated. 'Ah, she might not be able to take you up on the offer right away, she will need to recover.'

'They take it out of you, I'm told,' Cailer said dryly. 'Babies, that is.'

Missing her joke, Narin shook his head. 'That's not all. Her husband has demanded she be whipped for deserting him, one stroke only but it must break the skin and will make her recovery longer.'

'There's nothing more vicious or petulant than a man scorned,' Cailer said. 'No doubt it was a man's spite that made up the saying about a woman scorned. I'm in no rush, just so long as I'm not taken for a fool when she does come.'

'I promise,' Narin said, bowing as best he could without backing up the stairs. 'Dov is all that matters to either of us now. Letting you down would let her down.'

'Good. Wait – a moment more, Investigator.' Something had changed in Cailer's voice and Narin returned to her side with a puzzled frown, sensing this was something of greater import than a maid's work.

'Yes, Lawbringer?'

Cailer gestured for him to lean closer. 'There's a woman waiting down the corridor. Lawbringer Uledenin sent her to me from the front desk. If you walk to the bottom of the stairs and look right you'll see her.'

Narin did so, glancing along the high corridor where a dozen people in grey or white were walking. Off to one side was indeed a woman – warrior caste, with long red hair and an ornate red-and-white tunic. Her eyes were turned in the other direction, but Narin still ducked back out of sight with a gasp.

'Is that a Banshee?' he hissed in astonishment. 'I've never seen one in the flesh, not even while patrolling Leviathan District.'

Cailer inclined her head. 'So she appears.'

'What does she want?'

'To speak to the Lord Martial.'

Narin scowled. 'He's not in the finest mood.'

'More importantly,' Cailer said pointedly, 'she gave old Uledenin quite a tale, one he'd be inclined to dismiss if it weren't for what she is.'

'Well yes, Banshees aren't likely to get hysterical over something imagined.'

'Indeed. She claims she saw a man with features twisted beyond recognition entering a house on the Tier Bridge, the upper level. Given what she's heard from local gossip, she seems pretty sure it was a man possessed by a hellhound – a House Smoke mercenary.'

Narin nodded. That confirmed what he'd deduced about likely safe-houses used by the Etrage Merchant House. Now it was Cailer's turn to frown.

'You don't seem so surprised.'

'I'm not, only that whoever's behind this is sloppy about covering their tracks.'

'I'm glad I brought it up, then. My question's this: who should I tell?'

'Who? I don't understand.'

Cailer had a pained look on her face. 'Lord ald Har was most grieved by the losses the Lawbringers took as they assaulted the goshe island. He's wary of another such confrontation – quite aside from how House Dragon might act were we to impede them in asserting their authority a second time. Lawbringer Rhe, on the other hand, fears no conflict of any form and is something of a zealot in matters of what constitutes the Lawbringers' purview.'

'So you're asking who I'd take this information to?'

'Indeed. It's far from normal to take any such information to the Lord Martial, but I wonder if this is not an instance where protocol should be ignored? It goes against the grain for me to do so and I'd appreciate your opinion here, given you're unlikely to be involved either way.'

Narin was quiet for a long while, trying to weigh the two options. Rhe would indeed want to deal with it himself, but the Lawbringers and Investigators he drafted in could be bolstered by Prince Kashte's band of Imperial warriors, at least. If House Dragon got involved, they might have the greater power to bring, but Enchei would certainly have to keep clear and Narin suspected he wanted to be part of it if he could. Not only to be sure it was over with, but to know no prisoners would be taken to be interrogated by Dragon's Astaren.

'I don't know,' he admitted. 'It's a risk to our brothers and sisters, but I dislike hiding behind the skirts of House Dragon.'

'As do I,' Cailer said. 'If it was just a choice between the death of Lawbringers or the hardened killers of the Astaren, it would be simple.'

'Tell Rhe,' Narin said, finally deciding.

A fog of guilt seemed to fill his heart as he said it, but he knew Rhe would at least be careful in who he recruited to the cause. The criminals of the Imperial City were hardly a gentle crowd, so every Lawbringer knew the risks of their oaths.

'The choice should be his. He knows what forces he can bring to bear and he won't risk their lives if he doesn't believe it'll work. There are Dragon emissaries hounding him already; he'll always have the option to turn it over to them.'

'Do you think he will?' Cailer asked sceptically.

Narin shook his head. 'I think he'll find a way to do it under Lawbringer auspices. He's not one to accept any plan until he's certain of it.'

'And not just because he's House Brightlance originally?'

'He's House of the Sun now, as to-the-bone as you or I.' *And he's made a new friend in Prince Sorote too, perhaps.*

Lawbringer Cailer nodded and Narin guessed from the look on her face that her own thoughts had been along the same lines. 'Thank you, Investigator. Now get yourself to the shrine and meditate on your new life.'

She turned and eased her way back down the stairs where already there were Investigators waiting to speak to her. Narin watched her go then caught the bright eyes of Rhe's favourite novice, Tesk, beside the slate.

Will she be glad to see me back under Rhe's charge? I suppose so, better that way than he takes on another, younger, Investigator and she misses her chance while my replacement's being trained. Once I've served my penance I'm either back to Lawbringer or I spend my days as a senior Investigator, training others myself.

Narin shook his head. 'Getting ahead of yourself there,' he said quietly as he headed back up to the shrine of Lord Lawbringer where large stone tablets, positioned as the stars of the Ascendant God's constellation, bore the oaths of his order. 'Stay alive these coming days, that's the only plan right now.'

Lawbringer Cailer was right and also wrong, he realised as he crossed through the shrine and sat on the far side, at the narrow windows where the low sill served as a long stone bench. The reverential quiet was preferable there and he knew he wouldn't be disturbed other than by his handful of friends, but he felt every eye on him. There was nowhere to hide in the shrine and a constant stream of Lawbringers and Investigators passed on the other side. Enough would spot him sitting there like a child sent to the corner as punishment and the tongues would wag all the faster.

'*Protect the innocent*' Narin read from the first of the tablets. *Everything else is just words. Bring me your most hurtful words,* he thought, staring back at some of the curious looks. *My armour is* made of a woman's smile and a baby's cry. *Your hot air cannot hurt me, so try as you will.*

He closed his eyes and imagined his life as it was now to be. A smile soon appeared on his face and never left it until the Moon youth, Danshuer, returned with the grey clothing of his old life.

Enchei stood in the cluttered bedroom of his friend Pirish and stared into nothing. The debris of a life was scattered all around him, Pirish having lived half a century in the smokehouse, but his thoughts were on a more distant place. The two little girls he'd left behind, crying with their mother at the estate gate, and all that had been thrust upon them.

'*Tell us how – before anything else I want to know that.*'

Their conversation the previous day had been fraught – filled mostly with silences while Kesh kept a respectful distance. They were strangers, fumbling at threads he'd cut twenty years ago.

'*How? How this happened to me – to you?*'

'*Yes.*'

Enchei had been quiet a long while, forced back into uncomfortable memories. '*I was on a mission a few years before you two were born, far to the east.*'

'*In Shadowrain Forest?*'

He'd shaken his head at that. For most the thousand-mile-barrier of Shadowrain Forest, beyond the House Raven hegemony, was simply the furthest edge of the world – not just of the Empire.

'*Beyond Shadowrain. We crossed the great north mountains and skirted the forest where it met the snow-line. We knew of the kingdoms beyond the mountains, beautiful places but too remote to attempt to conquer.*

'*Beyond them, though, there was talk of a great inland sea and civilisation on the far shore – in the kingdoms we knew they called it the garden of the world. Most beloved of the old Gods, we were told, granted a paradise to live in and knowing only peace.*'

'*How?*'

'*There were guardians chosen from each generation, guardians given the power of Gods. We discovered inherited traits like the ones you have were in these blessed bloodlines – their rituals of adulthood involved relinquishing their powers to the priesthood who kept great repositories for the guardians to draw on.*'

'*And you broke into one?*'

239

'I did. We were outmatched and I took a risk. I was assigned to watch the unit's back, but we had evaded our pursuit and I saw an opportunity. I broke into a temple while the priests were elsewhere, but it was ancient. A walkway crumbled underneath me and I fell. I lay there half-dead, roused only by the screams of my unit in my ears as they were ambushed and slaughtered a few miles away.'

'So you contracted it like a virus?'

'Not quite. A guardian found me, the newest of their number. Just a girl, really, her name was Sarra — or rather it had been. The Lady of Mists was what she'd become. Whatever happened to me in the temple, it would have killed me had she not done something. I don't know how, but she healed me and changed me at the same time, sent me back alone to tell the tale of how the rest had been killed.

'Sarra didn't want a second, stronger expedition to be sent after us, but she warned me to keep my fall in the temple a secret even as I reported how dangerous the guardians were. She wanted me to glimpse the burden the guardians carried, how it turned each of them insane as the years passed. I didn't understand what she meant at the time, didn't know what secret she warned me to keep. I only knew that I believed her, that it would be the end of me and all I loved if my masters knew what had happened that day.'

'She gave you their greatest weapon and then warned you to keep away?'

'She gave me the secret of how they passed their weapons on through the generations, but no weapon of theirs. Each guardian was powerful enough to destroy an army — they had done so many times in their history before invaders learned they were invincible by any mortal standards.

'The changes made to my body — the blades, the mage-sight, the hardened bones, each of the hundred-odd adjustments the mage-priests made when I was younger — they didn't add up to enough to threaten the guardians, no matter how many of us there were. But Sarra used them as a warning and a punishment — she knew others within the Astaren would turn on me for personal gain just as she knew I wanted a family before I died. She twisted things inside me so those changes became inherited traits rather than just the tinkering of mage-priests. She cursed me with the prize we'd sought there, knowing what any army would do to its own to get their hands on such an advantage.'

'And so she tied your future and ours in a neat little bow. Once you had children, they would be always under threat from your own comrades.'

Enchei bowed his head, heart as heavy as lead.

240

'And then you abandoned us – walked away and told the world you were dead rather than face the consequences of what you had done.'

'Enchei?' called a voice.

He looked up, startled for a moment, before getting his bearings. 'Pirish? I thought you'd gone.'

The tiny old woman stood in the doorway, looking so hard at him he felt her gaze on his soul. She remained spry despite her age and a husband buried longer than Enchei's girls had been alive; the ravages of the years were visible on her face but didn't affect her mind.

'This is my house,' she snapped, 'I'll go when I'm good and ready.'

Enchei sighed. For all their differences there was a fierceness in Pirish that reminded him of the Lady of Mists – a bloody-mindedness and independence that could never be swayed. 'I need to get on here.'

'No you don't,' she said, advancing into the room and settling into a wicker chair so filled with cushions only someone of Pirish's size could fit in the remaining space. 'You need a friend to talk to. I've never seen you like that before; like the starlight just marked out your grave in front o' you.'

He shook his head. 'Maybe the opposite, actually. Feels like I've got part of my life back again, one I thought I'd lost forever.'

'Then why've you got a face like that on ya?'

'It's complicated.'

'Knight's balls "it's complicated". Folk always say that when they've dug 'emselves a hole, but it's rarely so complex.'

'You've no idea.'

'So tell me,' she said, shifting slightly in her seat to get more comfortable. 'I've no stake in this, not like your Lawbringer friend.'

'There's nothing to tell,' Enchei said in a hollow voice. 'I need people to forgive me and it doesn't matter what's right or wrong, true or false. I need 'em to forgive me in their hearts, not just say the words, and there's nothing I can do to help it.'

'Must be family then,' Pirish concluded, a smug look on her face. 'Nothing messes a man's head up more'n family. I thought you'd left yours a long while back, some scandal or the like?'

Enchei hesitated. He'd known Pirish for a few years now, longer than Narin, but had never told her his secrets and she'd been careful not to ask. Intimations of an insalubrious past were enough for Pirish – from how they'd met, Enchei guessed she'd known more than a few men

241

like that and would be fazed by little. But she was content not to pry and he had always been glad of it.

'That's right,' he said after a pause that was long enough for Pirish to notice. 'Left them a long time back, but they tracked me down.'

'A man can never apologise enough,' Pirish declared. 'For what he said, for what he didn't say – hells, sometimes just for bein' himself or having the face he does. Say you're sorry and say it again. Say it till you've run out of breath then bloody write it down instead.'

'Never been good at sorry.'

'Aye, doubt you've had much practice,' she said darkly, 'but mebbe you try and mean it this time, eh? My first husband never could sound sorry – arrogant bastard he was, always wearin' a grin like the Emperor himself would forgive whatever he'd done.'

'First husband? What did you do to him?'

'Hah, don't think I weren't tempted once or twice. As you're mebbe plannin', you shut a man in that pitch-dark smokehouse for five minutes and he's dead all accidental like.' She sighed. 'But though the Emperor might've forgiven him, turns out an Eagle warrior caste wasn't so accommodatin'. Never found out what he'd said to the man, only that the little sod was coming half-nekked out some floozy's house at the time. The Eagle put a bullet between his eyes and just kept on walkin' like nothin' had ever happened.'

Before Enchei could find the words to reply, there came the thump of feet on the stairs and Kesh's face appeared at the doorway.

'If you old buggers have finished your tea party, we've got work to do, remember?'

'Aye, I remember,' Enchei scowled. 'I'm on it.'

'Really? Because I thought you were going to nail planks across the inside of those shutters?' Kesh said, pointing to the wide window ahead of him.

'You filled all the buckets with water?'

'Just getting the last few now. There's six downstairs already. Pirish, I know there's a smokehouse downstairs, but why so many buckets?'

The old woman cackled. 'Can never have too many,' she said, 'not when you've got fires smoking day an' night.'

'They won't burn the place,' Enchei said, pushing thoughts of his daughters from his mind. 'They're warrior caste on a blood feud; they'll barge their way in and want us to see their faces as they kill us.'

'You sure they'll come in the other bedroom?'

He nodded. 'It's an easy hop up on to the smokehouse roof. We leave a lamp burning in this room and the other dark; it'll be the obvious entry point.'

'Unless they kick in my front door,' Pirish pointed out.

'They'll do that too, come at us from both directions. I'll set up a surprise for anyone getting through that door. My money's on the leaders coming up here, though – let the noise down below lure folk downstairs and give time for a little family reunion.'

'But they get that boy with the demons in his head instead?' Pirish asked. 'Tough you may be, Enchei, but you're no warrior caste.'

'There'll be no straight fight up here either,' Enchei said firmly. 'We're taking no risks today.'

'Glad to hear it.' Pirish hauled herself up out of the chair. 'So like the lady said, you've got work to do, which means I'm to the pub. Fetch me when it's all over an' it's my house again.'

'Thank you, Pirish.'

She waved it away as she headed down the stairs, calling over her shoulder, 'Just you keep my house from burnin' down, you hear?' She cackled again. 'And remember I'm always lookin' out for a fourth husband before I die!'

CHAPTER 27

Shonrey ground to a halt and watched the urchin trudge past the tavern up ahead. The light had been failing steadily and now dusk was upon them. The lamp that hung over the tavern door was lit, creating a bubble of warmth in the fog. He could just about read the tavern's name, the Broken Field, as the urchin passed it, eyes downcast but turned just slightly to the left.

They had taken an oblique route to get here, but Shonrey felt a quickening in his gut that told him finally they were where the Gods willed them to be. The Lawbringer had been demoted, Shonrey saw, but not stripped of his rank entirely. Another example of the weakness within the Lawbringers, the cheap blood that flowed in their veins. Either they were too cowardly to fully acknowledge their mistakes or they were so venal that they did not consider his crimes serious.

Shonrey ground his teeth in anger, feeling his hand tighten into a fist. He would show them what punishment was appropriate to one who betrayed her husband, her family, her caste. This Investigator and his whore, both would learn the wrath of the Wyverns before the night was out.

Investigator Narin was a grey phantom in the fog as he moved in bursts and constantly turned to check behind, but Shonrey had learned from their mistakes of days past.

Their missing kin, their failures in following the Lawbringer to his whore's lair – all solved by a single coin and a grubby low-caste boy with no honour. He was a local, no more than fourteen years old, and interested only in the silver coin he'd been promised.

Growing up penniless on those streets, the boy called Virin hadn't cared why he was to follow a Lawbringer, but even in this one day he had proved his worth at it. The man was watching for dark faces following him and it seemed he had not even noticed just another poor, white face walking behind. How the Investigator and his associates had managed to ambush his previous pursuers not once but twice remained a mystery, but it no longer mattered. Now he was undone by his own grasping, low-born kind.

The sound of boots on cobbles heralded Shonrey's youngest cousin, Toher, a gangly youth whose questions had been a constant irritant over the days they had spent in the Imperial City. They both wore dark blue cloaks over their clothes, enough to hide everything but their faces. Up ahead, the urchin in the ragged clothes had stopped past the tavern and turned to face them.

'Has he found it?' Toher asked, clouds of breath betraying the anxiety of one so young he had never been in battle.

But you're lucky, cousin, Shonrey thought, *you will survive your first fight. Perhaps you'll learn the sense to survive battle-proper. House Eagle's armies will prove more dangerous than this Investigator when the warhorns finally sound, and it's my duty to see you safe until then.*

He did not answer the youth for a long while, instead watching the urchin keenly. Virin waited a moment then retraced his steps, heading towards them with head again low. It afforded him one final glance at the side-street the Investigator had disappeared down.

'Return to Vosain,' Shonrey said at last, eyes never leaving the urchin growing steadily more real as he emerged from the fog. 'Tell him to come at once.'

Toher nodded. 'So close to Dragon District,' he breathed as he cast around to get his bearings. 'Astonishing.'

'Their choices will have been limited,' Shonrey said. 'The Investigator will have had little money and has likely never left this city in his life. His thinking will have been similarly limited.'

'And Kine will not have been able to travel ...' Too late did Toher realise his mistake and tail off.

Shonrey turned and grabbed the youth by the throat. 'Never speak that name,' he hissed with barely constrained fury. Toher croaked and shuddered as Shonrey's grip closed his windpipe but the tall warrior did not relent. 'She is dead to us. The whore was never part of our family, understand me?'

Toher's eyes began to roll up and Shonrey released him, letting the youth fall back to the ground where he gasped and pawed at his throat. Finally he heaved in a ragged breath, retching once noisily before he recovered himself.

'I'm … my apologies, cousin,' he managed at last, sitting with legs splayed in the slush and filth of the street.

'Get up,' Shonrey snapped, turning away. 'Bring Vosain to me, quickly now.'

As Toher fled, the urchin stepped forward – he had wisely decided not to get involved in the scuffle – and stuck out a grubby hand. 'Smokehouse, down behind the tavern.'

Shonrey pulled a silver coin from his increasingly depleted purse and held it up. The embossed Wyvern emblem on one side glinted in the feeble light of the street.

'You have one final task,' he said in halting Imperial. While it was the trade language of the Empire, Shonrey's family were warriors only, their need to learn anything more than House Dragon's tongue limited.

The urchin hesitated. Evidently he wanted to curse and demand his money, but he knew what that would bring from a warrior caste.

'What?' he said in a sulky voice.

'Scout the land,' was the best Shonrey could manage at first, falling back on words a warrior needed to learn. 'The smokehouse is big? Small? We can flank it?'

'Ah right,' Virin said, nodding as he understood. 'Aye, there's an alley behind. It's this way.'

'I wait here,' Shonrey said.

'Suit yourself, I'll go check. Been a while since I came this way, but I reckon I remember it okay. You'll get in easy enough round the back – some old woman owns it, I think. Probably rented her spare room out, it's not a big place, none of these round here are.'

'Find me a path,' the Wyvern said, fingers touching the butt of a pistol at his waist, 'and the silver is yours.'

It took Toher a half-hour to return with the remaining five of their number, Vosain at their fore as always. In that time Shonrey had himself ventured to the mouth of the side-street and scouted what he could of their goal. The smokehouse was a typical low-caste building; shabby and small, made from yellow clay bricks stained halfway to black by dirt and rain.

Virin, now paid and gone, had told him there was a workroom behind the main door and the smoke-room itself lay beside it. Above the workroom were two smaller ones where the owner lived, one looking out onto the street, the other over the smoke-room. An alley that stank of piss ran from the rear of the tavern all the way down behind the houses until it reached the wide street that served as the border with Dragon District. Their path was clear to Shonrey, the only problem being a large man he had seen entering the house after Investigator Narin.

'I was lucky,' he said to his cousin as they stood together, fifty yards from the side-street entrance. 'A minute earlier and he could have seen me there.'

The scarred veteran looked down at him. 'You are sure he did not?'

'I am sure.'

Vosain nodded, taking him at his word. The age between them was too great for them to have grown up as friends, but they had served five years together in the army. Shonrey had once been the foolish youth Toher was – perhaps not so foolish, given the skirmishes he'd survived in those early days, but still reliant on his elder cousin to see him through.

'He was warrior caste?' Vosain asked.

'No. A big man; he looked like a mercenary or hired thug, but no high caste.'

'We do not need to worry, then. Toher alone is worth more than a low-caste mercenary.'

Unlike most Wyvern warriors, Vosain's dark head was bald rather than a mass of braided or threaded hair. It accentuated the brutal bullet-scar and ruined upper-half of his right ear, making him appear even more fearsome than his size already indicated.

Shonrey glanced back at the youth, standing nervously to the rear. Vosain was right in that the youth had been trained to shoot well enough, but there had to be more at work here. They had all lost kin on this blood feud; sisters and brothers dead in some gutter, their corpses eaten by demons, he was forced to conclude.

'We must assume he is dangerous,' Shonrey pressed. 'We have too many dead to do otherwise.'

'You think one mercenary killed so many of our kin?'

'Not alone I'm sure, but what other explanation is there?'

'A dozen or more,' Vosain growled. 'Do you forget my brother was among our first to be lost? I underestimate no man.'

'Then what? Have we stumbled into something more?'

'That bloodless viper son of Brightlance is all my brother stumbled into,' Vosain replied, 'and he paid for such luck with his life. Lawbringer Rhe is a great warrior, this is known, but he is not here now. There are no guns inside, no true warriors. I had not thought you so anxious, Shonrey.'

247

'When we've lost the first skirmishes, I grow wary,' Shonrey said calmly. 'Your brother had four with him, none returned. Harai and Usern were assigned to follow Lawbringer Rhe the next day and they disappeared with our two watchers on the bridge. Until I know how they were ambushed, I remain wary.'

'Your wariness lets victory slip through your fingers,' Vosain spat. 'We have the rats cornered now. I will kill them both myself if needs be.'

'I am always at your side, cousin, you know that.'

'I do.'

They fell silent as Vosain considered the layout Shonrey had reported. With the divine constellations hidden by cloud, the diffused slivers of light from surrounding windows were the only light. The street itself was quiet, the side-street and alley deserted now.

'I will take Toher,' Vosain announced at last. 'He will guard my back and ensure no one from the tavern uses the alley. I will climb the roof of the smoke-room and wait at the window there. That front door should be easily kicked in – even barred, two of you should be able to break it down with your shoulders.'

'They have relied on ambush before,' Shonrey said slowly, knowing no other answer was possible. 'They will do so again.'

'It is so. Break in the door and fire on anyone you see, but do not enter. Lure them out if you can. Station one man at the window, ready to shoot should they use that.'

'Meanwhile you will enter and take them by surprise. I should be with you, though, not Toher. Better we both make the assault.'

'Either one of us will succeed or both will fail,' Vosain argued, putting his hand on his cousin's shoulder. 'When you hear my guns, enter cautiously. They cannot cover both sides effectively.'

'We should take nothing for granted. I have a grenade, I will use it. It does my honour no good, but until the whore is dead my honour can suffer no greater stain.'

Vosain's mouth thinned. 'Very well,' he said with obvious reluctance. 'You are right, cousin. They fight without honour and nor should we until she is dead.' He turned and beckoned the youngest of their group over. 'Toher, come with me.'

'You have to the count of a hundred,' Shonrey said, freeing his pistols from their holster ties. 'Then you must be in place, ready for when we breach the door.'

Vosain nodded. 'Lord Knight bless our cause.'

'Lord Executioner guide our hands,' Shonrey replied. 'The Gods be with us all, cousin.'

From beneath a cloak of rags, he watched. Hunched and pathetic, he was ignored by all in his hollow of broken boxes. Just another beggar too drunk or crazed to find somewhere more sheltered from the descending cold. Just another beggar who'd be dead by morning, whose corpse others would step over until one became sickened by the sight and tipped him into the river to feed the demons.

The fog grew thicker, the breeze off the sea a savage cold that left ice in its wake. Still the beggar did not move, did nothing but watch. He was motionless and silent, but for the voices that chattered in the depths of his mind.

We wait.

There are four.

I count ten.

Sea snakes.

Count the shadows.

I see flame and shadow.

The hounds call.

Dragons rise from the depths.

We burn.

Still he did not move, but he watched all and slowly the fog curling around him grew and thickened. A corona of vapour rose from his shoulders, then smoke. At last he moved, head bowing to look at his clasped grey hands. Each finger was inscribed with a prayer; hands, arms and entire body too, an ancient etched script that glowed faintly in the darkness. As he watched, the glow increased and the rags of his cloak continued to smoulder.

We burn, he called to the night.

Shonrey finished his count and made a small gesture with his hand. Each of the Wyvern warriors shrugged off the long concealing coats and shook their braided hair loose before they drew their pistols. One moved next to the lower window of the workroom, ready to shoot anyone who might throw open the shutters, and the rest headed straight for the door. The largest, Urern, led the way and broke into a run in the last few steps.

He dipped his shoulder and hit the door with the full weight of his body. The sound echoed like thunder around the street as something burst under the pressure. The door flew open and Urern staggered forward over the threshold, dropping to a crouch as Shonrey levelled his pistol at the room behind. A sour, pungent smell met him; smoked meat and fish mingled with something unrecognisable to a high caste.

The room was dark enough that he could only make out the regular shapes of packing crates arranged along the far wall. The door lurched drunkenly, one hinge ripped free of the wood. Ahead was an open doorway to a smaller room, empty chairs and a dead stove illuminated by weak lamplight from above. Just as Shonrey took a breath a dark shape edged around the corner of the doorway ahead and darted back. He fired on instinct, seeing his bullet strike the far wall.

He turned, leaving another to aim at anything that moved in the room and gestured to the cousin at the rear of them. He offered over a burning taper which Shonrey held to the stub of fuse on his grenade. They were untrustworthy weapons and disliked by all warrior castes, but he had enough deaths to account for back home without chancing more. When the first group of family had not returned from their mission to capture the Investigator, Shonrey had bought the fist-sized iron ball from a Dragon weapon-smith, aware of its power in the narrow streets of the Imperial City.

The breath caught in his throat as Shonrey watched the cord fizzle into life. Once he was sure it had taken he wasted no time and hurled the grenade through the door where it clattered against the stove. He held his position a moment longer, second pistol in his left hand, in case the figure made a break for it, then ducked back out of sight before the blast could shake the room.

It never came. One held breath stretched out and became a second, then a third. Caution kept Shonrey back a moment longer then he turned back around the corner, sinking to one knee to present a different target to anyone within. The view was empty, the grenade a dark and dead shape on the ground. The fuse was still visible – it had gone out somehow, rather than been dislodged. He doubted even a desperate man would have tried to gather and smother it.

'Come,' he breathed to the man beside him; Suken, the oldest of their group.

Together they edged forward, Shonrey silently drawing his longsword as they went. The smell worsened as they entered, filling his head with a heavy, sickly sensation. There was no movement ahead, no sign of the low castes they had cornered here. As they reached the middle of the room he found his limbs grow heavier and instinct made him grab Suken's arm, dragging the man back out with him into the open air.

They stumbled through the doorway, only to find the others similarly enfeebled. Shonrey forced himself to look around the street, to keep moving, but he saw no assailants, just empty shadows.

The city blurred around him, the fog wrapping its tendrils around his arms. It dragged him down like a demon's embrace and then the darkness took him.

The Firewind stood, burning rags cascading from his body. His second skin shone now, trails of incantation following the line of his body like cracks in a lava flow. Nearby he sensed his war-siblings do the same, the glow around each illuminating the bone-white struts and buildings nearby. From below he felt as much as heard the deep booming call of the Stone Dragons as those armour-clad destroyers rose to join them.

A curl of flame flickered into existence in the air in front of him before winking out again. The Firewind bent and grasped his grey spear, the edge a dull white that began to shine in the waxing light. Bursts of fire began to erupt from his second skin, flaring out as the prayers shone so bright they became unintelligible and the wood around him caught light.

A great whoosh of flame erupted from nearby, swirling streams of yellow surrounding a second Firewind and casting their brightness wide. Up ahead he saw a figure move in the shadows, raise some sort of weapon, and he threw his empty hand out towards it. A gout of flame raced forward, covering the twenty yards in a heartbeat. A ball of fire exploded around the figure and they fell, but the Firewinds did not advance. Instead the pair stood as sentinels, spears upraised, while the heavy tramp of feet appeared behind him.

The call of the Stone Dragons rang out again, the fury of some ancient monster awakened. Four of the armoured warriors advanced between the Firewinds, weapons ready to cast indiscriminate death. From further ahead he heard more calls, saw more burgeoning storms of flame reflecting in the fog.

The trap is complete, he thought, sending it out to his fellow Astaren of House Dragon. *Take them.*

CHAPTER 28

From around the corner Vosain heard the crash of the door, followed by the crack of a pistol that echoed through the small house. He waited a heartbeat for movement within the darkened room then slipped his knife through the shutters to lift the catch. He pulled the shutters back and peered into the room as best he could. Nothing moved within. He could see little but certainly there were no faces looking back at him, no naked steel pointing his way.

His knife worked its way around one cheap pane of glass easily enough and soon he had the blade behind it. A twist of the wrist cracked the glass and levered a piece towards him. He removed it and dropped it on the cloak he'd spread out on the roof below, quickly pulling more pieces away until he could slip his hand in and open the window silently.

It had taken him a matter of seconds. There were no more gunshots below but a shuffle of feet and a clatter of something on bare floorboards. Vosain didn't wait for the grenade to explode, confident enough in his ability to move quietly, so he eased his way over the sill and into the dark room.

It was a cluttered mess inside; opposite him a dresser of pale china shone in the starlight, four armchairs arranged around some low table covered in garish glass pieces. The chairs were pushed back against the walls, affording him a clear space to move in and no hiding places better than a battered glass-fronted cabinet.

Low castes and their pretensions, Vosain thought idly as he picked his way past porcelain figurines of Ascendant Gods and drew his pistol.

He took a step towards the door before some sixth sense caught movement behind him. He whirled around, bringing his gun up, but it was smashed from his grip by a numbing blow. The Wyvern warrior was already reaching for a dagger before he focused on his attacker.

For a moment he thought they were a Dragon from the dark colour, but then he realised it was a man swathed in black and masked.

Before Vosain could draw his dagger the figure rapped his knuckles with a short baton. He followed that up with a punch to the sternum that drove Vosain back into a chair. There he slumped for a moment, breathless and stunned, while the man grabbed the second pistol from Vosain's ornate holster across his belly and tossed it aside.

That done, the figure checked behind, glancing out of the window for any assistance he'd failed to notice, but saw nothing. Vosain realised Toher would be out of sight, watching the rear entrance of the tavern. A distant voice told him he was going to die unless he acted, but as he forced himself up the man gave him a slap around the head that set his skull ringing as he fell back.

Confusion filled Vosain's mind. He was far taller and broader than his attacker, but each blow had struck like a hammer. For a moment he just sat there, stunned and willing Shonrey to burst through the door and shoot this stranger down, but nothing happened.

His assailant cocked his head, lowering the baton in his hand as he looked Vosain up and down. The Wyvern warrior wore only functional clothes, no sign of military rank or honours sewn to his shoulder. He was there to execute, not fight honourably. Still, the other man nodded before he spoke.

'Guess you're the cousin, then.'

Vosain blinked once before anger forced his wits to return. This damn low caste thought to speak to him so, let alone be so casual when attacking a twice-titled warrior of the plain?

'I am the cousin,' Vosain growled, fighting to think and plan while the low caste enjoyed his moment of advantage. Something was not right here, but Vosain had dealt with stronger men than himself before. 'The whore told you about me, then?'

It seemed an idle flick of the wrist, but the man seemed to know which exact point on Vosain's knee to strike and a bolt of pain shot through his leg. The veteran soldier hissed with pain, coming close to crying out.

'That ain't nice, especially when she's your kin.'

'She is no family of mine. She has shamed us and must die.'

'No family o' yours?' the man echoed. 'Aye well, fortunately for her she's got a new family. We might be bit of a mix, but that's life for ya. Point is, family should stick up for each other, not hunt each other down.'

The man leaned forward and his tone turned menacing. 'And once you're messing with my family,' he snarled, 'the Gods themselves ain't going to be able to help ya.'

Vosain sneered at him. 'The Gods have cursed your family then.' He could see in the dark eyes glaring back that it scored a hit. The flash of anger distracted the man for long enough for Vosain to whip a stiletto from his sleeve and stab it into the man's neck—

Except the man was no longer there. Vosain's blade cut only air and he felt a jolt of shock. He'd not even seen the man move. One moment he was in the path of that lethal point and the next he was well clear. Before he could recover Vosain felt his wrist grasped and twisted back on itself.

The stiletto fell from his fingers and was scooped up by his attacker. He tried to move, lurch up from his seat and throw himself sideways, but another punch to his chest rocked him backwards.

Vosain fell back, mouth open and gasping at the sight of the narrow stiletto hilt protruding from his chest. Then the pain came; a fierce embrace of unbearable heat that flowed around his chest and up through his throat. He tried to breathe but could only manage an agonised wheeze as his chest filled with fire.

'Yup,' the man said distractedly, 'that'll hurt, but you're a big strong lad. You won't die for a while yet, so how about we talk some more?'

Vosain did his best to spit at the low caste. It fell short, but his defiance was clear.

'That's a shame,' the man said. 'I was hoping to spare some o' your kin. If you want me to kill 'em all as I find 'em, fine.'

The Wyvern tried to speak but the pain made every movement a stabbing jolt. With an effort of will he found the strength to lick his lips and draw in a shallow breath. 'We are warriors,' Vosain huffed. 'We die for our honour.'

'Can't persuade you? What about the young lad in the alley? Don't he deserve a few more years of life before some bastard cousin of his drags him to a fool's death?'

'He is a warrior.'

'How many of you are there?' the man persisted. 'How many like you? Kine says you and her brother, Shonrey, will be the ones in charge. Without you two, will the rest slope off back home?'

Vosain felt a moment of doubt before anger eclipsed it, but even as he replied he thought the man had caught the hesitation.

'They will die for the honour of family.'

The man sighed and shook his head. 'Where would our armies be if it weren't for boys too stupid to realise what they're getting into?'

He reached around the back of Vosain's head and clamped steel-clad fingers around the base of his skull. The pain increased as the man half-lifted him out of the chair, fingers digging into his flesh so hard it broke the skin.

'How many? Five? Six? Seven? Eight? Okay, seven it is. Would you trust them to see this through if Shonrey and your lovely self were dead? Excellent.'

Vosain didn't speak at all in reply, but the man – mage or shaman, he now realised – seemed uninterested in hearing anything.

'Doesn't look like I need you any more now, does it?' the man said idly, peering forward at him and releasing his grip.

A cold sensation slithered down Vosain's spine. He twitched his fingers, trying to be sure if his right hand was still strong enough to move.

'You hide your face,' he croaked slowly in response. 'You hide your name. I am a warrior of House Wyvern. It is my right to know who will kill me.'

'Right?' The man shook his head. 'You got no rights here.'

Vosain moved as fast as he could, grabbing the hilt of the stiletto embedded in his chest and yanking it clear with a cut-off howl. He slashed forward at the man and saw its edge slice the cloth around the man's head as a hot gush of blood spilled from his own chest. The masked man jerked back and Vosain threw himself forward, using what remained of his strength to propel himself on to his opponent.

His greater weight slammed down on the man as he stabbed at his face, but somehow the commoner twisted away. Half pinned by Vosain's massive frame, the man wedged a hand under Vosain's wrist to keep the stiletto from driving down into his chest. Vosain punched him in the side of the head with his free hand, but it was a feeble blow and the man shrugged it off, so he put both hands around the stiletto grip and all his weight behind the slim point.

The man punched him in the shoulder, a savage blow that felt like a knife wound, but amid the last moments of his life Vosain was oblivious to everything bar inching the stiletto point down to his assailant's chest. The man punched again, a second agonising blow, before he realised it wasn't enough. The stiletto crept a little further down, but then the man got his hand up under Vosain's own.

255

Instead of gripping the weapon, the man moved his hand up towards Vosain's throat and there came a small wet sound like a blade sliding through flesh.

'Her name is Dov,' the man whispered. 'A beautiful baby girl – and you'll never hurt her.'

Vosain barely heard him. His body was growing cold and all he could see was the stiletto in his hands. His whole being was devoted to driving it down into the man's flesh and ensuring he would trail him like the servant he was all the way into the afterlife.

'I don't think so,' the man commented as the stiletto edged a little further, pricking the material of his clothing.

With a snarl he pushed his free hand up and away, a razor edge tearing into Vosain's throat and chopping through his flesh to scrape on bone before it was ripped away. There was a moment of white-hot pain that seemed to fill the world and a gush of warmth from Vosain's throat – then nothing. No pain, no anger, no honour or regrets. The world vanished and he was no more.

Irato stalked through the still bodies in the street, the faint bitter smell of gas in his nose despite a silk scarf wrapped across his face. The Wyverns all lay like crumpled toys at his feet, while Narin held back. The Lawbringer – Investigator now – remained halfway up the stairs, waiting for Irato's signal that the breeze had dissipated Enchei's little concoction.

The gas proved stubborn, though, and it was only Irato's goshe Blessings that kept him upright. It felt as though the night's fog had slipped into his mind, a disconcerting glassy sensation as he picked his way through the unconscious fallen. As a Detenii, Irato knew he would have used gas when he broke into houses to dose newborns with Moon's Artifice, but the memories were lost to him, like everything else.

That time before remained a hole, a sucking emptiness at the heart of him. They had assembled fragments and guessed more, but *who* he had once been remained a mystery. To walk in that man's footsteps, however, sent a frisson down Irato's spine – a familiar echo in his bones but nothing more.

He looked left and right. A grey spectral figure stood at either end of the street, motionless and watching him. The city was an inverted woodcut to Irato's eyes, also changed by the goshe doctors. Shades of black and grey were all edged in white, picked out with breathtaking precision that the fog hid nothing of. Instead it only added a strange softness to the sharp white cuts of the city.

The daughters, Irato said to himself. *They're not worried about breathing this gas either, strange that.*

'You going to help?' he said quietly, the sound travelling easily in the still of night.

The one he was looking at nodded at the other, a twitch of the head that sent her sister off into the shadows. That done, she slipped the hood of her cloak back and stepped forward.

'I'll help, she'll watch our backs.'

'So which one are you?'

'You know which is which?'

'Not really,' Irato said, trying to make light of it.

'Then stop asking.'

He snorted. 'Kesh said one of you was a bad-tempered bitch.'

She didn't rise to the bait, instead gathering the pistols from the nearest fallen man. Irato watched her a moment then went to do the same, roughly turning one over to reach his guns. A young man compared to Irato, cheeks dimpled and scarred by some old illness, chest hardly rising as he breathed. He pulled the man's weapons – two pistols, sword and dagger – and moved on to the next, taking the same from that one.

'It will shame them to be sent home without weapons,' his companion commented. 'Father's sure this won't make them seek redress?'

'Dunno,' Irato said. 'He didn't say.'

'You didn't ask?'

'No. He said to take their money too.'

'All of it?'

'Aye – leave 'em their jewellery. Some of it might be family pieces they really won't want to leave without. The rest they can sell for their passage home, but there's no easy way for us to tell the difference.'

Irato rolled another on to his back, a big man with fleshy cheeks and a grazed temple where he'd fallen against the wall. He checked the Wyvern's pulse to ensure he was still alive then gathered his weapons. Arms full he went inside, stepping over the two who'd made it that far. The weapons he dropped in one corner of the back room, stepping aside for the daughter to do the same. From the stairs Narin watched them, looking anxious.

'Have you found the brother? Enchei's got the cousin.'

Irato shook his head and Narin pointed to the pair behind him. 'He's probably one of those two. Warriors like to lead from the front.'

Irato went to look, hauling up the limp body of the younger for Narin to see. 'This the one?'

'I, I'm not sure,' Narin said. 'He looks similar to Kine, but they're all family of some sort. Check his pockets.'

Irato did as instructed, but he found little of use there.

'The collar pocket,' Narin urged, 'Warriors in battle wear name-banners so they might be known to those they fight. Duellists too, I think. They might not have them on show when trying to kill low-caste scum like us, but they've probably got something to declare their family honour.'

'The fucking idiots,' Enchei added, appearing behind Narin. 'I'd write my name-banner really small so I could kill the buggers while they were still reading it.'

Irato pulled a fold of cloth from the small pocket and let it unfold, stitched to the rim of the pocket.

'Looks like they really did come ready for a fight,' he grinned as the name Sir Shonrey Tsudan Wyvern was revealed. 'Shame it didn't help 'em.'

'That's her brother,' Narin confirmed as Enchei headed down the stairs.

'Good.' With one violent jerk Irato snapped the Wyvern's neck and let him fall to the ground.

'Irato!' Narin gasped. 'What in the seven hells have you just done?'

'What?'

'You just murdered him in cold blood.'

'Easiest way.' Irato hesitated. 'We wanted him dead, right?'

'Well, ah, yes but …' Narin floundered for a moment, shocked by what he'd just witnessed. 'I'm a Lawbringer – an Investigator, I mean. You can't just murder people in front of me like that!'

'I should have waited till you were looking the other way?'

'Yes – no! Gods, that's not what I meant at all.'

'Easy up there, Narin,' Enchei said as he searched the dead man's pockets. 'He had to die, you know that.'

'But—'

'But nothing,' Enchei snapped. 'The Emperor's law has no place here, or did you forget? This is a blood feud sanctioned under House Dragon law; your law's trumped. If they'd killed you and Kine then been arrested, you know Lord Vanden would've successfully petitioned for their release. If the Lord Martial caused a fuss, the Lords of Dragon would get involved. A high-caste matter of honour? You can bet all our lives they would be set free – they'd demand it and they're the ones with all the guns round here. No other House would object. Foreigners or not, caste is what matters to those who matter.'

Narin stood resting heavily on the banister, head down. 'And the cousin?' he asked eventually.

'Put up a fight,' Enchei said gravely, 'but given how quick he was and the wounds he took without stopping, I'd have preferred he was unconscious too.' He was quiet a moment before adding, 'This was how it had to end, Narin. I know it goes against the grain, but we've got bigger problems, remember? Put the argument aside, lad, tonight ain't the time.'

That stopped Narin in his tracks. 'Gods on high, is it really as easy as that for you?' he said, aghast. 'You just put things out of your mind for when there's time to be upset or angry or … I don't even know what.'

'Best way to survive.'

'At what price?'

'Bugger the price,' Enchei snapped. 'Dov and Kine, that's all you need in the front of your mind for the moment.'

Narin had no rebuttal for that, though he still looked sick at the latest erosion of his childhood principles. His hand briefly shook as he made his way down the stairs and fumbled at the unconscious Wyvern's arm. Eventually he got a proper grip on it and helped Irato haul it out into the street. Just as they reached the door he jumped as a grey-hooded figure darted through, pistol and sword in hand.

Irato smiled at Narin's alarm, but it soon faded. The Investigator always looked so timid around violence, jolted from his usual self. By contrast, Irato never felt more alive and his mind seemed to wake from its usual slumber at such times.

Might be I envy him that, Irato thought sadly. *Not enough of me left to spread over the hours of the day.*

'Lawbringer's Light,' Narin breathed as he realised the newcomer was one of Enchei's daughters, her face half-hidden from them both.

'Not even close,' she said with a scowl. 'Father, there's one more in the alley. Enay's gone to bring him round.'

Enchei nodded. 'Time to dress the scene a little.' He yanked a long-knife from Irato's various sheaths and made a few shallows slashes across the dead Wyvern's clothing. 'Might need a packing crate dragged over for him to have broken his neck on—'

His planning was caught short by a deep boom echoing out through the night beyond – not a gunshot, but something far larger.

'Was that a cannon?' Narin asked as the four exchanged looks.

'Big bloody cannon if it was,' Enchei said. 'Enay, you hear anything?'

The young woman cocked her head. 'No, nothing close.'

'Come on.'

They ran out into the street, scanning the sky just as a second distant explosion roared out across the city. They looked around, momentarily confused by the echoes coming off the buildings around them, until a voice called down to them. Irato looked up to see the other daughter, Maiss, perched on a rooftop.

'Tier Bridge,' she called softly and pointed.

As one they rounded the inn on the corner and from the empty street they could see down toward the curved struts of the bridge that reached high into the fog-laden sky. The view was far from clear, even to Irato's Starsight Blessing, but he could make out enough at that distance. Clouds of yellow and orange illuminated the stark white of the bridge, the brighter light of flames engulfing one section of the upper tier as a third boom cracked the sky.

'A store of gunpowder?' Narin wondered aloud, only to have Enchei snort derisively at him.

'On the Tier Bridge? No House owns that, no House would store weapons there.'

'What then?'

'A trap, most likely. Pity's light, I don't like this shit. We should get these boys moved over the Dragon District border and make ourselves scarce.'

'I don't understand, what's going on?'

'Think, dammit! Where was the safe-house? Upper tier of the bridge.'

'Gods, you think Rhe is …?'

'Nope, but I'm starting to think we're being dicked around and he could easily be part of it. This can't be a coincidence.'

'Who's caught in the trap, then?' Irato asked, digging his nails into the palm of his hand to try and fight the sensation of his thoughts returning to their normal slumber.

'The one group who, if they were told the location of the safe-house, would march straight up there and kick the door in – confident in their ability to tear apart even a pack of hellhounds.'

'Dragon's Astaren?' Narin answered.

'Aye. Looks like someone decided not to make it a fair fight.'

'Stars of heaven, there must be more than a hundred people who live up there!'

'Not any more,' Enay said darkly.

'So they allowed us to find the safe-house? Oh seven hells, that Banshee. We'd worked out where the house was, but they sent someone to report a sighting yesterday to make sure it was found. She must have been in on it.'

'You're a trusting bunch, for thief-takers.'

'It would have been confirmation of what we knew, why distrust it?'

Enchei nodded. 'And then the Dragons only get told there's a confirmed location so they believe it too. Stupid of 'em, but they're keen to meet any threat with unassailable force so I'm guessing they were happy to wade into whatever sort of fight presents itself.'

'But what does it mean?'

'It means this ain't over.' Enchei grabbed Narin by the arm and pulled him round to look him in the face. 'But we've got tonight's problem to deal with, remember? You and Irato just killed two warrior caste who followed you here. We'll take the rest and dump them in some corner of Dragon without weapons or money. They'll wake with such headaches they can barely move and enough embarrassment they'll catch the first boat home. Without Shonrey and Vosain, they'll slope off with their tails between their legs. The knowledge we could've killed them will be enough incentive there.'

Narin took one final look at the bright glow of flames through the fog and nodded. 'Let's hope so. Gods, I should be running that way.'

'You're not welcome there, the Lawbringers made sure you aren't part of any investigation now, remember?' Enchei nodded towards the bridge. 'And look what happens in your absence.'

'Now you're getting ridiculous,' Narin said, almost laughing at the suggestion. 'Your paranoia's taken over.'

'Mebbe,' he conceded. 'All of a sudden I ain't feeling so paranoid, though. I know they're still out to get me, but mebbe their heart ain't so in it as I thought.'

'What's that supposed to mean?'

Enchei glanced at his daughter and shrugged. 'For once, just once, mebbe things ain't all about me.'

CHAPTER 29

It was well into the night by the time Enchei finally relaxed. A crawling sensation had followed him through the foggy streets as he and his daughters had dragged a handcart of insensate Wyverns. There was a rare anger deep inside his bones, something awakened in the fight with Kine's massive cousin. He could have killed the man silently and quickly, he knew that, but it wasn't just the questions he'd asked the man that had prevented that.

He'd wanted to hurt him, Enchei realised with a start, hurt the man badly. Old scabs had been picked over by the sight of his daughters – these two beautiful strangers in whose faces he saw painful echoes. The man he'd once been, the wife he'd loved and left – even the grandparents who had survived to see his girls born – there were ghosts of all of them hanging in the air. Faint wisps beyond the edges of sight and imagined scents on the breeze.

'I don't know about you two,' he said once they were well clear of Dragon District, 'but I could use a drink.'

Maiss grunted in response, Enay said nothing, so he took that as some form of sulky assent and turned east towards the Fett Canal.

'Come on, I know a quiet place.'

He led them almost to the canal itself before ascending a canopied stairway running up the side of a building that overlooked the canal. The frontage was adorned with red lanterns, gloomy and foreboding in the still white fog. The eatery was shuttered for the night despite the shining lanterns and soft strains of music filtering down from the room above.

Enchei thumped on the door and a few moments later it was jerked open by an oversized Dragon woman with enough earrings and neck-laces for a dozen people. She wore a rich blue coat half-open at the front to display a quite remarkable amount of cleavage, seemingly restrained only by the broad scarf tied high around her waist. She looked them up and down for a moment, reserving a hard look for the girls before speaking.

'Enchei, it's been a while.' Her voice was rich and deep, the accent of a woman brought up in the city but around true Dragon voices most of that time.

'Utrenne,' he replied warmly, 'you're keeping well?'

'No complaints. Who're these two?'

'A pair who've looked me up from the old country, looking for a local contact.'

'They better be,' she said dubiously, her words drawing an exasperated hiss from Enchei.

'Oh piss off, Utrenne – I ever brought that sort o' girl here? 'Specially ones young enough to be my daughters.'

She grunted and stepped back, having to flatten herself against the wall to make enough space for them all. 'Aye, you're right. Just had a few folk recently who didn't know the rules. Came close to a knife in the gut last Ascendancy.'

Enchei smiled. 'I'm sure he regretted his mistake soon enough.'

It wasn't that Utrenne was fat, for all that she indulged her considerable appetite often and frequently, but she was unusually tall and broad of limb. He'd seen men make unfortunate assumptions about her several times, seeing just a fat woman with a blue merchant caste collar.

'It was his whore with the knife!' Utrenne snorted. 'The Gods alone only know why, but she came ta regret events sure.'

She ushered the three inside and closed the door behind them. Enchei pushed a curtain aside to reveal a set of smoky rooms and led his daughters inside, past benches and round tables piled with the remnants of meals and towards the sound of music. The mournful strains of a zither accompanied a young man's voice, the music slow and wistful, while the smell of spiced meat mingled with tobacco smoke in the air. They passed through the main room, where a chestnut-skinned youth was surrounded by an enraptured audience, into the smaller rooms beyond where hanging drapes created booths around the various tables, the light of lanterns set on each table producing a lantern effect.

They soon found a corner where they could have a degree of privacy, the babble from the main room enough to confound idle listeners. Once Enchei had caught the eye of a local woman and gestured for drinks he finally allowed himself to stop and relax, to look his daughters up

263

and down with a refreshed eye. They endured it silently, shedding their cloaks in the warmth of the bar. Maiss watched him suspiciously while Enay kept an eye on those around them, assessing everyone within sight before she allowed herself to settle back into her wicker-backed chair.

'Thank you,' Enchei said at last, for want of another way to start the conversation. 'For earlier. It wasn't your fight, I know.'

'You expected us to sit back and watch?' Maiss tugged her dark hair back and deftly twirled it around before she fixed it with a long pair of pins.

'Doesn't mean I'm not appreciative, all the same.'

'Your thanks is noted,' Enay said acidly as a woman brought them a tall swan-necked bottle and three tumblers.

Enchei poured them each a drink and the girls took their glasses dubiously. Enay held hers up to the light and inspected the contents, a clear liquid with silvery swirls running through it. 'Moon's water?'

Enchei nodded as he fished a slim leather cigar case from an inside pocket. 'Had it before?'

'Never been this far west before,' Maiss said in reply.

'Well it's an acquired taste, but it goes well with a smoke and quiet music so it's the drink of choice here.'

Enay reached over the table and plucked the cigar from Enchei's fingers just as he pulled it from the case. 'Best we get the full experience then.'

Enchei raised an eyebrow but the young woman ignored him and opened the lantern to light it from the flame. Eventually he did the same, Maiss declining the offer of one, and raised his glass to them in toast.

'Your mother,' he whispered.

Maiss drank, but Enay's eyes flashed with anger. 'You left. You don't get to make that toast.'

'You know I had to leave,' he said calmly, 'and you know it was the only way. Didn't stop me loving her. Didn't stop me missing all of you. This is the first time I've been able to toast any of you aloud – first time in almost twenty years. Please, give me that at least.'

Her lips went tight, but eventually Enay relented and raised the glass herself. She took a long drink, frowning slightly at the chill taste as most did when they drank moon's water for the first time. It had a subtle, elusive flavour that seemed to turn cool on the tongue, quite opposite to the warmth of something like whisky.

'You sold the estate?'

Maiss nodded. 'Not really a neighbourhood we could spend our years in, was it? Too many sharp ears and sharp eyes, but Uncle helped us get a fair price.'

'We have a house in Oredenast, overlooking the Sourwater, and a small gaming house out on the water itself.'

Enchei pictured the place, a busy city in the lands of House Clearlake. It was an important trading hub, but best known for the series of lakes built in ancient times. It gave much of the city a relaxed, open air quite unlike the cramped, sometimes frenetic, streets of the Imperial City, and attracted artists and gamblers alike to its many pleasures. A good place to get lost in but also a good place to have a home, if you had the money to afford it.

'Gaming house?'

'Named in your honour,' Enay said through a cloud of cigar smoke.

'Oh Gods,' Enchei said with trepidation. 'Do I even want to know?'

'The Cards of the Broken.'

'You're fucking joking,' he snarled, leaning forward. 'Are you bloody mad?'

To his astonishment, the young woman's face dissolved into laughter and even Maiss smiled at his reaction.

'Of course she's joking,' Maiss reassured him. 'We're not idiots, Father!'

Enchei hesitated. 'Right, ah yes. How did you even know about that, anyway?'

'Uncle told us,' she said with a slow blink of her deep blue eyes. 'He said we deserved to know a little about you and what you'd done.'

'For one o' the Five he talks too bloody much, on top of the fact he dragged you two into this mess here.'

'He only told us a little, no real details, and better us to back you up than official Astaren, no? We've done unofficial work for him before, makes his patronage feel less like charity'

Enchei grunted and took a long drink, wondering how much of his career he would like anyone to know, not least his last remaining family. 'Did he make it sound good?'

'He made you out a hero,' Maiss said as Enay nodded, still smiling. The sight jolted him like a spark leaping from the fire.

'Stars in heaven,' he gasped, chest momentarily tight, 'those smiles ... Gods I've missed that. You've both grown up beautiful, but those are still the smiles of the little girls I remember.'

Maiss lowered her eyes, the glint of tears forming, while Enay scooped up her glass and drained it, looking away.

'Let's not get into the past,' Maiss whispered. 'Not here, not now. The present's hard enough, can't the past wait a few days?'

'However long you want,' Enchei said, reaching out to squeeze first her hand, then Enay's. The green-eyed woman tensed under his touch, but didn't yank her hand away.

'Seeing you two again has been a gift I never let myself truly hope for. It would've hurt too much if I'd kept that hope in me over the years. Seeing those smiles, I can't tell you what it means, but I'll be glad of whatever more time I get with you.'

Enay nodded. 'In that case, let's start with another drink.'

'It's done?'

Narin nodded as he stamped his feet, trying to force some warmth back into his toes. It hadn't been a long walk back to the house, but he'd taken an oblique route to pass through Enchei's cluster of spirit traps – Irato trailing along behind as normal.

'We weren't the only ones having a busy night either,' he said, peeling off layers in the warm kitchen before he sat at the table with Kesh and Kine. He rubbed his fingers as hard as he could, but they remained cold to the touch and his grizzling daughter didn't seem to appreciate his affection.

Kesh frowned at him. 'Who?'

'House Dragon.' He poured himself a cup of cloudy green tea and hungrily sucked the warm liquid down. 'Our hellhound mercenaries too. You didn't hear it?'

The pair shook their heads, Kine nodding down at Dov. 'This one's been howling for an hour or more. She's only just settled.'

'Guess you can't see the bridge from any windows here, either,' Narin said. 'Some sort of ambush, I assume – explosions on the Tier Bridge right where the mercenary safe-house was supposed to be. Enchei reckons the Dragons tried to take it and the mercenaries were waiting for them.'

'You don't know?'

He shook his head. 'All guesswork, but … you know. Hah, Enchei's particular form of arrogance must be rubbing off on me. Whenever something as bad as that happens, it's hard to doubt it has nothing to do with the shit we're in. It ain't bad luck or coincidence when everyone's out to get you.'

'Why didn't you go investigate?'

'I'm suspended from duty,' Narin said with a forced smile, made rather manic by fatigue. He gestured to his hip. 'Look, no sword. Can't be trusted with something as dangerous as that these days.' He sighed. 'Demoted and suspended, so the last thing I should be doing is showing up at a scene when I know Rhe'll be along soon.'

'Does this mean it's almost over?' Kine asked, her voice more sceptical than hopeful. 'For all of us?'

'Who knows? Your cousin's dead, your brother too. The rest of the Wyverns won't want to find us again, not after the way we left them. That's as much as I know at the moment.'

Kine's mouth fell open and Narin cursed himself for delivering the news so carelessly.

'I'm sorry, that was …' He tailed off as Kine shook her head and looked away.

She had never spoken of her brother except in passing and he knew they were not close, but still. He was family and she had effectively marked him out for death. Knowing it might happen, knowing he wanted to kill her and everything else about it, didn't stop Kine being a gentle soul. To be so involved in a man's death was a shock and Narin knew he should have realised that ahead of time.

The noblewoman bent over their daughter, kissing Dov once on the forehead before whispering a prayer for the dead. 'Lady Sailor carry them to rest, Lord Lawbringer protect them.'

Narin blinked at the mention of Lawbringer a moment before realising the Ascendants she invoked were both of the Dragon hegemony. Elsewhere the heritage would not matter, but he suspected proud Wyvern warriors would want to be attended by their own, even in death.

'Don't tell me Enchei failed to give an opinion for once,' Kesh said once Kine had finished.

'He's suspicious,' Narin agreed. 'Of everyone and everything. It's too soon to say what's true, but I don't think we need to be watching out for Wyverns any longer.'

'Then I must face my own punishment,' Kine said gravely. 'I will go to Prince Sorote in the morning and wait upon his command.'

'Go yourself?' Narin asked, startled. 'Why? I can go to him, ask when he wants you to present yourself. There's no need to trek over there with Dov and simply wait.'

'My husband will not wait to see me marked with the lash and my caste tattoo struck out,' Kine said, 'and I will give him no excuse to break his agreement. It will serve as an act of contrition on my part, to await their leisure. They do not know where we are, getting a message to us via the Palace of Law could easily mean a day's delay in me appearing before him.'

'So you're just going to—'

He didn't go any further as Kesh broke in. 'Shut up, Narin, she's right.'

'What the hell do you know about it?'

Kesh raised an eyebrow at him. 'I've seen enough to know a few things about men and their bloody pride. If Lord Vanden's forced to wait a day, he could easily take offence and renegotiate the deal. So let's make it fifty lashes, or he takes Dov to be raised as a labourer on some Wyvern farm. Whatever angry little thought crosses his mind, do you think your Imperial friend will bother to put up much of a fight?'

Narin found himself frozen on the all-too-easily imagined possibilities. The longer he knew Prince Sorote, the less he trusted the Imperial to show any shred of humanity except when it served a purpose. For a moment he made no response, but at last he nodded and lowered his head.

'In the morning then. Your remaining family'll be waking up with headaches so bad they won't be watching the streets for you. Getting to the Imperial Palace should be simple enough at least.'

He studied Kine for a long moment, the unusual sight of grim determination on her face giving him pause. Already she was adapting to life outside the strictures of Dragon and Wyvern society – she would never have allowed herself to look at a man in so challenging a way before. Kine would have trained for adulthood just as carefully as Siresse Myken, every gesture and word as perfectly timed as any warrior's, to negotiate the male-dominated nation around her. Her beauty and charm requiring the same deft use, the same balance and subtlety a duellist needed to succeed. You did not face a proud Wyvern warrior down, you manoeuvred around him with eyes averted as though he was a dog ready to snap.

Or maybe this is just how she deals with low castes like me, Narin joked privately.

'Time for some sleep, then,' Kesh announced, pushing up from the table just as Irato thumped on the door to be let in. 'There's a long day ahead.'

CHAPTER 30

Senior Kobelt Geret Hoke woke and blinked up at the incantations that adorned the ceiling above. He slowly rose and lifted his hands, staring at the aged, bronze skin for a while before smiling. There was a tattoo on the palm of each hand, twisted symbols worn only by shamans of House Gold.

'Good,' he said in a soft voice. 'This will serve.'

He rose and dressed, the movements awkward at first as though he were unfamiliar with the body he wore. As he pulled on his heavy robe there came a knock at the door.

'Father, are you awake?'

'Father? Ah yes,' Geret muttered under his breath, searching his memory before a tight smile appeared on his lips. He reached to open the door. 'Ulesh. Yes, here I am.'

There was a younger man on the other side, looking anxious. Also House Gold, his long blond hair hung loose over his tattooed cheeks. 'Something's happened.'

'What?'

'The wardings, several shattered in the night.'

'Do you know how?'

The man shook his head. 'The acolytes swear no one has been up there – I checked the central shrine, it's intact. It was no demon, but something passed this way in the night.'

'Is anyone hurt?'

'No, but—'

'If it's just a few wardings, I suggest you don't worry.'

That seemed to startle the younger man. 'Not worry? Are ... what's wrong, Father? You look strange?'

'Strange?'

'There's something different about you this morning,' the man insisted. 'What is it?'

Geret smiled and shook his head. 'Merely a recent awakening. Ulesh, my son, come here.' He ushered him into the room and stood with one hand on his shoulder.

'What's happened? You sound different too.'

'I will explain,' Geret said, the smile never leaving his face. He took his son's face in his hands. 'It is like this.'

Before either of them could speak again Geret slid his left hand around the back of Ulesh's neck and punched the man in the throat. Ulesh stumbled back, half-falling but for the grip his father had on him. Geret let the flailing man down to the ground and pushed his knee into his throat. Now Ulesh tried to fight him properly, tearing at Geret's arms but the older Kobelt put all his weight on to his knee and something gave under the pressure.

Ulesh's strength lessened, he pawed weakly at his father's leg but could do nothing but give a strangled squawk before slowly succumbing. His hands fell limp. Geret held him there a little longer, making certain Ulesh was dead before standing and dragging the body towards the bed.

'A shame you had to notice something was different,' Geret commented as he shoved the body under the bed and draped the blanket over it so it wasn't visible. 'But perhaps you'd have needed to die anyway. Your father's memories say you'd notice the ritual I'm planning wasn't right. Best you die quietly here.'

With that, Geret left the room and headed for the acolytes' dormitory. He was met in the corridor by a fat, bald man who was sweating profusely – fear and exertion combined.

'Master Hoke!'

'I know, I know – the wardings.'

'What is it? What do we do?' the fat man pleaded.

'It's an attack,' Geret said briskly, 'the summoner has turned on us. Get everyone up to the shrines, there is an old ritual I know – a broken summoning that will pry the hellhounds from the summoner's control.'

'Where's Ulesh?'

'I've given him a mission I can entrust to no other. Don't worry about him; we're *all* in danger right now. We must realign the shrines, move every chain and charm there is. We have no time to waste – go fetch all the Kobelen and acolytes, now!'

'Yes Master Hoke.'

The fat man turned and ran back the other way, shouting almost incoherently the names of various Kobelen. Geret watched him go and allowed himself a small, secret smile.

'So Priest, you had best be ready,' he said to the empty corridor. 'You want mayhem in the city and House Eagle always delivers on its side of a bargain.'

A cold winter sun worried at the last of the morning mist as they set off for the Imperial Palace. Kesh had hired a large curtained litter for Kine, Dov and Narin to travel anonymously in, four massive bearers taking their weight with practised ease. Kesh herself was happy to play the role of servant trailing along behind while Myken, in a plain green jacket, acted as a mercenary bodyguard alongside the litter. There were enough rich merchants and factors who travelled in such a fashion that they drew no interest on the Public Thoroughfare, and once they reached the Tier Bridge there was more to look at than passers-by.

Kesh moved closer to the litter and leaned in so she could talk quietly to Kine and Narin. 'We're reaching the bridge; looks like most people are stopping to stare. It might take us a while to cross.'

'How bad is is?'

She could hear Narin shift slightly to try and peer out through the folds of cloth that hid them, but there was little room to move.

'Hard to say. There's smoke still coming from some of the buildings on the upper tier, and even the struts look flame scorched.'

'Gods,' Narin breathed. 'There have been fires on it before, but the structure's always been untouched.'

'There are Investigators blocking the path to the top, ah – House Dragon soldiers too. Two dozen of them maybe and they don't look so happy.'

'If it was an ambush as we suspect,' Myken added, 'they will be in panic. Lord Omteray will try to lock the whole tier down and recover the bodies.'

'Which Rhe won't like so much, he'll see it as a crime to be investigated.'

'If Rhe is there,' Myken said gravely, 'he will fight a duel by the end of the day. Every warrior caste knows they must consider the bodies of Astaren to be sacred, so they will not allow any Lawbringer to remove anything. Let alone take instructions from a son of Brightlance.'

'Which always goes down well with Rhe,' Narin muttered. 'Bloody Eagles and Dragons, always looking for an excuse.'

'We're taught from an early age that they are the enemy,' Myken said, sounding pointed but not defensive, 'just as we are taught they see us the same way. In times of peace, it's only ever a matter of time before we're at war again.'

Narin growled from within the litter. 'If you seek war, make sure a large chunk of the population isn't allowed to do anything but prepare for war.'

'Narin,' Kine broke in, 'perhaps now isn't the time for an argument about a thousand years of the caste system?'

Kesh smiled as Narin muttered an apology, but returned her attention to the bridge as they shuffled forward behind a slow column of traffic. Myken made her way around to the front and used her presence to part the tide, speeding them up a touch until they came up behind another litter and couldn't work their way around it.

From beneath there was little to see of the upper tier; a concave ceiling forty yards above their heads, patchily grey after millennia of enduring the wind sweeping off the sea but bearing no sign of the firestorm that had been unleashed above it. They made better time across the main body of the bridge and soon were out in the bright sunlight again.

Kesh craned her head around to look back at the other end of the upper tier and gasped. 'Stars above, the buildings are gone.'

'Completely?' Narin demanded.

'There's just rubble,' she confirmed, 'I can't see – wait, there's one. Maybe the nearest two or three buildings each side are destroyed. This end's been levelled, there's nothing taller than a child standing.'

'There's smoke rising from further in,' Myken added from the front of the litter. 'Something burns there still.'

'But the nearer ones are destroyed? How much gunpowder would it take to do that?'

'More than a few barrels, more than anyone would store there. It seems your friend was right.'

'Why?'

'The power needed to erase those buildings,' Myken explained, 'is more than an accident. But if you're setting a trap, you have one bomb to make your enemy fall back and a second to catch them in retreat. They draw together to regroup and re-evaluate, making themselves more vulnerable.'

'I didn't think Dragon soldiers ever ran away,' Narin said.

'Not fearing death is different to welcoming it,' Myken replied. 'Victory is the greatest virtue, one you cannot achieve while dead. If they discovered the enemy was waiting for them or more powerful than expected, falling back before they were too deep in the hole makes perfect sense. It's not as though there was anywhere for their prey to flee to, so they thought they had time to reassess their attack.'

'And didn't that work out well for them. Or us, come to think of it – if that's the biggest threat to them gone, the hounds will be bolder than ever.'

'It's Enchei's problem for the moment,' Kesh declared as the pace picked up once more. 'Today we finish with our other situation, put the whole thing behind us.'

'Let us hope so,' Kine said in a quiet voice.

Kesh's heart went out to her as she heard the noblewoman's attempt to control her apprehension. It was not just the stroke of the lash she would endure today, but the painful erasing of her tattoos too – quite aside from, most likely, the bitter anger of her husband. Kesh could hardly comprehend the stilted, formal world of a noble-caste woman, but it was clear enough that honour and decorum were powerful forces for those who lived in it. Status and a position within society were intrinsic to such a life, so this rare lowering of caste would cut as surely as the lash.

Once on the Imperial Island they continued north, up the grand boulevard of Knight's Path Avenue until the road branched and they turned right towards the Imperial Palace. At that hour, traffic was light, but Myken was careful to direct the bearers well clear of any other litters – affording those of higher status a careful measure of respect. While she wore red on her collar, Myken was dressed as a mercenary still, so any liveried House soldier would consider her inferior and Kesh could see the Siresse had no intention of letting carelessness delay them.

The Sun Avenue comprised the last stretch; a wide road that led directly to the Hundred Houses, the ornate tower-like structure standing on a hundred pillars that marked the entrance to the Imperial Palace. Flanking the Sun Avenue were the grandest temples in the city – huge structures devoted to the six Greater Gods and Goddesses, each flanked in turn by small temples of their five subordinate Ascendants, but all dominated by the vast Imperial Palace ahead.

As they passed the first pair of temples, Kesh found old instincts turning her head right to look towards that of Lady Jester's. All the greater temples were six-sided buildings of white stone walls, with friezes set between tall windows and topped by two levels of black-tiled roofs. At the very centre of the upper roof was a cornea-like glass disc five yards across through which the light of their god would be focused on the altar below.

Despite the magnificence of a building that Kesh rarely saw, having grown up believing low castes were not allowed on this avenue, her gaze went to the smaller temples flanking it, their sharp spires rising like upraised spears. From where they walked, the temples of Lords Cripple and Duellist were closest to the road but, as they continued on, Kesh could see the spire of Lady Chance rising behind Cripple's.

Look down on your sister, Kesh thought, finding her lost piety slip on again like a favourite coat. *Lady Chance, favour her – bless little Dov and see her safe. She deserves none of this. Lapsed I may be, but I will teach her every prayer to her namesake Ascendant if I live to hear her speak – I swear it on Emari's memory.*

Kesh blinked hard, feeling tears threaten at the reminder of her lost sister, and returned her attention to the litter until they were past. There was a hushed reverence on the avenue as they continued down it, Lord Knight's temple on their left, Lady Shaman's on the right, before finally they passed between those of the God-Emperor and God-Empress. They headed though the Gate of the Sun, a pair of eighty-foot-high ruined pillars that had until the Ten Day War served as the entrance to the palace, before finally leaving the litter at the Hundred Houses and continuing on foot.

Despite their wariness of being seen in public, the cold ensured most people wore hoods or fur hats along with heavy winter coats. There were plenty of lower castes in anonymous clothing to blend into. Even the unusual sight of the swaddled and sleeping Dov nestled in a sling across Narin's chest was barely noticeable to those not paying close attention.

Narin and Kesh led the way through the trading district that had flourished around the palace's great towers. Kesh knew they would end up at the Glass Tower, a wonder she would have been childishly eager to witness under different circumstances, but Narin took them to the Office of the Catacombs. First they had to find Prince Sorote and then, no doubt, a message would be sent to Lord Vanden.

Their pace was slow, but Kine would accept no assistance and had no intention of arriving in a manner permitted only to high castes. By the time they reached the curious, isolated building that seemed to serve as Prince Sorote's offices, Kine's teeth were gritted in discomfort and her feet shuffled along the snow-carpeted ground. Still she made no complaint and waited in silence as Narin hammered his fist against the door.

After a pause, they heard the sound of boots on flagstones and the door was opened a shade to reveal the bald head of a servant of Prince Sorote's.

'Investigator Narin,' the man acknowledged cautiously, inspecting Narin's companions in turn and bowing to Kine after a moment's hesitation. 'My Lady Wyvern, Siresse,' he said rather more formally, before adding, 'Mistress,' as an after-thought to Kesh.

She pursed her lips and left matters up to Narin, not wanting to reply to an off-hand greeting, while the two high castes were not expected to greet a servant.

'Ah, Hentern, is it?' Narin hazarded.

'Indeed, Investigator,' the servant replied in a flat tone. 'You honour me by remembering. I shall summon Prince Sorote.'

He made to close the door again but Myken reached out and slapped a flat palm against the wood, stopping it dead. 'Fetch your master,' she said sternly, 'but my Lady must sit. You do not want to impede us.'

Hentern hesitated a moment then stepped back, recognising the cold certainty in the warrior's voice. 'Of course, Siresse. Please, enter, and ensure my Lady Wyvern is comfortable.'

Kesh and Narin stepped aside while Kine shuffled forward and, assisted by Myken, eased herself down into the nearest armchair. The room was chilly and dim – the building's high windows admitted precious little of the winter sun while the stove was clearly recently lit. There was no one else in the room, but one of the reinforced cellar doors that stood at an angle on the far wall was open. Weak lamplight shone up the steep steps, illuminating only a turning flight that led underground.

There was an uncomfortable expression on Hentern's face as the door closed behind Narin and he pulled a chair over to beside Kine's, sitting as gently as he could. All Kesh could see of Dov was the top of the baby's head, but from the complete silence it seemed as if she was happily asleep.

'I ... Might I offer you refreshment, my Lady?'

'Don't you have to fetch your master?' Myken demanded.

'He is coming, he sent me ahead to light the stove.'

'But still you were about to fetch him,' Myken pressed, 'with the door shut too. He's downstairs somewhere? Just how far do the cellars extend here? Is there a tunnel all the way from Prince Sorote's palazzo?'

'I am not permitted to leave outsiders alone in here, Siresse.'

Myken took a step towards one of the nearer desks then looked up at the mezzanine above the cellar doors, where a beautifully crafted desk stood beneath a pile of papers and books. 'Nor are you able to prevent a warrior caste from investigating anything she chooses,' she pointed out, indicating Sorote's desk, 'so perhaps fetching your master would still be the best use of your time.'

Hentern's anxiety deepened, but he only spoke when she took a pointed step towards the stairs leading up to the mezzanine. 'Siresse, I beg you ...'

'Don't worry,' Myken said, turning back towards Kine, 'I only read when I am bored. Be back soon and these papers will remain untouched – on my *honour*.'

At Myken's emphasis on the final word, Hentern's expression turned pathetically grateful and he bobbed a small bow before heading back towards the cellar. The scuff of his feet on stone steps echoed up to them for a surprisingly long time and then there was only quiet. Keen to evict the cold, Kesh went to feed more coal into the stove and stoke the flames, but once that was done she found herself in the middle of the room, eyes drawn to the open works on the nearest desk.

'Kesh, I have given my word,' Myken warned.

'I know, I know,' Kesh grumbled, glancing over to the cellar door. 'You didn't say anything about what's down there, though.'

'For pity's sake, Kesh,' Narin said, 'now isn't the time to anger Prince Sorote!'

'When you're the lord of me,' she replied, 'you get to give orders like that. I've been the good little servant caste enough recently, but your friend's been holding out on you more than a little.'

'Not my friend,' Narin said. 'Just a relation of the Emperor's with the power to destroy my life.'

She shrugged. 'Just want to see what's down there, whether it leads to a tunnel or something more.'

'Please, Kesh!'

She ignored him, suddenly gripped by a fierce desire to see past the few steps she could make out. Narin hissed angrily after her but she padded forward and peered through the open door at the stairway beyond it. There was little of anything to see, just well-worn cut stone with a groove hacked into the inside wall for a handhold.

Feeling like a child, Kesh took a tentative few steps down, moving as quietly as she could manage. The stair turned back on itself before opening out on to an empty room that bore only a lantern hanging over a high peaked doorway. She crept through that and found more steps that branched left and right. It was darker down there, the only light coming from the lantern above her head, but the left-hand path seemed to continue down and open out into some larger space while the right levelled out into a tunnel of some sort.

She took a step forward, craning her head to peer over a short balustrade that the left-hand stair stretched around. Kesh blinked once, twice, to try and make out anything in the not-quite blackness below, but before she could a hand grabbed her by the bicep and hauled her back.

On instinct Kesh twisted and punched up at the arm holding her. She felt a lurch sideways as she was dragged off-balance, but delivered a second blow with greater intent and managed to dislodge her attacker's grip. In the gloom she couldn't make out who she'd struck before a heavy kick to her ribs slammed Kesh into the smooth stone wall. She dropped down, ignoring the pain, and stamped back towards her attacker's shin, catching them a glancing blow. Throwing herself sideways she avoided a second kick and came up with dagger in hand, but before she could find a target a stinging blow smashed it from her hand and in the next moment she'd been slammed against another wall, cracking her head against the stone.

As the stars before her eyes slowly cleared, Kesh realised there was a sword-edge at her throat and she froze. Eventually the rest came into focus and she realised it was Prince Kashte holding the weapon. The Imperial's face was more alive than she'd seen it before, a dangerous glitter to his eyes that told her his blood was up.

'So we meet again,' Kashte said in a husky growl. 'I should kill you for striking an Imperial caste.'

'But you would die in the next moment,' called a voice from behind him.

Kesh saw his jaw tense before sense took over and Kashte eased the pair of them slowly around enough to see Myken standing on the stairs with a levelled pistol.

'You sure you'd make that shot before I opened her throat, Siresse?' Kashte said, voice tight as he tried to restrain his fighting instincts.

'No,' she replied simply, 'but I would not fire unless you harmed her. She struck an Imperial caste, yes, but she believed she was being attacked and did not hesitate to defend herself. That instinct I honour as a warrior.'

'She's just a servant caste.'

'Nonetheless – she has a warrior's soul,' Myken continued, much to Kesh's surprise. 'She stands beside her friend Narin despite knowing all those she faces will have either superior weapons or training, mostly likely outmatching her in every way. Still she has shown no fear at the prospect and so I stand at her side as any warrior should.'

Kashte grinned wolfishly. 'Then I should honour it too,' he said in a slightly forced way, releasing Kesh and stepping back. 'Mistress Kesh, best you take greater care in future. It is most unsafe in these tunnels.'

Kesh stepped back and waited until Myken had holstered her gun again. 'So it seems,' she said quietly. 'Is that why the door's reinforced from the outside? Because of what lurks down here in the darkness?'

'I mean there are disused tunnels and crumbling stairs,' Kashte said, 'all unsafe in the darkness. You don't believe in children's tales, do you?'

'Which ones? The ones I was told growing up in the Harbour Warrant were about ancient gods and demons living in the deepest parts of the sea. You might say those got confirmed by the highest authority, so I'd believe anything you had to tell me about this place.'

'Growing up in the palace, I heard different stories,' Kashte said dismissively. 'I had thought they were better known than they clearly are.'

'Something about your catacombs?'

'Something, yes.'

Before Kesh could ask him anything more a voice came echoing from the tunnel. 'Telling tales of horror, Kashte?'

The three of them turned to see the faintly smiling Prince Sorote emerge from the gloom, dressed as soberly as ever with a strangely academic-looking cape over plain tailored clothes. Close on his heel was Hentern, doing his best to contain his anxiety, but if Sorote was angry at any of them he betrayed no trace of it. What did strike Kesh as surprising, however, was the fact that while his clothing was far less expensive and flamboyant than Kashte's – who was the perfect image of the rakish noble warrior – both carried a pair of pistols in ornate sheaths.

When she had first encountered Sorote back in the summer, he had obviously been a high caste from the House of the Sun and, following tradition, had carried only a rapier on the streets of the city. The rapier remained on his hip; she could see the gold detailing on pommel and guard glinting in the lamplight.

What's changed since then? she wondered as she knelt to the high caste, hands folded over her chest. *Are more Imperials flouting tradition these days the way Kashte does, or do you prefer a gun to hand in these tunnels?*

Neither possibility was comforting, but as Prince Sorote joined them he seemed in no great hurry to escape up to the surface.

'I was just delivering a warning,' Kashte replied as Myken bowed to the Imperial and received a nod in reply. 'These ancient parts of the palace are not for the idly curious.'

'Indeed not, as treacherous as they are convenient,' Sorote said, looking fixedly at Kesh. 'Now your curiosity regarding our cellar has been sated, however, shall we return to the plane of the living?'

Kesh frowned at his choice of phrasing, but didn't hesitate to follow the man's directions. She trooped up the stairs after Myken, ignoring Narin's furious look and moving well to the side to let the high castes perform their own greetings.

'Prince Sorote,' Narin began, 'I apologise for—'

The Imperial held up a hand to stop him. 'It is done and it was not your fault, Investigator. The tunnel is no great secret; I merely choose not to advertise something that might one day be useful if it is unknown.'

Ignoring the hands reaching for her, Kine pushed herself up out of her seat and curtseyed as best she could. 'My Lord Sun,' she said in a breathless voice, 'I am honoured to be in your debt.'

'My Lady Wyvern,' Sorote replied formally, 'please, do not rise – sit. I realise you must be in discomfort so soon after giving birth. This is the child, I assume?'

'Indeed, my Lord,' she said as Narin turned slightly to afford him a view of Dov's face. 'Dov Deshar, born of the House of the Sun.'

'Certainly by the time we are finished with her,' Sorote added. 'She is healthy?'

'She is, my Lord.'

Sorote gave a curt nod of approval, one that made Kesh think he cared nothing for Dov but wanted to be sure his own efforts were not wasted on a sickly child.

'In that case, let us be off.'

'Off?' Narin echoed.

'Lord Vanden will not be gracing us with his presence,' Sorote explained. 'His steward shall serve witness in his place. The Lord Vanden feels attending will be a waste of his valuable time and has important matters of betrothal to attend to. Matters await us at the Glass Tower.'

'Steward Breven is at the Glass Tower already?' Narin shared a puzzled glance with Kine.

Sorote hesitated. 'I see you didn't, in fact, receive the message sent to you at the Palace of Law. I had wondered at your alacrity given your suspension.'

'I've not been back yet,' Narin confirmed, 'nor home, but Kine wanted to wait upon your leisure.'

'Of course she did,' Sorote said with a small bow to Kine. 'Please ensure, my Lady, that your daughter learns a sense of propriety from your good self. Her father occasionally displays a certain lack.'

Narin scowled. 'Have you been comparing notes with Lawbringer Rhe, my Lord?'

The twitch of a smile on Sorote's lips was the only response he received, but it was enough.

'In any case, Steward Breven waits upon my leisure with a sanctioned tattooist close to the Glass Tower. If you are able, my Lady, we will go directly there and ensure this matter is put to a close as swiftly as possible.'

'I am,' Kine confirmed.

'Excellent. Given the events I hear took place on the bridge last night, I'm sure the next few days will bring some measure of excitement to the city. By star's turn I'm sure this whole situation will be forgotten and we can all go about our lives in peace.'

Kesh watched the man with a mounting level of distrust. She expected high castes such as Sorote to be dispassionate, but he seemed to be enjoying the play of events just a little too much for her liking. But if anyone else felt the same, they had the sense to keep quiet and as a group they headed back out into the chill morning air for the short walk to the looming Glass Tower.

CHAPTER 31

Lawbringer Rhe nudged what had once been a wooden beam with his boot. Now it was merely a sculpture in ash. The fire that had consumed it had been so quick and hot that there had been no time for it to crumble. Under his touch the ash fell away and collapsed into nothing, merging with the heaps that were slowly being carried away by the sea wind.

'How did it burn so hot?' Law Master Sheven commented from nearby, joining Rhe within the shattered remains of a house. 'In the freezing cold of winter?'

'The wind drove it,' Rhe said, looking out through the curved, soot-scarred struts of the bridge to the white peaks of the sea beyond, 'but this wasn't natural. Remember the goshe firepowder?'

'I wish I could forget,' the aging Law Master said sourly. 'Barrels of the stuff?'

Though his head was bald and his long beard white, the burly senior Lawbringer was an able fighter still. He and his brutal scimitar had led the assault on the goshe island alongside Rhe in the summer, and Sheven himself had been scorched by the goshe weapons.

'There were explosions reported,' Rhe said by way of agreement, 'and the goshe used their firepowder to burn the bodies of their dead in the days beforehand. It burned hot enough to hide the enhancements they had made to the bodies of their soldiers, the Blessings they had granted themselves.'

He gestured around at the scene of utter devastation; that entire end of the upper tier a flattened wasteland. Some part of Rhe wanted to see movement, some phoenix rising from these ashes and shaking off the horror done there, but none did. The Dragon soldiers had picked it through and removed some bodies, but no survivors. Not even their Astaren remained. Some perhaps had escaped – if anyone

281

could survive a fall of hundreds of feet it was an Astaren warrior-mage in battle armour – but Rhe had heard no reports of anyone rising from the shores of the Crescent.

'How many died here?' Sheven asked, aghast at the idea.

Rhe shook his head. 'We may never know. Scores of innocents I'm sure, but I doubt even the Imperial rent collectors have much more than an idea of how many people lived in these houses. Witnesses speak of a dozen Stone Dragons and beings of flame too. Whether those were allies of the Dragons or hellhounds I cannot say, but no living were taken from this place. The remains of the Astaren have been removed by Dragon soldiers, battered and burned beyond recognition. I doubt there will be remains of anyone not in armour left, after this heat.'

A gust of wind spun up around them and a funnel of ash rose from the uneven ground. Rhe closed his eyes as the still-warm ashes swept over his face, coating his white Lawbringer's coat in all that was left of the homes and bodies. Once it had subsided he looked down at himself.

'I am become an Investigator again,' he said without humour.

Sheven grunted, rusty-red skin tinted grey, and brushed at his clothes. 'And I am become Ghost,' said the man of House Salamander. 'We are both brought low by this.'

Rhe found himself unable to reply. *Only one of us is brought low,* he thought. *Your skin can be brushed clean. I am not so sure of my soul.*

'Is this an end to it?' Sheven continued after a while.

'I suspect not,' Rhe said. 'This was a deliberate act. To scour this place so utterly, the master of these hellhounds must have known the Dragons were coming – must have gathered the weapons to deal with them. In that case the attacks will continue unfettered until this city becomes overrun with Dragon Astaren and then …'

Sheven sighed, knowing only too well how the sentence ended. 'And then we shall witness savagery not seen on the streets of the Imperial City for five hundred years.'

'Unless this is the first blow of war.'

Sheven looked startled at the idea. 'You think this might have been engineered by your kin?'

'There is no trace of them that I have seen, and yet I still wonder,' Rhe admitted. 'We all know war is looming – why not prelude that with atrocities to diminish the numbers of your enemy's Astaren?'

'And the deaths until now were merely senseless killings designed to draw the Dragons out?'

Rhe thought of Administrator Serril, dead in his office, and shook his head.

Enchei Jen, where do you fit in here? Are you the phoenix that rises from these ashes? Is this part of some long-running plot of yours, a plot of many threads and planned over years? House Dragon and House Wyvern, what have you involved yourself in and why? Or have your masters truly come for you and simply knew they would come into conflict with House Dragon in the process?

'Perhaps not,' he said at last. 'Perhaps it is another House and a different agenda entirely. I doubt we'll ever know.'

'What will you do, then?' Sheven asked. 'How do we investigate crimes we're not permitted to even understand? If this is all an Astaren game, how do we track down this summoner of hellhounds?'

'I don't know, but I must try. This is the Emperor's city and *his* law will rule its streets. *His* citizens have been murdered and if there is anyone to answer for it, they must.'

'And now you do it alone, with Narin demoted and suspended.' Sheven shook his head. 'A Wyvern noblewoman of all things? What was he thinking? He's lucky to be alive.'

'Narin is fortunate in his friends,' Rhe said coldly. 'How far he chooses to stretch that remains to be seen.'

Inside the Glass Tower, the passage of a cloud across the low sun was a strange, elusive thing. Light and shade seemed to slip at random across every surface, cracked walls running contrary to the million fractures of ceiling. Narin had not been the only one to gape as they entered the lowest level of the tower and from there it had only got more astonishing.

They ascended in a brass cage operated by four burly labourers turning a massive crank on the ground floor, glimpsing a different sight through the tall, narrow doorways at each level. Long banks of copyists and clerks laboured on several levels, while one was mostly filled by an incomprehensible intertwining sculpture made of the same fractured glass as the floors and walls.

Slowly they arrived at their destination where a tall, shaven-headed young Imperial stood on guard at the doorway. Dressed immaculately in white and gold, he would not have looked out of place at a formal ball, but he carried a broadsword on his hip and pistols across his stomach. Even more telling, as the man stepped aside for them, Narin

283

saw a pair of long, ragged scars down the side of his head – signs of an injury that must have come close to killing the man.

There was something of a delay as the newcomers were forced to bow or kneel to the man, despite the fact he was clearly there to serve as a guard, but eventually they found themselves in a large barely-furnished room, just a single table – where a tattooist's tools were laid out – and a pair of chairs made for giants out of the fractured glass. Narin found himself reluctant to even walk on the cracked glass that comprised the tower interior, but he kept dutifully close to Kine as she made her way in.

From somewhere a pair of stools were produced for Kine and the tattooist, a hawk-faced local woman with a carefully blank expression. Narin guessed someone like Prince Kashte had explained her job that day and made it clear she was neither to notice nor repeat anything she witnessed. She barely looked any of them in the face despite the fact that her caste scarf was blue, signifying a higher rank than Narin or his friends, but for once he found himself grateful for the effect of Sorote's inherited authority.

Kine sat and there they waited while the tattooist made ready, Hentern having been sent to fetch Steward Breven, and before long they were joined by the two men. Narin found himself tense at the sight of Breven, a man he had come to know well enough in the last year and a half, but the steward was his usual efficient, reserved self. If the man possessed any opinion on the subject he betrayed no trace of it and he was carefully respectful of all he was obliged to greet, taking care to offer the correct level of deference to Kine.

'My Lady Wyvern,' Breven said as he bowed to her. 'I am pleased to see you in good health.'

'Thank you, Breven,' Kine replied in a faint voice that told Narin she had been somewhat dreading the encounter still. 'It seems I will be bowing to you before the morning is out, though.'

Breven might have been a servant caste, but he ran the Vanden palazzo around his master with an unquestioned authority and skill. He was perfectly capable of humiliating her within the bounds of protocol, but his expression didn't change at Kine's self-deprecating words. Narin guessed that loyalty to his lord was one thing, but he disliked his master's desire for retribution.

'I would not ask such a thing, my Lady,' Breven said in a short tone. 'I am here solely to witness what is done, nothing more.'

284

'Then I thank you for that – and all that you have done for me these past few years. I am glad my … Lord Vanden has a man of your quality at his side.'

Breven pursed his lips and nodded, but if he had anything to add it was precluded by a clap of the hands by Prince Sorote.

'Let us be under way, then,' he said briskly, 'Tattooist Evresh, you are clear in what you are to do?'

'Yes, my Lord Sun,' the woman said, bowing. 'The mark of noble marriage to be struck through, the caste mark to be corrected to that of servant caste, the House mark to be struck and made an Imperial sun.'

'Just so.'

Evresh set to work as briskly as she could, her inks and a variety of bone needles arranged neatly on the table. Kine endured it without making a sound, while Narin found himself biting his own lip as he watched Evresh deftly prick at Kine's dark skin. All those assembled found themselves watching in uncomfortable silence, Breven and Myken staring down at the tattooist with stony expressions that she felt were hostile, by her wariness every time she looked up.

Dov woke and it was with some relief that Narin was forced to walk around the room, trying to let the movement settle her. Her cries were insistent, however, and at last Kine called him over, her voice sounding strangely loud after the long, tense silence.

'Bring her here.' With a small gesture she got Evresh to stop and rearranged her clothes so that she might begin to feed the squalling child as the tattooist continued to work on her shoulder. Myken stepped forward at that point and turned her back on Kine, one look at the princes and Breven enough to ensure they retreated to a safe distance. Once Narin had eased Dov out of the sling on his chest, Myken's expression was enough to make him retreat with the others as soon as she was settled in her mother's arms.

Kashte grinned at him as he joined them, Kesh taking up a position at Myken's side to further obscure the view so only Kine's bare shoulder was visible as Evresh recommenced her work.

'You're just marrying one of them, right?' Kashte muttered to Narin.

'He has yet to ask any such thing,' Kine called from behind the screen of attendants. 'But I think three wives might be too much for him and their prospects are somewhat brighter than my own, so they may prove more discerning. However, it looks as though I *am* at least now unmarried. Mistress Evresh, I commend your work.'

Kashte's grin only widened at Narin's startled expression, but it was Sorote who replied and in less jovial tones. 'Perhaps not today, Mistress Kine, given the ink of your annulment remains wet.'

'You are right of course, Prince Sorote, my apologies. I should not have spoken of it in such careless tones.'

Silence again reigned for the remaining time Evresh was at work, the only interruption being a briefly renewed burst of wails from Dov. The nature of caste tattoos was such that they followed a single form with the curved Imperial caste mark as the basis for all of them – each additional curve downgrading the caste a further step. An upgrading was impossible except by notation of marriage or Imperial decree.

At long last they were done and Dov was happily sated, asleep at the breast. Evresh took up a different bottle and her smallest bone needle at that point and, with Kine's assistance, scraped a red mark on the baby's shoulder with the needle's edge. Once the marks of the House of the Sun and the craftsman caste, to match her father's, were traced out on the flesh Evresh rubbed a rag soaked in the bottle's contents over the mark. The mark would be renewed every few months for several years, staining the broken skin until Dov turned six and was deemed old enough to be tattooed properly.

Once that final piece was complete Kashte began to unbutton his braided jacket, beckoning Kesh forward to hold it for him while he rolled white silk sleeves up in preparation for the final indignity of Kine's failed marriage.

Narin found himself gritting his teeth at the sight, more so when Kashte pulled a long bullwhip from inside his coat and let it uncoil at his feet. He looked away, knowing he could make no objection now, but as he did so there came an uncomfortable cough from Steward Breven.

'I … I must apologise, Prince Sorote – and to you, my— Mistress Kine.'

He opened his own coat and from inside brought out a second whip – a different one. Narin couldn't restrain a growl of anger when he saw what it was. The bullwhip would leave Kine bloodied and bruised, but Lord Vanden had clearly decided that was not sufficient for him. Breven carried a scourge, a lash used for the punishment of low caste soldiers serving a military term. A fat handle with seven leather thongs attached, the tip of each tapered and threaded through a hole in a flattened metal teardrop. It was a brutal weapon, even one stroke of which would prove agonising, and imagining it tearing down Kine's slender back took Narin's breath away.

'You cannot be serious, Breven?'

'I perhaps would not choose it this way,' Breven said, not meeting Narin's eyes, 'but my master has instructed me thus.'

'This was not what I had agreed with him,' Sorote added, lacking Narin's anger but his cold tone having a greater still effect on Breven's manner.

'My master feels it is within the bounds of your agreement, my Lord Sun,' Breven said, ducking his head in some sort of makeshift bow as he spoke. 'One stroke of a lash, the nature of which was not discussed, but Lord Vanden feels it only right the lash belongs to him.'

'He just happens to have a Priest-Sergeant of the Ascendant God, Lord Executioner, within his household retinue?' Sorote asked. 'I had not realised Vanden was quite so military minded.'

Breven could only bow again at that, clearly unable to either refute or confirm Sorote's words without telling an outright lie. Sorote was quiet a while, bottom lip caught in his teeth as he looked from Breven to Kine.

'Very well, proceed, Kashte,' he said eventually.

'What?' Narin and Kesh almost shouted in the same breath, Kesh quickest to continue as Sorote's expression hardened. 'That's outrageous, my Lord! She's servant caste now, floggings are reserved for the army or ship discipline – even then I've not seen one of those used on anyone but a pirate!'

'Your concern is noted, *Mistress*,' Sorote snapped, 'and now you will hold your tongue.'

'I will bloody—'

'Kesh,' Kine broke in. 'Enough.'

'What?' she demanded, rounding on the woman as Kine began to slip her left arm from the plain dress she wore.

'I will not argue, the decision is Prince Sorote's.'

'Kine, that thing will strip the flesh from your damn back! It's a brutal weapon, I've seen the mess it makes.'

'Then we should be quick about it. I do not wish to dwell on the image. Prince Kashte, if you would?'

The elegant nobleman had lost his smile, but he didn't hesitate from taking the scourge from Breven. With his sleeves pushed up, Kashte revealed muscular arms that would be able to put a great amount of force into the single prescribed blow. Despite his usual warlike bearing the man held it reluctantly, well aware of the damage he could do with it.

'Kine, you don't need to do this.' Narin insisted, catching her arm. 'The bullwhip is more than enough to satisfy Vanden's anger. Breven, I can see you're unhappy with this too. Would you really report it back if we used the bullwhip?'

The man looked miserable at the prospect, but Kine shook herself free before he could answer. 'This is how it must be, Narin.'

'What if Kine was to take a strike of the bullwhip, enough to mark her as agreed, and I take the scourge? There would be blood enough to carry back to your master.'

'Narin,' Kine said firmly, 'I was born warrior caste, whatever it now says on my shoulder. I have not fought in battle, but that does not mean I do not understand duty.'

'This isn't duty, it's childish spite!' he yelled, bewildered that only Kesh had spoken against it.

'This is my path and I will walk it,' Kine said. 'I have promised as much.'

'What are you talking about?'

'The night Dov was born,' she said, 'when Myken carried me out of the palazzo. Before she reached me, the doctors were about to kill me. I prayed in that moment, to the God-Empress and Lady Chance, for the life of my child. They granted just that and this is their price.'

'This isn't their price, that's madness. This is the price of a mortal man enraged at the direction his life has taken!'

'Narin – think of every picture you have seen of Lady Chance,' Kine continued calmly. 'What does she carry?'

'Carry? She ah, oh, you cannot mean that!' he protested. 'That proves nothing, it's mere coincidence!'

'A flail of six chains, tipped with blessings and curses,' Kine said. 'I feel the will of the Ascendant Goddess in this and so I agree. It is my flesh to offer and I will gladly use every scrap of it to shelter my child.' She lifted her head slightly and adopted a more aristocratic poise. 'Steward Breven, this will be an end of it, make sure of that. I have jewellery gifted to me by Lord Vanden still, several valuable pieces I do not intend to sell. Instead I will hide them away, so he should be aware I will always have the means for retribution, should he decide blood off my back is not enough.'

'I shall keep that in mind,' Breven said hoarsely, 'should my Lord need reminding it is beneath him to pay any further attention to the life of a servant caste.'

'May he always profit from your advice,' Kine said with a bow of the head. 'Now, my Lord Sun?'

Narin was left flabbergasted as Kine turned to face the far wall and slipped her underclothes down to her waist so the perfectly smooth skin of her back was exposed. Kashte stepped forward and gave the scourge an experimental twitch while the others withdrew from the vicious weapon's reach.

'You're ready, Madam?' Kashte asked.

'Your teeth,' Kesh called and Kine nodded, gathering up the sleeve of her dress and slipping it into her mouth to bite down on. That done she lowered her head and tucked her elbows in.

Kashte grunted and cast a baleful look at Steward Breven before returning to Kine. He wasted no time, drawing the scourge behind him and lashing out to whip the metal barbs down her back with a crisp wet crack.

Despite the bit in her mouth, Kine's scream echoed through the room and a thin spatter of blood darted away from her to dot the great glass chair nearby. Narin flinched as it struck and then ran to Kine with Kesh alongside, the young woman already reaching forward with a clean strip of white linen.

As it touched her, Kine shuddered and shrank away, two then three and four near-parallel lines of blood blossoming on the cloth. Her cry faded to an agonised whimper and she slumped a little, Narin slipping an arm under her shoulder as best he could with Dov back in the sling across his chest. Eventually she lifted her head and somehow managed to draw her shift and dress back up so she was covered again. With Kesh's careful assistance she stood and turned to face the men behind her, looking from Breven to Sorote with teeth gritted.

'Let that satisfy wounded pride,' she whispered. 'We are done here.'

CHAPTER 32

Enchei lifted his fingers gently off the wire and paused. Nothing happened – no bright flash, no fiery death. A relieved smile appeared on his face.

'Finished yet, old man?' hissed a voice in his ear, making him jump.

'Breath of Winter!' Enchei exclaimed, hurriedly pulling his fingers away from the wire. 'Don't do that, Enay!'

'You've got twitchy in your old age,' she chuckled, easing back and dropping down to the ground. 'Maybe you should stay in with the baby, leave the younger generation to deal with anything that comes in the night?'

Enchei turned as best he could without falling off the ledge he perched on. He looked his daughter up and down, struck by the transformation she had undergone that morning. Even the grey cloak she wore was now one embroidered with purple and lilac. Underneath that was a dark green quilted arming jacket, cinched by a sword belt at the waist then flared like a skirt to the top of her knee-length boots. On her belt hung a plain pair of short rapiers in the House Ghost fashion while a pistol sheath sat proud across her belly in the usual Imperial way.

Everything was expensively tailored and Enay looked every inch a wealthy warrior caste – right down to the four golden constellation brooches to the Ladies Archer and Chance, Lords Knight and Shield.

Enchei gave a nod of approval. 'Just remember your manners when you're dressed like that. We don't need either of you picking fights.'

She raised an eyebrow at him. 'Thank you, but we don't really need advice on something we've done a dozen times before.'

'Aye fair enough, I'll shut my mouth then.' He paused and doffed a pretend cap at her. 'Siresse.'

'Damn right you will, bloody low born,' she snapped, accent taking a sharper tone to suit her new mode of dress. 'Maiss is inside, dropping off the rest of our purchases.'

Enchei grunted and eased himself down to the ground. They were in one of the small communal courtyards that backed on to the rented house. The feeble sun didn't seem to have reached these parts and Enchei's fingers were chilled as he finished the last of his traps.

'Give me a hand with this?'

He pointed to a length of copper-threaded twine coiled neatly on a patch of trodden-down snow. Handing one end to Enay he carried the other to a nearby wall and used a makeshift ladder to reach the hanging eaves.

'What is it?' she asked as Enchei fixed one end to a gutter. 'A nightingale line? It's like no soul trap I've ever seen.'

'This old dog's still got a few tricks,' he said, adding, 'Keep your end high!' as Enay let the twine sag towards the ground again. 'Not spent much time on the south continent then? That script's Salamander.'

'I know that much,' she muttered, inspecting the short wooden tabs strung along the twine, 'but that doesn't mean I know what this is supposed to do.'

'It's a warding line. Will only keep out minor spirits like Irato's fox-demons, but it'll trip a hellhound coming this way. Not enough to banish it, just make it stumble a moment.'

'And that's useful?'

Enchei grinned and produced a metal box from one pocket. Battered and pitted with age, there was still a slight shine to it and enough to highlight the raised circular plug in its centre. 'Means there's a good chance they'll pull it down to get rid of the annoyance.'

'And pull that from the box,' Enay said in realisation. 'Some sort of Starflare, right?'

'Pretty much. Tucked up inside some person or not, any shadow hound standing here is going to be hammered into the next Ascendancy.'

He fixed the box to the opposite wall while Enay carefully let the twine play out so they could string it across the courtyard well above head height.

'The locals won't mess with it?'

Enchei shrugged and looked around at the empty courtyard. 'Doubt it, even the kids round here are keeping their heads down. What happened on the bridge has spooked 'em and, after the summer, they'll stay cautious. This Starflare won't hurt anyone, just leave 'em dazzled for an hour or so. Anyone messes with the windows it's a different story, but that's tough shit for any thieving bastard who tries their hand.'

Heading through several arched walkways, the pair went inside the little rented house to discover Maiss sorting through the contents of a long canvas bag in the kitchen. She was dressed similarly to her sister; warrior-caste clothes in the House Ghost style, her hair plaited tightly and fixed with a half-dozen silver clasps.

'So what do we have?'

Maiss gave him a sharp look, but after a moment it softened and he realised there was no malice in it, just a lifetime of trusting no one but her sister. She removed a small pistol-bow with ornate gold scrollwork from the bag and placed it on the table.

'A small sting, to keep Kine reassured. We'd have got her a proper Lady's Companion, but what with this being a Dragon-controlled city the only one for sale was an ornate piece the gunsmith had on display.'

'And it was too expensive, just on the hope she'd still be willing to use it,' Enay added. 'Especially now she's newly low caste.'

'Suspect you're right there, yes. What else?'

'Apart from our guns and new clothes? A musket and some mercenary kit for Myken, an Imperial-style longsword for Narin. We even found a veil for Myken like the sort indebted soldiers from House Greenscale wear. In the dark she'll pass well enough for a Greenscale now her hair's cut.'

'Good.' He hesitated a moment then pointed back towards the front room. 'There's also a sack in there, just in case we need it.'

'If we need a sack, we've got problems.'

'Inside the sack,' Enchei continued with a level look, 'is something I picked up a while back. *Do not* use it unless we're in trouble, understand me?'

'What is it?' Enay asked, doubling back to go and investigate.

'Careful,' he called after her. 'You don't want to mess with it. I've rigged things so it's safe to fire, but don't touch it any more than you have to.'

'Stars in heaven,' she exclaimed from the other room, 'is that a Stone Dragon's lance?'

'Aye, so if you use it, folk might notice. Obviously still being alive is more important, but don't burn holes in the walls just because you can't be bothered to reload your pistol. Damn thing is heavy. Irato would be able to use it, but not Narin or Kesh, and I'd prefer one of you had it before him. I don't know if he'll have any of those fox-demons in his head by this evening but either way …'

'So now what?' Enay asked as Enchei tailed off.

'Now? We wait. I'm sure as dammit I didn't pick up any sort of trail today, but Narin's coming back from the Imperial Palace and it's hard to say if they're going to be followed. Irato'll be watching our web of spirit traps so we should get some sort of warning, but I'm not making any assumptions. Either they come after us or, frankly, we sit here while shit happens to someone else and we find out about it in the morning. After that trap on the bridge I don't know what's being planned next. It's their move and we just need to be ready to deal with it.'

Voro, Second-Major of the Firewind Exalted and last survivor of his unit, flexed his fingers and winced. Two failed to move, not broken but encased in armour that was now rigid. The slate grey carapace covered his entire body, now scored and gouged in parts, flame-scorched all down one side. The prayers carved into it were dark, but unevenly so. Some were black, others shades of grey that verged on white. Voro could not command them all and his armour served him only fitfully now. A glow arose from his arm as he tested it out, an invocation of Lord Lawbringer, and reassured him he had some weapons remaining to him.

The corridor was cold and dark; his only light the last scraps of dusk's glow from under a bowl of grey cloud outside. Ahead of him was a wide terrace with plants in fat terracotta pots down both sides – a space reserved for the high caste ladies of Lord Mereto Dragon's great household. In deference to winter it was unlit with no benches or tables out, just a broad space that looked on to the Tier Bridge, where Voro's fellow Astaren had been slaughtered.

Even a warrior caste would not venture out on to that particular terrace, but Astaren were beyond caste, whatever deference they chose to offer. Voro headed out through the open archway and felt the starlight of the Gods settle on his second skin like gentle pinpricks. There was a strip of clear sky above the horizon and through it shone two Ascendants – Lord Shield leading the Order of Knight across the sky with Lady Pity in close attendance. The only Dragon in the sky, their Brother-under-Knight, was hidden by a band of cloud so neatly it seemed deliberate.

They will come for us, Voro said to himself, a mantra he had repeated a dozen times that day. *They will come for us. I must be ready.*

It had felt like an age, the course of that day. A Firewind was no lover of winter, no friend of the pervasive cold that gripped this city. For hours he had lain in the shallows of the Crescent, as still as driftwood, while the cold bodies of hunting demons drifted by. Senses scrambled by the explosions, he was unsure how long he'd called to his comrades – searching for them through the ice-bound night by every arcane manner he knew – only to finally accept the numbing realisation they were all dead.

Somehow he had been saved. Just a fraction further from the nearest building that exploded, chunks of stone had flown just past his eyes. Voro had been bodily hurled from the bridge, afforded only a single glimpse of the horror through the struts he'd somehow been hurled between while his sister-in-flame was cruelly broken around another.

Despite his burning armour, the fall to the water had nearly killed him. Voro felt his body tense and curl at the memory of striking the surface and being dragged down. The stiffening pain in his knee intensified as he remembered, the piercing sting in his ribs a remorseless reminder. Voro closed his eyes, falling back on the rituals of his training a decade past.

He pictured a flickering candle, his blade-like hands cupped about the flame. The warmth grew, intensified into pain, but a Firewind could not fear such pain. The fire was part of their very being, the heat and light echoed by the spark in their soul. It settled over his skin, searing hot but not burning – becoming part of him, drawn deep inside.

Fire and pain he repeated, taking long slow breaths, *they are one, we are one.*

He stayed motionless for a long while and when he started off again, the pain was dimmed. Still present, still insistent, but no hindrance to his movements – no distraction to the languid, deceptive grace the big Dragon could bring to bear if they attacked again. Voro pulled his grey spear from its sheath on his back and went to the terrace edge to look over.

Lord Mereto's fortress was a solid, unforgiving building that had never before been assaulted, but something told Voro that was about to change. The Astaren of House Dragon were used to being the aggressors, the hammer-blow that stopped a brawl from spreading into a battle. That they had been attacked was unlikely enough; that they had been nearly wiped out was astonishing.

Such a thing does not happen by chance, he reminded himself, scanning the shadowy streets below. The packed snow and ice gathered every sliver of starlight and illuminated the streets for him, but picking out the details of the dark shapes below required a brief mantra spoken in the quiet of his enclosed helmet.

Not by chance, he repeated, *and given that this has been planned, they will be ready to press their victory.*

Behind him rose a needle-sharp tower, one of two that burst abruptly from the blockish fortress. Two dozen more studded the perimeter of the central keep and the square barbicans that flanked it – almost decorative by comparison, large enough only for a pair of gunners to stand and shoot over the perimeter wall. Embedded into the walls of those towers were long sweeps of glass that faintly shone green and blue, a modest trick of the Astaren the locals marvelled at – ignorant of the wardings that were their true purpose.

That nearer tower was Voro's domain alone now, until his call for reinforcements was answered. There, secure from the rest of the fortress, they kept an array of whispernets and hawkeyes to spy on the city, while steel panels hid armour and weapons enough to decimate an army.

But not enough to defeat these Gealann mercenaries, he reminded himself bitterly. *If they are truly mercenaries. Have House Ghost lied to us, or were they unwitting tools to dupe us? I heard no Eagle voices there and our whispernets have snared nothing of the kind in weeks, but who else would be so determined to destroy an Astaren force? Could they really be so crazed to set that trap merely to buy themselves time?*

Below him there were running footsteps in the street beyond the wall, but it was only a detachment of soldiers moving in an ordered block. For a moment he was almost persuaded that he had been mistaken and dusk would not herald any further bloodshed. Then he heard a distant howl roll across the city.

Voro kept very still, letting the sound fade as he tried to unpick the demon sounds in his mind, a second howl coming from the south of the district a few heartbeats later. The howls were subtly different to Astaren ears, one building on the other like a rising tide. A third confirmed his suspicion and in the next moment his exoskeleton began to glow. Prayers to the Gods shone out over the terrace, traced in light over the smooth stone floor, and then an arc of flame erupted from his arm to spiral down the length of his short grey spear.

In response, a growl echoed across the terrace behind him. Voro restrained the urge to dodge to one side and turned towards the sound. Spear-tip levelled he surged forward, only to find nothing waiting. The terrace remained empty, the only movement the twitching end of a canopy imperfectly secured away.

Again there came a growl, this time from Voro's left — a stretch of ground he knew to be empty. The ball of loss in his stomach lessened a shade and the ache of his injuries faded as an unseen grin stole across his face. The stern, stylised expression on his face-plate betrayed none of that, but when he spoke the words carried unimpeded over the terrace.

'Come here, little dog, come out into the light.'

Voro exploded into flames, a burst of white light that tore across the terrace. Against the fire, dark shapes were cast like an afterimage that fought to escape. The fighter's instinct rose up in him as shadow fangs snapped from his right and he rolled away from the attack even as he brought his spear to bear. The grey metal now glowed white and the blade cut the night apart — a sickle-like trail searing through the hellhound's maw.

The darkness closed in on both sides but Voro slipped gracefully forward and slashed behind him as shadows burst upon his armour of flames. He crouched as one went high and brought his weapon up under it, lunging and slashing with the precise strokes of the fanatically devoted. And then they were gone, the shadows torn apart and he stood alone, balanced in mid-stroke for the next killing blow that was never needed.

Voro turned around, spear held high, but he knew in that instant that he was alone — his foes dead or banished back to the plane of dark fire. In the next moment the flames died down and he returned to the white-grey figure of glowing incantations. The hushed hiss of night's mist turning to vapour on his second skin was the only sound.

They have entered the fortress, Voro reminded his newly-protesting body, forcing back the warrior instincts that had momentarily taken him over. *Lord Omtoray — they must be here for him. If he dies it will compound our weakness in the eyes of the other Great Houses.*

He set off at a sprint, no longer interested in the high vantage of the terrace. Now he had just one goal, one mission, whether or not it cost his last breath.

The streets will be red with the blood of the fallen, he realised as he raced down the corridor and turned into a narrow spiral stair. *But I can do nothing for them. Lord Omtoray is all that matters now.*

Despite that, he called to the servants of the Astaren still in the fortress, both slaved and willing minions of House Dragon's destroyers.

Unheard by all but a select few, his instructions soon spread through the fortress and the standing body of warrior-caste soldiers readied their weapons. Even as the first howls and death-cries rang out through elegant halls and cramped servant rooms alike, torches were lit and blades heated.

Through it, Voro ran, almost shot by his comrades a half-dozen times before he reached the private rooms of Lord Mereto Omtoray Dragon, the highest representative of his people in the Imperial City. The guards were blessed with quick wits; as the glowing unholy figure burst through the outer door, they recognised the blank face of a Firewind and stepped back. Voro shattered the inner doors to Lord Omtoray's court and found a pair of shadows closing silently in on two grey-haired high castes.

Both men had their guns drawn, but were clearly unsure whether what they saw was the threat itself. The nearer man was called Rhoen, Lord Omtoray's bodyguard – an exceptional fighter whose skill had kept his lord alive for almost forty years. Once the Firewind was inside the room, Rhoen seemed to make up his mind that what he was seeing was real, albeit a mystery that might require an Astaren. He put a bullet through the head of each wolf-shaped shadow and as the hellhounds faltered he had his sword drawn.

From behind him Lord Omtoray, a barrel-chested man even by Dragon standards, shot also, but by then Voro was close and twin streams of flame wrapped around the hellhounds. The demons howled and writhed, clawing their way free but unable to move fast enough to evade Voro's blade. One blow, one parry, one final strike – and they were alone again, shadows dissipated.

'We are under attack?' Lord Omtoray demanded.

Obeying the training beaten into him decades before, his hands were already instinctively mimicking Rhoen's, reloading one gun and then the next.

'I believe they come for you,' Voro replied, skirting around the ruler of that district to check the rear of the room. Behind him, the guards had their guns levelled – faces trying to mask their anxiety at their lord being attacked while they stood outside.

'How many more of you remain?'

'I am the last.'

Rhoen made an angry sound as he realise the gravity of the situation.

'Where is the nearest standing force?'

Voro stopped. Lord Omtoray had authority over all Dragons and subjects of the hegemony here in the city, with the exception of the Astaren, who were exempt from all oversight. What the day-to-day rulers of the Great House knew of their warrior-mage protectors was limited, and instinctively Voro wanted to ignore him, but right now the truth was more pressing.

'Trokail Endir,' he said, 'two days' journey. The call has already gone out.'

'How many of them are they?'

'I do not know.'

Lord Omtoray's face hardened. 'Then you will protect me with your life.'

Voro nodded. The man was no cowardly nobleman, but the third-highest-ranked noble in the entire Great House. He knew the importance of his own life, the consequences of it ending that evening. Compared to all the Dragon warrior castes in the district, Lord Omtoray's life was more significant.

'We all will.'

CHAPTER 33

'Something's happened.'

Narin looked up as Enchei's daughters pushed up from the table, reaching for their weapons. 'How do you know?'

'We just do.'

Beside Narin, Kesh gave a snort. 'Fine explanation – they must get that from their father too.'

While Enay glared at her, Maiss sighed. 'Actually yes, in the same way we know something's happened. I'd explain it, but you wouldn't understand a fucking word and then you'd just be sitting there looking even more stupid than usual.'

'Next time you see that man,' roared Enchei before Kesh could reply in kind, stamping his way down the stairs and into the kitchen, 'clip the bastard round the head from me, will you?'

'What's going on?' Narin asked Kesh as Enay and Maiss grinned at their father.

'No bloody idea, but apparently it's funny.'

'The old boy doesn't look like he's laughing,' Narin muttered. 'Hey, will one of you talk sense for a moment? Maybe use conversations that don't take place in your head or mention people we've never heard of?'

Enchei's face remained tight with anger a moment longer before he raised his hands in apology. 'Sorry, just got taken by surprise is all. It turns out an old friend of mine's more arrogant than I thought possible.'

'He just sent the three of us a warning,' Maiss added, 'in a way no one would be expecting, so it's about the safest way possible.'

'And the fact it felt like an elder god just tramped its way in one ear and out the other was just a happy little bonus,' Enchei said with a grimace.

He shook his head as though trying to dislodge water from his ear, but the look of patient expectation from Kesh and Narin made him stop. 'Ah, the message, aye. From what he can see, some damn fool's unleashed a pack of hellhounds over Dragon District and it's all going to shit pretty bloody quick.'

Narin frowned. 'You have a friend watching Dragon District?'

'Is that really the most important detail here?' Enchei demanded. 'Or the fact folk are getting torn apart a dozen streets away?'

'Not a whole lot I can do about it now, is there? Your girls brought me a replacement sword, not a magic wand. How useful is a sword against a hellhound?'

'Not a whole lot by itself,' Enchei admitted, 'but I reckon we can do something about that. Kesh, you got those spark pads still?'

The young woman nodded and pulled two flattened bundles from one pocket, offering them over the table.

'Now your sword, Narin, and your long-knife, Kesh. Flames work just as well, so bring a few torches if we've got any – anything of light and heat that'll cut their shadows – but these you'll be able to control better. If there are any possessed still around, you'll want a blade to hand more'n a torch.'

Once they had handed their weapons over, Enchei set them all down on the table and bent over them while his daughters belted on their swords and guns.

'So are we safe?' Narin hazarded as he watched the former Astaren unpick blackish metal wires from the cloth pads and begin to prise the thin strands of metal apart.

'Safe?' Enchei shrugged. 'Looks like it, seems I'm not so important as I thought. Bit of a kick in the crotch that, come to think of it.'

'So we've been hiding here all afternoon and evening for no useful reason?' Kesh gasped. 'Oh Monk's stained habit, that's just bloody perfect.'

'How was I supposed to know? There was a good chance we'd be hit. This all started with 'em looking for me, how was I to know they'd give up?'

'If you put it like that,' Narin said, 'it sounds pretty suspicious.'

'Aye, I know, but given the storm that just exploded over Dragon, we're safe. Sounds like there's a lot of hellhounds there – and I mean one whole bloody lot of demons. Unless you've got the power of a Great House behind you, you don't set something like that off when you're planning a second assault on someone like me elsewhere.'

Narin smiled at that. 'If you were anyone else …' he said. 'Not even Lawbringer Rhe could sound so arrogant – oh Gods, Rhe!'

'What about him?'

'When he hears about this, he'll be leading the Lawbringers out. They'll be slaughtered!'

'Good thing we've got a jump on 'em, then,' Enchei said grimly. 'The Lawbringer won't have heard yet and it'll take a while for 'em to get organised. None of your friends are dying yet, Narin. Myken's friends, however, them I'm making no promises about.'

'They are warriors,' Myken joined in as she also descended the stairs. 'They will die with blade and gun in hand. That is what's important.'

'If you say so,' Enay said dubiously. 'I prefer to be the one standing at the end myself.' She checked the clasps holding her hair in place then pulled her hood forward so her face was in shadow. 'And we have a tool to allow us to do just that, don't we, Father?'

Enchei went very still. 'Don't be so foolish,' he said quietly. 'Use a Stone Dragon's lance on the streets of Dragon? Are you looking to draw as much attention to yourselves as possible?'

'I was thinking we just used it in front of whatever hellhounds were out. They surely believe they've killed all the Astaren in the city if they're acting in the open now. Given Dragon are known for meeting threats with the full weight of force they can bring to bear, it's a fair assumption the entire city's garrison of Astaren were involved. If word gets back to the summoner they might've failed to kill them all, there's a chance they'll pull back. Luring Dragon's Astaren into a trap is a far cry from wanting to face some on their own ground.'

A smile slowly worked its way across Enchei's face. 'That's my girl,' he murmured. 'And by the same logic, if there's any safe time to use it, that'd be now, when Dragon's got no Astaren left in the city. Good idea.'

'If you pat me on the head, you'll lose a few fingers,' she warned.

His smile widened. 'Fair enough. Kesh, fetch your dog and tell him to be ready. It won't take me long to rig spark pads around these two blades and give them enough of a sting to hurt the hellhounds. Going via Dragon means you're not coming with us though, Siresse Myken. We can't take that sort of risk. Bad enough we have Narin around, but you've lived there for years. I'm guessing your face is better known than his is noticeable.'

The Wyvern woman inclined her head. 'I would not leave Lady Kine alone in any case.'

Kesh patted Narin on the shoulder. 'Don't worry; this boy's got Lord Cripple's own luck. He'll drag you into something dangerous one day; you won't be missing out for long.'

'Piss on the lot of you,' Narin said darkly, rising from the table. 'I'll go say my goodbyes, then bring my luck to accompany all of you into hellhound-infested streets.'

Sorpan stood motionless in the darkness, frost forming unnoticed on his clothes. For a man used to the blunt end of operations, he was disquieted by what he saw and heard. Only a week ago his purpose had been clear. Only a week ago he had been preparing the way towards a new life outside of Astaren constraints.

And now I find myself caught in the selfsame webs.

A break in the clouds heralded a blade of starlight sweeping across the city to illuminate the mist filling its streets. The Order of Jester was rising towards its midnight zenith, Lady Dancer leading their progress across the night sky. Sorpan watched the fog-veiled lines of Dragon District as distant howls echoed all around and asked himself once more what he was doing there. His instructions were clear, his sense of preservation too strong to question them, but murder on the streets of Dragon District brought them no closer to the renegade.

I remain another man's weapon, but to what purpose?

He had heard it only faintly, just as he arrived in Dragon District that evening, but the distant song that had echoed through his head had confirmed all of his suspicions. It was a Ghost voice, garbled and unintelligible but as familiar to Sorpan as the faces of his parents – embedded just as deep in his mind. What it said he could not fathom, but the effort had told him enough as he searched the parts of his memory the mage-priests of Ghost had given him. There was a sense to each such song, a common rhythm of composer those implanted memories could recognise, whether or not he could understand each note.

And yet this one's as alien as it is familiar, Sorpan mused, still stunned by the realisation. *It's as though I've heard a new note after years of musicianship, only to find it's one that doesn't place on any scale I've seen. My mind knows it, yet is prevented somewhere from understanding it.*

The thought left his mouth dry. Wherever there was secrecy and danger, there were rumours. He'd heard more than a few in his time, but one came immediately to mind now. Old-timers, retired and half-mad in some cases, hinting that the cipher-songs of the Astaren had more than once been changed. Rumours they had heard as novices themselves, then had confirmed as those younger than them could not hear the songs in the same way – as such a note on the musical scale might be erased. It had happened in the wake of the Fields of the Broken and some suggested one was now a song that only gods were permitted to hear; erased for future generations of Astaren.

His eyes drifted up to the divine constellations shining down upon him. *But those gods have their own cipher-songs, songs no Astaren can even hear. Whatever gods obliterated three hundred thousand soldiers, they were older and stranger than any mortal-born Ascendant. If I were one of the Five, I might be tempted to exclude all but a few from any such conversations. But if any of that's true, why doesn't Priest seem to care?*

Footsteps echoed in the street, ending his tangled thread of thoughts. Sorpan didn't move, content to remain and let whoever it was draw closer. A dull black cloak as thin as silk hung over his clothes. He stood within the arched shadow of an overhang – invisible to natural eyes behind the cold starlight that was slicing down on the street cobbles and illuminated the curtain of fog. Under the cloak he held a stiletto ready, listening to the district around him and waiting for the right moment.

It never came. The footsteps stuttered to a halt as a low growl echoed around the houses. A muttered curse told Sorpan his prospective victim was indeed a Dragon and very carefully he turned to watch events unfold. It was hard to tell what caste he was under his enormous greatcoat, but the man was no warrior, that much was obvious. Bundled up against the cold, it took the Dragon a moment to dig through his layers of clothing and pull a short sword from his belt.

Sorpan watched him carefully look all around him, staring straight through the hidden Ghost Astaren. Finding nothing, the man took another two paces closer before another threatening, deep growl rolled over the street. Sorpan saw it then, his eyes more attuned to the shadows than a normal man's. A shape on the wall behind the Dragon, a shadow slipping forward, invisible to its prey though the man turned full about. Despite himself, Sorpan watched with his breath caught – a frisson of primal terror prickling down his spine.

Too frightened to continue any further up the street, the man waved his weapon blindly before him, but only when a huge hump of shadow seemed to detach from the wall did he see anything. By then it was too late, by then glowing red eyes stared straight at him and the growl became a snarl of deadly intent.

The Dragon gasped, knees buckling, before some instinct made him turn to run. A blunt shape of nothing darted down and caught his leg. The man howled as he was hauled off his feet, scrabbling madly at the ground as shadow claws tore great rents in his coat. Again his leg was seized, the flesh sliced deep by half-seen teeth and he was dragged back, shaken like a rat and tossed aside. The man fell and for a moment his cries became louder. Then the huge shape bent over him and Sorpan could no longer see those glowing eyes, only make out the impression of an enormous paw pressing down on the man's chest.

The Dragon stared back at his death for a moment, transfixed by the ember glow. The demon bent lower over him and he started to scream, his voice blunted and weak as the hellhound pressed down on his chest. A hiss and crackle followed as wisps of smoke began to rise from the man's face; the dirty porcine stink of burning flesh soon reached Sorpan's nostrils. The hellhound grew more animated as the man fought it, struggling madly under an unnatural grip, while the smoke and sizzle only intensified. Ugly, excited growls replaced the rage-filled snarls as the demon prepared to feed on his victim's soul. The smoke intensified and one final cut-off shriek heralded the man's demise, but the demon remained bent over the body for a while afterwards as though savouring the scent of its kill.

A gunshot rang out, loud and shocking. Even Sorpan flinched in surprise and the hellhound reeled from the shot. Far from being driven off, the demon retreated a step or two and resumed the deep growl that had heralded its first attack, but the newcomer seemed to not care. She strode forward, sheathing one pistol and drawing the second with a practised movement. In her off hand she carried a blazing torch that cast its own light over the street and that, as much anything, drove the demon further off.

Sorpan noted her clothes as she moved past him, the red, green and blue livery of Lord Omtoray himself. She was tall and well-built, wearing the decorated brigandine of a warrior caste and mail-sheathed sleeves. A musket was slung across her back, but she knew enough to carry a torch and with it levelled she advanced on the demon – clearly there remained someone in Dragon District who knew enough to brief the rest.

The hellhound snarled and retreated a few paces, while Sorpan shrugged inwardly and checked to see if she had come alone. He could see no one following, hear no other movement on the street beyond, so he stepped silently forward as she levelled her second pistol.

The steel plates sewn into her brigandine proved no match for an Astaren's strength. Sorpan punched the stiletto through her shoulder-blade and into the lung behind. The woman staggered forward under the impact and would have fallen to her knees had Sorpan not caught her. He pulled the dagger out and from habit pulled it across her throat to ensure no last cries betrayed him, gunshot notwithstanding. That done he let her fall, pistol clattering to the cobbles while the torch hissed and half-extinguished on the ice-rimed cobbles.

As soon as the torch's light had dimmed, the growls of the demon increased. Sorpan looked up to see it take one tentative pace forward, but before it could decide whether to attack he drew his rapier too. Tiny bursts of light began to wink in and out of existence around his fingers, darting threads of lightning that swiftly grew larger and in moments were racing down the length of his steel blades.

'Go find easier prey,' Sorpan advised in the plainchant of demon kind. 'We're both here to kill Dragons, but I don't care what darkness I cut tonight.'

The hellhound crouched slightly at his words and for a moment Sorpan was convinced it was about to attack, irrespective of how dangerous he might prove. The moment stretched into two, then three and more before finally it slunk away instead and the shadow of its body faded into the wall behind, becoming one with the shadows there and slipping from perception.

Time to investigate further, Sorpan decided as he gave the wall one last glare and sheathed his sword. That warrior knew at least something about fighting hellhounds; it might be there are still some Astaren left here. Priest might be using me the same way my old masters did, but tonight's not one for complaints. For now I will be the good servant and see her plan to the end. I can worry about anything more if I'm still alive to do so after this night.

CHAPTER 34

Even before they reached Dragon District, they could hear the gunfire. Narin exchanged a worried look with Kesh and her face told him she was thinking the same thing. Up ahead, Enchei and Maiss ranged twenty-odd yards beyond the rest of them, scouting the path, while Enay silently lugged a canvas sack beside Kesh, and Irato brought up the rear.

'We should've brought Myken,' Kesh muttered to Narin.

He nodded. 'I think you're right, panic's already taken over there. It could be none of us have the right face to be welcome right now.'

'Warrior castes panic?' said Enay, gaze never leaving her sister's back. 'That's seditious talk, Investigator. Want to be busted down to novice, do you?'

'That's the least of our problems right now. In fact, running into my superiors just got a whole lot more attractive.'

Through the tangle of streets and shroud of mist Narin couldn't gauge distance or direction for the shots, but he recognised the different reports of muskets and pistols. Nothing about the sounds suggested a pitched battle of any sort; it was more likely they were mostly firing at any shadow that moved, if hellhounds were stalking the streets.

At the border of Dragon District, Enchei and Maiss waited for them to catch up in the lee of a covered shop front. The mismatched pair stared intently at the streets beyond, but as they arrived Enchei turned and nodded at Narin.

'Looks like you're right.'

'It does?' Narin asked in confusion, before realising Enay had relayed their brief conversation to her sister.

'Aye, Lawbringers might be our best chance at getting in there without Dragons taking potshots at us.'

'But we don't want to use that thing in front of anyone else,' Kesh said, nodding at the canvas sack Enay carried. 'Are we going to just crouch here and hope some demon comes to meet us? I was hoping one of you'd manage a more sophisticated plan than that.'

'Problem is, we don't belong there,' Enchei said. 'Might be we turn a corner and find ourselves facing a dozen guns whose owners are spooked. If they've been shooting at shadows all night, we don't want to be the first real target they come across.'

'If you don't count any unlucky low castes they might've already come across,' Narin said darkly. 'So what, then? You go by yourself and scout it out? Have Irato following you as backup?'

Enchei was silent a moment. 'I scout it myself. I won't go far, but before we wait for Lawbringer Rhe to turn up so we can hide behind his skirts, we might as well know what we're dealing with.'

'I'd put my year's pay on everything west of the bridge being clear, a dozen-odd streets up to the Fett Canal too,' Narin said. 'Or free from warrior castes at any rate. Good thing we're a few days off Dancer's Festival or the district would be full of people heading to the park amphitheatre.'

'You think they'll set up a perimeter around Lord Omtoray's fortress?' Maiss asked. 'Keep their back to the Crescent docks and let the hell-hounds come at them?'

'I think they don't care about where the poor people live,' he said with a shrug. 'Why would they defend those parts of the district? It'd mean patrolling and getting picked off as much as anything.'

'Pride might force it,' Enchei said, 'but right now we know nothing. The rest of you wait here.'

'You need someone watching your back,' Enay protested. 'You're still a target, remember?'

'I'm used to going alone,' he countered with a shake of the head and pulled his all-enclosing helm from a bag he carried.

Narin had seen the veteran use it before, when they had crept onto the goshe island in the summer, but still had no idea how the man could see in it. There were several lines and seams breaking the smooth curves up – but it hinged only at the back, just enough to fit his head inside before being clipped back down. The face-plate was a single piece with no eye or mouth holes but as Enchei eased his head inside and closed it up, he looked straight at Narin for a moment before returning his attention to the streets of Dragon.

'I'm going to look, see what's going on down the nearest few streets,' Enchei said, voice perfectly clear despite the helmet. 'Then I'll be back and we can decide our next step.'

Enchei didn't wait for a discussion, just checked left and right down the street before crossing into Dragon District. He was dressed in dark servant's woollens under a long concealing cloak, all unobtrusive but able to accommodate his flexible mesh armour underneath. Slung across his back was a shapeless leather bag, while a variety of weapons sat snug in pouches and sheaths strapped around his body.

It's how I've walked into battle a hundred times or more, Enchei reminded himself as the light around him dimmed, the cloud-cover thickening overhead. *And this time they're not even trying to kill me. That's a much better way to start off.*

High above the dragon-adorned buildings ahead he could make out the very peaks of the fortress towers, picked out in dulled lines of eldritch green. He reached a corner and checked around it, secure in the black shadows of his cloak, only to find nothing there. The street was indeed quiet, with precious little light escaping the drapes that would be covering the inside of every window and door in winter.

He moved on, all of his unnatural senses alive for anything that might tell him he was not alone in the street, but as he cut down an alley it was something rather more mundane that caught his attention. The flickering light of a bonfire reflected off the buildings around it up ahead, a small crossroads set around a well-shrine, if his memory served correctly. The nervous voices of Dragon soldiers carried well through the night and Enchei stopped short – careful not to be seen and mistaken as a threat, but more concerned with what other watchers there might be. Before he could see the bonfire itself, Enchei spotted a pair of bodies in the street and then a large shadow sliding down the wall behind them.

The soldiers saw it too and a stuttering volley of gunfire peppered the wall – several shots bursting through the shutters of a window to screams from within. Something smashed and fell, a lamp Enchei guessed, which prompted more screams. Chillingly, they were followed by distant howls echoing around the streets and Enchei felt his hand tighten as he realised some hellhound had discovered a family plunged into darkness.

Before you could get there, they'll all be dead, Enchei reminded himself and turned away. Soldiers came into view, hesitantly following the cries that were cut short with chilling speed. One wore Omtoray's colours, but not as a uniform so Enchei took the young man to be some sort of relation sent out to take charge of these streets. The rest were warrior castes of Dragon and Wyvern, eleven young men and women all told, wearing the badges of their Houses on a variety of light armour.

Slowly, they circled around the building, each reluctant to lead the way. It took the nobleman's order to get the largest of their number to kick the door in, whereupon the young noble himself edged inside – pistol and a flaming torch in hand.

Whatever he saw there Enchei could only imagine, but the nobleman found no threat and soon retreated back into the safety of the bonfire's proximity. Despite the cold of night and haze of fog, Enchei could hear it burning fast.

No doubt they covered it in lamp oil, he thought as he moved forward to the extent of his cover. *Damn fools haven't realised it'll burn itself out long before morning if they let it go like that.*

From where he crouched, Enchei could see the entrance to a half-dozen streets or alleys thanks to the haphazard layout of this part of the district. Aside from the soldiers he couldn't perceive any people in the area; Dragon District was unnaturally quiet and he was just about to retreat when one of the soldiers ahead began to shout a warning.

Almost immediately there came a long echoing growl, then another – racing around the twisting lines of houses, seemingly coming from more than one direction at once. Enchei turned a full circle, mage-sight shifting through colours and greyscales as he sought the hellhounds, but all he detected were traces on the wind like the scent of a real hound. Nothing recent, but criss-crossing trails that told of demons roaming freely.

Abruptly, the calls of the hellhounds broke off and Enchei found the hairs on the back of his neck prickling. Something had changed in the air – almost imperceptibly, but where the demon hounds had brought a sense of threat and flame, this was entirely different. Without meaning to, he glanced up, sensing some looming presence as though great stormclouds had rolled in overhead.

The sky was veined with star-speckled darkness – rogue constellations visible through the breaks of cloud. With the Order of Jester in zenith, it was Emperor rising in the West, and Lord Huntsman's light seemed to flash a warning to Enchei. His hand tightened on his baton as he continued to cast around for danger behind him, but then

309

footsteps echoed clear and steady from one of the other streets leading to the crossroads. The soldiers scampered back to their bonfire and the bubble of protective light it offered, while Enchei watched the end of the street with increasing trepidation.

A pale figure appeared, walking without haste towards the bonfire. The buckles of a fitted white coat glinted in the darkness, showing a feminine warrior figure – a suspicion confirmed by long trails of hair hanging free from within a red hood. The silver tip of a scabbard glittered faintly behind her, shining pistol butts at her stomach, but she held no weapon as she silently stared at the soldiers ahead of her.

Enchei's stomach tightened. *A Banshee*, he thought, before correcting himself. *No, she was once a Banshee. That's no woman now.*

As though to confirm his fears the light of the bonfire guttered under a wind Enchei couldn't feel and the faint light of the Gods seemed to stutter. Moments of blackness broke over the street, once, twice – some form of unholy opposite of lightning from the realms of demons. In those glimpses of utter dark, Enchei saw a huge shape massed around the Banshee – an overwhelming presence that his arcane senses could barely fathom, but one he couldn't deny, even once the Gods had reasserted themselves.

Stars above, that's no mere hellhound.

Enchei looked down at the baton in his hand and the bulge on his left wrist where his darter sat. He wasn't confident either would do much more than irritate such a demon – not one of that size. As commands and panicked voices rang out ahead, unanswered by the Banshee, he searched his memory for what he'd seen in that fragment of shadow-silhouette. The hint of great wings high in the air, a humped back and body larger than the biggest of bulls, vast forelimbs and hooked claws, a ridge of three great horns on a long head.

'A Terim,' he whispered to himself as musket and pistol shots split the night. 'Merciful Gods, how is any one summoner strong enough to bring a greater demon into the world?'

Some of the bullets struck the Banshee – Enchei saw the impact on her clothing, at least – but they had no effect. The Apkai claimed the dark crown of greatest of demons, the most long-lived and powerful of all those outside of the ocean's depths, but the varied Terim were just as unassailably powerful by human standards.

She swept her arm forward towards the soldiers and Enchei reeled under another stuttered after-image of darkness. Behind the building there was a crash of timbers and a burst of sparks rising high in the sky. As Enchei found his balance again he found himself watching a figure charge for the Banshee and his mouth fell open. The nobleman, guns spent and discarded, ran as though into a gale and Enchei could only marvel at his crazed bravery.

Out of his sight Enchei heard piteous wails; the enfeebled cries of the broken and the high, frantic shrieks of a man watching his life's blood run out. He found himself frozen to the spot, unable to tear his eyes away as the nobleman fought through an unseen storm – great two-handed sword drawn and ready to strike – but it was taking all his strength just to come within cutting distance of the Banshee.

Just as he neared her, the Banshee stirred herself to action, moving as though she was just a marionette of her demonic possessor, reaching out with a splayed palm. Enchei was ready for that shudder of darkness and just about managed to keep his eyes open, his knees steady, as a shadow-claw the size of a cutlass tore down through the man's body, bursting through him from shoulder to hip. The pieces of nobleman spilled to the ground and if there were any of the soldiers left alive by the bonfire, they had fled by the time their leader was dead.

Enchei gasped, but old instincts kicked in – old memories of a winter far worse than this one, of other dead things walking and horrors worse than this, conjured by the dreams of a slowly-waking god.

It'll tear the district apart. That damn summoner's unleashed it on the Dragons like some monstrous revenge.

He stepped out from the lee of the house and levelled both his weapons. Tiny flashes of starlight raced across the street as a half-dozen darts tore into the Banshee's flesh. The demon was slow to react, though, and it was only when he levelled the baton at her that it lurched around to face him. The night air twisted and roiled as he activated it, another stutter of darkness but this time the shadow-form of the demon was briefly diminished wherever the distortion seemed to touch it.

Enchei had a better look at the Banshee's face now. Her features were contorted under the pressure inside her, the monstrous creature too vast to inhabit the mind of one mortal. Already blood trailed from her eyes and nose, but it only added to the horror of her presence. Enchei realised the Terim would have more than enough time to kill him before its vessel failed.

Slowly the Banshee began to raise an arm, the movements awkward and jerky, but it was enough for Enchei. He didn't stay to fight, merely

311

turned on his heel and fled as fast as he could. Showing an Astaren's weapons to the demon should prove enough for it to pursue him rather than rip the district apart, but there was something of a downside to that.

From behind him there came crashes and a great bellow of rage as the demon took his challenge and began its hunt. The beams of the building he'd crouched beside splintered and shattered under its touch, roof tiles falling like brittle rain.

Oh hells, I blame Narin, Enchei thought madly as he ran as fast as he could back the way he'd come. *I was never this stupid before we became friends. Enay, Maiss – I hope you're on your toes, otherwise we're all dead!*

'What are you doing here?' Enay demanded, keeping her gun levelled at the woman who'd walked up behind them.

Narin whirled around to see Myken standing there, musket resting loosely in her hands. Dressed in the dull grey and brown of her new mercenary garb, a grey veil loose over her nose and mouth, Myken's eyes and the polished brass of her guns stood out all the more in the darkness.

'My Lady instructed me to,' Myken said coolly, gaze fixed on the pistol until it was sheathed again.

'She's alone?' Narin scowled and made to return but Myken stopped him with two fingers touched to his shoulder.

'It is her instruction. The threat to her is done with – if any remains, they will not get inside the house past Enchei's traps. Her concern is for your safety now.'

'Mine? What about the rest of them?' Narin said, gesturing at his companions.

'They're either more skilled at arms or less adept at getting into trouble. You're the one who needs watching over.'

Narin scowled while out of the corner of his eye he could see Kesh grinning. 'She said that?'

'She expressed concern for your safety, I extrapolated the reasons.'

'Woman's got a point,' Kesh whispered. He continued to ignore her.

'Fine, I guess—'

'Quiet,' Enay snapped suddenly, 'what's that?'

'Feet – running,' Maiss replied, though Narin could hear nothing. 'And some sort of demon-cry?'

'Running this way,' Enay added. She looked left and right. 'Kesh, Narin, fall back. Irato and Myken, take cover there.'

Narin watched the former goshe and Wyvern move without a word, but it took Kesh yanking on his arm to spur him into movement. Maiss peeled away to a large brick well with a stylised sun canopy while Enay headed the other way and settled into the lee of a water butt. The winter weather had split its timbers and a sliver of ice shone out of its belly, a moment of death preserved until the thaw came. As they retreated to cover, Kesh and Narin watched Enay free Enchei's plundered Astaren weapon from its sack and ready it to scorch the night.

Narin felt an ache in his gut as he saw the Stone Dragon's lance again. That very one had almost seared the flesh from his bones before he'd taken another beating from Synter, commander of the goshe's secret elite. He was in no hurry to see the Dragon's Breath employed again, even if it was by an ally this time.

'What's going on?' he muttered, drawing his sword but feeling foolish as he did so.

The sword only emphasised the paucity of weapons permitted to a man of his caste, even if Myken's guns were feeble compared to the lance, but he still felt better for something in his hand.

'Shush,' Kesh chided, pulling out her long-knife and hatchet as she settled into a crouch behind a low wall, ready to attack or flee.

Narin looked down at the sword. The Lawbringers used straight broadswords with a single edge and short point. The over-long handle meant it handled in a not-dissimilar way to the staves Investigators trained with, ensuring those promoted adapted quickly to the weapon. The sword Enay and Maiss had found for him was more traditional, but Rhe had been teaching him classical sword-craft for six months now and it felt familiar in his hand.

The only detail Narin was unsure about was the cloth and wires of the spark-pad Enchei had rigged around the sword's guard. Gingerly he took a proper grip of the weapon so his index finger and thumb pressed into the cloth. A crackle of light immediately danced down the edge of the sword, but his fingers registered only a faint tug.

'Enchei,' Kesh breathed, nudging Narin.

He looked up to see a dark, faceless figure racing towards them. For a moment he didn't recognise the veteran in his armour. It was only once Enchei shouted, 'A Terim!' at his daughter that Narin was sure.

'What's that?'

'Whatever it is, *he's* running from it,' Kesh said, the nerves evident in her voice.

313

Narin felt his skin grow colder. 'Gods above.'

Up ahead, Enchei sprinted to his daughter's side with a speed that belied his age and skidded to a halt. It appeared Enay had understood what he'd shouted because she didn't even look at her father, just hefted the pale, stubby lance and braced herself.

The explanation came soon enough, surging around the corner on boiling wings of shadow. A great mass of something huge yet insubstantial, bearing on its wave a figure clad in white and red which it then deposited in the centre of the street. The air stuttered and flickered around it – her, Narin realised a second before recognising her clothes. It was the Banshee he'd seen at the Palace of Law, the one who'd brought them news of the summoner.

'In case we hadn't found them,' he muttered, 'or kept the news from the Dragons.'

Looking at her now he recognised something of the black aura around her, having seen Irato possessed by fox-spirits half a dozen times or more. Different to be sure, but a charged air of power surrounded both. The greatest difference was that this woman looked like an animated corpse hung on strings, rather than more alive and vital as Irato was. From what Enchei had said of the hellhound-possessed men he'd found, this was an order of magnitude greater; perhaps the demon did not so much need her body to use as serve as a conduit.

The Banshee stood watching Enay and Enchei for a moment, arms hanging limp at her side before she began to jerkily raise one. A musket shot immediately rang out around the street and her head twitched back under the impact. Narin turned and saw a small cloud of smoke in front of Myken while the woman calmly went about reloading.

Maiss fired in the next moment from the other direction, one pistol then the other. They had less impact than the musket but it was enough to distract the demon-possessed woman. Enchei followed up with both his weapons, the strange distorted stream of air buffeting the Banshee back before Enay unleashed her own horror. The Dragon's Breath gouged a hole through the misty air and then struck with the force of a hammer. The Banshee was rocked back as she exploded into flames, but it wasn't enough to stop her.

Narin gasped as the woman took a step forward, silent despite being entirely engulfed by fire, and reached out. Enay and Enchei threw themselves aside as jagged whips of darkness seemed to lash the ground where they had stood and tore furrows in it. Enay rolled and fired a second time before ducking round a corner to avoid another blow. The roof of the building shattered under the impact. Even as he shrank lower behind the wall, Narin saw lines carved through tiles and timbers alike, as though gigantic claws were ripping through them.

The fires engulfing the Banshee raged furiously now and her next step forward was awkward, but the light of the flames seemed to cast her demon shadow with renewed strength. Narin could see great wings raised up in the sky, a broad animal's body and a horned head above the burning woman's. Before anyone could attack again, however, there came a shuddering, deep roar that seemed to rise from the very stones beneath Narin's feet. He looked around in confusion as the earth began to shake and the whistle of wind eclipsed the crackle of flames.

'Oh seven hells!' Kesh gasped.

Narin realised the sound was coming from the well where Maiss was sheltered just in time to see a mass of twisting white lines erupt from the well mouth. Maiss fell back in shock, scrabbling away while a column of unfolding light blossomed above the well – moving too quickly for Narin to make any sense of the shapes being formed and reformed.

'What is it?'

'The Apkai,' Kesh replied, gaze fixed on the strange writhing mass of light. 'Don't you remember? Out on the sea when Lord Shield tried to claim the goshe's artefact?'

'Gods, yes – but what's it doing here?'

With a sudden whip-crack speed his question was answered. The light flew across the street towards Myken and Irato like the wrath of Gods. Before Narin could say anything more, the former goshe was surrounded, barely able to make any move to defend himself before being hauled bodily into the air. The light then contracted and drove inside Irato – forcing itself into his eyes and mouth until only a writhing corona remained. Held five feet off the ground, Irato went rigid, limbs outstretched and head tilted up in a voiceless shriek.

Gods – of course it would take him. The goshe's poison washed away his memories, most of who he is, to make space for the god they were trying to create. He'll be the perfect tool for a demon like the Apkai, especially as he's already been used as a vessel by the fox-spirits.

A moment later the goshe was lowered almost to the ground again and Narin saw the demon's light shining from his eyes and mouth, feeding an angry swirl that now wrapped around his entire body.

315

Unnoticed at his feet, Myken scrambled up from the ground having fallen in her fear and wonder, barely retreating in time before the shadow-demon attacked.

Great claws of darkness crashed down on Irato's head. Where they missed and struck the ground, cobbles burst and the ground was torn, but as they hit him they exploded in an eye-watering burst of light. The Apkai and Irato both seemed unscathed and a roar of rage rang out across the street as the demon attacked again. It drove forward, the burning Banshee staggering along at its heart. Narin could just make out the shape of the demon – *a Terim, a distant voice noted* – surrounding her, raging and slashing at Irato.

Every blow caused another flourish of blinding sparks, but the Apkai weathered the assault without a backward step. After a dozen heartbeats or more, it finally seemed to gain full control of Irato and looked down to face its enemy. Irato leaped forward at the Terim, thrusting spears of spitting light into the demon's shadow-body. The Terim howled at this retaliation and struck back but Irato dodged and struck a second and third time. Each blow punctured the Terim's body and ripped away chunks of shadow until finally Irato jumped high over its claws and stabbed down at the Banshee's face. The spear punched right through the flaming mass of her head and something seemed to give inside her.

All at once the shadow-form of the demon folded in on itself with a crack of thunder and vanished from view. Only the charred corpse of the Banshee remained to crumple dead to the ground. Narin gaped as Irato, still shining with unnatural light, regarded the body a moment longer then turned to face them.

For a moment no one moved. Almost reluctantly, Enchei hauled himself up from where he'd taken cover and pointedly motioned for Enay to set the Stone Dragon's lance on the ground. That done, he approached the Apkai-possessed man and knelt before him. He didn't speak and while he didn't glance around him, first his daughters then Myken did the same. Narin and Kesh were the last, Narin feeling some faint pang of guilt in his heart, though he had never been too devoted a servant of the Gods.

'*Fools declare war,*' the Apkai pronounced. '*Gods end them.*'

'Great one,' Enchei said, head bowed, 'I thank you once more.'

'*The shadow-kin trespass and kill among my aligned. My patience is at an end.*'

'Kill?' Narin said abruptly, taking a step forward. 'Who are your aligned? Samaleen's murdered priests? Or have they attacked the city's demons too?'

Enchei turned and gave Narin a furious look while Irato's light-filled eyes slowly turned to him.

'*You were once marked by the Ascendant, Shield,*' it intoned. '*A young god's regard means little to the ancient.*'

While it spoke in a level tone, Narin heard the rebuke and faltered. Lord Shield had once marked him, it was true, but it was no divine blessing. If he angered the Apkai now, Shield would not care for his fate.

'Great one,' Kesh said, advancing past Narin and dropping to one knee. 'We crave your indulgence once more.'

Narin and Enchei both frowned at her, but Kesh was not paying attention to either. Most likely she was remembering her own interaction with this god-like being, when she had frustrated the plans of both the Apkai and Lord Shield.

'*The bold one,*' it said at last, voice rolling over the street cobbles like distant thunder. '*What demands have you now for immortals?*'

'No demands, great one,' she said carefully. 'I beg only that you do not allow your shadow-kin to provoke you.'

'*My kin? Your ignorance betrays, mortal who brings starlight.*'

At that, Narin suspected he could see a faint flush in Kesh's cheeks. Having tricked both a god and demon, she had faced them down with unashamed anger and grief. In honour of that, Lord Shield had promised to write her deceased sister's name in the stars for one night every year. They were yet to see if the Ascendant God kept that promise, but if a demon-prince remembered surely a god would not renege on it?

'She is ignorant but honest, great one,' Enchei broke in. 'There is a summoner in the city who hunts me – who has set hellhounds on my scent and killed without regard. But the Terim was not set on my trail. Until I attracted its attention it was here only to kill at random, I believe.'

'*Action without reason is a fool's impulse. There is purpose here.*'

'The same reason why House Dragon's Astaren were lured into a trap,' Enchei replied. 'To weaken Dragon's hold on the city, to humiliate Lord Omtoray and show them as something other than unassailable. This demon was here to kill and destroy, to show the Dragons could not defend themselves.'

'But your followers were also killed, great one,' Kesh added. 'Targeted, even. What if their goal is to not only show the Dragons as weak, but also an irrelevance? To have you openly fight Terim on the streets – to have the warriors of Dragon attack both hellhounds and fox-spirits and be attacked in turn. They want chaos, nothing more, and as they drag you in, great one, their goals are furthered.'

The Apkai did not speak. The cold white light shining from Irato's eyes and mouth dimmed, as though its attention was elsewhere, before eventually it waxed strong again and raised Irato up off the ground once more.

'*You are all as children playing with vipers. How soon before the bite?*'

'Not yet,' Enchei said, 'not if there remain some of us to stop it.'

'*I withdraw in favour of my aligned among your kind. They shall bring light to this District in my place and fill every shadow.*'

'And the fox-spirits? The people are frightened; they'll attack any demons they see.'

'*My chosen shall bring light in its myriad forms. My light shall bring peace.*'

Enchei bowed a little lower, obviously realising that was as much of an answer as he was going to get. 'Then we will go to stop the summoner.'

'*You carry a weapon of Dragons. You go to preserve their name of power.*'

The former Asteren blinked and looked back at his comrades. The Apkai was right – any indication of House Dragon continuing the fight would lessen their humiliation, and even the greatest mortal power in the world would not object to impersonation there. 'Mere chance, great one, but I'll not complain when fortune favours me.'

'*This one I claim as my own,*' the Apkei continued. '*His mind is like none of my aligned.*'

'Can … can he survive that?' Kesh asked. 'That woman the Terim was using – she looked half dead even before we shot her.'

'*Her mind was a door ajar. This one has been prepared and a fragment of my greater self can serve so close to my sancta.*'

Narin opened his mouth to argue that they were casually selling Irato's mind to a demon, but the words died in his throat. None of them had a choice in the matter, he realised – quite aside from the fact Irato had already been claimed by its lesser kin, the fox-spirits. Their opinion wouldn't sway a godlike being that had found Irato a useful tool, and what did it change? They could do nothing to stop it and perhaps Irato was actually safer in the control of something so powerful.

As they watched, the light dimmed and Irato returned to the ground. The Apkai withdrew in streams of twisting light, surging back to the well mouth to disappear underground once more. Abruptly, the former goshe crashed to his hands and knees, panting madly, while Enchei and Kesh ran over to him.

'Irato – can you hear us?'

Narin followed Kesh, watching warily as she hauled the big man upright. As she did so, Kesh gave a gasp. While the alarmed expression on his face showed that Irato was back in control of his body, his eyes continued to glow.

'Shitting Gods,' Irato croaked. 'Am I just a plaything now?'

Enchei laughed and clapped a hand on the man's shoulder, almost knocking the wavering Irato back down. 'We all are, my friend, there's nothing new here.'

Kesh slipped one of Irato's arms over her shoulders and stood, hauling him up and holding him steady until he seemed able to stand by himself again. It took him a while, his enormous strength nothing without control over his drunken limbs, but eventually he stood upright and looked around. The lambent shine in his eyes remained as his cheek and brow twitched – the man's fractured soul struggling to remember emotions and expressions with a demon-fragment woven through it.

'You're good?'

'I, ah – I can walk at least,' Irato said, taking deep breaths to steady himself. 'What happens when the demon wants to go in a different direction, though?'

'I think we've just seen what happens when the demon wants out to play,' Narin muttered. 'When it happens, I reckon we're the ones who need to look out.'

Irato nodded stiffly. 'It doesn't care for any of us. I can feel its rage. But it sees this as a mortal concern; it'll allow us a chance to end things before it tears the city apart.'

'So what now?' Enay demanded from Narin's left. She held the Stone Dragon's lance casually, despite its bulk, and kept her eyes firmly on Irato.

'We trust the Apkai,' Kesh said. 'We leave the hellhounds in Dragon District to its followers and go find the summoner. Even if they can't stop the hellhounds they'll slow them at least, distract them. It should buy us time.'

Enay scowled and gestured to the city around them. 'Where exactly? Irato – the god-fragment inside you giving any clues?'

'It doesn't need to,' Narin said suddenly. 'I know where they'll be.'

'What? When did you work that out?'

He shrugged. 'Just now. That demon, the Terim, that's not something you can easily bring into this world, right?'

'Aye, maybe an Astaren could manage it, but some mercenary summoner who's already dragging a pack of hellhounds too? Not alone – you're right, this is a bigger job than we'd realised before.'

'The shrines Rhe and I went to in Iron District, the priests or whatever they were there. They said the same thing, that it was hard enough to bring in a couple of hellhounds and control them.'

'Shrines?' Enchei mused. 'I see what you're getting at.'

'What?' Kesh exclaimed. 'Those priests are actually involved? How can you trust anything they've said, then?'

'Chances are they weren't,' Enchei said. 'Gods, it has to be!'

'What?' Narin and Kesh said together.

'Shrines and priests dedicated to these hellhounds and their kin,' Enchei explained. 'All that's easy enough to turn to a different purpose if you know what you're about. Oh seven hells, that explains it.'

Seeing the faces of his friends he raised his hands to ward off their questions and explained. 'You come to this city to hunt someone like me, you're going to come into conflict with House Dragon, right? To risk doing that, you need to get some protection and your first stop's the hegemony that would *already* be at war with Dragon if it hadn't been for the goshe affair distracting folk. So you find a friend in House Eagle and they might have a few suggestions that serve their cause as the price of protection.

'I'd guessed something along those lines, but this part the Gealann simply don't have the power for. Their summoner's strong, but not strong enough to do all this. House Eagle, on the other hand, they've got Mindwalkers among their Astaren – you get one of them in the head of the high priest – the Kobelt did you say? – right, in the Kobelt's head and use him to turn those shrines into a summoning circle instead.

'The city fills with demons and House Eagle get everything they want. Most likely this's their way of recruiting allies for the coming war, keeping their hands clean in the process. There's no evidence to present to the Emperor and turn opinion in the other direction, just some rogue mercenaries and a shameful loss of control from the Imperial City's protectors.'

'So we have to kill these priests? Priests whose minds have been stolen by Astaren? Novices too? This just gets worse and worse,' Kesh groaned.

'You want to walk away, you've every right,' Enchei said. 'This ain't your fight.' He pointed to his two girls. 'I've got my orders, however – these two've been living off credit extended from a man who once owed me. This is the price of getting my girls back, far as I'm concerned, and I'll walk into that demon's jaws if I have to. Don't think Irato's got much choice at this point either, but Narin, Kesh, Myken – you three should walk away now.'

Kesh jabbed a finger in the man's chest. 'We've had this conversation before, remember, old man? Next time you tell me to walk away I'm going to cut one of your balls off, understand?'

Enchei grinned and looked askance at Narin. The Investigator shrugged. 'What she said.'

At that, Myken took a step forward and shouldered her musket. 'I am warrior caste,' she said simply.

'You lot'll be the death of me,' he sighed theatrically.

'Really?' Kesh said, pointing at the charred corpse of the Banshee. 'My money's on one of them.'

'Aye, you could be right,' Enchei said with a nod. 'Iron District it is, then. It's a long walk, mind. Normally I'd say we steal a boat and skirt the Imperial Island – given Irato's going to be scaring off any hungry demon we might meet on the Crescent – but that'd mean going into high-caste parts of Dragon.'

His face hardened. 'Just remember it'll only get worse from here on. There's more'n a few nasty tricks waiting for us at these shrines, assuming Narin's right and I reckon he is. The Apkai mightn't have noticed it happen, given the shrines'll stink of hellhounds anyway. It's not just hellhounds we'll find there, though – you come across a Ghost or Leviathan and there's a good chance they'll be Astaren, so keep clear or run away. Beyond that, stick together and watch your backs.'

CHAPTER 35

They skirted Dragon District until they reached the Public Thoroughfare that led up through the district to the Tier Bridge. The skeletal fingers of birch trees fractured the mist that filled the city's veins, jagged shapes against the star-lit air. Narin felt the cold grow sharp on his skin as the clouds slowly splintered and the Gods were revealed alongside a sullen, yellowed moon. The Order of Jester was past zenith now, Lord Cripple trailing in the wake of his fellow Ascendants across the sky.

The Investigator looked around at his comrades for the fight to come. Enay and Maiss led the way, Enchei behind them, flanked by Kesh and Myken, while Irato and he himself took up the rear.

Some would say that was a message from the Gods, he thought to himself. *That we've fallen into something like the shape of a divine Order. Or is that just the natural order of things? The Empire teaches its children obedience with every breath, to conform to its structure. Are we all slaves to that?*

Seven of us; six Gods and a Dark Week where one might yet be raised. Which means Enchei's playing the heartless bastard, Lady Jester, and no one's surprised there. He checked the stars again, reminding himself of the Order's positions. *Lady Dancer leads the way – well that's Enay, ready with her lance. Maiss is Lady Spy, that makes Myken the Lord Duellist and Kesh the Lady Chance. Irato, who may or may not be there inside his own mind, is the Dark Week.*

He sighed inwardly. *And that makes me Lord Cripple.*

Unprompted, he heard his mother's voice in his mind – a memory of when he was very young, several years before he was orphaned into the Lawbringers. She had told him the tale of Cripple and the Three Knights whenever he'd come home bruised and battered by older boys in the neighbourhood, which had been often enough. That memory, along with the story's message of forbearance and forgiveness, had served him through the noviciate dormitories and beyond.

When Narin had allowed himself to be riled by high-caste peers, he'd always felt more guilty for failing his mother than any shame at acting above his station. As they walked on and the smooth arcs of the Tier Bridge began to emerge from the mist, Narin again felt that guilt in his heart – a nebulous worry that there was a lesson he'd failed to heed.

They travelled to kill the aggressors, the bullies of this adult life – hardly in the spirit of gentle Lord Cripple. But the stories she'd told him had been done in front of a wall hanging that bore the oaths of the Lawbringers. Those oaths had been even more of a constant in his life, a truth he felt to his very core, so with a silent apology to the Ascendant God above, Narin trudged on in the wake of his fellows.

The jangle of thoughts and doubt he kept deep inside, hoping the others would not read it in his face and wondering if they felt them also. Kesh perhaps, but since they'd first met Narin had admired her sense and pragmatism. With the violence Enchei had done, it was hard to tell where the scars ended and the man began – and that went more than doubly so for Irato. But Kesh had heart coupled with a will and purpose Narin knew he'd not been born with, one he was still learning to put on with his Investigator's jacket.

On impulse he reached out and quickly squeezed Kesh's hand. She glanced back, startled for a moment before seeing something in his face that made her understand. Offering him a smile, she squeezed back then returned to the mission at hand. Irato noticed the move-ment and shot them a blank look – not protective, as he often looked towards Kesh, or slow to comprehend as his damaged mind sometime was. The man's expression was far from human, the shine in his eyes making Narin shiver and look away.

As they reached the deserted market that flanked this end of the bridge, they stopped at the sight of a makeshift column of men and women coming the other way, ghostly in the whites and greys of their Lawbringer ranks.

There were a good hundred or more, by Narin's judgement, and more than a few of his friends were within those ranks. It was a forest of faces he knew and he felt a wrench of guilt in his chest at not being among them. He wore his heavy grey coat, but the clothes and weapons underneath were more mercenary than Investigator.

It was only belatedly that he felt the shame of his demotion – of the gossip that would have raced through the Palace of Law. Such an occurrence was rare, still more so given the circumstances. In the dark it was hard to gauge the expressions of most, but he saw stony disapproval on more than a few faces.

At their fore was Law Master Sheven, even broader than usual in a thick white coat, his bald head covered against the cold. Narin looked up and down the column as his small group moved aside to let them pass – he couldn't see Rhe. What was in evidence, however, was fire and light, none of the Lawbringers or Investigators walking with their usual weapons in hand. Instead they carried lamps and makeshift torches, staves with oil- and tar-soaked rags wrapped around one end.

'Law Master,' Narin called, bowing low to the senior Lawbringer.

Sheven nodded at him and raised a hand for the column to halt. 'Investigator Narin, why am I not surprised to see you here?'

Narin ducked his head. 'Because suspended or not, I am still one of the Lawbringers. I cannot stand aside while others die on our streets.'

'Good.' Sheven cocked his head at Narin's companions. 'But where are you going? We heard only that Dragon District was assailed.'

'As have we, but … ah, Lawbringer Rhe isn't with you?'

'So that's it,' Sheven said. 'No, he is not – and I'd wager you know where he's going. He may not welcome your help, however. You have disappointed him.'

Narin shook his head. 'Lawbringer Rhe isn't a man to let his own disappointment incur casualties. He'll want us to follow.'

'Perhaps, perhaps not. He's taken all the high-caste Lawbringers and sent word for our new Imperial-caste allies, Prince Kashte and his warrior cousins.'

'Summoned Kashte, eh?' Enchei mused behind Narin.

The Investigator understood the man's tone, but pressed on, knowing there was more he needed to say to Law Master Sheven.

'Who suggested the torches, sir?'

Sheven frowned at him. 'Lawbringer Rhe. Is there a problem?'

'No,' Narin said with a shake of the head. 'He's right. We, ah, you won't be alone in driving these demons out. There are trigger-happy warriors out on the streets, but also some sort of pagan cult. There's no time to explain all about them, but their leader's probably a woman called Samaleen – Rhe and I met her a few days ago in our investigation. They're enemies of the hellhounds; I think they'll have some sort of magic to ward them off with.'

'Some sort of civilian militia?' Sheven growled. 'Armed Imperial castes is one thing, but—'

'Not a militia, but shamans and other occultists – not the same as this summoner, but they know more about demons than we do. Please, sir, listen to them if you come across them and don't let anyone go looking for a fight.' Narin glanced back at Enchei. 'I think I'm right that the torches can hurt a hellhound and can drive them off, but I don't think that'll be the same as being able to kill them. Don't let anyone go looking for a fight or we'll have even more dead on our hands.'

'How bad is it here?'

Narin looked helpless. 'We've barely gone into the district, we skirted around when we saw how bad it was. There are … things, worse than hellhounds – much worse. You can't fight them. We barely got away and we had help.'

'Help?'

The Investigator was silent for a moment, trying to work out how to explain without prompting more questions. Law Master Sheven knew much about what had happened during the Moon's Artifice affair, but he was a member of the Vanguard Council and they'd been careful to hide some details. Enchei was, to him, just an experienced ex-soldier and Narin had been rescued with the help of Lord Shield. Though Narin was sure they could trust Sheven, bringing in talk of demon princes and Astaren helped no one.

'The fox-spirits you saw on the island – they helped us escape. Think of them as the local spirits of the city. The hellhounds are invading their home ground.'

'And we're to ally ourselves with shamans who worship them?' Sheven growled, his expression reminding Narin that the Law Master had been born into the religious caste.

'Doesn't order take priority, sir? Stopping the deaths on our streets?'

'At what cost? Our souls?' Sheven snapped.

'The oaths care nothing for our souls,' Narin said as meekly as he could manage. 'Lawbringer Rhe once said that to me.'

Law Master Sheven took a breath as though ready to shout or strike Narin, but he caught himself before anything could happen. 'The oaths,' he said slowly. 'It is true. We serve the Emperor, whose blood is of the divine. Our oaths are our bonds to him.'

Sheven gestured for Narin and his comrades to move on. 'I'll not delay you any longer if you go to catch up Rhe.' He turned to one side. 'Lawbringer Kohen.'

A large woman broke away from the column, as broad as most men of House Dragon were and taller than most of her compatriots. 'Law Master,' she said in the deep, rolling accent of one born in the Dragon homeland rather than the city district.

'Form them up into their units. I need to address them before we go out into the streets.'

'Yes, Law Master,' she said and bowed.

Narin did the same. 'Thank you, Law Master.'

'Stop this at the source, Investigator,' Sheven said sternly. 'Do not force us to fight these hellhounds all night.'

Narin nodded and wasted no time in setting off, skirting the massed Lawbringers while Kohen started giving orders to a group of designated lieutenants.

'Rhe's going for the shrines?' Enchei asked, the rest of them having kept a respectful distance from the conversation. 'And he's made friends with Prince Sorote – enough that Kashte's at his disposal?'

'Rhe's always been determined to have Imperial power rule the streets of the city,' Narin said through gritted teeth as they started up the slope. 'I can't help but wonder if he was happy to tell House Dragon about the summoner's likely safe-house. Their power in the city gets momentarily crippled and the Lawbringers are there to restore order.'

'Is that what Sorote's about? Increasing the Emperor's power?' Kesh asked sceptically.

Narin exchanged a look with Enchei, who scowled. 'I doubt Sorote's really the public-spirited sort.'

'Man's playing a dangerous game,' Enchei added, 'but he's good at it, I'll give the bastard that.' He looked up at the empty road ahead, running down the centre of the Tier Bridge with darkened shop fronts on either side. 'More importantly, Rhe'll get there ahead of us.'

'No he won't,' Maiss declared, hitching up the sheathed rapier at her side. 'I'll get to him first. If I run I can make up the ground, maybe catch them at the Iron Bridge.'

'He doesn't know you,' Narin said. 'He'll be especially suspicious at some warrior caste running through the city alone on an errand.'

'He wants to see my caste tattoos, fine. He wants to interrogate me about who I am, where I'm from, he can whistle for it.'

Enchei nodded. 'He'll assume she's my Ghost handler. The man always thought I was lying to him about being retired. Now I guess it's closer to the truth than I'd like anyway. What the Imperials will make

326

of her I couldn't say.' He nodded to Maiss. 'Go. Send the humourless sod my love.'

The young woman sprinted off, sure-footed despite the rime of ice and packed snow coating the city. Narin and the others upped their pace without anyone saying a word, but it was only moments before Maiss had disappeared into the fog. It was normally dangerous out on the streets late at night, but Narin doubted any footpads could trouble her.

While there was little breeze coming off the sea, the exposed bridge was even more intensely cold than the freezing streets and Narin found himself glad of the faster pace. They couldn't run all the way, or at least Narin and Kesh couldn't, but with the starlight of the Gods lighting the city they could at least walk with a forced briskness. He coughed to clear his throat, the sound echoing strangely around the deserted lower tier of the bridge, and began to relate to his comrades all he could remember about his visit to the strange House Gold shrines.

Whether they appreciated the distraction from what horrors they might find, Narin couldn't tell, but he kept on regardless and pushed thoughts of his new-found family right to the back of his mind. He was cold enough without feeling that all-too-familiar chill of fear return.

Narin finally spotted the tall, motionless figure of Lawbringer Rhe waiting for them with Maiss on the far shore as they crossed the final step of the Mason's Bridge. The high sides of the bridge had sheltered them from the breeze, but the stone itself radiated a fierce cold. By the time he had reached the shore of Iron District, Narin was yearning for another layer under his coat. All he got was the expected look of frosty disapproval from Rhe as he knelt to the Imperial castes then bowed to his superior.

His companions did the same except Myken and Enay, who merely bowed as high castes, grey scarves wrapped around the Ghost's face – as much to hide her from the Imperials as against the cold.

'You have new friends, Investigator,' Rhe said coolly. 'I had not thought you a man to share your exploits so freely.'

Narin suppressed a wince, knowing Rhe was aware he'd taken the credit for Enchei's feat of arms on more than one occasion.

'They are friends of the highest discretion,' he assured the Lawbringer. 'I trust them as highly as your new friends.'

'*Your* new friends?' echoed Prince Kashte at Rhe's side. 'Are we no longer your friends, Narin?'

Even in the cold of winter, the young Imperial managed to convey an image of being effortlessly, thoughtlessly, rakish and handsome. His scarf and hood shone gold in the light of the torches they carried – the intricate embroidery of black and gold on his coat reminiscent of Lord Shield's clothing when Narin had met the Ascendant God on the streets of Dragon.

'My apologies, Prince Kashte,' Narin said with another bow. 'I meant my benefactor, whom Lawbringer Rhe has only recently met.'

'A famous name does make quite an impression on us all,' Kashte smiled, fluttering his eyelids. 'Do your companions have names?'

'Keel and Holin,' Maiss supplied before anyone could contradict her.

'Mercenaries who owe a favour or two,' Enchei added, 'yer prince-ship. Don't you worry about them.'

Kashte's smile never wavered as he inclined his head. As an Imperial he could hardly fail to recognise the given names of the Ascendant Gods, Lady Spy and Lady Dancer, but he made no objection to the pseudonyms.

'So you've had the same notion as I, Narin?' Rhe said.

'We did after what we saw in Dragon,' he replied. 'No single summoner's managing all that.'

'Do you propose a plan of attack?'

Narin shrugged and glanced at Enchei. The veteran nodded. 'Same as before.'

Rhe raised an eyebrow. 'As on Confessor's Island? I seem to recall we took all of the casualties that day.'

'Doesn't mean you took all the risks,' Enchei said, pointing at the assembled party behind Rhe. 'And you had every Lawbringer you could muster then, now you've only got trained fighters.'

With Prince Kashte there were two dozen more Imperial castes carrying the beautifully-crafted rifles they had employed to great effect against the goshe. On top of that, Rhe had assembled a similar number of high-born Lawbringers and perhaps a dozen gun-carrying Investigators. Narin recognised many faces among them, but none he considered friends.

He was not in the habit of befriending his betters and being raised to Lawbringer by Imperial writ would have galled many. There were precious few friendly looks among them and all Narin could be sure of was that Rhe had selected only those he could trust completely.

'So we attack and draw their fire,' Kashte recalled, 'while you sneak in the back and try to cut the summoner's throat.'

Enchei scowled. 'Before they drag some demon prince through the veil to tear all our faces off, yes.'

Kashte gave Enchei and Irato a searching look, clearly trying to work out what he didn't know. Narin had downplayed their efforts at foiling the goshe, putting success down to the efforts of the fox-demons and the majority of guards facing the Lawbringers. Enough of that had been true to make it plausible, but it was stretching matters to expect to get away with it again. Narin just had to hope they could find an explanation – or threat – to ensure Enchei's secrets were kept, but surviving this was going to be hard enough.

'Go, then. We'll give you time to get into position then follow and announce ourselves,' Rhe said.

'You're going to tell them they're all under arrest first, aren't you?' Enchei said wearily.

'I am not a soldier, I am a servant of the Emperor's law,' was Rhe's stiff reply. 'If we act no better than the soldiers that rule our streets, what's the point of claiming we are different?'

'Aye, there is that,' Enchei said.

Narin pointedly brushed past his friend as he set off, heading for the interior of Iron District, and Enchei got the hint, falling in beside Narin without another word. The others followed along and none of them spoke until they were past the Lawbringers and out of earshot.

'So Rhe brings out your good side, eh?' Maiss asked from behind her father.

'Mark my words,' Enchei said darkly, 'the hypocrisy of that one'll kill more'n a few of his fellows. *Now* he claims superior authority, with high-born guns at his side? Mebbe if House Dragon had oppressed this city he'd have a case, but they've protected the Emperor's position as well as any.'

'On our side now?' Myken called from the rear.

He glanced back, clearly surprised she had spoken up. 'On no one's side 'cept my own, but I won't ignore truth. Dragon's been this city's protectors for centuries and the wealth has flowed in, not out. I've seen conquest and oppression – this ain't it, not by a long shot. That the high castes of the city might not like it ain't the greatest problem in—'

'Let's start with problems like hellhounds then, shall we?' Kesh interjected. 'Do you have a plan like last time?'

Enchei shook his head. 'Unless killing everyone and everything in our path is a plan?'

'There's only seven of us,' she pointed out. 'How about we find something a little more clever than that?'

'Like we're outnumbered, they probably know we're coming for them, and this'll be a trap of both demons and Astaren?' Enchei's sour response was met with silence.

Narin glanced back at Kesh and forced a smile. 'Something better than that,' he said. 'Something that involves our own demons – our own Astaren.'

'Who made you officer in charge, eh?' said Enchei.

'You did, every bloody time you made me take the credit.'

Enchei laughed at that. 'Good point. Guess that makes me the sergeant who gets all the important stuff done.'

'Are you both finished?' Enay demanded.

Narin and Enchei exchanged a look.

'Don't have daughters,' the veteran said. 'She was this bossy even as a child. Ah, too late for you, isn't it? Well then, don't have two.'

CHAPTER 36

Oh brother of mine, what have I done?

Sorpan crouched on the roof of the Minerild in the lee of a shrine recently desecrated with bloody symbols. He was not alone, but of the other figures up there only one possessed a soul and Sorpan considered that a tattered, pathetic thing.

A little treachery, you would not have begrudged me that, Sorpan thought, picturing the grey-haired veteran he'd met the year previously. *Such is the nature of our lives. Those of us not destined for greatness must still make our own way.*

He bowed his head, unable to look out at the mist-veiled streets through which, he was sure, the hero he'd betrayed was approaching. The city was quiet, cowed to silence by the demons that haunted its shadows and the brutal cold of winter. Distant echoes brought the voices of hellhounds to him, faint on the feeble breeze, while the occasional gasp and moan of pain came from a figure much closer to hand – one he wished he could not see.

And it turns out they were right about me. Whatever flaw they identified, whatever led to the quiet, painless stalling of my career, that seems to have been my undoing. I never intended this – as the Gods are my witness, I did not.

A pale figure ascended the stairway behind Sorpan and moved up beside him. 'You're quiet,' he commented.

'I'll be dead soon, Kebrai,' Sorpan replied. 'That makes a man want a few moments with his thoughts.'

The Leviathan made an amused sound. 'You think us so vulnerable?'

'Expendable, not vulnerable.' He looked up at to meet Kebrai's disconcerting lilac eyes. 'Even you.'

'Who is not expendable in this world?'

Sorpan looked away. 'I'm Astaren. I've no use for feeble fatalism.'

'Very well. Answer me this – why would Priest plan to throw our lives away?'

'Because all this has little to do with my countryman. All that's happening in the city, the tattooist and I are both incidental to it.'

'You think Priest cannot pursue two goals at once?'

'I think I will not survive to see either.'

Kebrai was quiet a moment. 'Priest is not wasteful, certainly not with those of value. Do you doubt your worth, whether or not we take the mind of this tattooist?'

'My value comes with a danger – I don't know what the Sea Lords think of their Astaren striking out on their own, but I doubt Priest wants such attention from House Ghost too if she's already antagonising House Dragon.'

'That is Priest's problem.'

'And my life.'

The Leviathan smiled unexpectedly. 'Perhaps this will cheer you then, I have orders for you.'

'What? Where's Priest?'

'Nearby. We anticipate the tattooist and his friends will be coming here. When that happens, you will ensure the Senior Kobelt escapes and heads toward the river. There's a palazzo at the far end of the Steel Steps bearing the family arms of Sultatrair – the family are wintering elsewhere. Priest will meet you there.'

'We're to be bait?'

'Priest remains determined to take the tattooist. That has not changed and there's no conflict with any other plans she might be pursuing. One might even complement the other, but what's certain is that Priest isn't foolish enough to waste a man of your skills. Bait you might be, but the sight of you is bait enough. Not your death.'

Sorpan pursed his lips as he thought. 'Why the Kobelt? If he's an agent of Priest's, he can take care of himself. If not, why is he important?'

'He has a further role to play.'

'Like Sharish?'

Sorpan forced himself to look to his right across the roofs and shrines towards the raised crescent of wall that rose around a quarter of the Minerild's perimeter. His mage-blessed eyes meant he could see every detail of the shamaness' pain – chained to the brick wall and linked to the rooftop shrines.

Her clothes and flesh had both been torn by shadow claws and her blood ran freely, but it was the spiked crown that fixed her to the wall and linked her to the shrines that was the greatest horror.

He knew he could do nothing for the woman, but the sight of her reduced to a mere tool to engineer horror sickened him more than the experienced Astaren would have expected. Or perhaps it just reminded him of his betrayal, and he found that harder to stomach than expected.

The entire summoning effort was being directed through her mind. Priest had turned on her suddenly and without mercy. Sharish had stood no chance of escape before she was handed, crippled and stunned, to the strange pagan priest who had welcomed them here – Senior Kobelt Geret Hoke – who had acted as though he had always been party to their plans, had known what was going on better than Sorpan. He had been the one to draw more and more horrors from the shadow realms, to the brief astonishment of his own Kobelen and acolytes. And then they had succumbed almost all at once, their souls swallowed by the hellhounds driven into their minds.

And he has done it better than I could have ever expected from some civilian pagan, certainly when he called a demon-prince of their realm. Sorpan paused. *Which is the whole point. Gods, what a fool I am!*

'The Terim,' he said slowly. 'Such a powerful demon is too great for most minds, it would destroy them almost immediately. But if a mind was already enslaved by something lesser beforehand, that might prepare it enough for a demon – for a time at least.'

Kebrai gave him a level look. 'I see you understand.'

Understand? Oh yes. I understand Priest is in bed with House Eagle and their Mindwalkers. If ever I doubted how expendable I might be, I'm sure the twisted soul of the Mindwalker inside Geret Hoke will be happy to confirm it as it watches me die.

'Where is he?'

'In the central forge, down below.'

Sorpan nodded and returned to his vigil. 'I will see it done.' *Too late to go back now.*

'This isn't going to be easy.'

Narin glanced around at his comrades. 'Did anyone expect that?' he asked, clenching his fists less in anticipation of the fight to come than an effort to keep them warm.

Enchei shrugged. 'I'm reminding you,' he growled. 'Given the numbers we just saw back there, it's worth saying twice.'

'How many?'

'On view? Half a dozen novices prowling the rooftops, all possessed. Patrolling the perimeter you've got teams of guards, Sea Snakes if my guess is right.'

'Astaren?'

'More like pets of Astaren,' Enchei said. 'A warrior cult from Leviathan, trained from birth to work as a unit – brains half-fried on drugs, but all the more dangerous for it. They get sold in broods to work as mercenaries. Given what I was told about there being a Benthic Knight behind this company, it's no surprise they brought Sea Snakes with them.'

Maiss nodded. 'We came across a handful in Sight's End once – skin so pale they look dead already, they take wounds like it too. Don't notice injuries until you put them down.'

'And what if we come across this Benthic Knight?'

Enchei scowled. 'Run – all of you.' He looked pointedly at his daughters. 'I'm serious, unless you got that one dead to rights with the Dragon's Breath, run away. Maybe with your new passenger, Irato, you can take one, but not the rest of you. I ain't so keen on it either, but the choice ain't mine.'

'We've got all the skills you have, Father,' Enay objected, but Enchei just raised a hand to stop her.

'No – you really don't. Your body's been changed the same as mine, that's all. Don't mistake that for twenty years' training and battlefield experience, let alone my armour.'

She bit her lip and nodded. 'Just don't think we're precious and helpless.'

'I've seen you in action, remember?' Enchei gave a brief, fierce smile that gave Narin a cold sensation in his gut. 'You'll be getting your hands bloody.'

His friend was an irreverent and calm figure most of the time, but now he had the look of a bone-deep killer. It was disconcerting to see the man strike a match and ignite that part of his soul, the part Enchei had now been running from for decades.

Is that how he was chosen? Narin wondered. *For the ability to choose which self he wears, or is it just something buried in his mind by the mage-priests who changed him? Gods, which would I even prefer? I still see the faces of those I've killed, but would I want a dead corner of my soul like that?*

'Irato and me lead,' Enchei said as he readied his helm again. 'Narin, Kesh and Myken behind us. Watch our backs and follow us

334

up to the top. The summoner's likely to be up there with the shrines. We go when the guns start, with luck it'll distract them and give us room to move.'

'And us?' Enay asked.

'You two take the rear. Maiss, take Enay's pistols and cover her. That lance is slow to move and they could be coming from all sides. Enay, leave a trail of destruction in our wake – make it clear for anyone investigating tomorrow that Dragons were here and dealing with the threat to the city. I'm no fan of House Dragon, but anything that pisses on our enemy's plan works for me.'

'What if they *are* here?' Narin asked suddenly. 'What if we meet Dragon Astaren?'

Enchei shook his head. 'They'll be back in Dragon District; they've got enough on their plates. Their remit's to protect their own, protect Lord Omteray. If they hadn't been ambushed, sure, but they don't have the numbers to rule the city right now. Their only goal is ensuring the ruling lord of Dragon District lives through the night – if they can't protect their own, the shame'll be doubled.'

'And Iron's Astaren?'

'Most likely killed before the shrines were activated, or they're keeping their heads down. Only Dragon keep units of combat troops in the city, so far as I've ever heard, the rest mostly have just spies. They're much tougher than normal soldiers, but they're not here to challenge Dragon's authority. You don't piss off the prime hegemony in the Empire unless you really need to.'

He slipped his helm on and readied his weapons, tucking back the sleeve of his left arm to uncover twin holes the width of a knitting needle that could spit darts hard enough to punch right through a man. In his hands were his Astaren baton and a triangular-bladed dagger of the same dark metal as the rest of his armour.

'Now we wait.'

On the western flank of the Minerild, Lawbringer Rhe glanced left and right at the figures waiting in the shadows. The gaudily-dressed Imperials had split into two groups and flanked Rhe's Lawbringers, pulling on nondescript grey capes that blended into the smoke-blackened stones of Iron District. Through the mist he caught Prince Kashte's eye and the young Imperial nodded to him, the jewelled hilt of Kashte's broadsword protruding from his coat while his rifle nestled in his hands.

Rhe set off, moving swiftly through the narrow side-streets until he reached the broad cobbled road that surrounded the Minerild. His neck prickled as he felt the predatory attention settle on him, but he strode on regardless until he was out in the most exposed part – a looming ghost in the starlight.

He looked around, seeing faint red glowing eyes in the shadows of a darkened archway, then two pairs, then three. The outline of a head appeared over the high wall almost directly in front of him.

'You are all under arrest,' he called loudly. His voice echoed around the deserted streets, met by a low growl just on the edge of hearing. 'You will receive no second warning. The summoner and all members of the Etrage Merchant House are to surrender immediately.'

Behind him the Lawbringers and Investigators emerged too, guns already drawn. He couldn't see the Imperials but Rhe knew they would be there, keeping to the shadows themselves and readying a volley if the Lawbringers were attacked.

There was no reply. Rhe drew his sword and transferred it to his left hand. All nobles and warriors were taught to use both gun and sword in either hand, but the pistol holsters were traditionally angled towards the right. Few became more than competent with either in their off hand; Rhe had even seen one youth manage to stab himself when ordered to switch hands in duelling practice. For Rhe there had never been such problems, never anything more than puzzlement that skilled fighters could be reduced to childish helplessness that way.

'No answer?' he said, almost to himself. 'Very well.'

He didn't get a chance to take a step forward. A small figure burst forward from the archway, blond hair flying, face contorted and distended as it leapt for Rhe. Such was its shocking, unnatural power that it covered the ground in the blink of an eye. With blurring speed Rhe drew and fired. The figure's head snapped back as though on a leash, black blood exploding from its throat as the bullet tore through and shattered its spine.

It fell like a broken toy, but Rhe was forced to dart to one side to avoid the tumbling bundle of fangs and ragged limbs. He almost didn't see the second possessed novice charge out, but behind him, Investigator Soral was the first to aim and fire. She caught it dead-on, a black flower blossoming on the possessed's chest before it staggered back.

Rhe made up the ground in two steps and brought his sword around in a long arc before the novice could right itself. He slashed up at its armpit and opened a deep cut, but didn't wait to see if that was enough to kill. He brought his blade back around to chop into its nape hard enough to break bone. It fell.

From the roof of the building off to his right a pair of pale, hairless figures dropped. Rhe left the Lawbringers there to deal with them and one was spun right around by the double-crack that split the night. The second ducked down and leapt like a hunting dog, scampering forward at the nearest Lawbringer and ignoring the shot that grazed it. The pale man drove up at the Lawbringer, daggers outstretched as though for leverage before he bit at the man's face.

The Lawbringer howled – the first cry to part the night – and fell. What happened to him Rhe couldn't say, as the sound seemed to herald a dozen more possessed novices and pale ones emerging as one from the shadows of the Minerild. Rhe sheathed one gun and fired again, taking one of a pair through the forehead. From both sides the night was shattered by a volley of gunshots – both pistols and Imperial rifles.

Many of the newcomers fell but the second of Rhe's pair zigzagged towards him, thrown off-balance by the lead that ripped through its ribs but did not slow it down. Powerful strides covered the ground so swiftly that Rhe only just had time to drop his spent gun before it lurched within cutting range, hooked daggers slashing wildly.

Instinct drove Rhe forward. He slipped both hands around the sword's grip and thrust straight. He caught the man high in the chest, felt the crackle of bone parting as the tip drove through and into the vital organs behind. Such was the pale man's momentum he drove right up the blade, still flailing with his daggers, and Rhe felt a burning pain open on his bicep as his coat and flesh were sliced open. He gave ground, startled more by the unnatural ferocity than anything else, before finally managing to raise a leg and kick the staggering man in the gut.

The kick drove them apart, Rhe almost falling as the pale man finally came to a halt. Both were still for a moment, Rhe afforded a clear view of the man's rounded face, strangely thin lips and lolling black tongue. His eyes were black, no gleam of infernal light there, but the light of the Gods illuminated slender fangs in his mouth and Rhe didn't wait to see any more. A second kick and a renewed grip on his sword shoved the pale man off it before Rhe spun and slashed in one fluid motion.

Nearby there were others not faring so well, several of his comrades taken to ground by the attackers. No more rushed from the Minerild, however, and the remaining Lawbringers quickly went to their comrades' aid, impaling the snarling defenders until they were at last silent.

All was quiet for a moment. Before anyone could speak or Rhe could assess the dead and wounded, a haunting howl rang out from somewhere deep within the great circular building. Despite himself, Rhe felt a tightening in his stomach at the unnatural sound. He straightened and let his sword fall so the guard rested on his boot, ready to flick up again in case of attack, hands already moving to reload his pistols.

'Ready yourselves,' he called and a cold knot of anger twisted inside him. 'These streets are the Emperor's own, we do not suffer demons to walk them.'

He finished one pistol and sheathed it, picking up the second and quickly reloading that too. One quick jerk of the foot and he caught his sword again, advancing forward with pistol and blade ready. If the others were behind him, he did not notice. He saw only the shadows ahead. As he entered the Minerild, the light of the Gods went with him.

CHAPTER 37

Enchei didn't speak. He didn't need to; the stuttered whip-crack of gunshots told their own tale. With Irato close behind he ghosted forward, footsteps silent and weapons ready. Emerging into the open ground he found no one waiting for him, only the white flash of a Sea Snake devotee rounding the curve of the Minerild towards Rhe's troops.

It didn't last long. Just as they reached the nearest archway, recessed between a shuttered bakery and a blacksmith's, a possessed novice came sprinting in the other direction. Barely an adult, the young woman had red burning eyes, huge lower canines and every finger had morphed into a hooked claw. She bounded towards them, hurling herself through the air.

Enchei shot her in the face, but it did nothing to slow her flight. He twisted, battering at her reaching arms as he dodged. She fell heavily, but landed on all fours. Before Enchei could bring his darts to bear a second time, Irato reached out and almost lazily grabbed her by the scruff of the neck.

The possessed snarled and wrenched around, scrabbling to tear Irato's face open. The former goshe looked unperturbed—

—*no*, Enchei corrected himself, *Irato's not even there now.*

A blank expression on his face, eyes and mouth shining with bluish light, Irato swatted away the flailing claws and shook the novice like a rat. Enchei heard the crack of her spine breaking, saw the shudder of air around her as the hellhound inside was half-dislodged by the death of its vessel.

Should've run, Enchei thought idly as some shadowy limb reached up from the dead novice's body. *It'll get you now.*

Irato somehow grabbed the insubstantial limb and yanked it forward, hauling the hellhound out into the night's sky before a bright flash of light tore through it and the shadows evaporated. The Apkai, or whatever fragment of its self it had left behind, let the corpse fall from its fingers – already forgotten – and stalked towards the arched entrance to the Minerild.

Enchei watched it for a moment as the scent of snow filled his mind, quite separate from the freezing weather that surrounded him. Memories of a mountain valley with fresh snowfall and glimpsed figures in the darkness. The place that would become known as the Fields of the Broken, the fragments of a waking god's thoughts that brought horror and ruin to five armies.

A sudden and powerful sense of hatred filled him, though he knew the Apkai was nothing like what had been found in the valley tombs. For a moment it didn't matter and he felt his arm rise, ready to fire at Irato's back. Some scrap of revenge for the pain and death, the nights of horror that had strained the minds of even the Astaren among them, but he quelled the thoughts and forced his hand down again.

You killed it, there's no more revenge to be had.

With an effort, he stopped his hand shaking, old instincts screaming in the cage of his memories until he was back in control. Just the memories were enough to nearly paralyse him. Every second he watched some demon avatar hunt in the darkness brought fresh reminders of those months he could not forget.

Enchei glanced back at the people following him. Wide-eyed Narin scurrying behind and veiled Myken moving with drilled purpose, Kesh taut and tense, his daughters standing tall and ready as they watched their flanks.

Always leaving folk behind, Enchei, he said to himself. *And you left a part of you in that snow-choked valley. How much is left of the girls you once knew? Of the father they once knew? The dead lie in my wake, that's what a survivor carries through the years, but sometimes I feel like more. Like some avatar of destruction – I break what I touch and leave the pieces of lives behind me.*

He shook his head. His purpose was clear. Whether this was his last mission or not, success would make those girls a fraction safer. Whatever part of him had broken, the fracture had created enough jagged edges for a weapon and like it or not, that was how he was most comfortable. He turned and followed Irato into the Minerild, the edge of Irato's long-knife laced with starlight even in the dark.

The blackness closed around them like the advancing grave. Enchei felt a tremble in his eyes as they sought to adjust, settling on

340

a washed-out grey view just in time for another attack. Four Sea Snake devotees burst through a doorway in the side of the curved tunnel wall, daggers in their hands. He fired the baton at one and the man folded like a child's toy, falling stunned under his comrade's feet and getting trampled in the other's desperation. That one Enchei dodged, rolling right around the reaching blades. He popped the man's shoulder out of joint with a deft swipe, jerking the drug-fuelled warrior to a halt long enough to jam his dagger up through the base of his mouth. As the devotee dropped, Enchei was already finishing off the unconscious man.

Beyond him, Irato whirled and slashed with swift, awkward movements, his skill with a blade superseded by the demon avatar's brutal speed and power. One Sea Snake threw himself under the blades and buried his fangs into Irato's arm, only to be half-decapitated in the next instant and never see the venom of his bite fail.

'Move,' Enchei yelled, pointing towards where the brick passage opened out on a sliver of star-lit ground.

A set of stone steps led up the side of one building and Enchei ran past Irato to reach them. Another possessed was descending but it stumbled under the twin effects of the baton and darts ripping through its body. Enchei left it for Irato to finish as it tumbled down the steps, vaulting the first few as he ran for the rooftops.

Up there the starlight burned in his mage-sight – white against a dirty red haze around the shrines. The columns of pale stone fragments hummed with power, the wire surrounding them seemingly part of some complex web that snared power from the air. His eyesight fluttered again, shifting through complex colours and forms as it sought to identify a surge of power in the air so great that it set Enchei's teeth on edge.

He could hear the calls of hellhounds more clearly from here – the howls and rushing wind of their home just a step away as the shrines thinned the wall between the worlds. He looked around, shot once, twice at a possessed creeping forward at him. The impact threw it off a rooftop to the ground below and won him a moment to properly inspect his surroundings. The configuration of the shrines had been changed, that much was obvious – the cone-shaped ones having been connected in a double prism, the columns in a horseshoe form. The heaviest chains now formed a gathering rune that led to a bound figure at the back wall, while lesser ones had been jury-rigged into a summoning rune with bent metal struts forming the vertices where there was no stone shrine.

As he took it all in, he sensed movement in the shadows. Great shapes circling around them. Enchei turned once then raised his arm and sent a volley of darts into the figure bound to the wall. It was a woman, he guessed, maybe House Gold by the look of her, but horribly injured and twitching under the force of the power being driven through her. Whether she was the summoner or not, what flowed through her needed to be stopped.

It wasn't. Even though the woman stilled, the power continued unabated – but now it all flowed down, like water draining away. Behind him, Irato rose up, a contrasting light in Enchei's mage-sight. The demon avatar turned left and right, inspecting the shrines and the shifting bulky shadows beyond them. He outstretched a hand and the nearest of the shrines burst apart in a flare of sparks.

Snarls came from the shadows; deep and threatening growls from the guarding hellhounds. In response Irato gathered more light to his hands, forming a cat o' nine tails of spitting energy that he used to flay the nearer shadows. The hellhound there was torn open by the force of the blow and Enchei was already moving – content to leave Irato to deal with the remainder.

He ran over the rooftops, quick jumps taking him between buildings, until he was at the centre of the Minerild. There the power still flowed, running down through the roof of one unremarkable structure. He plunged forward, leaping for the small brick parapet around its half-rotten, pitch-stained roof. Whoever controlled the hellhounds, whoever was using the woman on the roof as a lens for their workings, had to be here.

Before he could drive down through the roof, it exploded. Enchei's mage-sight went white as a hammer-blow of noise and roof fragments struck him face-on and threw him backwards. All-consuming white light, then the studded black of night, then a second impact and a long moment of silence.

Narin was halfway up the steps when he heard the explosion. He reached the top in time to see the after-glow of fire vomit up into the sky and a dark figure pinwheeling into the crumbling dirty brick of a neighbouring house. A section toppled inward under the impact and the body fell in a cloud of dust through the wall. Narin ran the last few steps up, Myken on his heels, and dodged around Irato. Light blazed from the former goshe's hands, long spitting streams that raced around the rooftops with a will of their own.

A clamour of lupine sounds assailed Narin's ears, howls of rage and pain, while shadows burst under Irato's assault and the dust and embers of the shattered roof spiralled through the cold night air. He staggered forward through it all, trying to blank out the shrieks and growls, the gunshots echoing through the guts of the Minerild, and pushed on after Enchei.

He reached the edge of the rooftop and looked down. The central structure was burning, twisted fragments of metal glowing inside what remained of its walls. Just beyond that were two figures – a pale-skinned man poised in the act of firing a pistol at someone below Narin while supporting another, darker one. Nearer, half-inside a broken building, lay Enchei amid the rubble.

Something about the pale-skinned man demanded Narin's attention. He was House Ghost – both his clothes and features confirmed it. That he was Astaren seemed likely when he fired a second time, then a third, with the same pistol. One glance up at Narin and he raised the gun to shoot. Narin found his body wouldn't react at first – he was hypnotised by the slow, smooth movement, while around the man grey flowers of dust burst into life where the Lawbringers' bullets struck brickwork.

At last his limbs obeyed and Narin dropped to his right as the man fired. His shoulder was slammed back as the crack of the pistol rang out and Narin realised as he flopped backwards that he'd been shot. A strange prickle ran through his fingers, then the numbness of a stinging punch filled his arm. Only then did the pain come and Narin gasped at the shock of it, too surprised to even cry out.

Sprawled on the edge of the rooftop, almost directly above Enchei, Narin watched the pale-skinned man direct one more shot in the direction of the Lawbringers down below. After that he fled, one arm slipped around the chest of his presumably-wounded companion. Narin watched them run into another dark archway tunnel before he found himself unceremoniously yanked back from the edge by Kesh. Above him, like some vengeful goddess, Myken stepped over his body with her musket levelled. She fired after the pair, but from the slight twist of her features, only half-hidden by the hanging cloth, Narin could tell she had missed.

'Damn fool,' Kesh snapped, closing her hand around Narin's shoulder. 'When are you going to learn some sense?'

The Investigator howled at that and squirmed under her grasp, but the pain was too great to wriggle free and he submitted.

343

'Move,' commanded another voice from behind Myken.

The Wyvern glanced back then stepped away, hands already moving through the motions of reloading her gun. Narin looked up in confusion, not recognising Irato's voice until the man with shining eyes was staring down at him.

Irato crouched and removed Kesh's hands from Narin's wound. Narin's vision blurred for a moment at that fresh stab of pain, but then Irato was touching two fingers to it and the Investigator properly understood what it was to scream with his every ounce of strength.

'He will live,' Irato stated once the red shadows of pain had receded and Narin once more gasped for air, that now stank of burned flesh.

'Enchei,' Narin croaked, flopping towards the edge of the rooftop again.

Kesh peered over. 'He's moving,' she commented, far from concerned for the veteran. A grin flashed across her face as Narin heard a voice from down below – not clearly enough to make out the words, but the tone spoke volumes. 'Oh aye, man's back to normal already.'

'The summoner,' Narin pointed towards the tunnel he'd seen the two men retreat down. His arm was numb now – entirely absent and limp, but mercifully free from pain. 'They went that way.'

'The summoner is there,' Irato said, pointing across the rooftops to a bloodied, brutalised body that seemed to Narin to have been nailed to the wall. 'She is dead,' the demon stated in a flat, lifeless tone.

Narin gave up trying to focus too greatly on the dead woman Irato pointed at. The sight was horrific in any case and making out details in the dark made his head swim.

'The Ghost … he escaped that way. Had someone with him, injured I think.'

Enay's sharp voice emerged through the staccato sounds of gunshots. 'Ghost? The one who betrayed Father?'

As she spoke, Maiss crouched and extended an empty hand over the edge of the building. A moment later she hauled back and pulled the swearing, blank-visored Enchei back up on to the roof. The former Astaren looked unsteady to Narin, but with the world lurching underneath him, Narin was envious that Enchei could remain standing.

'Bastard almost got me,' Enchei growled. 'Must be old to fall for somethin' like that.'

'The summoner is dead,' Irato intoned. 'Destroy the shrines and the remaining hellhounds in the city will be banished. Then my duty is done.'

'As simple as that, eh?' Enchei snapped. 'You're coming with us, I tell ya. That worm Sorpan tried to sell me to Gealann mercs and until I cut his balls off, nothing's done.'

'Narin saw him, he went that way.'

Enchei followed Kesh's direction. 'Good.' He glanced down. 'Got yourself shot?'

Narin coughed and nodded.

'Tough – you ain't dead, so you're coming with us.' With his finger he traced a path through the air, following the line of rooftops to work out where Sorpan's tunnel would emerge. 'He was heading west?'

'They.'

That took Enchei by surprise. 'They?'

'Had an injured man with him, was helping him.'

'Don't seem likely. Was the other one even paler than a Ghost?'

All eyes turned to Narin, who shook his head. 'Looked a local – some House under Iron. Hair wasn't grey, but he was from round here.'

Enchei grasped Narin's good arm and pulled the Investigator upright. 'Could it've been one o' the priests you met before?'

'I ... maybe.'

'Doesn't sound like your job's done yet after all, Irato,' Enchei said. 'Sounds like we've got a second summoner to kill – one that used the first like a weapon.'

He started to skirt the open ground where the shattered building stood, heading west over the rooftops towards a stairway.

'It could be a trap,' Myken called after him as the others moved to follow. 'The defenders here were no match for us.' She pointed down to demonstrate her point, to where Lawbringer Rhe had emerged into the starlight at the heart of the Minerild, looking left and right for more Sea Snakes and possessed.

'Aye, could be,' Enchei replied without any of his usual levity, 'but I want the bait all the same.'

Before anyone could argue, Enay hefted her Stone Dragon lance and gave the remaining shrines a speculative look. 'Best you all get to the ground,' she said with a cold smile on her face, and levelled the weapon at one of the nearest. '*Right* now.'

Narin hurried to obey, Kesh helping him along as Myken led the way to the stairs. Irato simply stepped off the roof while Maiss stayed with her sister, a pistol in each hand. Before Narin had reached the stairs he heard the dreadful, hushed sound of the Dragon's Breath turning the air to flame and metal to slag. He quickened his pace, despite his now-useless arm.

Once they got to ground level Narin looked around for Lawbringer Rhe, but the man had disappeared already. Prince Kashte flashed him a smile as he arrived briefly in the starlight – rifle now stowed on his back and broadsword dripping blood. Then more gunshots came from the northern part and he was off again, two more gold-scarfed Imperials prowling in his wake.

'Looks like they're enjoying 'emselves,' Enchei growled. 'I guess Imperials don't get much chance to brawl like commoners.'

With Irato leading the way, they moved through winding tunnels and open alleys that echoed with gunshots, shouts and cries. Narin saw nothing block their path as they followed the Ghost's trail. He heard only the whispers of Enchei's darts and their clatter against brick, swiftly followed by the meaty crack and thump of Irato killing something out of sight.

He tried to keep his eyes on the person ahead, Myken, and do little more – apart from keep his teeth from chattering in fear, or shock, or the memory of pain, he was no longer sure.

Kesh continued to give him anxious looks, but it was his left arm that Narin could no longer use. He tucked it inside his tunic to stop it working at the wound as he moved. His right hand tightened sufficiently around the hilt of his sword that Narin refused to be told to wait behind.

Not that anyone has suggested that, Narin noted in a distant, dazed fashion as they emerged into a street. He saw Irato point towards movement perhaps a hundred yards away. *Enchei wants me on hand to recognise the priest. Is that it? Or something else?*

He shook the questions from his mind, finding no answers in the fog there. It was easier simply to follow, to leave the decisions to his friends and stumble along behind as they hurried down the street. Ahead, Narin could see the pale golden pinpricks of magical light that adorned the towers of House Iron's nobles.

The Spines, he recalled, remembering the six white columns around which the largest palazzos were built. It was a sight he'd rarely seen at night, but he knew the mages of House Iron in generations past had set sigils of magic-imbued glass – invocations of divine favour – on the columns and the peaks of those palazzos. A lesser display than the long shapes that adorned House Dragon's towers or the eyries of Eagle perhaps, but beautiful against the stars of the Gods none the less.

346

'There,' Enchei said, pointing down the street.

Narin could see nothing, but Enay and Maiss both nodded as more gunshots rang out behind them. The houses on both sides were dark and silent, the people of Iron District no doubt cowed into silence while rare violence reigned outside.

'Who's the other one?' Maiss asked.

'The priest here,' Narin said abruptly as though jerking awake. 'Senior Kobelt Hoker, something like that. Bastard's one hell of a liar. Even Rhe believed him, but he was with them all along.' He spat. 'Pillar of the community, hah.'

They reached a fork in the road and Enchei stopped to look for their quarry as Narin and Kesh panted for breath.

'Towards the river,' Irato said. He pointed down to the dirt-packed ground as though it was as clear as day.

Enchei frowned and tugged a chunk of metal from the darter on his wrist, slapping an identical one back in its place a few moments later. 'You sure? Something's messed my senses up proper, I can't see any traces anywhere.'

'I am.'

They continued in that fashion for five hundred yards, taking an oblique path towards the palazzos looming on the nearer bank. The largest, those built around the ancient columns, looked like cog wheels stacked one atop another, irregularly sized with scraps of pale golden light inscribed on the walls between shuttered windows.

Around them were lesser palazzos that echoed the style and Irato led them to one at the Crescent flank of the noble streets – a light-less building of five storeys inside a yellow brick perimeter. Noble sigils in the Iron tongue were embossed on the bronze-sheathed gate that stood ajar, square pillars spaced along the wall topped alternately with stylised hammers and anvils.

Enchei glanced at his daughters and nodded to the wall. Maiss knelt at the base, making a cradle with her hands that Enay stepped into. Without any great effort Narin could see, she stood and lifted her sister, lance and all, up until Enay could see over the wall.

'Empty,' she reported as she dropped back down again. 'Main door's open.'

'Why would they go to ground?' Kesh wondered aloud.

'They haven't,' was Enchei's grim reply. 'We ain't that lucky.'

'So what, then?'

'Enay, Maiss – skirt the perimeter. See what other exits they got and if there's any mischief you can get up to. There's power here, enchantments in the stones, I can smell 'em. This place has been prepared.'

The two young women broke into a silent run, as swift and silent as the foxes used as vessels by lesser demons.

Narin exchanged a look with Kesh. 'You're just going to walk straight in, aren't you?'

That elicited a grunt. 'If this is a trap, I doubt they had Irato in mind.' Enchei flexed his fingers and a burst of lightning crackled hot and fierce over his armoured hand. 'You three stay here – keep this gate open. Myken, you shoot anyone you see and don't like the look of, understand?'

With that he pulled the gate open and stalked through, Irato again following close behind. Beyond them, Narin saw a great stone basin a few yards past the entrance, ice gleaming inside it. The light of the Gods illuminated frosted gravel paths between fractured boulders half-covered with grey mosses. Under starlight the formal garden looked like a long-dead corpse of some fantastical beast entombed in ice, the broken edges of stone arranged in some complex, organic pattern.

Myken raised her musket, a practised position of readiness from which she could aim in an instant. Despite his wound Narin found himself holding his breath as he waited for some new attack, but what came was quite unexpected.

From the doorway a grey figure walked out into the starlight. Narin felt a jolt – the figure was insubstantial and ghostly. A young woman, barely as old as Kesh, with painfully thin limbs, a blurring grey dress hung down over her feet. Her gaunt face looked serene, at peace with death – though if she was truly a ghost, she had died of prolonged starvation. Her empty hands trailed through the air at her sides, a gesture of peace that revealed her clawed fingers.

'You want me, I'm here,' Enchei growled, apparently unperturbed.

The ghost opened her mouth to speak but no words came out. Her hands described some complex gesture, more a dance than communication, but it was enough to stop Enchei in his tracks and glance back at his demon-possessed friend. If Irato had an opinion he did not share it so Enchei hurried to meet the ghost, weapons ready and armour crackling with power, rather than be left standing in the open.

Without warning, the ghost lunged forward. Enchei evaded its grasp easily, but in the next instant Narin saw it was not after him but Irato.

The possessed goshe reached out and grabbed the ghost by the arms while the echo of a howl seemed to rise up from the ground. The ghost struggled a moment, unable to break Irato's grip, then relaxed and bowed her head before bursting apart.

Suddenly, two more ghosts leaped up from the gravel beneath their feet and seized Irato. A savage open hand swipe tore right through one and it instantly evaporated into nothing, but more followed – a sudden eruption of grey blurs appearing on all sides and falling forward into Irato's body, flailing and clawing at him. In the next moment a burst of bluish light erupted from Irato's back and Narin heard the man howl – not the demon, the man.

Irato turned his head to the sky as half a dozen spitting whipcords of light appeared from inside him and lashed at the ghosts, but they continued forward and somehow they bodily hauled the twisting, folding shape of the demon's avatar from Irato's body. The former goshe screamed as the demon was ripped from his body and mind, the massed ghosts wrapping themselves around it and bearing it down into the ground, where all of a sudden it vanished.

The lights faded. Irato gave one final croak of pain and sank heavily to his knees then all was silent. Myken didn't wait any longer and marched through the gate, musket levelled. Enchei turned in a circle as she came, looking for a target for his darts, but at last went to check on Irato, who looked about to topple face-first to the ground. The stricken man stared off at nothing in the distance, shuddering at what had just happened.

Behind Enchei the door crashed open and the shadows were split with light. Narin recoiled from the white fire silhouetting his friend even as Myken aimed and fired. If the bullet struck, Narin didn't hear it. A surge of wind whipped up over the ground as Enchei rolled and fired. Stuttered white light seemed to flash across his faceless helm then something caught hold of him and yanked the former Astaren off his feet.

Myken dropped her musket and fired a pistol, but failed to stop whatever force was dragging Enchei towards the door. He twisted in mid-air; throwing his body through an impossible horizontal flip and landing upright with his baton tearing the air apart ahead of him. Again he was snared and dragged off his feet, spun about as his body made a furrow in the gravel.

'Oh f—'

Narin blinked and Enchei was gone.

CHAPTER 38

Enchei crashed heavily to the flagstone floor and rolled sideways. He pushed himself up into a crouch and spun away, expecting some sort of attack, before realising he was in a still, dark room. Shades of grey fluttered across his eyes as his mage-sight fought to readjust. The lines of an atrium enclosed by narrow archways slowly unfolded before him.

Through the central arch he saw a grand hall that rose to almost the height of the entire building – a central space penned by curling staircases and partitions in the House Gold fashion of hollowed-out caverns. Directly in the centre of the room, a figure of nightmare regarded him. Once it had been a man of House Gold – the Kobelt, he assumed – but now there was little left of the man he'd once been. Black trails of blood marred his cheeks, welts and fissures in his skin spilled blood and smoke-like trails. Where there had been something darkly magnificent about the possessed Banshee, haloed by a demon's shadow, here it was monstrous as the forces slowly tore their vessel apart.

Enchei checked left and right as incantations buried deep in his memory began to sing and he rubbed the metal of his gauntleted fingers together. He could feel the armour chime and radiate tiny pulses of sound as the shape of the palazzo's interior began to develop in his mind's eye – the line of stairs and semi-defined rooms, four solid chimney stacks and curved beams that supported the roof. It was a warren with few obvious exits; the lower windows too small to escape through, the winding staircases all leading down to the centre where the demon waited. The demon's presence distorted it all, offered Enchei only a twisted picture with a deep well at its heart, but he saw enough.

No point dragging this out, Enchei thought as more incantations activated. His muscles began to ache with building power, runes on the metal edge and ball of his gauntlets glowing white. Without waiting he fired a stream of darts at the Kobelt. The possessed man didn't bother to dodge, letting the slivers of metal punch through the flesh without effect.

Enchei continued to fire, volley after volley until the man's face was a lacerated mess – it wouldn't stop the demon, he knew, but anything that weakened its vessel might be worthwhile, if he could stay alive for long enough. He had no intention of getting into a straight fight, not when there was a tangle of obstacles to get lost in, but torn flesh and arteries forced the demon to expend more energy to maintain its link to the mortal realm.

When he stopped, the demon hadn't moved. In the strange washed-out twilight of his mage-sight there was a moment of stillness. Even the air was caught between breaths and Enchei found himself frozen, watching the demon from halfway behind a stone pillar.

'You realise you can't win,' called a woman's voice from somewhere above Enchei. 'Not against both of us.'

Enchei suppressed a curse.

'Your point?' he replied after another furtive check.

He could see no one and the voice seemed to echo from three different points on the upper floor – she was clearly masking her location. The incantations in his mind changed to staccato pulses flooding around the building, but the demon was a vast sucking hole in the world. The outline Enchei saw was so warped by its presence that he could make little sense of it, and certainly not find the speaker.

'You do not need to die.'

Enchei paused. 'You got a weird fucking way of selling that one. I'm all for foreplay, but days o' hellhounds chasing me is a step too far.'

'I'm a practical woman. I recognise you're adept at staying alive and I would prefer to be out of this place quickly and clean.'

'You mean before House Iron's Astaren come?' Enchei felt a moment of hope as he spoke. However problematic the presence of Astaren might be, if she was keen to avoid them that gave him something to work with.

'Don't get your hopes up, Master Tattooist. Their presence in the city is modest and they know the dangers of the Terim.'

'Who, then?'

'I am not here to kill Lawbringers, not if I can help it.'

'Doesn't help the recruitment effort, eh?' Enchei ventured. 'Your Eagle paymasters might be unhappy if the Emperor turned against them.'

She laughed, a thin and dead sound. 'Paymasters? I'm sure I don't know what you mean.'

'Right, my mistake.' *Keep talking, give the others time. I'm not getting out of here without a distraction.* 'Still – best only Dragons die while you're hunting me down, eh?'

'Say what you like about House Dragon, they don't whine about casualties.'

'They do seek revenge, though.'

'I intend to be somewhere they cannot find me.'

Aye, unless the coming war goes disastrously and if that's the case, the whole Empire's in chaos, so you're well down the list of priorities.

'What do you want, then?'

She sighed, a whisper of breath that raced up and down the length of the palazzo. 'You know that – and now your time is done. Give yourself willingly or have the Terim rip your memories out of your eyes as you breathe your last.'

Enchei started to move towards a slightly more protected corner, watching the demon shift slightly to follow him. 'You think my mind's as easy to crack as all that?'

'I will manage.'

The certainty in her voice made him believe her. Whatever failsafes and defences had been implanted into his mind by the mage-priests of Ghost, he wasn't willing to gamble they'd stand up to the combined efforts of a higher-order demon and the most terrifying of Leviathan's Astaren. They spoke to the Gods of the deep, legend told, and Enchei was one man who knew the terror of a god's presence in his mind.

'Guess you won't take my word there's nothing of value in my memories? That you'd never make it through the valley passes?'

The tiniest of flutters sparked in his gut – one he quelled instantly, but enough to make Enchei linger on the thought. The Fields of the Broken – the god he'd killed. Even the Ascendant Gods had been kept from that valley while the various armies tore themselves apart; it hadn't just been snow and ice cutting them off from the rest of the world.

'I like a challenge, if the reward's sufficient.'

'It's dead. I killed it before it fully woke,' he said more in hope than expectation. If there was nothing of value or danger left in that valley, it wouldn't have been sealed off.

'That hardly matters. Your answer is no, then? As you wish.'

'Wait!' Enchei yelled as the Terim took a step forward.

Her impatience was palpable and icy. 'Yes?'

Enchei looked around for inspiration, desperate to prolong things even a few more moments, but the gilt-edged furniture, wire-bound lanterns and long curtains provided him with nothing. The moment stretched out until Enchei felt a manic grin slip on to his face. He whispered an incantation and felt the warmth against his skin as the armour obeyed.

'Nah, I got nothing,' he muttered and broke into a run.

As he ran, his boots crashed down on the flagstones in a shower of sparks that seemed to ignite the air around him. From under his clothes burst a glittering smoke, pouring from his armour with a threatening hiss as he moved to disperse it as far as he could manage.

Bursts of utter dark came from the possessed man in reply. Through the peripheral haze and smoke, Enchei glimpsed the after-echoes against the smeared grey of his mage-sight. A tall upright body and long fore-limbs, curved neck and spread wings – the size of a true dragon and just as terrible to behold.

The Kobelt ran forward just as Enchei ducked behind a staircase and checked his stride. A darting claw of shadow smashed forward across his path, slicing neatly through a wall-hanging before smashing a sideboard to splinters. Enchei hit back with darts and baton, cutting furrows through its shadow wing and studding the man's tattooed cheek. Neither seemed to slow the demon but Enchei was already moving, smoke billowing in his wake.

Up ahead a grey figure appeared, causing Enchei to lurch to one side, darts spitting as he went. They passed through the ghost without effect as it advanced with claws raised. He dropped and skidded on a rush mat, sliding into the grey figure as it struck. Claws caught his forearm and screeched down the armour while Enchei's blow met no resistance. He spun and drove up to face the ghost again, but now his metal fingers were surrounded by spitting light.

One swipe gouged through the ghost and sent it reeling, one step and a lunge burst it apart. Grey tatters billowed briefly in the smoke-laden air then dropped back into nothingness but as Enchei turned to resume his charge around the palazzo he caught sight of a huge shadow limb grab a fretwork partition and rip it away.

He turned and retraced his steps as the possessed Kobelt stepped forward, ducked down in echo of the hunched demon shadow that surrounded it and reached claws after Enchei. One came within a whisper of hooking his leg and Enchei checked his stride, seeing an opportunity. He twisted and chopped down with his open palm, hammering a glow rune against a shadow-claw as long as his forearm. It connected with a burst of light and sound that made Enchei reel, the detonation driving him back against the outside wall as the claw exploded. A terrible screeching rang around the palazzo but the demon's fury was only increased and it raked furrows in the stone walls as it struggled forward in the cramped space behind the stone stair.

It was increasingly hard to see anything with the glitter smoke still billowing from his armour. Enchei was forced to fire his baton blind, knowing it would do nothing more than slow the demon. From his belt he pulled a misshapen metal ball. It was an ugly and crude weapon, but as the trails of lightning around his fingers ignited the fuse and he tossed it, the veteran wasted no time in diving clear.

The grenade exploded in an even brighter light; a sputtering orb of white forming on the flagstone floor and shredding a limb of the demon. The explosion was more palpable this time and the force pitched Enchei into a panelled cupboard set to one side of the atrium.

Stars above! Enchei thought blearily as he shrugged free of the wreckage and fought his way upright. *At least we know those work.*

The grenades were a recent creation. After Narin's recognition by the Emperor himself, Enchei realised the chances of meeting another Astaren had just got greater. He'd sacrificed his battlefield weapons when he faked his death all those years ago, knowing what his comrades would be looking for if anyone required confirmation. Until now that had been a risk worth taking, but the goshe's firepowder weapons had reminded him that he might one day need to pierce Astaren armour.

Before he could move, another ghost materialised and leaped for him. Claws scored the armour at his throat as Enchei was driven back. He twisted frantically then slammed his palms together in a burst of light inside the ghost's head. It vanished in the same storm of tatters but behind it was a greater danger still. While the demon's howls of pain and fury shook the stones under his feet, there was a moment of quiet in Enchei's mind. At the far end of the hall was a figure – a living person who paid the demon no mind. A woman; the Benthic Knight.

She wore a long black coat that would have been severe except for the ornate filigree of its collar, buckles and cuffs. From her dead white skin and hair he could see she was a Leviathan and, as he looked, the air trembled around her. There were faint ghostly images of figures flanking her but Enchei's attention was more drawn to the slim black cane resting gently in her hands. She flicked it idly in his direction and Enchei felt the impact like a slashing sword across his chest.

He reeled sideways, glimpsing a dull reddish light in the tip of the cane as it was twitched back across him and another blow struck his helmet. A volley of darts in reply was swatted aside and then Enchei was running again – the demon's rage building to shuddering proportions behind him.

As he went left and right, cloth was slashed open and wood splintered under the impact of her unseen lash, but Enchei kept his head down until he reached more secure cover. At another staircase he pulled one of his precious grenades from his belt and tossed it blind into the centre of the hall, but as it exploded he heard no cries or alarm from the Knight.

A *little help, girls,* he thought frantically, knowing his daughters couldn't hear his thoughts – chillingly aware he'd been cut off from theirs since being dragged into the palazzo. *Narin, Kesh – any of you. Win me a chance – Gods above just give me that!*

Enay signalled to her sister and readied her lance. Maiss pulled herself up to the top of the palazzo's rear wall and levelled a pistol over it. Before her head was up, a bullet had struck the crest next to her and her own shot was hastily fired. A second bullet spat up from the stone by her fingers, but in the next moment Enay was up and the Dragon's Breath churned a path of flames across the memorial statues standing in the moonlight.

A flash of movement attracted her eye and she moved with it, pulling away just in time as a zip of air sliced the side of her head. In the rear garden of the palazzo, the renegade Ghost, Sorpan, dived out of the skewed path of her weapon. He came up shooting again, his pistol inexhaustible it seemed, while Enay knew her sister only had one loaded gun left.

Enay spun away, feeling the trickle of blood down her ear as she went. The Dragon's Breath was her best defence, she knew – its indiscriminate and terrible power forced the man into haste. As she fired again she sensed Maiss drop down over the wall and crouch behind a broad urn-topped memorial. Sorpan saw it too and directed a shot in her direction but then had to hide again as Enay swept the searing heat lance across his hiding place.

'Sorpan!' she called as she joined her sister over the wall. 'Give yourself up!'

That threw him, she sensed it almost as clearly as she did her sister's advance. The strange powers they had inherited made them an effective and lethal hunting team. Though Sorpan would be counting on being able to hear any directions they gave to each other, the twins didn't need to do any such thing. Their connection was bone-deep and instinctive – Enay had an understanding of how Maiss would move or act that went beyond communication.

In the palazzo beyond, she could sense her father moving again. She couldn't reach him with her thoughts, but his last gift to the pair of them had been the ability to sense him wherever he was. It was a lesser bond than the one with her sister – just a tiny scratching at the back of her mind when she focused on him – but one she knew was the product of Astaren magic.

He hadn't been able to be any more of a father and it was a feeble gift by some standards, but in the low moments that happened in every life, sometimes it was enough. Though Enchei might have been on another continent and had buried a compulsion to stay away, all their lives they had been able to at least face in his direction.

'You're here for me?' Sorpan shouted back at last.

As he spoke, he tossed a bag high in the air. On instinct Enay raised the lance and caught it with the Dragon's Breath – only to have the bag ignite in an eye-watering burst of glittering fire. She recoiled from the blinding light as long sparkling trails streamed down through the air and obscured anything beyond them. She changed position almost blind, having to feel her way to another carved standing stone. Blinking furiously, Enay realised from its height the stone was one of the largest in the garden – a robed Lord Pilgrim with arms outstretched in supplication.

'We're here for you,' Maiss replied on her sister's behalf.

'Without second skin or armour?' Sorpan called. 'No guns or darters? No snares or stings?'

'We don't choose the missions,' Maiss said. 'No trace of Ghost, that's the order we got here.'

'But a Dragon weapon's allowed?'

Enay answered that with a burst from the lance that scorched a path up the wall behind, a slit window bursting inward under the intense heat. The curtain of glittering light still hung between them, the breeze

356

shifting it slightly while the Dragon's Breath cut a furrow that dragged trails inward in its wake.

'You don't need to die,' Enay added, though she accompanied it with another burst from the lance. 'You have his word on that.'

Again, a slight hesitation. 'Whose word?'

'The one you went to.'

'No – no, it's too late for that.'

Enay felt a moment of panic as Sorpan rose from behind a memorial – not the one she was expecting – and fired two shots in quick succession at her. She flinched away, the shallow wound down the side of her head flaring hot at the movement. Before she could aim the lance again, Sorpan was running forward with Maiss closing on one side. Something detonated with the blinding flash of a starflare as Maiss passed an oval memorial, smashing her sideways out of his path. As Maiss fell heavily Sorpan dodged away, rounding a chunk of stone and lunging for Enay with a glittering blade.

She barely managed to parry with the body of her lance, the impact throwing it to one side and giving him an easy shot at her belly – had it not been for the crack of a musket. Chips of stone exploded by Sorpan's ear and Enay saw her chance. She dropped the lance and grabbed his arm, levering the pistol away as she punched up at his armpit. The blade inside her palm flashed in the moonlight as it shot out – only to skitter off the second skin Sorpan wore under his clothes.

He struck back with a boot to the gut, but Enay rode the mule-kick blow and twisted in to slash inside the reach of his short-sword. She headbutted the man and swiped a second blade across his throat, but something in his neck resisted the edge and it failed to tear his gullet open. A second gunshot interrupted their struggle and Enay felt it through his body as she sensed her sister pull the trigger from a dozen yards away.

The bullet struck him in the small of the back and she could tell it penetrated his second skin – a lesser armour than the soldier's one her father wore – but Sorpan only slowed for a moment. He crashed an elbow down on her shoulder and Enay screamed as it jolted from the socket. The impact drove her to her knees, Sorpan almost leaning on her as he pulled back for the killing blow.

With a shriek of anger and pain Enay punched up with her remaining good hand. This time the rigid blade in her fist slammed into the man's throat and burst the pale mesh of his second skin, driving right through his jugular. Sorpan's head snapped backwards, hands suddenly weak and feebly pawing at the wound. His oval eyes widened as the pain struck him and then he toppled unceremoniously, limbs enfeebled and unable to support him as his blood gushed black in the starlight.

Scooping up Sorpan's pistol Enay awkwardly levelled it, determined to make sure of the kill. The blade protruding from her hand made the grip difficult, but she managed to put the gun to his face and fire. The dead Astaren spasmed and kicked before abruptly falling limp, but now Enay moved in even greater haste.

She peeled away and slipped behind the nearest monument as a hiss began to rise from the corpse – spells woven into the second skin releasing the power stored inside it. Out of the corner of her eye a fierce light shone from under his clothes, followed by the *whump* of them igniting and the hiss of his flesh starting to burn.

Enay averted her eyes as the searing light intensified, the heat painful even by her levels of endurance before, within a few heartbeats, the power was spent and the light was replaced by the stink and crackle of skin burning, the acrid stench of super-heated metal scraping at her tongue.

Enay looked up towards her sister. Maiss was sitting up, spent gun in her hand, with blackened streaks and bloody strips of cloth marking her right side. Advancing towards them was the Wyvern knight, Myken, her musket discarded in favour of pistols now, but the woman's attention was on the burning corpse on the ground rather than Enay.

'Is that the renegade?' Myken asked. 'What did you do to him?'

The young woman grunted and hauled herself up to drape her arm over a stone sleeve of some ancestor of the palazzo's owners. Using it as a fulcrum she tugged down on her useless arm, inwardly howling at the pain as her shoulder jolted back into place. She leaned on the statue a few moments, panting and fighting the pain.

'I killed him. The magic inside his armour did the rest. Maiss, you good?'

'Will that happen to you?'

She looked sharply up then shook her head. 'No armour for the likes of us. Easiest if we don't get killed.'

Myken sniffed at that, a rare quizzical look on her face. 'And people say the warrior caste have a strange attitude towards death.'

'It's a family thing,' was Enay's sour reply.

'From what I've seen of your father, I can well believe it. Will his armour do the same?'

Enay ignored her and went to help her sister. Maiss was hurt worse than Enay, but it didn't look life threatening. Blood ran freely from a series of gashes down one side of her head as Maiss tugged a fragment of something from her skin and tossed it aside with a growl. Her left arm hung limp at her side, the clothing and leather armour torn to bloody strips, while a grey splinter protruded from the meat of her thigh.

'Let's hope he doesn't need us,' Enay said as she wadded up some cloth and pulled the splinter free, jamming the cloth into the wound. Despite her Astaren levels of endurance, Maiss whimpered as between the two of them they tied a strap around the wound. The pain forced her to ease back on the monument she'd been thrown against by Sorpan's bomb. Enay checked her over for further injuries while Maiss set about reloading a pistol with awkward, stiff fingers, jaw set against the pain.

Myken turned towards the palazzo as a deep roar echoed out over the crash of timbers. The upper windows shuddered and cracked as reverberations shook the stone walls. Enay gritted her teeth and picked up the lance, dragging it over to where her sister leaned.

'How bad is it?' the Wyvern knight asked.

'I can shoot,' Maiss said through gritted teeth. 'Just don't ask me to run.'

Enay nodded and raised the pistol she'd taken from Sorpan. 'You shouldn't need to keep loading this one.'

She turned the gun over to inspect it. It looked like any other – well crafted, with a polished brass butt and trigger guard, but lacking any ornamentation. Peering down into the barrel Enay could see it taper inside to a far smaller bore than any normal pistol would have. To check she cocked the weapon and aimed up at the nearest first-floor window. A crisp crack echoed around the stone monuments as a neat hole was punched through the shutter covering it and the tinkle of falling glass followed.

'That'll do,' Maiss declared and reached out to take the gun. 'Tie something round my arm now?'

Enay nodded and pulled a thin bandage from her pocket – a long strip of cloth ready prepared to slip around an injury and pull tight. In moments Maiss grunted her approval and waved Enay away, finishing the job one-handed herself.

'Now that back door,' she said, half to herself.

The palazzo's rear door was clad in embossed brass – a single sheet depicting rivers and mountains that covered all but an inch around the edge. Levelling the lance, she fired a near-invisible stream of heat and cut through the metal in moments, but just as the wood behind blackened the air around, it seemed to twist and distort. All three women sensed the danger and dived for cover just as a thunderclap and a blinding flash erupted across the garden.

Enay felt something lash over her leg like poison barbs – just a sudden moment of searing pain, but as she blinked away the after-glare she saw her trousers were torn and blackened strips marked her skin. Whatever that had been, she didn't want to get caught in the full force of it.

She picked herself up, leaning heavily on a cherub-faced stone soldier until the pain ebbed and she trusted her legs again. Next Enay aimed the weapon at the stone wall – testing what effect it had on the stone blocks there, given that the windows were too small to get through. The Dragon's Breath washed searing light over the ice-rimed stone and a great crack echoed around the garden. Where it touched, the stone blackened and brittle fragments sloughed away. Enay lowered the weapon and peered at the steam-wreathed damage.

There were fissures in the stone, but even as she raised the lance again a reddish glow appeared through them. The light stole around the broken lines and straight edges of the stone blocks, filling them before spreading a dull patina over the damaged surface of the blocks. Enay didn't bother testing the Dragon's Breath on it, not wanting to find out what would happen this time or waste the lance's power on enchanted defences.

'More bloody traps,' she said with a wince, 'I'm really starting to hate these Gealann.'

'So what now? Upper window?'

Enay inspected the wide wooden frames of the window above. Without replying, she aimed at the one she'd shot through, Maiss and Myken already stepping back. The shutters crumpled under the assault and the window behind burst inward, but there was no explosion of light. Through the wreckage she saw movement, however – a grey ghostly figure that was not lit by the yellow flames dancing around the wrecked window frame.

It looked like a child but Enay wasn't fooled. As though in confirmation its clawed fingers pulsed briefly red just as an identical light spread around the flame-edged aperture. The ghost moved back out of sight, away from the savage power of the Dragon's Breath, but Enay saw the warning still.

She held off firing again. The last thing her father needed was the palazzo on fire any more than it was already. Another deep, muffled detonation came from inside, then a renewed monstrous roar and the sound of wood shattering under inhuman violence.

But we're kept out, she realised, *that Benthic Knight has him where they want and they've made sure they're not disturbed. Climbing through a window's not going to be easy with ghosts patrolling – we need another way in.*

CHAPTER 39

Enchei thought of death and its shape unfolded in his mind. A warm glow appeared on his chest as a twisting, faceted rune pulsed its readiness. The mantras tumbled through Enchei's mind without effort – complex lines of prayer engraved by the mage-priests into his soul. He felt the warmth of a lesser rune glow beside the first, one denoting memory, then a third for immobility and a fourth for fury.

Try to take me, you fucking overgrown bat, Enchei thought savagely, *and I'll burn your shadow into the wall with my death. Along with this whole palazzo.*

He dropped an echo-stone behind him and vaulted a broken table, the echo-stone falling with a stuttered, chaotic clatter of noise that didn't fade in his wake. He'd left more around the palazzo, forming a cacophony of distraction through which he could creep unnoticed, but now he sprinted for a doorway into the servant quarters on one side of the palazzo.

Inside a wide kitchen he paused, darkly glittering smoke still trailing in his wake. Not far away the demon thrashed in fury at a landing, tearing timbers from the wall above. The smoke was hampering it for certain, but he suspected the Benthic Knight was having to restrain it from tearing the building apart.

A chilly realisation ran down his spine. *Which means she'll be coming herself.*

He moved on instinct, darting to one side just in case that moment's pause had been enough for her to line up the lash of her cane weapon. A slashing line of nothingness failed to tear a path through where he'd been standing and a small manic smile crept on to Enchei's lips. Then he glanced down at his chest, where a long tear in his shirt revealed glimpses of a scored line across his chest-plate.

The groove was neat and near-perfectly straight – and deeper than Enchei would have liked to see. Whatever the weapon was, he didn't want to see the effects of it striking elsewhere. He crossed the kitchen and checked the next room – some sort of antechamber with drape-covered doorways on three sides. As he stepped into the room the right-hand drape was sliced through, a darting red eye carving a path across the table before him. The drape fell amid smoke and darkness, but instead of fleeing Enchei hurled himself through the doorway. Sliding on the ground he fired another volley of darts as he went, arms raised to take any slashing blows that caught him.

The Knight was just a few yards away, her long cane cutting furrows in the stone floor as she brought it back around. Enchei pushed up to sprint the last few yards and get inside her cane's reach, dagger ready. The Leviathan whipped a glittering swirl of blades forward in her other hand and he only just checked in time, knife and baton held high as he dropped down and stamped forward at her knee. The blow connected in a shuddering burst of sparks and then Enchei was parrying and cutting upwards.

Running half on instinct, incantations of speed and strength flooding his mind, he slashed and battered with inhuman speed at the woman. Shuddering trails of light flared around her face as his blows were stopped by magic of her own, flashing fractures in the air. They traded blows, the clatter of her cascading blades ringing out on his arms and shoulders while he struck up and down her body, trying to find a weak spot before the demon intervened. Through the blur, grey ghosts flourished and disappeared a moment later – a succession of clawing, grasping hands, but he was faster and more savage than them all as the magic sang in his veins, driving him faster.

Enchei punched the glowing runes on his fists into one elbow and was rewarded with a stutter in her movements. Faster than the Leviathan, he twisted away and caught the elbow again from a different angle with the knife. He dipped his shoulder and put all his weight into hammering down with the baton just as her arm was at an awkward angle and something snapped under the blow.

Another slash sent blood spraying up, the impact jerking the knife from his hand even as it spun her half around. Enchei felt a spark of elation as he swung a ponderous fist around to slam into the small of her back. It threw her off-balance but still she had the poise to spin and swipe at him with the cane as she went. Anticipating the blow – heavy enough to shatter the skull of a normal man – he'd already pulled back and it glanced off his helmet.

Enchei rode it and stamped into the side of her knee. She buckled but found the strength to backhand Enchei across the face so hard he was thrown from his feet. Lights and colours burst inside his helmet as his head snapped back, the stone floor rising to hit him like a giant's punch. He felt his bones creak under the impact and the incantations in his mind wavered as the power of his armour started to fail.

He rolled, avoiding a slash from the cane that split the flagstone apart. Something thudded against his thigh and instinct made him stab down with his knife to dislodge whatever had latched on to his armour.

He dodged the whirling blades but couldn't avoid a thrust of the cane, only catch it on his arm and fire darts in return. It burned right through his armour and into the flesh within. A moment of blinding pain obscured everything before Enchei sensed looming shadows surround him and instinct tried to hurl him sideways. His leg betrayed him, heavy and unmoving, and it took a second attempt to stab at the spider-like object attached to his leg before it burst apart.

The drain on his strength lessened, but all he could do was drop to his knees and send the surging trails of light surrounding his body into a single flare through the runes on his fists, up into the great claws of shadow descending. Everything went white and still he was nearly crushed by the impact, sledgehammer talons closing around his back before the light could strip their power.

Enchei tried to strike back but his limbs felt leaden and standing upright was enough of a struggle. All around him were swirling trails of smoke and shadow, punctuated by shattered walls and spitting fires. The shell of the palazzo remained intact, a dull red skein covering the more damaged sections, without which it would surely have collapsed.

Ahead of him, the Leviathan woman was unsteady, her fine clothes torn just as his were. The gaps exposed grey scale armour flecked with gold, like some fantastical sea creature. Her arm was twisted at an unnatural angle, turned out at the elbow, but as she retreated he saw her stow her cane before she jerked her injured arm back towards a healthier position. Not a sound broke her lips as she retreated, leaving the enraged demon to do its work.

The Terim's human vessel was a bloodied mess now – lacerated flesh hung from its body, ghastly wounds showing the white of bone and glistening bulbous innards. None of that mattered to the demon surrounding it, rearing high above the dead man anchoring it to the world while new claws unfurled from the dark. To see a man walking with such monstrous injuries caused memories of the valley to flower again in Enchei's mind. Then it had been boldness that had kept him alive, patience for the right moment and not a step back until it was done.

Enchei hesitated a moment, on the point of attacking and pressing the advantage, but he could feel that the flow of power in his limbs had dulled. This was draining him, too fast for him to be able to take them both. He retreated into the feeble safety of the service rooms behind him while the demon threaded its shadow-form back together, trusting the tangle of walls and smoke to give him a measure of cover. The flow of smoke had faded to a shiver and with a thought he silenced the runes, conserving all he could as he tried to recover his strength.

'Clever, tattooist,' called the Benthic Knight from behind the dark veil, 'but how long can you keep that up?'

'Enough to take a limb or two,' Enchei replied. He tugged a sliver of metal from his collar and jammed it into a wooden pillar. When he spoke again it would echo his voice around the near-collapsing palazzo – another precious moment of distraction, perhaps. 'How's the arm?'

'Healing,' she said baldly.

The words made Enchei scowl. He'd heard Leviathans could manage something far in excess of his own magic's battlefield patching, but this was the first time he'd fought one.

Your flesh can heal, he thought savagely, *but flesh's easily broken once the shell's cracked. I've got my own tricks to play and you didn't see me play that hand.*

'You see you cannot win, don't you? You don't have the strength, not to take both of us.'

A small voice at the back of his mind cried desperation, but Enchei knew the Leviathan was right. He was burning through his magic far faster than she was. Most likely he'd manage the Terim, given the state of its vessel, but he'd have nothing at all left for her. Injured arm or not, she had her ghosts and more strength than him in reserve.

'Will you consider my offer again?'

'Offers from a woman whose name I don't even know?' Enchei replied, hearing the whispers of his voice reverberate around the outer part of the palazzo. 'What would the wife say?'

There came a sound akin to amusement, but from a throat unsuited to it.

'My name is Priest,' she said, her soft footsteps almost masked by the rumbling growls of the Terim that echoed from the roof. 'Come forward and you will survive. That is the only way. My wards are strong enough to keep your friends out long after your strength has failed you.'

'What do you think my answer's going to be? I killed a god, remember? I squeezed the life out of it with these two hands.'

'And I look forward to seeing that memory,' Priest said, 'as I tear it from your mind.'

'Enay, Maiss!'

Narin straightened as Kesh spoke, needing a hand from her to steady him. At his feet, Irato lay slumped against the outer wall – limp as a sack of potatoes, propped where they'd dragged him and unaware of what was going on around him.

He'd not wanted to touch the man at first. Some voice of caution had stayed his hand, the scene so reminiscent of when he'd first met Irato on the streets of Dragon District. When Kesh had tried to rouse him the former goshe had toppled backwards and stared unseeing up at the tattered shroud of the sky. Only the sight of Irato looking up at the stars, twitching and blinking like a man stunned, had stirred Narin to movement.

This time there was no god to give him orders, only a man who was his friend lying in need. They had dragged him from the palazzo, but got no sense out of him. The goshe's powerful hands tightened around Narin's as they hauled him back, but he had looked straight through Kesh when she'd spoken to him. Irato continued to mutter under his breath, short and urgent sounds, but neither Narin nor Kesh could make sense of it.

Narin stumbled forward as the two young Ghosts rounded the palazzo towards them. Myken followed a few paces behind, musket level and ready. Both of Enchei's daughters were injured, Maiss blackened and bleeding from half a dozen wounds.

Kesh gasped at the state of the two House Ghost women. 'What happened?'

'The renegade,' Enay growled.

'Is he dead?'

'And then some.' She shook her head. 'There's no way in round the back. They've set some sort of defences that're keeping us out.'

'The Dragon's Breath?'

'Might cut through the wall given time, assuming we don't exhaust its power. They've got magic protecting the walls; this place has been prepared as a trap for Enchei. Some sort of ghosts or demons are patrolling the upper floors – we put in a window, but anyone climbing up there's getting their throat ripped out.'

They all turned towards the house as more sounds of chaos came from within; splintering wood, cracking stone and furious roars – but all blunted by either the stone structure or the magic protecting it.

'Well, we can't just stand here,' Kesh snapped. 'So find an answer, one of you!'

'Now's not the time to be picking a fight with me,' Enay said in a quiet, dangerous voice. 'I'm not done killing tonight.'

Maiss put a hand on her sister's arm, though her face was scarcely less thunderous. 'The lance is likely to set the place alight before it cuts an escape route. We need a way to help Father stay alive in there.'

'What, then?' Kesh said. 'Throw that lance through the window you broke? Do you have any other weapons?'

The sisters looked at each other. 'Uncle?' Maiss asked softly.

Enay shook her head. 'Won't get here in time.' The young woman winced at her wounds and cast around as she thought, teeth grinding in frustration.

'Who?' Narin demanded.

'Best you don't know,' Enay snapped. 'Safer for you, that's for sure.'

'What about the Gods?' Kesh said, more in hope than anything else. 'How is it they're not interested in the Imperial City any more? Lord Shield might not be in Ascendancy at this time of year, but his stars still pass over and I doubt he's paid us no mind since the summer. He traced Narin for us, for pity's sake!'

'Oh, I'm sure they're watching,' Enay growled. 'They like to watch more'n get involved, though. Especially when the Astaren are part of things, so I've heard – they'll keep clear and watch only. Your goshe conspiracy was one thing, that's entertainment and possible profit for them. They meddle in the games of nations, though, and they're taking sides all of a sudden. That gets more serious, that gets more dangerous for all involved.'

Narin shook his head. 'She's right. Lord Shield or any of the others aren't going to help us here.' He paused and looked to his right.

'The gate,' he said and turned ponderously, his whole arm now numb and stiff.

The dried blood on his clothes was crisp in the cold night air, black in the starlight. He and Kesh had between them managed to rig some sort of sling to cradle his damaged limb, but the dull throb of pain was eating its way through his shoulder.

They dragged the gate open to reveal a ragged column of figures hurrying towards them. Rhe led a depleted-looking group of Lawbringers and Investigators, while Prince Kashte and his gold-scarfed relations trotted alongside them. Narin wasn't sure of their numbers, but they seemed to have a fair few more than the Lawbringers now.

'He needs help,' Narin said, pointing towards the palazzo. 'Enchei got dragged in and the doors have some sort of protective warding.'

Rhe nodded. He turned to his remaining Lawbringers and lifted his chin to address them all. 'Spread out around the perimeter wall. Arrest anyone attempting to escape and do not ask them twice.'

As they ran to obey, scattering left and right until none were within view, he returned to Narin. 'A window, then.'

The Investigator shook his head. 'There's some sort of ghosts inside. They dragged the demon from Irato and they're guarding the broken windows.'

'So our guns won't work?' The Lawbringer hesitated.

For a moment Narin saw fatigue in Rhe's eyes and at last noticed that the man's clothes were not quite perfect. Trails of blood stained his sleeve and one hand was pressed against his ribs. Under Rhe's fingers Narin could see torn cloth and, by the way he was standing, he must have had a cracked rib or two. In the starlight his pale face and hair remained ethereal and emotionless to most, but Narin had spent two years watching that face for signs of life.

'You need to do something!' Kesh demanded, stepping up beside Narin.

Rhe stiffened. 'Suggest something,' he said coldly.

She jabbed a finger towards him, then off to his right. 'Not you – you.'

The Lawbringer turned to where she pointed. Prince Kashte sniffed and carefully brushed an imaginary speck of dust off the hilt of his sword.

'Be careful where you point that thing,' he said lazily. 'Especially towards your betters. It might just come off.'

'You know what?' Narin joined, shifting forwards half a step so Kashte was forced to change his focus. 'I don't think we need to be careful. You and your friend – it's time for the both of you to stop pissing around and get involved.'

The Imperial's eyes narrowed. 'What do you think we've been doing thus far?'

'Playing, playing with us all. But now Enchei needs help and there's no time for playing. He'll be dead if you don't do something *right now.*'

Kashte titled his head to one side. 'And why was your tattooist friend the one taken?' He nodded towards the palazzo. 'By the sound of it, he's got some rather angry company – yet he's still alive to be rescued? How about you tell me what's so special about your friend first?'

Maiss barged her way forward and levelled a gun at Kashte. Behind him half a dozen Imperials drew their pistols, but then Enay limped forward and swung the lance from her back.

'If you can save him, how about you get on with that and worry about answers after?'

'Ah, your mercenary friends; mercenaries with Astaren weapons, I see. What were your names again?'

Despite its bulk, Enay raised the lance so it was in line with Kashte's face and the prince was staring into its oversized barrel.

'Bugger our names – what's Narin talking about?'

Lawbringer Rhe raised a hand. 'All of you, lower your guns,' he commanded.

'Fuck off,' Enay responded. 'I want answers and I want them now, otherwise the lot of you aren't going to have faces much longer.'

'Now now, children,' called another voice from the street. 'I think we can dispense with the harsh language and posturing.'

Narin turned in astonishment to see Prince Sorote emerging from a side-street, two more armed Imperials in his wake. A thin strip of gold ran around his collar but beyond that and the pistol at his waist there was little indication of the man's caste. His tunic, trousers and coat were all plain and dark, the slim cane in his hands just topped with a small silver sun.

'Who's this?' Enay demanded.

'I think the question is more who are you, my dear?'

Narin raised a hand before she had time to get even more angry. 'Prince Sorote, time's pressing and our friend's not going to last much longer. I need you to do something to help him, or to get us inside.'

'What makes you think I have that power?'

'Because I'm not a bloody fool, whatever you high castes might think!' Narin snapped. 'All your interest, all your little questions and curiosity in the unnatural – don't fucking lie to me. You can do something and I warn you, now's the time to do it.'

'You warn me? Be very careful, Investigator Narin. You have a history of turning your powerful friends into enemies, one that may prove the death of you soon.'

Narin shook his head. 'Not this time. My friend needs help and you'll do it right now or your secret will get out – I promise you that. The Office of the Catacombs, isn't that what you call yourselves? Just another tiny little corner of the vast Imperial family, eh? I don't know if you found something in those catacombs or it's just a useful place away from prying eyes, but you've shown me enough of what you're doing.

'Between you and Rhe, you let House Dragon know about the safe-house faster than was necessary. Might be you even tipped the Gealann off about the attack, made sure it was an ambush. You want them to fight because only then'll House Dragon's hold over Imperial lands weaken enough to maybe break.'

'But only if you have your own Astaren,' Kesh continued. 'And while you know Dragon's spies are always on the lookout, there's a respect afforded to members of the Imperial family itself – so if you could hide your new Astaren anywhere, it'd be in your catacombs.'

'No, not hide,' Narin said. 'Recruit. All those young men and women trained to fight but kept in a gilded cage. They must have jumped at whatever was offered, secure in the knowledge that Astaren retribution probably won't be the same for their caste if you're caught.'

Narin shook his head. 'I've no problem with what you want to do, but you better damn well believe me that if Enchei dies I'll make sure the Houses hear about it.'

'Or have they already?' Prince Sorote asked, glancing at Enay and Maiss. 'Your friend is clearly no mere tattooist. If we had secrets, as you suggest, and the power to save him, it would expose us. One might reasonably assume it would be safer to kill you instead.'

'Firstly, these two are House Ghost,' Narin said. 'So they'll not be part of any war between Eagle and Dragon. Secondly, they're not alone in the city. If they die, their friends will know it. Right now this conversation's only between us.' He glanced at Enay and Maiss as the pair glared at the Imperials. 'And it'll stay that way if we all play nice. Their mission – and Enchei's – doesn't cross your plans.

'There's no need for any of us to fight here – most likely rising Imperial power will be good for House Ghost anyway. Distract some of their competitors, even. Either way, if Enchei lives he owes you a

370

favour and these two have an incentive to keep your secrets. If Enchei dies, all bets are off and Ghost'll be crawling over this city, I promise.'

Prince Sorote paused, then looked at Kashte. The belligerent young prince made no indication either way, but something seemed to decide it for Sorote. Narin's years on the street had taught him when someone was about to throw a punch and when they'd decided against it. The fastidious, academic-seeming Sorote was far from a brawler, but men under pressure acted in similar ways whatever their background.

'You ask for a lot of faith,' the prince said, in a carefully controlled voice.

Narin felt a flush of relief. It wasn't agreement, but tacit acceptance that there was some truth in his suspicions. Up until now he'd not been certain of anything, but Sorote hadn't laughed in his face and called him deluded, as Narin had been half expecting.

He gestured for his companions to lower their weapons and once they had done so the assorted princes and princesses of Kashte's Imperial cadre did the same.

'Faith from both sides,' Narin said carefully. 'Enchei's identity has been years in the making; they don't want to throw it all away now.'

There was a long, taut moment of silence, but finally Prince Sorote nodded. 'Whatever his mission, it's taking place in a city controlled by House Dragon, so I doubt we would object to his goals. It appears we have a deal, Investigator.'

Narin sagged with relief, the tension that had been holding him upright suddenly draining away to leave his injury feeling like a lead weight.

'Thank you.'

'One condition – you two,' Sorote said, pointing at Enay and Maiss, 'retreat outside the compound. Unless you're willing to show me your secrets in turn?'

To Narin's surprise, the fierce young women made no objection; they showed no sign even of surprise. Without a moment's pause they both limped through the gate with an Imperial escort until they were out of sight.

'Shout if there's something to kill,' Enay called softly over her shoulder as she went.

Prince Sorote nodded to his lieutenant. 'Kashte – spread them around this face of the palazzo. Give the tattooist a chance against this demon.'

'What are you going to do?' Kesh breathed as the Imperials ran to obey.

'What we can,' Sorote said curtly. 'The rest will be up to him.'

Narin watched as each one took position around the palazzo wall, stopping two yards short of the wall itself and dropping to their knees. Weapons sheathed, they each bowed their heads and stretched out a hand towards the wall. Behind them, Kashte paced like a caged lion, sword and gun at the ready and watching the door and upper windows. Without being asked, Myken moved to a few paces behind him, musket at the ready. As she passed, Prince Kashte gave the warrior caste a small nod.

At first nothing happened, but still Narin found himself holding his breath as he waited. After a dozen heartbeats he felt the anxiety bubble up inside him but as he opened his mouth to speak Prince Sorote raised his cane warningly. The words died in Narin's throat and in the next moment he felt a strange prickling sensation on his skin.

He felt the hairs on his neck rise, then a creeping greasiness as the sharp winter air became alive and charged. Tiny flashing threads of light began to creep around the kneeling Imperials, thin sparks disappearing up towards the night sky. The air between them and the palazzo began to shimmer with some weak lambent light as their hair lifted and twitched in a non-existent breeze. The haze of light and darting slivers rose steadily, forward and up until they reached the grey stone walls and pushed on through without any sign of resistance.

'Is that it?' Kesh demanded in a whisper. 'What good will that do?'

'Your friend's a born fighter,' Sorote replied, 'if I'm any judge. Master Narin's feats of heroism always seemed to take place alongside his aging friend, as I recall. This will level the field for him, I believe – diminish the power he faces. I doubt we can meet this Leviathan Astaren head-on if your friends cannot; these defences are as powerful as anything I've ever seen. And so we change the game, make it about skill in combat rather than power – that is where your friend has the advantage, we must hope.'

'For your sake you'd better be right,' Kesh warned, nodding towards the gate. 'Those two aren't in a forgiving mood tonight.'

CHAPTER 40

Enchei felt the change like a mouthful of air to a drowning man. The smoke-filled palazzo was a wreck inside. His silver-dust smoke mingled with raging shadows and darting ghosts as though he was already dead and inside one of the seven hells. Fires burned behind the shroud, while the splinter of beams echoed from the roof overhead.

He looked down at his hands and watched the crackle of lightning between his metal-clad fingers stutter and fade. A sudden sense of fatigue washed over him as the power in his limbs waned – not washed away, but sapped by some strange, nebulous emanation behind him. This time it wasn't something Priest had done, though, it was a dull cloud hanging in the air that dulled everything.

Looks like Narin's finally found a use for his betters, Enchei thought, with a manic sense of hope.

He turned his hand over and watched the light fade from the rune engraved underneath – the power stored there bleeding out into the smoky air to dissipate. One by one he sensed the echo-stones he'd scattered around the palazzo flicker and die and quickly he thought a silent mantra to still the magic running through his armour. He was unsure how much remained, but it would fade to nothing if he kept his defences high.

Somewhere not far away the demon roared once then retreated, driven back by the sapping radiance. A sense of quiet fell over the palazzo – the confused clatter of the echo-stones and heavy footfalls of the demon fell away to leave an ominous silence. He tested his baton and watched the stream of distorted air fracture then diffuse into nothingness just two yards away. He didn't bother testing his darts, just sheathed his baton and checked his knives instead.

Let's hope it's not just me, he thought as he rose and moved around the sideboard he'd been using for cover, *otherwise this may be over a little quick.*

Enchei skirted the wreckage of a staircase, keeping low and weaving from side to side as he searched for the others. From nowhere a ghost leaped up, claws red and reaching, but as he dodged and slashed back, the ghost faded to nothing. Enchei threw himself forward to where the ghost had been, rolling back up on to his feet but not moving quickly enough to avoid a blur of red light washing over him. This time the blow wasn't so heavy, a bundle of canes cracking down on his back rather than a giant's sword, but still it threw his balance off.

He struck blind as he wheeled, catching nothing but evading another stroke. At last he saw her – torn and bloodied, but closing with a dancer's speed. The cane slapped down once, twice, then she whipped her spinning blades up at his riposte. Enchei lunged at her and on past, happy to distance himself for a moment then changing direction again. A pillar stood between them but he had his own target in mind – the demon.

A huge black shape stood off to the right of the main door and Enchei ran for it with abandon. Great claws descended sluggishly but he wove a path through to the ruined corpse beyond. Still he was lashed with tendrils of shadow that buffeted him left and right while he made no attempt to retaliate.

Only when he came close enough to the corpse did Enchei do anything more than evade and deflect, taking blow after blow on his armoured arms. He could barely see, feeling the great mass of shadow as a choking, overwhelming presence and using that weight itself as a guide to the demon's heart.

The demon scratched and tore at his mind, ripped the air from his lungs and scourged his back with terror's claws, but the Imperials had done enough. He stabbed again and again, muscles screaming as he chopped through flesh and bone – the demon too weak to utterly engulf his mind. The shriek of demon song stripped at his mind's defences so savagely that he felt the death rune on his chest pulse once with readiness. And then with one final blow he severed the corpse's spine and sent its head tumbling to the ground. Summoning his reserves, Enchei whispered words of light into the tempest of demon song and a brief, blinding flash erupted from his chest.

The shadow-form was cut through, slashed to ribbons which melted away on the winds of that strange haze cast from outside. With one final monstrous howl the Terim abandoned the dead flesh that anchored it in the world and seemed to explode around Enchei, rushing shadows that melted into nothing and left only an acrid stench around the fallen corpse.

'And then there was one,' Enchei called, blinking the afterglow of light and shadow from his eyes.

His ears rang with the last traces of demon-song, his normally-infallible balance reeling amid the whirl of movement and unknown incantations.

'One?' Priest replied, stepping out into the debris-strewn hall. 'Hardly.'

A ghost stepped out from her body, then another and another. A cold fear flickered in Enchei's heart as that became five then six, then he lost count as they charged as one in a dizzying blur of half-real movement.

He let his body move in automatic response; not thinking about the pattern of parries and strikes, but only responding with a dance he knew in his bones. The ghosts were enfeebled by the Imperial song outside, but every slash and blow nudged and distracted him. He whirled around as he fought, one eye still on Priest as she waited for an opening but concentrating all his efforts on the storm of ghosts.

Whether one came, Enchei could not tell, but suddenly Priest was there – launching forward with every scrap of strength and power she had remaining. The cane slapped against his leg like an iron bar, the cascading blades worked their way along his chest towards the joints and bit. He threw his all into a flurry of slashes and followed it up with a savage knee-strike to her back. Even as the ghosts tore at him, Enchei felt the crack of armour underneath his blow and the gasp of pain from Priest.

Through the blur, Enchei saw the dull metal disc he'd planted earlier fall away, along with pieces of her armour. With a flicker of elation in his gut he wrenched himself free of the grasping hands and raised his dagger. Red light flashed like a rapier across his face but the armour held and in the next moment Enchei hurled the dagger at Priest.

On instinct she threw her hands up and blocked the weapon, but it gave Enchei time to dive forward under her guard. Grappling furiously, he hammered half-lit runes against her armour, stabbed and slashed with his knuckle-dagger while she tried to twist and throw him. The ghosts swarmed over his back but Enchei continued his reckless assault, face pressed into her chest as he pumped his legs and drove her backwards.

He slipped his hand down to his belt and was punished immediately by a blade slamming into the back of his shoulder, through his armour. Flames of pain raced down his arm but he didn't stop, yanking the last of his grenades from his belt and pulling it round to the damaged part of her back. He called whatever power was left in his hands and felt a hiss of lightning briefly surround his fingers. With a last burst of strength in his legs he finally tipped her back and over.

Priest's balance gave out as she tried to work her blade further into his shoulder and down they went. Enchei dipped his head and slammed her into the stone flooring, howling with pain as her dagger twisted violently in his wound. As his vision blurred he hauled with all his strength to free his hands and at last they—

Everything went white. He didn't hear the explosion; just felt the gut-punch as he was hurled up. His hands were thrown out wide by the force of the explosion, his body snapped up and around to tumble in a heap beside Priest. More pain came, then a slap of darkness as the grenade's flare receded. Lights and colours swam before his eyes. He sensed movement, grey shapes pouncing forward, but no claws pierced his shuddering, defenceless body. As one they were hauled through the air, the unseen radiance of the Imperials casting them back once more as Priest's strength failed.

Enchei wrenched around and screamed as his weight went on to his left hand. Again his eyes blurred, overtaxed strength taking an age to dull the blinding agony. With a gasp he found himself able to see again, levering himself up to his knees with his one good arm and not daring to look at the other.

Beside him, astonishingly, Priest stirred and looked up, her mouth forming an O of pain and wonder. Enchei found himself unable to stand for a moment, struggling under the weight of his own body. He could only watch in amazement as the woman slowly focused on the failing roof above and turned her head towards him. Her clothes were flayed to nothing, the strange scale-patterned armour now cracked with dark fissures from which blood flooded.

'Slayer of gods,' she whispered, shuddering under the agony of movement.

Enchei stared back a moment, awed she could manage to speak at all, but at last he nodded.

'Slayer of gods,' she repeated, a small smile appearing on her lips, 'it is time to run.'

He looked down, eyes widening. The rents in her armour began to glow, red light shining out over the expanding pool of blood around her. More cracks began to appear, rapidly spreading all the way across her chest as the light intensified to magma-red. The light filled his mind but Enchei could only scrabble backwards, his exhausted body failing him as Priest's scraps of clothes were consumed by flames. Even through his armour Enchei could feel the heat.

'*Come on, old man!*' roared a voice inside his head.

He tried to look around but the searing red light was everywhere, filling his mind. Distantly, he felt a jerk and a burst of renewed pain as his arms were grasped by strong hands. Suddenly he was surging backwards, dragged like a ragdoll through a crashing obstacle course of wreckage while the ball of red light rose and expanded before him. He felt the heat and light consume him, blotting out the world around—

And then he was hauled free, the light no longer red but instead the unfeeling ice-white of the Gods above. The ground beneath him became rough and clattering rubble instead of smooth flagstones and at last he made out shapes around him. The looming bulk of the palazzo, lit red from within like the belly of the seventh hell. The shattered front doors, one torn entirely from its hinges, flashes of white and gold on the figures staring aghast down at him, his blood-stained and panting daughters each standing with one hand under his armpit.

Maiss ducked down and slipped his arm over her shoulder, bringing Enchei upright while the veteran tried not to cry out again at the too-slowly-receding pain in his hand. With his one good hand he fumbled at the hidden clasps of his helm – the armour now constricting with its power so sapped.

Enchei pulled the helm off and gasped at the shocking slap of cold air on his skin. He felt himself tilt sideways and had to grab at Maiss' shoulder until the world righted itself under his feet.

'How bad?' he croaked at his daughter.

'You or us?' she said with a snort.

'I ain't dying,' he wheezed. 'I meant you.'

She patted his shoulder. 'Better'n you – so long as we get out of here.'

Up ahead the first of the roof timbers began to fall, Priest's body invisible at the infernal heart of dancing flames. Nothing of the inside at all was visible and even at the mouth of the gate, twenty yards from the palazzo's stone flanks, Enchei's skin stung with the heat. He sensed movement and drunkenly brought his punch-dagger up, realising a moment later it was just the Imperials being driven back by the intense heat.

'Now now, Master Jen,' Prince Sorote said from behind him. 'Let us not part on unfriendly terms.'

'Part?' Enchei echoed, looking around at those assembled and noticing Narin, Kesh and Myken for the first time.

Behind them, Irato sat with his back against the wall – still reeling from the demon-fragment being torn from his mind no doubt, but the man looked straight back at him and gave Enchei an unsteady nod.

'After all that, you'll just walk away?'

Sorote gave him a half-bow. 'I am a man of the Imperial caste,' he said solemnly. 'My word is my bond. Without that assurance, what would the Imperial family have?'

Enchei coughed, wincing at the pain it provoked. 'More'n I'd have suspected a few days ago.' He waved away any reply from the prince. 'You'll get no argument from me – just thought there'd be some bargaining to be done.'

'It is concluded. Your friends are quite capable without you.' Sorote smiled. 'I wish you luck in whatever your mission is in the Imperial City,' adding, with an inclined head towards Prince Kashte, 'so long as it doesn't interfere with our own endeavours.'

Enchei looked up at Enay, lance slung easily beneath one arm, then exchanged a look with a pale-faced Narin. 'Our mission? Guess I can agree to that easily enough.'

Sorote bowed. 'Then we shall leave you. I suspect House Iron's Astaren will eventually creep from their burrows to investigate this, so it's time we were elsewhere.'

At his gesture, the Imperials swept away and disappeared into a side-street far from the eyes of the district, leaving only Lawbringer Rhe standing in the street beyond.

'The scene is mine,' Rhe announced, looking straight at Narin. 'You, Investigator, are suspended. You should leave now.'

The six friends looked at each other, all too tired to laugh at the absurdity.

'Gladly,' Narin said with a weary nod. With Maiss supporting her father and being supported in turn, Enay hauled Irato up to his feet and steadied the former goshe.

'I'm not carrying him home again,' Narin commented. 'Once is enough.'

'I'll walk,' Irato groaned, 'I just need an arm to steady me.'

With half their number propping the others up, they began the long trudge home. Enchei offered Rhe a grateful nod as they passed, but the

Lawbringer was already looking past him at the flames shooting from the palazzo roof. A small smile crept on to Enchei's face, but then he caught sight of his mangled fingers and that faded again.

'What mission do I have?' he whispered once they were past the Lawbringer. 'Am I likely to get in Sorote's way?'

Narin gave a snort. 'Your mission? Same as all of ours, just to keep on living and look after your own. Prince Sorote can imagine what he likes, I'll not correct him.'

Enchei grunted. 'Keep on living?' He drew his daughter in close and embraced her as best he could. 'That I could probably manage, though you two might be looking after me for a while. I tried death and it never sat right for me.' He brightened. 'Dov'll need a sensible eye to watch over her in the years to come, though.'

'And she shall have me to do so,' Myken said firmly.

Enchei managed a weary grin. 'Aye, mebbe I'll teach Narin then – once I remember how to be a father. Can't have been too hard, these two turned out okay.'

'Keep talking, old man,' Maiss grunted, 'and you can walk the rest of the way unaided.'

'See, they don't suffer fools. Dov'll need to learn that if she's to spend any time around you.'

EPILOGUE

It was a week later and no one had died in between. The days passed slowly and the wounds began to heal. With the threat to their lives lifted, Kine and Dov moved with Narin to Kesh's temporary boarding house – the jewellery from Kine's former life sufficient to pay their way for many more weeks to come. There had been tears and angry words, delight and relief, between Kesh and her mother Teike upon their reunion, but at the sight of Dov, Teike's anger had faded like the morning mist.

Enchei and his daughters had taken over the other house in the meantime, to recover and reacquaint at their own pace. Both Enchei and Maiss had been grievously injured – so Enay had told them on her one visit – carrying wounds that would have killed lesser mortals, but they were now healing fast.

The only incident had come four days after what was already being called the Night of Wolves in parts of the city, a night that had claimed more than a hundred innocents before they stopped it. A large dark-skinned woman with two armed attendants had appeared suddenly at the boarding house. It had been enough to make Kine cry out in alarm, fearing Lord Vanden had gone back on his word, and Kesh and Irato had drawn weapons before realising their mistake.

Only the magnitude of the error had prevented it escalating. The two attendants had drawn their guns before Kesh and Irato could do anything more, moving between their mistress and the onrushing pair but so confident of their superiority that they had no need to shoot. In the next moment Kesh had realised they were Astaren and dragged Irato to a halt. By the time Narin had appeared, both were kneeling before the high castes and making their apologies.

The interrogation had been remarkably brief, given the grilling they had received in the wake of the Moon's Artifice affair. It was, in fact, a formality only – Lawbringer Rhe had given his account, as had Prince Kashte, and while it was never mentioned, they all knew about House Ghost's bargain with House Dragon. The Astaren had seemed careful not to intrude too far on any subject there, painstakingly so to Narin's mind. It was quite unlike the impression of Dragon's rulers he had grown up with, but Narin knew they had a war brewing in the north and even the position of neutral Great Houses would be significant. Belligerent House Dragon might be, but they were neither ignorant nor foolish.

Inside half an hour the Astaren had announced the matter closed and stood to leave. She had hesitated a moment over Dov, making a point of congratulating Kine on her birth, and then they were gone – back out onto the frosty Harbour Warranty streets, leaving a warm sense of relief in the low castes they left behind.

In what seemed like no time, Narin's suspension was over and he rose early to wash and have Kesh help re-bind the dressing on his shoulder. The bullet had broken a bone and his arm had to be strapped to his body to give it time to heal, but they all knew he couldn't let that be an excuse to stay away. He was close to fainting with fatigue by the time he returned home that first day, but that melted away with the cold once he stepped through the threshold of the boarding house.

At the table, beside Dov's wicker cradle, sat Enchei. One side of his face was yellowed with bruising and dotted with dark scabs, his left arm was in a sling and a cane leaned against the table. Kine and Irato were with him, peeling vegetables with short knives with varying degrees of success, while Kesh ducked her head out through the kitchen doorway briefly having heard the door.

'How was your day at work, dear?' the veteran called with a sly smile.

Narin grinned. 'Long. Where's my dinner?'

'There's some soup left over, Kesh's dealing with it. As for supper – I've got something rather more impressive planned, but my helpers are slowing things up a tad.'

Narin made his way over to the table and Irato jerked a chair out for him to slump into. Narin ignored it at first and shuffled over to Kine, who was now making her way around the cradle. Her smile sent a flush of warmth through his body, the barest brush of her lips electric against his cheek.

'How are you, my love?' she breathed into his ear.

'All the better for seeing you,' he said. With Kine's help he managed to extricate his one good arm from his coat and settle into a chair. 'All's well here?'

'A happy home,' Kine confirmed, 'and Enchei tells us Maiss is recovering well.'

'Aye, that she is,' Enchei said. 'My girl's starting to claw at the walls today, though – bed-ridden doesn't suit her any more'n it does me – but it won't be long before she's strong enough to leave it.'

'And you?'

'Pah – I've had worse.'

'You shattered most of the bones in your hand and wrist, no?'

Enchei shrugged. 'Bones are easy to heal if you're like me. Not saying it's a whole lot of fun, but broken bones are better'n the sliced sinew and ripped ligaments elsewhere. Just takes time, and the three of us are eating enough for ten in the meantime, but we'll end up better'n you, most likely.'

'And what then?'

Enchei gestured at the others in the room. 'I was just telling the others. Winter's got a way to go yet so we've all time to recover before travelling's much fun. Once spring's with us I'm thinking I'll travel back with my girls – stay with them a season or two. Moving back to any part of the Ghost hegemony is foolish, even if House Clearlake's lands are a long way from Ghost's own, but a few months will give us time to work each other out a bit.'

'I intend to persuade Myken to go as well,' Kine said as she returned to her butchery of supper, domestic duties not coming easily to the former noblewoman. 'Otherwise she'll waste her life watching over me.'

'Aye – she'll do well there,' Enchei added. 'There's a cachet to having Dragons and the like as overseers there. She could do nothing more than glare at the customers in their gambling house and within days she'd get others trying to tempt her away.'

'No news from your old friend?'

Without meaning to, Narin had lowered his voice before remembering that they'd taken all the available rooms at the boarding house, using Kine's jewellery to secure rooms elsewhere for the current guests. It afforded them some much-welcome privacy and allowed Kesh and Irato to spend every daylight hour working at their old house.

'Eh? Oh, him. No, no word, which I'm assuming is a damn good sign. Enay did the Dragons a good turn burning half of Iron District with the lance – to any Astaren it'll be as obvious as a dog checking the scent on trees. Makes it look to those who count like Dragon cleared up the mess themselves and neither they nor Ghost will correct that.'

'We couldn't have asked for more, really,' Narin said, pleased. 'And while he was as formal and stiff as you might expect, Lawbringer Rhe's holding no grudge against me. At least he never cared about his own standing, unlike some Lawbringers, so my shame in the eyes of our colleagues means little.'

'His legend didn't do badly out of it,' Enchei said. 'It'd be cheap of the man to complain after all that.'

'Maybe now life will quieten down for a while,' Kesh announced, emerging from the kitchen carrying a clay pot topped with a flatbread. 'I don't know about the rest of you, but I'm looking forward to watching this little one grow while absolutely no one's trying to kill us.'

Enchei snorted. 'I'll drink to that.'

Kesh set the pot down in front of Narin and gave Enchei a hard look. 'Be my guest, but you're fetching the drink yourself.'

'Irato—'

She reached over and cuffed Enchei around his head. 'Irato, you stay where you are. The old sod can fetch his own drinks, one hand or not. It looks like Narin could do with a cup of something as well, Enchei, Kine too.'

'That would be lovely,' Kine said with a sudden radiant smile. Enchei burst out laughing at that and grudgingly nodded as he hauled himself up.

'Move away,' he hissed at Narin. 'That one'll be a bad influence.'

'Oh, shut up and fetch the wine,' Narin replied. 'I spent the day with Rhe and wasn't annoyed once by his damned noble attitude or any of the looks I got from the high castes – that deserves a celebration, I reckon.'

'Your heroics continue to amaze us,' Kine said in a level tone. 'We all know how much you despise your betters.'

Narin hesitated a moment then leaned over the table to kiss her once on the cheek. 'Lucky you're servant caste then, eh?'

Kine raised an eyebrow at him. The dark-skinned woman brushed an errant trail of hair back and looked over towards Kesh. 'You're right, he's already getting airs about it.'

'Told you.'

'Told her what?' Narin demanded.

Kesh grinned at him and headed back towards the kitchen. 'Oh, just a few things us servants know about the craftsman caste.'

'And Kesh and I have agreed,' Kine added, 'that the imbalance must be corrected at once. It's really the only way to stop you getting yourself into trouble.'

'Eh?'

'We'll be getting married, the sooner the better.'

'Married?' Narin exclaimed, half in jest but feeling ambushed all the same. 'Don't I get a say?'

She frowned at him. 'Why would we allow something like that?'

Narin couldn't help the smile that broke across his face. He nodded and closed his eyes, leaning back in his chair with a gentle sigh. When Enchei slipped a cup of wine into his hand he raised it in silent toast to his friends. Dov shifted and snorted in her sleep, a sound that filled his body with a warmth he'd never known before. He felt hands slip gently over his shoulders and breathed in Kine's faint scent as she hugged him close. Narin drank with a heart lighter than he'd ever known, the pain and fatigue in his body dwindling as that perfect moment stretched on and on.

The Hegemonies of the Empire and their subordinate nation-Houses in order of standing beneath the Great Houses

HOUSE DRAGON

Major	Minor
Wyvern	Longtooth
Willow	Leopard
Darkcloud	Greenscale
Smoke	Highash
Greydawn	Quicksilver

HOUSE WOLF

Major	Minor
Forest	Battle, Greathorn
Bear	Centaur
Mist	Heron
Diresong	Scarab

HOUSE EAGLE

Major	Minor
Falcon	Mantis, Hornet, Plainsdevil
Fox	Breakwater
Brightlance	Chimera
Icewind	Cavern

HOUSE LEVIATHAN

Major	Minor
Storm	Steelfin, Proudsail, Shark
Kraken	Siren, Hightower
Armourback	Flood

HOUSE RAVEN

Major	Minor
Crow	Bat, Greeneye
Ironoak	Rattletail, Greyfang
Threehorn	Starlight

HOUSE REDEARTH

Major	Minor
Whitemountain	Redhood, Horse
Stag	Greatclaw
Condor	Tiger
Wildhunt	Fireant

HOUSE MOON

Major	Minor
Silver	Glass, Owl, Polecat
Rain	Swallow, Poisontongue
Shadow	Ibis

HOUSE SALAMANDER

Major	Minor
Redstone	Lion, Jaguar, Flame, Knife
Phoenix	Blood, Sunfire
Arrow	Amber

HOUSE IRON

Major	Minor
Gold	Bull, Osprey
Thunder	Minotaur
Tusk	Longhammer
Redeve	Porcupine

HOUSE GHOST

Major	Minor
Snow	Crab, Otter, Greykeep
Talon	Mink, Bone
Bear	Darksky
Clearlake	Blackhare

The Celestial Orders of the Ascendant Gods

(Specifying the order of Ascendancy throughout the year and mortal names of the lesser Gods)

Order of God-Emperor (winter)

General – Abeh Falcon
Huntsman – Besh Wolf
Navigator – Ganstal Leviathan
Artist – Sia Proudsail
Magistrate – Kest Diresong

Order of God-Empress (spring)

Healer – Deno Raven
Archer – Cheseirr Storm
Assassin – Baran Knife
Trickster – Miall Swallow
Thief – Dirugi Greenscale

Order of Knight (spring-summer)

Lawbringer – Toro Dragon
Sailor – Diss Leopard
Ranger – Hatarian Greycloud
Shield – Ehn Redhood
Pity – Kolobehn Glass

Order of Shaman (summer)

Shapeshifter – Gerra Chimera
Piper – Teprell Salamander
Pilgrim – Forilend Iron
Acrobat – Im Condor
Monk – Kho Ghost

Order of Smith (autumn)

Farmer – Verghy Rattletail
Mason – Leam Greykeep
Executioner – Poleton Redearth
Wright – Sel Whitemountain
Scholar – Neyal Bone

Order of Jester (autumn-winter)

Cripple – Holass Longtooth
Chance – Dov Moon
Spy – Holin Eagle
Dancer – Keel Ermine
Duellist – Kiro Raven